Hunt for a Hometown Killer

A Novel

Small towns can have secrets and skeletons...

What happens when a sinkhole uncovers them?

Mary Dodge Allen

Name: Mary Dodge Allen
Title: Hunt for a Hometown Killer/ By Mary Dodge Allen
Identifiers: LCCN: 2021908795
ISBN: 978-1-952369-81-0
Subjects: 1. Fiction/Christian/Romance/Suspense
2. Fiction/Mystery & Detective/Amateur Sleuth
3. Fiction/Christian/Suspense

Published by EABooks Publishing, a division of
Living Parables of Central Florida, Inc. a 501c3

EABooksPublishing.com

Dedication

To Monty, my true happy ending.
To Dave and Alison,
and my entire family, including my dearly loved friends.

"Even though I walk through the valley of the shadow of death, I will fear no evil, for you are with me..."

Psalm 23:4, ESV

"Again, Jesus spoke to them, saying, 'I am the light of the world. Whoever follows me will not walk in darkness, but will have the light of life.'"

John 8:12

"The light shines in the darkness, and the darkness has not overcome it."

John 1:5

Riverside Bay, Florida
Thursday

Roxy Silva breathed out a relieved sigh as she finished the last delivery on her mail route. She was looking forward to going home and cranking the air-conditioning down to the sub-zero range. It had been a difficult day—the second anniversary of her husband's unsolved murder. And for the past several hours, while delivering mail in the scorching June heat, Roxy couldn't stop thinking about the fact that the person who killed Vance was still out there, somewhere.

She brushed strands of damp hair off her forehead as she walked back to her mail truck, parked near the huge retention pond at the end of Dolphin Lane. Sunlight shimmered on the pond's rippled surface, highlighting a strange patch of swirling water a few feet offshore. The whirlpool's funnel shape reminded her of water circling around a bathtub drain.

"Hello there, Rox!" Mae Sims waved to her from the sidewalk bordering the pond. The elderly woman was pushing a pink baby stroller, and her small poodle was riding in the stroller seat, as usual. Mae stopped under the shade of a tall laurel oak and held up a plastic Cool Whip container. "I baked sugar cookies today. Want to try one?"

Roxy hesitated. Her thoughts flashed back to last year's church bake sale, when Mae's banana bread sent several people to the

ER. "Thanks... but I can't, right now. I'm running late, and I need to get back to the post office." Roxy gave the woman a smile and a quick wave.

As she unlocked the truck's driver's door, a loud rumbling sound rang out. The pavement beneath her feet began vibrating. A towering geyser erupted from the whirlpool near shore, spraying her skin with cool droplets, like a misty rain.

Mae let out a panicked scream as chunks of the pond's grassy shoreline slid into the convulsing water. The laurel oak nearby cracked and splintered as it toppled over, creating a massive splash.

Roxy broke into an icy sweat. "Mae! Get away from there!" She threw down her shoulder bag and ran toward the petite woman.

Mae visibly trembled as she stood on the cracked sidewalk next to the oak's gigantic root ball, which was still clinging to the soil at the edge of the steep muddy bank. Water dripped from her short gray hair as she stared into the hole.

"Mae! Come with me—"

"No!" She shook her head and let out a sob. "Not without Trixie! She's stuck in that tree!"

Roxy looked down. The pink stroller bobbed in the swirling water near the fallen oak. Something sparkled like diamonds in the oak's leafy branches—Trixie's rhinestone-studded harness. The tiny poodle sat wedged between two thick limbs, just out of reach. The dog's high-pitched whimpering was barely audible over the rushing sound of the turbulent water. Roxy turned to Mae. "If you leave with me right now, I'll come back and help Trixie. I promise!" She guided the frail woman to the spot where she'd discarded her mail bag. "Stay here, okay?"

Mae nodded. Her wrinkled face wore a dazed expression.

Roxy ran back and stood next to the huge mass of tangled roots and soil. She took a deep breath as she gripped a thick, dirt-caked tree root with her sweaty left hand and stepped off the sidewalk's broken concrete. Her steel-toe athletic shoes sank into the damp, unstable dirt. Roxy tightened her grip on the root as she leaned down and stretched out her right arm toward Trixie. She gently slid her fingers under the sparkling harness and felt the poodle's rapid heartbeat beneath her soft fur. "It's okay, girl. I've got you." Twigs snapped as she freed the tiny dog.

The dirt under Roxy's feet abruptly shifted, and she lost her grip on the tree root. She held the small dog in the crook of her right arm as she slid downward. Branches scraped her left arm as her hip slammed against the trunk. She realized she was pinned against the limbs that had held Trixie.

Adrenaline surged. Roxy's heartbeat accelerated as she grabbed a thick branch with her free hand. Using all her strength, she pulled herself up the slippery dirt wall and scrambled over the crumbling sidewalk. She ran toward Mae and picked up her shoulder bag before escorting the frantic woman further away from the sinkhole. When Roxy finally stopped, she was gasping for breath and trembling almost as much as the poodle in her arms.

Mae reached for Trixie and cradled her tiny dog like a baby. Tears formed in her eyes as she tenderly plucked stray twigs and leaves from Trixie's dirty white fur. "She doesn't look injured, but I'd better take her to the vet to make sure." Mae looked up. Her lips quivered as she said, "Thank you."

Roxy nodded and smiled, still too out of breath to speak. She heard the sound of voices and turned. Residents had gathered in the street, several feet away. She knew all of them well, since they had been on her mail route for years. A few waved to her, but most of them wore shocked expressions as they stared at the sinkhole. Mae hurried over and joined her neighbors.

The ground shook again. Roxy turned back to the pond and let out a sharp cry as the oak's root ball slid out of sight, along with the cracked sidewalk. The pavement under her mail truck's front tires disappeared. The truck slid forward and abruptly stopped. Its rear tires gripped the edge of the hole.

"Someone needs to call the police!"

Roxy startled, as if she'd been awakened from a trance. With shaking hands, she reached into the torn pocket of her postal uniform shorts and pulled out her phone. She hesitated when she saw the spider web of cracks, and then she whispered a quick prayer as she double-tapped the damaged screen. Relief surged when her phone lit up. She pressed a familiar speed dial number. When Kyle answered, she blurted, "A sinkhole opened up in Riverside Bay Estates! You need to send officers out here! My mail truck slid into the hole, and it's caught on the edge—"

"Rox! Are you inside the truck?" Kyle sounded panicked.

"No... I'm okay. Sorry, I should have told you that first." She blew out a shaky sigh, as her heartbeat thundered like a jackhammer.

"Is anyone hurt?"

"No... at least I don't think so. But my mail truck fell halfway inside the sinkhole. You need to send a tow truck."

"Where exactly did the hole open up?"

"In that huge retention pond at the end of Dolphin Lane. Part of the shoreline is gone, but the sinkhole isn't near any homes, yet. The water level has gone way down." She stopped, as something on the opposite shore caught her attention. "Kyle! You need to send another tow truck! I see a black car stuck in the muddy bank across the pond, near the entrance to the wildlife refuge—" Her words caught in her throat as she made the connection. Two years ago, a witness saw a black Mercedes sedan speeding away from the scene of her husband's fatal hit and run.

"Is it a Mercedes, Rox?"

"I don't know. The front of the car is still underwater... but it's definitely a black sedan."

"We're on our way," Kyle said.

Roxy's hands were still shaking as she made a second phone call to Mack, the manager of the Riverside Bay Post Office. She quickly described how the sinkhole had opened up and partially-swallowed her mail truck. "It happened right after I finished my last delivery, so there's no mail in the truck. I put all the outgoing mail I collected inside my shoulder bag." She assured him she wasn't injured and told him a tow truck was on its way. After she ended the call, she looked across the pond and stared at the black sedan. A cold shiver slid down her spine as she thought about Vance's murder.

"There you are, Rox! Am I ever glad you're not inside that mail truck!"

Roxy turned and saw her cousin Jo Marshall hurrying toward her, carrying a red first-aid kit. Her green nursing scrubs were cinched at her slender waist, and strands of her blonde hair had come loose from her topknot.

"Jo, how did you find out about—"

"Kyle called the Clinic, and I rushed over." Jo's blue eyes opened wide. "Rox, your left arm is all scraped up, and you're bleeding."

Roxy glanced down at the red stream leaking from the gash in her upper arm, just below the sleeve of her postal uniform shirt. Blood. The sight of it triggered a wave of nausea. She became aware of a throbbing pain as she swayed on her feet.

"Come over here and sit down, so I can examine you." Jo guided her to the curb and sat next to her.

Roxy cried out as Jo probed the wound on her arm.

"This cut looks deep, Rox. I'll close it with stitch strips, but I'm sure it needs stitching. Charlie's on duty at the Clinic this afternoon, so he can do it."

Roxy sighed. She'd worked for hours in the scorching heat, and she'd almost fallen into a sinkhole. Now she needed stitches. She glanced at her damaged mail truck and wondered if the day could get any worse. She yanked off the elastic band securing her ponytail. As she finger combed her long wavy hair, she felt sharp bits in the tangles. Shards of tree bark and crushed leaves clung to her hand.

"Sit still," Jo said, as she began cleaning the wounds with sterile wipes.

Roxy winced. It felt as if Jo had plunged hot wires into her left arm. She glanced up when she heard the rumbling of approaching vehicles. The crowd in the street separated like waves in the Red Sea, clearing a path for two Riverside Bay police cruisers. They parked at the curb.

Kyle Ransom and Sam Boney got out of the first cruiser. Both detectives were dressed in the typical summer uniform, light blue police polo shirts and dark trousers. Their detective shields were clipped to their belts, next to their holsters. Kyle glanced at Roxy and gave her a nod. His gaze lingered for a long moment.

Three officers in dark blue uniforms emerged from the second cruiser. One of them began herding the onlookers further away from the sinkhole. The other two retrieved a stack of orange cones and a roll of yellow caution tape from the trunk. The detectives walked with the officers as they placed the cones and yellow tape around the sinkhole perimeter.

Kyle turned and caught Roxy looking at him. His handsome face relaxed into a grin. He pointed to her truck, perched at the edge of the sinkhole. "I guess it's safe to say you've had a stressful day."

She smiled and nodded.

Kyle walked over to Sam. After a short conversation, they turned and headed toward her. Sam's compact body sported a middle-aged paunch at the waistline, and his longish dark hair curled over his ears. At six three, Kyle's athletic body towered over Sam, and his thick brown hair held light sun streaks, thanks to his love of boating and fishing.

"Rox, you didn't tell me you were hurt," Kyle said.

Sam wore a cynical grin. "Looks like you fell in that sinkhole."

"She almost did, Sam!" Claudia Silva-Gardner strode up, looking like a willowy fashion model in a sleeveless dress and high-heeled sandals. Straight black hair fell to her shoulders, framing her attractive face, which bore a strong resemblance to her brother, Vance. She turned to Roxy. "You almost fell inside that sinkhole when you rescued Mae's dog, didn't you?"

Roxy glanced up at her sister-in-law. "That's not what hap—"

"Yes, it is!" Claudia put her hands on her hips. "Mae's been telling everyone how you jumped inside that sinkhole and rescued her dog from a fallen tree. She said you slipped and fell and barely got out of there before that tree slid out of sight!"

Kyle and Sam exchanged stunned glances.

Jo stopped working and stared at Roxy.

Claudia frowned. "I can't believe you risked your life to save a poodle!"

Roxy tensed. "I didn't jump into that sinkhole! Trixie was stuck in the branches, within arm's reach. I couldn't just leave her there. I kept thinking about how I'd feel if Buddy was caught in that tree."

Sam shook his head. "Rox, it's hard to imagine your big golden retriever stuck in a fallen tree."

A ringtone sounded. Kyle retrieved his phone and glanced at the screen. He walked away as he answered the call and waved at Sam to follow him.

"Oh! That reminds me..." Claudia pulled her phone from her designer purse. The words Riverside Bay Realty were engraved in gold on the phone's shiny black case. "I need to tell dad you're okay. He's still in Tallahassee at that realty conference. I called him when I heard about the sinkhole, and he got worried when he found out your mail truck was involved." She paused, and her features softened. "I was worried about you, too. That's why I got so upset when I found out about Trixie."

Roxy smiled at Claudia, and her tension eased. She had always been close to Vance's family. She barely remembered her mother and father. They were killed in a head-on collision when she was six. Roxy survived with minor injuries, and she was raised by her aunt and uncle—Jo's parents.

Claudia aimed her phone at the sinkhole area and snapped a photo. "Dad's never going to believe this. Before I call him, I'll text a picture of your mail truck." As her fingers tapped on the screen, she breathed out an exaggerated sigh. "I've been working hard to sell a gorgeous house on Blue Marlin Lane, two blocks away.

This sinkhole is going to drag down the value of every property in Riverside Bay Estates."

"What a tragedy," Jo muttered.

Roxy gave Jo an elbow nudge and glanced up. Claudia had already turned away to make the call. Kyle stood nearby, with his phone still pressed to his ear. His deep voice mingled with Claudia's higher-pitched nasal tone.

A police cruiser pulled away from the curb and made a quick U-turn. Roxy recognized Sam behind the wheel. She glanced at the growing crowd and caught sight of Vance's cousin, talking to one of the uniformed police officers. Burke Devlin was easy to spot for two reasons; he was the only person dressed like a lawyer, and he bore an eerie resemblance to Vance. The two men had often been mistaken for brothers because of their remarkably similar Latin good looks.

"Okay, Rox. I've finished applying the stitch strips." Jo closed the first aid kit. "You're lucky. That cut on your arm is the only one that needs stitching. Since nobody else appears to be injured, I'll drive you to the Clinic."

Roxy slid the elastic band off her wrist and then flinched as she tried to lift both arms to gather her hair into a ponytail.

Jo smiled. "Let me do that for you. Remember when we used to fix each other's hair when we were growing up?" She quickly formed Roxy's hair into a ponytail and secured it with the band. "When was your last tetanus shot, Rox?"

"I don't know."

Jo stood and helped Roxy to her feet. "You'll need to get one, then."

Roxy sighed. The day just got a little bit worse.

Claudia tucked her phone back into her purse and looked at Roxy. "Dad's leaving the conference early. He's flying back tonight." She glanced at Kyle as he rejoined them.

"The tow trucks are on their way," Kyle said. "Sam drove to the guard shack at the gated entrance to wait for them. He'll send the first truck here, and then he'll escort the second truck to that black sedan near the wildlife refuge."

"What black sedan?" Claudia asked.

"It's over there, across the pond—" Roxy gasped when she saw how low the water level had dropped. The sedan's shattered windshield, crumpled hood and mangled front grill were now visible, proof of a violent impact. A knifelike pain shot through her heart. Tears stung her eyes as she pictured Vance's smile on that last morning, just before he kissed her good-bye.

"It's Greta's Mercedes!" Claudia let out a choked sob and turned to Roxy. They reached out and hugged each other.

After a long moment, Roxy felt a hand resting on her shoulder. She looked up at Kyle through blurred eyes. He stood close, with his other hand resting on Claudia's shoulder. Roxy blinked to clear her vision and read the grief in Kyle's sky-blue eyes. He and Vance had been best friends since childhood.

Kyle lifted his hand from her shoulder and pulled a folded white cloth from his back pocket.

"Thanks." Roxy dabbed her eyes as a hiccup escaped. "You're the only person I know who carries an old-fashioned handkerchief."

"I usually carry two," Kyle said. "They come in handy when I need to examine evidence and I don't have gloves."

Claudia looked up, sniffling. Her mascara had run, creating black smudges under her eyes.

Kyle handed his second handkerchief to her.

Roxy hiccupped again as she turned toward Jo, who was standing nearby. She wore a stunned expression, and she was biting her lower lip, something she always did when she was struggling to hold back tears.

Burke Devlin stood several feet away. His ashen face appeared frozen in shock. Two years ago, he narrowly missed being killed with his cousin Vance. Burke—the only witness— recognized Greta Wilder's black Mercedes sedan as it sped away from the hit and run.

Roxy opened her back door, and Buddy rushed toward her, wagging his entire body. His enthusiastic greeting lifted the weight of fatigue off her shoulders. "There's my sweet guy!" She stroked the thick golden fur around his neck, setting his collar tags jingling. After she snapped on his leash, she ventured back out into the heat and took Buddy for a walk in the neighborhood park along the Indian River.

As they walked back to her house, Burke Devlin's black BMW drove past them and pulled into her driveway. He got out and strode down the sidewalk to meet her. His white shirt and dark trousers looked freshly-pressed, despite the heat and humidity.

Buddy lunged his wagging body toward him.

"Easy now, Bud." Roxy stroked the retriever's bobbing head as she gently pulled him back. "Sorry about that. He's full grown, but he's still a puppy at heart."

Burke leaned down and brushed the golden hair off his creased trousers.

"This is a surprise," Roxy said.

He glanced up. "I know you don't like surprises—"

"That's okay. Come inside. I need to get out of this heat."

Buddy dashed inside the kitchen as soon as Roxy opened the back door. He galloped to his water bowl and began making loud lapping noises.

Roxy hung up the leash. "Would you like something cold to drink? I have iced tea in the fridge."

"No, thanks." Burke sat down on a barstool at the large kitchen island. "I just came over to check on you. How's the arm?"

"Seven stitches... and a tetanus shot in the other arm. After Charlie took care of me, Jo drove me to the post office, and I checked in with my supervisor. My mail truck will be in the repair shop for a while." She felt a nudge on her leg and looked down into Buddy's big doggy eyes. Water dripped from the fur around his mouth.

"Okay, Bud. I'll get your dinner."

Buddy danced on his paws like a racehorse at the starting gate as he watched her scoop his favorite dog food into his bowl. Several kernels fell on the floor, and he inhaled them like a furry self-propelled vacuum cleaner.

"Are there spare trucks at Riverside Bay's post office?" Burke asked.

She closed the pantry door. "There's only one. It's an older model with sky-high mileage. Nobody likes driving it."

Buddy stayed close to her, brushing his furry body against her legs. When she set down his bowl, he tore into his food as if he hadn't eaten in weeks.

Roxy sat at the island, across from Burke. "I wonder how much damage that sinkhole did to my truck. Did you see it after it was towed out?"

He shook his head. "I left shortly after you and Jo, and I'm glad I did. Two media vans drove into Riverside Bay Estates as I was leaving. Both were from Orlando TV stations."

Anxiety rippled through her stomach. "I didn't think about that. Sinkholes are always big news... and it'll be even bigger news if that Mercedes is tied to Vance's hit and run." Roxy sighed. "I dread being caught up in another media frenzy. I barely survived the last one. You know how depressed I was after Vance was killed..."

He nodded.

She caught a shift in his expression, and her mind pictured the shocked look on his face. "It was hard for me today, seeing that damaged car. But it had to be even harder for you..."

Burke frowned and glanced away. When he turned back, his expression brightened. "I think we both need cheering up. Let me take you to dinner."

Roxy shook her head. "Look at me, Burke. I'm all scraped up, my hair's a mess—"

"You always look good to me." He flashed her a smile.

She broke eye contact. Burke resembled Vance the most whenever he smiled. And today his resemblance pinched a raw nerve.

"I can wait here with Buddy while you get ready."

Roxy ran her hand over the island's smooth marble top as she silently rehearsed a gracious and firm refusal. She glanced up. "I appreciate the offer, but I have to say no. I'm still a little shaky after everything that happened today."

Burke looked at her a moment, and then he gave a nod as he rose to his feet. "Okay, I understand." He moved to the back door and then turned, resting his hand on the knob. "So... have you changed your mind about Saturday night?"

She shook her head. "I don't think—"

"We'd have a great time, Rox. Give it some more thought, and I'll talk to you tomorrow."

After Burke left, Roxy shook her head and let out a weary sigh. She poured herself a glass of iced tea and then stood at the counter as she took a long, refreshing drink. Buddy trotted over, licking his lips. She leaned down and stroked the soft fur on his head. "Hey, Bud. Looks like you enjoyed your dinner. I have no idea what I'm going to make for my—"

A knock sounded at the back door. Roxy glanced up and smiled when she saw Jo's face in the door's porthole-shaped window. "Come on in. It's unlocked."

Jo walked inside, wearing a striped t-shirt, dark shorts and flip flops. She set a large covered salad bowl on the island. "The cavalry is here with dinner, Rox. Mom's right behind me with two huge pizzas, one pepperoni and one veggie."

Roxy's aunt entered, balancing two extra-large pizza boxes in her arms. Nell Dowling was wearing one of her signature all-denim outfits—stonewashed capris and a blue denim shirt. Strands of gray ran through her short blonde waves, and her pretty face looked like an older version of Jo. She gave Roxy a motherly smile as she set the pizza boxes on the island. Nell had always treated Roxy like her own daughter.

"We picked up grandpa at the Senior Center," Jo said. "He's carrying our dessert inside his walker basket."

"Grandpa Leo's here, too?"

"Of course," Nell said. "You gave us all quite a scare!" She opened her arms and pulled Roxy into a quick hug. "I was shocked when Jo told me you almost fell into that sinkhole."

"Aunt Nell, it wasn't that dramatic." Roxy shot Jo a look. "You know how Claudia exaggerates."

"Yeah, I know how Claudia loves drama," Jo said, briefly frowning. "That's why I checked out her story. You said Mae was going to take Trixie to the vet, so I called Pet Wellness and talked to Sal at the front desk. Mae gave Sal all the details while Matt examined Trixie... and her story matched Claudia's exactly." Jo paused and smiled. "Trixie wasn't injured, by the way. She has a few scratches, but probably not as many as you, Rox."

"There's my Roxy-girl!" Leo Patterson smiled as he pushed his walker through the open doorway. He stood nearly six feet tall, even though his arthritic spine curved forward. His silver hair held conspicuous natural waves; a trait Roxy had inherited.

Roxy wrapped her arms around her grandpa's stooped shoulders and gave him a kiss on the cheek. He was dressed in khaki trousers and a blue shirt with a repetitive pattern of WWII airplanes. He had served as a pilot in the war, and she and Jo had given him this shirt on his 96th birthday. "Grandpa, you're looking handsome today."

An impish gleam flickered in Leo's blue eyes. "Looks can be deceiving, Roxy-girl."

Roxy held his walker steady as he sat on a barstool at the island. She glanced at Jo. "Is Charlie coming over?"

"He has to work late at the Clinic, but he'll try to join us for dessert." Jo lifted the walker's basket lid, which served as a padded seat and retrieved a plastic container of cookies. "We saw Burke's car leaving as we drove up. What was he doing here?"

"He wanted to check up on me," Roxy said. "He's still trying to convince me I'll have more fun if I take him as my date to our class reunion."

"Maybe he's right, Rox." Jo rolled the walker to a corner of the kitchen.

"No... Burke seems to want more than friendship, and I'm not interested. Besides, Vance was with me at our tenth reunion, and it would be weird to take Burke to our fifteenth. I mean, he looks so much like—" She stopped as her throat tightened.

"Rox, you've had a rough day," Nell said. "Go upstairs and get showered. We'll keep the pizzas warm in the oven."

The shower refreshed her. Roxy slipped on a lightweight blue sundress and then finger combed her long hair. She frowned when she detected remnants of tree bark in the damp waves. When she walked back into the kitchen, Jo and Nell were working at the counter, and her grandpa was sitting at the large oval island, chatting with them. Plates, utensils and a frosty glass of iced tea sat at four of the six barstools.

Leo glanced up. "You look nice, Roxy-girl."

She smiled. "Looks can be deceiving, grandpa. I still have bits of tree bark in my hair."

He chuckled.

"How did the bandage over your stitches hold up?" Jo asked, as she placed two trivets on the island.

"Fine. I was careful not to get it too wet."

"Good. Are you still planning to go back to work tomorrow?"

"Why not?"

"You'll risk pulling out those stitches, Rox. You shouldn't lift anything heavy with that arm for the next couple of days."

"I'll lift the heavier packages with my right arm."

Jo shook her head. "Rox, you can be so stubborn."

Nell removed two platters of pizza slices from the oven and set them on the trivets.

Roxy breathed in the delicious aromas of warm bread and melted cheese as she sat next to her grandpa. Buddy trotted over and sat between their barstools. Leo gave the retriever a pat on the head.

"Grandpa," Roxy said. "You're not going to feed Buddy under the table again, are you?"

Leo grinned.

After Nell sat down, they all bowed their heads as she said grace. When she finished, she passed a platter of pepperoni pizza to Roxy. After taking a slice, Roxy passed the platter to her grandpa. Then she stood and retrieved a bottle of ketchup from the refrigerator.

"I'm ashamed of myself," Nell said. "How could I forget something so vital?"

Roxy smiled. A familiar knock sounded on the back door, and her smile widened when she saw Kyle's face in the window. As she pulled the door open, a blast of hot, humid air rushed inside.

Kyle's eyes locked onto hers, and he smiled. "You look... better." He held up the small cooler containing her water bottles. "I pulled this out of your truck before they towed it away."

"Thanks," she said, as she took it from him. "I'll need that for tomorrow."

He pointed to the large bottle of ketchup in her other hand. "I see you have dinner all taken care of."

She laughed. "Come and join us. I'll bet you haven't eaten, yet."

He stepped inside and greeted everyone as Roxy shut the door. Buddy trotted over, wagging his tail. Kyle leaned down and stroked the dog's floppy ears.

Nell had already set another plate and utensils in front of an empty barstool. She handed Kyle a glass of iced tea. "Take a seat. There's plenty of pizza."

"Thanks... this looks great."

"I baked oatmeal raisin cookies for dessert," Jo said. She glanced at her grandpa. "They're Grandma Anna's recipe, of course."

Leo nodded. "They're the best, Jo-Jo."

Roxy set her soft-sided cooler next to the sink. After she sat down, she poured a generous amount of ketchup over her pizza slice.

Nell passed the salad bowl to Kyle and frowned when he put a small helping on his plate. When he took one slice of pizza, her frown deepened. "You have to be hungrier than that. Take two or three."

He grinned and did what he was told.

Leo looked at Kyle. "What have you found out about that Mercedes you pulled out of the pond? Have you tied it to the hit and run?"

"Not yet. The sedan was towed to the County Sheriff's forensic garage. They have jurisdiction, because it was found on county property near the wildlife refuge. Our forensics team will work with theirs, comparing it with the crash debris we recovered two years ago. We should know by tomorrow if there's a match." He took a large bite of pizza.

"Have you checked out the VIN number?" Leo asked.

Kyle nodded as he finished chewing. "The Mercedes is registered to Greta Wilder." He glanced at Roxy.

She sighed. "So... it's true. Greta was aiming for Burke, and she killed Vance by mistake."

"That's been our theory," Kyle said. "But we still need to confirm her Mercedes was involved in the hit and run."

Nell took a sip of tea and set her glass down hard. "I wonder where Greta ran off to."

"She had enough money to go anywhere she wanted," Roxy said.

Kyle frowned. "What I don't understand is why she hasn't left any kind of cyber trail. It's practically impossible to change your identity and just disappear."

"I can't believe Greta's living somewhere remote, off the grid," Jo said. "That's not her style. She'd want every luxury money can buy."

Roxy nodded as she finished chewing a bite of ketchup-soaked pizza. "Greta couldn't survive without social media. She loves being in the spotlight."

"More than that, she loves being in control," Nell said. "When she married our former mayor, she practically took over his job."

"That's true," Jo said, as she took another helping of salad. "But you have to admit Greta breathed new life into our town, by revitalizing our shabby downtown district. I love all the new restaurants and upscale shops."

"My uncle almost closed his diner a few years ago," Kyle said. "But now he's turning a good profit. Our downtown district has become a real tourist magnet."

"Tourists!" Leo spat out the word. "Riverside Bay used to be a quiet, friendly town. But all the pushy tourists are ruining it. I'm glad our art deco buildings were fixed up, but I don't like seeing those fancy restaurants and stores mixed in with the old family businesses. It makes our town look like a cross between Mayberry and South Beach."

Roxy and Jo glanced at each other and smiled.

Kyle's ringtone sounded. He pulled out his phone and glanced at the screen. "It's the Sheriff's Office. Sorry, I need to take this." He stepped into the adjoining family room as he answered the call.

Jo and Nell started clearing plates. Roxy stood and began helping.

"Sit down and rest your arm," Nell said. "Jo and I can handle it."

"I can clear plates with my right arm."

Nell gave her a look. "Sit down and rest."

Roxy plopped down. "Aunt Nell, I'm not an invalid."

"Don't give me any attitude, young lady." Her face wore the hint of a smile.

Kyle walked back into the kitchen. "I'll have to skip dessert. I need to head to the Sheriff's Office."

"Did they match those car parts with the Mercedes?" Leo asked.

"Not yet." Kyle's voice tone sounded casual, but his expression looked troubled.

Roxy stood. "We'll pack some cookies for you."

"Already done." Nell held up a bulging zip-top plastic bag.

"Thanks." Kyle said, as he took the bag. "And thanks for dinner, too."

Roxy walked him to the door. "Something's wrong, I can tell."

He shook his head. "I'll call you tomorrow."

Friday morning

The stitches in Roxy's left arm burned as if they were on fire when she entered the post office. As soon as she walked into the sorting area, the other mail carriers gathered around her. They peppered her with questions about her sinkhole experience, while teasing her about her truck falling inside it.

It took her longer than usual to sort the mail for her route one-handed. Roxy placed the plastic trays and boxes of sorted letters, magazines and packages into a large wheeled cart and then rolled it to the rear doors leading to the postal vehicle lot. When the double doors opened, she pushed the heavy cart outside, into the sweltering embrace of heat and humidity.

The other mail carriers had already driven off to begin their deliveries. She rolled the cart toward the only mail truck left in the lot, a battered relic that happened to be the oldest postal vehicle in Riverside Bay's fleet. She opened the truck's cargo door and stepped back as a rush of superheated air escaped. This truck wasn't equipped with air conditioning, and the afternoon temperature was predicted to break another June heat record. Roxy sighed, feeling a twinge of regret that she hadn't taken the day off.

After she loaded all the trays and boxes of mail, she slid open the driver's door on the right-hand side of the truck. Ragged cracks in the vinyl driver's seat exposed large areas of foam padding. When she sat down, she let out a surprised cry as she tilted backward. The driver's seat squeaked and swiveled like a carnival ride with every movement. She almost slid off the cracked seat cushion as she placed the soft-sided cooler containing her water bottles beneath the platform on her left, which held the mail trays for the first stops on her route.

Roxy fastened her seat belt and struggled to maintain her balance as she drove out of the lot. The old truck rocked, rattled and rolled over Main Street's uneven brick pavement, and she bounced in the squeaking driver's seat like a rodeo rider strapped to a wild horse. A humid breeze blew in through the truck's open windows, while a small fan mounted to the dashboard blew a steady stream of hot air at her face. Roxy felt as if she was driving a truck-shaped convection oven, adorned with the blue eagle logos of the U.S. Postal Service.

The traffic light turned red at the intersection of Main and Central, and she braked at the crosswalk. Tourists carrying takeout cups and shopping bags brushed shoulders as they passed each other, while hurrying across the street. Roxy looked to the right, out the open driver's window and gazed at Smith's Barber Shop. A vintage striped barber pole stood next to the shop's entrance, and a yellowed sign taped to its front window advertised: Cheap Haircuts and Free Advice. The chairman of the town council was sitting in the barber chair closest to the window, and the shop's owner was trimming what was left of his thinning hair. Roxy smiled. She had recently begun delivering packages from a hair restoration company to the chairman's fancy house in Riverside Bay Estates.

She waited a few seconds after the traffic light turned green and watched as several tourists sprinted across the street, against the light. When she bounced forward through the intersection, she spotted Kyle and Sam up ahead, standing in front of the blue art deco building housing the police station. Both detectives were dressed in business casual, and she assumed they were scheduled to testify in court today.

Kyle caught sight of her and smiled. He lifted his hand to his ear as if he was holding a phone, signaling he planned to call her.

Roxy gave him a 'thumbs up' sign as her truck rattled past him. She turned left onto Marina Drive, drove a half block to Bayside Plaza and then parked in her usual spot, near Duke's Donuts. After filling her shoulder bag with pre-sorted bundles of mail, she got out and opened the rear cargo door. She aimed her hand-held scanner at the barcode on every package addressed to Bayside's businesses and stacked them inside a portable rolling box. Then she locked the truck and towed the rolling box to her first delivery stop, the donut shop.

Two women walked out of the shop, dressed in yoga outfits bearing the logo of the fitness center next door. Both of them worked as realtors with Claudia, and Roxy stopped a moment to chat. When she entered the shop, a rush of cool air greeted her, laden with the delicious aromas of sweet baked goods and coffee.

A blonde realtor dressed in a yoga outfit stood at the bakery counter with her back to the door, chatting with Duke Murphy, the shop's owner. His extra-large baker's apron wrapped completely around his body, and its overlapping tie strings emphasized his trim waistline. For the past several months, Roxy had been delivering packages of diet-plan meals to Duke at his shop. He glanced up and smiled. "Hey, Rox. I hear it's going to be another scorcher today."

She smiled. "It's already a scorcher, Duke."

The realtor turned. "Oh... hi, Rox." Melody Manor's greeting held an artificially sweet tone. Her smile lacked warmth, and her blonde hair exhibited roots as dark as her eyes.

Roxy responded with an unsweetened greeting.

Melody smirked as she eyed Roxy's scraped and bandaged arm. "Look at you. I hear you fell in that sinkhole yesterday—" She stopped when her ringtone sounded. After glancing at her phone, she tossed them a quick good-bye and answered the call as she walked out the door.

Roxy gathered a thin stack of bills from her shoulder bag and placed them on the counter, along with a box from the diet-plan company. "Duke, I thought you reached your weight goal last week."

"I did. I'm on the maintenance plan, now." He set the bills on top of the box and carried his mail into the back room he used as his office.

While he was gone, Roxy pulled her travel mug from the outer pocket of her shoulder bag and set it on the counter. Duke returned and picked up her travel mug. "I just made a fresh batch of iced coffee." He moved to a large stainless steel dispenser and began filling it. "Where's Claudia this morning? She didn't come in for coffee with the other realtors after yoga class."

She heard the wistful undertone in his voice, and it triggered a rush of sympathy. Duke and Claudia had dated on and off for years, until she met Paul Gardner. Shortly after Claudia married Paul, Duke's massive weight gain began. Roxy cleared her throat and said, "She's catching up with work at the office today."

Duke nodded as he added cream to her travel mug.

Roxy hoped Duke wouldn't press her for details. She didn't have the heart to tell him that Paul's submarine is returning to King's Bay Naval Base tomorrow, and Claudia was clearing her desk so she could spend time with Paul during his extended leave.

Duke handed her the travel mug. "Here you go, Rox."

She took a sip of the cold creamy brew. "Thanks. This will help me beat the heat."

His gaze shifted to her arm. "Did you really fall into that sinkhole?"

She sighed. "It's a long story..."

Duke nodded, and his expression darkened. "I heard about the Mercedes they found... it has to be Greta's! I hope they'll finally bring her to justice!"

Roxy caught the flash of anger in his eyes. During the years Duke dated Claudia, he and Vance had developed a close friendship.

After she finished her last delivery at the plaza, Roxy returned to the truck and drank the last of the lukewarm coffee in her travel mug. The ice had melted quickly. She placed the empty rolling box inside the cargo area, locked the door and then drove to her next stop, the Riverside Bay Marina. She parked in a spot near the marina office, shaded by a stand of tall palms. Her ringtone sounded, and she pulled her phone out of the pocket of her gray uniform shorts. Kyle's name appeared on the cracked screen.

"Rox, have you recovered from your sinkhole adventure?"

"More or less." She smiled, even though she knew he couldn't see her.

"I heard from our forensics team," Kyle said. "They matched the crash debris with Greta's Mercedes."

Roxy gripped the phone a little tighter.

"It's strange... we've been looking all over the country for Greta's car, and it's been here all along, in that retention pond."

"It's even more strange that the sinkhole drained that pond yesterday."

"Yeah," Kyle said. "Two years to the day..."

Roxy slumped against the back of the rocking seat. "Now we know for sure... Greta killed Vance—"

"Rox, we know Greta's car was involved, but we can't say for sure she was the driver."

"Who else would it be?" Roxy sat up straight. "Everyone in town knew how much Greta hated Burke. She went crazy after they broke up! She knew what time he ate breakfast at the diner every morning. It was early, the alley was dark, and she mistook Vance for Burke—"

"Calm down, Rox! We can't jump to conclusions. We have to examine the evidence and let the facts lead us to the driver." He paused. "I promise you... I won't rest until I find out who killed Vance."

She breathed out a long sigh. "I know. I didn't mean to get so upset."

"That's okay." His deep voice softened. "Look, I need to give you a heads up. The Sheriff's Office is getting ready to release the forensic results to the media today. Reporters will probably want to contact you for your reaction."

Roxy's heartbeat quickened. Vance's fatal hit and run had ignited a wildfire of news coverage, mostly because Greta's Mercedes was involved. Greta had become a media celebrity during the years she was married to Quint Wilder, the town's former mayor. When Greta divorced Quint to be with Burke, the press covered every lurid detail. And months later, when Greta and Burke's stormy break-up was followed by Vance's murder and her sudden disappearance, the media coverage burned red hot for weeks.

"Rox, you okay?"

"Yeah, I just needed a moment."

"How are you holding up, working in this heat... after everything that happened yesterday?"

She let out a frustrated laugh. "Well, you know me. I live by the postal creed. Nothing keeps this courier from her appointed rounds."

"Neither snow, nor rain, nor heat, isn't that how it goes?"

"Don't forget the gloom of night," Roxy said.

"Who wrote that postal creed? It sounds old, maybe the late 1800's, with that antiquated wording."

"It's much older than that... around 500 B.C., when the Persians and Greeks were at war. The Persians used a system of mounted couriers, and that was their motto."

"No kidding?"

"No kidding. Mack tells that story to every new postal employee." Roxy glanced out the open driver's window and looked up at the cloudless blue sky. Through the waving palm fronds overhead, she caught blinding glimpses of the sun. "Kyle... if you think about it, delivering mail in the gloom of night makes a lot more sense than working in this crazy heat."

"Rox, why don't you have lunch with me at the diner? You know Uncle Milo keeps that place as cold as a meat locker during the summer. It'll be my treat."

"Lunch at the diner is always your treat. You never let me pay."

"That's because I get a steep family discount. So, what do you say?"

"Well... I'd be a fool to turn down a free air-conditioned lunch."

As Kyle ended the call, he heard a knock on his open office door. He swiveled his desk chair around.

Sam stood at the doorway. "What's with that smile? You look like you just won the lottery."

"No chance of that. You have to buy a ticket to win, and I have too many other interests."

"Seems like a certain mail carrier has become one of your primary interests." Sam grinned. "I heard you talking to Rox."

Kyle glanced away, surprised by Sam's comment. Were his feelings for Rox really that obvious? He had only realized them himself, a few weeks earlier. He looked up and said, "I called to give her the forensics results on Greta's car."

Sam's grin faded. "Have you heard anything more about the body they found in the trunk?"

"Not yet. The autopsy is being conducted this morning."

"Think they'll have an ID today?"

"It's possible. The body's badly decomposed, so they've requested dental records." Kyle paused. "They've confirmed it's the skeleton of a petite female..."

Sam nodded. "Yeah... it's probably Greta."

Roxy slipped her phone back into the pocket of her shorts and then pulled a water bottle out of her soft-sided cooler. After taking a long drink, she leaned back in the rocking seat and closed her eyes as she pressed the chilled stainless-steel bottle against her forehead. Drops of cold condensing water rolled past her eyelids and down her cheeks, refreshing her. She placed the bottle back in the cooler and then loaded her shoulder bag with bundles of mail for the marina complex.

She locked the driver's door and stood a moment, gazing at the rows of yachts and sailboats moored in the marina basin. Rigging cables clanked against the tall masts, while colorful flags flapped in the humid breeze. Her gaze traveled across the choppy blue surface of the Indian River; a briny lagoon that stretches over one hundred miles along Florida's east coast and serves as part of the Intracoastal Waterway. Roxy spotted a deep-sea charter boat heading toward the marina, presumably returning from a half-day fishing trip in the Atlantic. Seagulls screeched as they flew in tight circles over the boat. The catch must have been good today.

Roxy opened the cargo door and scanned several packages before placing them in the rolling box. As she slipped the scanner back into her shoulder bag, she heard someone approaching.

Quint Wilder ambled toward her, wearing ragged cargo shorts, a faded marina t-shirt and flip flops. The town's former mayor had inherited the profitable marina from his father years ago, and even though the business had made him a wealthy man, he looked like a sloppy beach bum. Quint's leathery face, shaggy hair and graying beard added twenty years to his appearance, giving him the look of a man in his sixties, rather than his forties. His father had named him after the grizzled boat captain in the movie Jaws. And now Quint looked the part.

Roxy smiled. "Hey, Quint. How do you like this heat wave?"

He let out a wheezing laugh. "It's good for business. People want to get out on the water and catch that ocean breeze." As he stepped closer, his right eye began twitching.

She caught the sour odors of sweat and beer and took a step back.

Quint eyed the packages she'd just scanned and lifted them out of the box. "I'll carry these to the office."

Roxy normally declined offers of help. But every package was addressed to the marina, Quint was the owner, and her stitches throbbed with a burning ache. She locked the truck, slipped on her shoulder bag and walked with him toward the marina office.

"I heard about Greta's car on the news." He paused and let out a raspy cough. "She was a real beauty... but inside, she was no good."

Roxy glanced at Quint, and her mind brought up an image of him, years ago, looking handsome and well dressed as the town's newly-elected mayor—before he fell for Greta. They married as soon as his divorce was final, and after that, she pulled all the strings in his life. For years, Greta and Quint hosted a merry-go-round of well-publicized social events as the town went through its revitalization. But their carousel came to a sudden stop after Burke Devlin moved back to Riverside Bay. When Greta filed for divorce, Quint collapsed like a puppet without his puppeteer.

"Have you talked to Kyle about the investigation?" He looked at her and his eye twitched again.

Roxy wondered if he had come out to help, so he could pump her for information. "Kyle called me this morning—"

"I figured he would." Quint shot her an anxious look. "Do the police have any idea where Greta is?"

"He said they're still processing evidence."

Quint balanced the packages on his hip as he opened the office door for her. "I think Greta probably left the country. She had a boatload of money stashed in bank accounts in the Cayman Islands." He frowned. "A lot of that money used to be mine."

Roxy read Quint's bitter expression. Greta had added insult to injury by hiring Burke as her divorce lawyer. He negotiated a generous settlement for her, including fifty-percent ownership of the marina business.

The marina's office manager was on the phone when Roxy entered. The plump woman glanced up and nodded as they exchanged smiles. She had worked at the marina nearly forty years, and she'd become a sort of mother figure for Quint. When his appearance began its quick downward slide, she encouraged him to step into the background, while she hired a savvy team of employees to interface with the marina's wealthy clients.

Roxy unlocked the mailroom door and then left it open for ventilation as she worked inside the cramped room. Two mailbox panels had been set into the wall, one for the marina's staff and the other for residents of Marina View Resort, an upscale condo tower Greta convinced Quint to build on the marina's property, in partnership with EverNorm Development.

While Roxy filled the mailboxes, Quint paced the hallway outside the open door. From time to time, he'd step inside the mailroom without saying anything. The anxious look in his squinty, twitching eyes disturbed her.

Roxy left the marina's parking lot and headed to the Silva Building, a yellow, two-story art deco structure at the corner of Main Street and Marina Drive. Her father-in-law Earl Silva purchased the building several years ago and renovated its four second-floor condos for family members. Earl moved into the largest condo, and Claudia took the smaller one next door. Burke moved in across the hall from Earl, and Roxy and Vance moved into the condo next to his.

When Roxy moved into a newly-renovated house six months ago, Earl insisted she keep her designated parking spot, because of the lack of adequate parking downtown. She used her personal remote to open the Silva Building's gated underground garage and then parked the rattling mail truck in the spot marked with her name.

After taking another water break, Roxy gathered the personal mail for the Silva family, along with the mail and packages for the Silva Building's first-floor tenants: Riverside Bay Realty; Burke Devlin's law office; the non-profit Community Clinic and its adjacent resale store, the Clinic Thrift. When Earl purchased the building, he generously offered to provide rent-free space for the Clinic, so it would have a convenient downtown location. Greta Wilder, who was managing the town's revitalization at the time, tried to block the Clinic from moving in. But she backed down when she realized the level of community support.

Roxy's rolling box had room to spare, so she gathered the mail and packages for the police station, since it was located next door. When she towed the box toward the garage's elevator, she noticed a red Ferrari convertible parked in one of the spots reserved for Riverside Bay Realty clients. Its license plate holder displayed the name and phone number of a Ferrari dealership in Miami.

She rode the small, dimly-lit elevator to the first floor, and then she blinked as she stepped out into the bright air-conditioned lobby. The rush of chilled air gave her an invigorating shock, like diving into a pool of cold water. Sunlight streamed in through the windows facing Main Street, creating rectangular glare spots on the lobby's black marble floor.

Roxy entered the Community Clinic's small reception area and left a stack of mail and two packages with the receptionist. Before leaving, she glanced through the window behind the desk and saw a number of patients in the waiting room. Her thoughts flashed back to the months when she'd attended a grief counseling group at the Clinic. She recalled one tearful session when she mentioned her two miscarriages and wondered how much richer her life with Vance might have been, if even one of their babies had lived.

In the very next session, a woman in the group gave her a book of quotes attributed to Epictetus, a Greek philosopher. Roxy's snapshot memory brought up the image of her favorite quote: "He is wise, who does not grieve for the things which he has not, but rejoices for those which he has." Another image surfaced, a Bible verse the woman had written inside the book's front cover: "The Lord is close to the brokenhearted and saves those who are crushed in spirit." Psalm 34:18.

Roxy left the Clinic and towed the rolling box across the sunlit lobby. She stopped at the Silva Building's ornate brass mailbox panel and unlocked it with an old-fashioned brass key. Hinges squeaked as she swung the heavy door open, exposing the mailboxes. She filled them quickly, paying minimal attention to the echoing voices and clicking footsteps behind her. As she closed and locked the brass door, she heard a familiar voice call out her name.

Earl Silva walked toward her, wearing a white Riverside Bay Realty polo shirt and khaki trousers. His hair had gone mostly gray, and fine lines crisscrossed his handsome face, which bore a close resemblance to his only son.

She looked at Earl and a thought struck her, "This is what Vance might have looked like in his sixties, if we'd had the chance to grow old together." Her throat tightened.

"Are you okay?" Earl's face wore a concerned look. He had always been more like a father, than a father-in-law.

Roxy nodded as she cleared her throat. "I'm fine..."

"You shouldn't be working so hard in this heat. Why don't you quit this job and join my staff? I've always said you'd make a top-notch realtor."

"Dad, we've gone over this before—"

"Rox, your mail truck fell into a sinkhole yesterday!" He glanced at her stitched arm. "Claudia said you almost did, too!"

"You know how she tends to exaggerate…"

Earl paused and grinned, as if he couldn't argue with that. Then his expression went serious. "Speaking of the sinkhole, I assume you've talked to Kyle?"

She nodded.

"He said we can't assume Greta was the driver. They have to examine all the evidence! What evidence?" Earl lifted his hands in frustration. "That car has been underwater for two years—" His voice caught, and he bowed his head.

"Kyle said he won't rest until he finds out who did it."

Earl nodded and looked up, meeting her gaze. "I know. He and Vance were as close as brothers."

For a moment, Roxy thought Earl was going to say something else about Kyle. Instead, he reached for her hand and gave it a gentle squeeze. Impulsively, she leaned forward and kissed his cheek.

A mechanical ping sounded as the elevator doors opened.

"Hey! I like the way women deliver mail in this town!" A pug-nosed bald man walked out of the elevator, followed by a blonde woman dressed in a pink spandex outfit that clung to her top-heavy body like a second skin. Claudia stepped out behind them, wearing a tailored white silk blouse and a black pencil skirt.

The bald man wore a lewd smile. "Do you ever make any special deliveries?"

Roxy thought of a sharp response, but she held it back when she read the look in the man's dark eyes. It was a cold look; the look of a shark sizing up his prey.

Earl stepped forward. "That's no way to talk to—"

"Dad!" Claudia said. "They're our clients."

"You must be Earl Silva." The bald man extended his hand. His enormous gold dragon ring flashed as it caught the light streaming into the lobby.

Earl wore a disgusted look as he shook the man's hand. "And you are…?"

"Harmon Doyle."

The name caught Roxy's attention. She'd seen it before... but where?

"We have something in common," Doyle said, as they broke their handshake.

Roxy almost laughed out loud, thinking, "What could Earl possibly have in common with a crude man like you?"

Earl raised his eyebrows, as if he was thinking the same thing.

"We're both related to Burke Devlin," Doyle said.

A look of doubt crossed Earl's face. "Burke is my nephew, my sister Lydia's son. How are you—"

"He's my nephew, too. I'm Red Devlin's brother."

"I wasn't aware Burke's father had any siblings."

"Well... I'm Red's half-brother, if you want to get technical. I was hoping I'd get a chance to see Burke today, but I hear he's gone off to some meeting in Tallahassee."

"He volunteered to take my place at a realty conference," Earl said.

The woman in pink spandex stepped forward. As she rested her hand on Earl's arm, her gaudy gold bracelets made jingling sounds. "Hiya there, Earl. I'm Isabel McGraw. But you can call me Izzy... everyone does." Her voice held a high-pitched, baby-doll tone.

Claudia was standing behind Doyle. She caught Roxy's attention, pointed to Izzy and then clutched her throat as if she was gagging.

Doyle looked over his shoulder.

A smile instantly appeared on Claudia's face. "Dad, I just took this lovely couple up to the rooftop terrace. They want to rent a condo in town, and I pointed out the Marina View Resort, across the street—"

"What about that empty condo on the second floor, the one next to Burke's?" Doyle turned back to Earl. "When I made the appointment with Claudia, she said that condo was for rent. Now she says it's not. I'll pay the going rate. Money's no problem for me."

Claudia's eyes widened, and she shook her head.

"It isn't available," Earl said. "But you'll like the condo at Marina View."

Relief flooded Claudia's face. "That's right. It has a great view of the Indian River. Let me take you to lunch at the marina's restaurant, and then I'll show it to you."

Doyle focused his predatory gaze on Claudia and gave her a nod. Then he turned to Roxy. "I hope to see a lot more of you, real soon."

Roxy looked at him and thought, "I hope your lunch gives you indigestion."

"We can go in my car," Claudia said, as she pressed the elevator's down button.

Roxy waited until the elevator doors closed, and then she turned to Earl. "Did you find a tenant for my old condo?"

Earl shook his head. "Claudia's been nagging me to list it for rent, but I can't bring myself to do it. I don't need the income, and there are a lot of memories there..."

She nodded.

"I'm glad I kept that condo off the rental market. I don't want someone like Harmon Doyle living across the hall from my daughter."

"But if he rents that condo at Marina View, I'll have the misfortune of being his mail carrier."

Earl looked at Roxy and smiled. "You can always come and work for me."

Roxy entered the police station's small lobby and waved to the blonde receptionist, sitting at her desk behind a bullet-proof window. The young woman smiled and nodded. She pressed a button on the wall next to her desk and a buzzer sounded, unlocking the entry door.

After she completed her deliveries in the mailroom, Roxy retrieved a small purse from her shoulder bag and then locked the bag, her scanner and the rolling box inside the room. She took the stairs to the second floor and used the restroom down the hall from the Investigation Division. As she washed her hands, she frowned at her reflection in the mirror. She dampened a paper towel, added a squirt of soap and washed the perspiration off her face. Feeling revived, she reapplied foundation with sunscreen and a fresh coat of lip balm. Her text chime rang. When she saw Burke's name on the cracked screen, she shook her head and slipped her phone back into her pocket.

When she walked out, she spotted Quint in the hallway, talking to Sam. The marina's owner looked even older and shabbier standing next to the detective, who was dressed in a shirt, tie and trousers, in shades of gray.

Quint let out a shout. He abruptly turned away from Sam and kept his head bowed as he strode toward Roxy. She moved, but not quickly enough. Quint ran into her, trampling both feet as he pushed her shoulder against the wall. He quickly recoiled, and then he stared at her, as if he was wondering how she had suddenly materialized. Before hurrying away, he mumbled, "Sorry, Rox."

Sam walked up. "You all right?"

Roxy glanced down, surprised her feet didn't hurt. "The good news is; I'm wearing steel-toe shoes. The bad news is; they're ugly."

Sam barked out a laugh. "You're lucky Quint was wearing those ratty lightweight flip flops." He reached into his pocket and held out a handful of round red-striped candies. "Want some peppermints? I have a desk drawer full of them."

"Thanks." Roxy slipped the candy in her pocket. "How long has it been, Sam?"

He patted his empty shirt pocket, where he used to keep his cigarette pack. "Three months since my last one." He tore the plastic wrapping off a peppermint, tossed it into his mouth and then rolled it to one side so he could talk. "Every time I get a craving, I eat one of these. The first month, I was eating them like crazy. Now, not so much."

Roxy rubbed the sore spot on her right shoulder. "Good thing my stitched arm didn't hit that wall. Why was Quint so upset?"

"That fool! He came here asking if we knew where Greta was. When I said I couldn't tell him anything that hadn't been released to the public, he blew up." Sam's expression shifted as he chewed on his peppermint. "Ah... don't get the wrong idea. I'm not saying we know where Greta is—" His desk phone rang, and he said a quick good-bye over his shoulder as he hurried back to his office.

Roxy walked to the end of the hallway. Kyle's office door stood partly open, and the deep sound of his radio announcer voice drifted outside. She hesitated, thinking he might be in a meeting. When she didn't hear other voices, she peered inside. Kyle was sitting at his desk, holding his cell phone to his ear with his right hand and scribbling notes with his left hand. He was wearing the blue shirt and patterned tie she and Claudia had given him last Christmas. He glanced up and smiled as he waved her inside. He pointed to the corner of his desk, where a bottle of iced tea sat on a coaster next to his nameplate: Lt. K. Ransom.

She mouthed, "thank you" and then took a long drink. It was her favorite brand of tea, and ice cold. She carried the bottle to his office window, which overlooked Main Street. Tourists crowded the sidewalks, one story below. Roxy's gaze wandered across the street and settled on the town's bookstore, The Yellow Book Road. Its colorful sign depicted Dorothy's ruby red slippers dancing on a road paved with yellow books. The bookstore's adjacent coffee shop, The Brew-Be-Sippers, was popular with the locals, who simply called it, The Brew Be.

The middle-aged bookstore owners stood on the sidewalk, dressed in their usual Wizard of Oz costumes; Dorothy and the Scarecrow. Earlier that week, while delivering mail to the bookstore, Roxy overheard the married couple bickering about how shabby his costume looked. She smiled, wondering how a Scarecrow costume could possibly look too shabby.

Her gaze moved to Shyanne's Boutique, next door. A woman walked out of the clothing shop carrying a garment bag. Roxy gave herself a mental reminder to pick up her dress for the class reunion after work. Shyanne had called her last night and said the alterations were done.

She took another sip of tea as she turned toward Kyle's corner bookcase. His diploma in Criminology from Florida State University sat on the top shelf, behind several framed photos. The largest photo featured a much younger Kyle, standing with one arm around his petite wife April and his other arm around their young son Josh. April was looking up at Kyle and smiling. Shoulder-length blonde hair framed her pretty face, and she looked several months pregnant. Roxy felt a pinch of sadness, knowing the photo was taken a few weeks before April died.

Two smaller photos were displayed in a double frame. The photo on the left had captured Roxy and April laughing as they stood on a dock at the marina. In the photo on the right, Vance and Kyle were standing in front of the fishing boat they had purchased together. Each of them held an enormous red snapper. Roxy couldn't see any visible size difference between the two fish, but she guessed by Vance's proud smile, he had won their fishing bet that day.

Another framed photo drew her attention, one she hadn't seen before. She was sitting at a dining table between Kyle and Josh. Recognition kicked in. Claudia had taken that photo two weeks ago, during Josh's sixteenth birthday celebration at Gemelli's Italian Café.

Roxy sensed she was being watched. When she turned, she met Kyle's blue-eyed gaze, and a soft thrill rippled through her—something that had been happening lately.

Kyle had been glancing up at Roxy, in between taking notes. She'd surprised him when she turned in his direction. After they exchanged smiles, he shifted his full attention back to his conversation with Lt. Jay Boyd at the Sheriff's Office. The two men had been co-workers before Kyle joined Riverside Bay's police department.

"… as you know, the body was found wrapped in a tarp and locked in the trunk," Boyd said. "Since the skeletal remains are consistent with Greta's petite size, I'm confident her dentist will confirm her ID." He paused. "Judging by the position of the driver's seat, the last person who drove the Mercedes was around six feet tall. That person was probably her killer."

"I agree." Kyle had been keeping his responses short, ever since Roxy entered his office.

"The autopsy revealed a hyoid fracture in the neck," Boyd continued. "I know you're aware the hyoid bone is well-protected by the lower jawbone. Most hyoid fractures require the use of considerable force, like strangulation. In the absence of any other injury to the skeleton, the coroner listed this as the probable cause of death. Since Greta's car was used in the hit and run, I think we can assume that the person who killed her was also involved in Vance's murder."

"That's what I'm thinking," Kyle said. "Now we're dealing with two murd—" He caught himself and glanced up at Roxy, who was standing at the bookcase with her back to him.

Boyd didn't seem to notice his clipped ending. "I'll call you as soon as I hear back from Greta's dentist."

"Make sure you call me on my cell. I'll be in and out of the office today."

"Okay..." Boyd paused. "I know you and Vance were close, Kyle."

"We were," he said. "This case is personal." Kyle ended the call with Boyd and then stood and stretched his back muscles, which had tensed after sitting so long. He stepped around his desk. "Hi, sunshine. I'm sorry you had to wait. I know you don't have much time for lunch."

She looked up at him and broke into a dimpled smile that quickened his heartbeat. "Mack said he'd cut me some slack on my route schedule because of my arm. If we take the alley short cut to the diner, that'll save time."

"Are you sure? I mean, you've avoided that alley ever since—"

"I'm sure," Roxy said. "Yesterday, when I was making my down-town deliveries, I decided it was time to start using it again." She paused. "It's kind of spooky that the sinkhole opened up a few hours later, exposing Greta's car."

They left the police station through the rear exit. When they entered the alley, a familiar burning pain ignited in Kyle's gut, fueled by the bitter knowledge that Vance's fatal hit and run had been a deliberate act. He glanced at the spot where he'd found his wallet. It could have landed there after the impact, and Vance's driver's license could have slipped out in the process. But that missing license still bothered him.

Roxy stopped suddenly and rubbed her arms. "I got chill bumps yesterday, when I walked down this alley. It was like... I felt close to Vance, somehow. And today... I feel his presence again." She looked up at Kyle, her expression calm. "Do you feel it?"

He shook his head. "Every time I walk down this alley I get angry, thinking about the cold-blooded way Vance was murdered."

Roxy nodded. "I've felt that way, too. My counselor said that anger and grief are closely connected."

When they reached the employee entrance to Milo's Diner, Kyle punched in a code and unlocked the door. He led the way through the storage area and pushed open the kitchen's swinging door. He waved to the tall, portly man standing at the grill. "Hi, Uncle Milo. Rox and I are here for lunch. We'll have the usual."

Roxy peered into the kitchen. "Hi, Milo."

"Hi, you two." Milo Ransom saluted them with his long spatula. A fringe of graying hair covered his forehead, beneath his red base-ball cap. The words Milo's Diner were stitched on the cap, over the silhouette of a classic car. A grease stain partially obscured an identical logo on his red bib apron. "I'll have your orders up, pronto." He flipped a row of burgers on the grill, and the sizzling sound intensified.

Kyle's mouth watered as he breathed in the delicious aroma of grilling meat. It brought back memories of working with his uncle in that kitchen, during high school and college breaks. He opened the door leading to the dining area and followed Roxy inside. The diner's décor screamed 1950's, with posters of classic cars, chrome tables topped with red Formica, and seats upholstered in black and white checked fabric. As he walked past a booth, someone tugged his shirt sleeve.

"Hey, good-looking. What's your hurry?"

He stopped. "Oh... I didn't see you, Melody."

Roxy tossed a greeting over her shoulder and continued walking toward their usual booth, at the far corner of the diner.

Melody Manor ignored Roxy. She looked up at Kyle and patted a spot on the bench seat next to her. "Want to join me for lunch? I'm waiting for my sister, but she might be a no show."

He shook his head. "I'm having lunch with Rox."

Melody frowned. Then she flicked her long blonde hair behind her shoulders and gave him a wide smile. "It's been ages since we went out, Kyle. My class reunion is tomorrow night, and my date had to cancel. If you're free, would you like to go with me?"

He hesitated. He'd been hoping Rox would ask him to go as her date.

"Kyle?" Melody touched the back of his hand.

He pulled his hand away. "Ah… I'm not sure. There's a lot going on at work."

"You don't have to give me an answer right now. I'll stop by your office later."

"Okay," he said. "Enjoy your lunch."

Roxy was reading her phone screen as he approached the booth. She had taken the seat facing the back wall, as usual.

He slid into the bench seat across from her, which gave him a full view of the diner. As a police officer, he always sat in the best spot to observe the activity around him. He never sat with his back to the door.

"Aunt Nell just texted," Roxy said, without looking up. "She wants to know how I'm doing. I'll send her an answer right away, so she won't worry."

Kyle watched her as she thumbed the message. Light streamed in through the window, highlighting the reddish tint in her wavy auburn hair. Stray locks had come loose from her ponytail, and she paused to tuck them behind her ear. When she glanced up, he focused on her pretty hazel eyes. Today they held a deep emerald green color with amber flecks. Some days they radiated the warmth of burnished gold.

She set down her phone.

Kyle pointed to the cracked screen. "Rox, you have the worst luck with your phones. Did that happen yesterday?"

"Yeah, I'm lucky it still works."

"You weren't so lucky the last time, when you backed your mail truck over your phone."

She did an eye roll. "Or the time before that, when I dropped my phone in the grocery store and ran over it with a full cart. And the time before that, when a wave hit the fishing boat and my phone fell over the side—"

"You mean, the burial at sea?"

She smiled. "Good thing I back up my phone data every week. I've also learned how to find the best deals on used phones." Her text chime rang, and she glanced at the screen. "It's Jo." She frowned as she read the message. She thumbed a quick reply and then slipped the phone into her pocket. "It's something about our class reunion. I'll call her back, later."

"Is there a problem?"

Roxy sighed. "Jo's in charge of registration. She just warned me that Trent's flying in from Minnesota tonight. He made a last-minute reservation."

"Trent...?"

"Thorson," Roxy said.

Kyle nodded, making the connection. "Vance and I knew his older brother. Seth graduated two years behind us, in Claudia's class." He paused when he read Roxy's troubled look. "Why would Jo need to warn you that Trent's coming to the reunion?"

"He and I..." She looked down at her hands. "We were engaged."

"You were engaged in high school?"

"Only for a few months. It... ah... ended suddenly." Roxy kept her focus on her hands as she flexed her fingers. "But that turned out to be a blessing. After graduation, I was free to move to Orlando and help Grandma Anna while she went through chemo. When she died, I helped Grandpa Leo sell their condo and move into the Senior Living Center here in town." She paused and looked up at him. "Trent is divorced, and he asked Jo a lot of questions about me. She's convinced he wants us to get back together..."

Kyle tensed.

"...and I really don't want to see him again! Not after the way he—" She made a fist and shook her head.

Her sudden anger sparked his curiosity. He opened his mouth to ask her what happened, but something held him back.

"How are things with Melody?"

Kyle blinked. It took a moment to redirect his thoughts. "Fine, I guess."

"You guess? The way she talked to you just now... I assumed you were dating again."

He shook his head. "She's not my type."

"Oh."

Kyle thought he saw a look of relief cross Roxy's face, and then he dismissed it as wishful thinking. He glanced up as Thelma Ransom approached their booth, carrying a tray of food. "There she is, my favorite aunt!"

Thelma grinned. "I'm your only aunt. That cuts down on the competition." A frizzy mass of salt and pepper hair framed her plump face. She rested a corner of the tray on the table as she set down their plates. "Rox, here's your BLT on whole wheat. And Kyle, here's your double cheeseburger." She set down two sides of sweet potato fries and two iced teas. "Can I interest you in fresh apple pie for dessert? I baked a batch of pies this morning."

"Sure, bring a slice for both of us," Kyle said. "You'd better put them in takeout boxes, in case we run out of time."

"Coming right up." Thelma walked away, carrying the tray at her side.

Roxy opened her sandwich and poured ketchup over the bacon strips.

Kyle suppressed a grin. She used ketchup on almost everything. It was a quirky habit he found endearing.

"I couldn't help overhearing your phone conversation while I was waiting in your office," Roxy said. "When I heard you say, 'this case is personal' I figured you were talking about the hit and run investigation. Have you found out anything new?"

He shook his head as he picked up his cheeseburger. "Just reviewing the case." He took a large bite, savoring the juicy flavors of grilled meat and melted cheese. They went quiet for a few minutes as they ate. A high-pitched wail caught his attention and he glanced up. A young woman stood at the diner's entrance, holding a fidgeting toddler. Kyle instinctively shifted his gaze toward the row of booths on his left. He caught Melody and her sister leaning out into the aisle, staring in his direction. As soon as he made eye contact, their heads disappeared behind the tall booth seats.

Roxy took a sip of tea. "Kyle, I'm glad Greta's car has been found. But seeing it... how damaged it was... brought back a lot of sad feelings. When I saw Earl this morning, I thought about how I'll never have the chance to grow old with Vance—" She paused and shook her head. "Here I go again."

When he saw the tears welling in her eyes, his own feelings of grief shot to the surface. Kyle pushed back his emotions as he handed her a handkerchief.

"I haven't returned the one you gave me yesterday." She hiccupped as she dabbed her eyes.

"Don't worry, I have plenty of handkerchiefs. April used to give me a boxed set every Christmas, partly as a joke. I still haven't opened the last box she gave me."

She nodded. "That's because you're sentimental. You don't talk about your feelings that much, but I know they run deep."

He smiled. She had no idea how much his feelings had deepened for her. "So... how's your arm? Is it very sore?"

"This morning I could hardly lift it, but my stitches aren't as painful this afternoon. I was worried I'd have to skip the camping trip with my friends. Now I think my arm will be fine."

"Rox, what gave you the idea for this trip? Did you and Jo go camping when you were growing up?"

She shook her head as she tucked the handkerchief inside her small purse. "We never camped. Aunt Nell and Uncle Cal always rented a beach house for our summer vacations. Sal Whitlock is the only one in our group with any camping experience. She and Matt go camping in the Ocala National Forest every chance they get. This trip was her idea. I guess our class reunion made her nostalgic."

"How many are going?"

"Six, including me. We were all on the majorette squad." She took the last bite of her sandwich.

"You were a majorette?"

Roxy nodded, chewing. She raised her hand to indicate she'd explain in a minute.

Kyle ate the rest of his burger and thought about how little he knew about her early life, even though they'd grown up in the same small town. Their six-year age difference partly explained it. And their relationship had remained superficial during the years she was married to Vance. But after his murder, their shared grief had drawn them close.

Roxy took a quick sip of iced tea and said, "Jo and I got hooked on baton lessons as kids. We even invented our own routines, like twirling a baton in each hand and tossing them to each other, like jugglers. Sometimes we'd spin around in circles as we tossed them."

"I never knew you had that kind of talent."

She smiled. "Hard to believe, isn't it? Especially since I can't seem to keep a phone very long without destroying it."

Kyle chuckled. He salted his fries and popped a few into his mouth.

"I'd never tell Jo this, but she was actually a better majorette." Roxy paused as she drenched her own fries with ketchup. "I was klutzy, but she rarely dropped a baton. Since we were raised together, there's always been a sort of competition between us. Jo was better at athletics, but I have a snapshot memory, so I got better grades. She'd say, 'I'm a month older,' and I'd say, 'I'm an inch taller.' It was always like that."

"That's normal," Kyle said, chewing. "It's the kind of sibling rivalry that happens when you're close to someone. Remember those fishing bets Vance and I had?"

"How could I forget?" She pulled a fry from the ketchup mound and ate it.

"Which campground are you using in the Ocala Forest?"

"None of them. They allow primitive camping on the Ocklawaha River, and Sal's taking us to a site she and Matt always use. She said the area is so remote, it's one of the few places where you can see Florida's true natural beauty." She looked at him. "Doesn't that sound cool?"

He thought it sounded a little crazy. "Rox, you don't have any camping experience—"

"That's part of the appeal, Kyle. It's a chance for me to challenge myself... to get away and spend time in the beautiful forest with my best friends." She stopped and studied his face. "Don't look so worried. We've arranged to stay at a lodge on the river for two of the three nights. We're only camping out one night, because Bri Thorson has health problems."

"Bri.... Trent's sister?"

Roxy nodded. "Bri and I have never let the broken engagement come between our friendship." She ate a few more ketchup-soaked fries.

Kyle went quiet as he thought about the snakes, bears and alligators in the Ocala Forest.

Roxy wiped ketchup off her hands and glanced up. "You really are worried about me." She smiled and reached for his hand.

He placed his other hand on top of hers.

"What would I do without you, Kyle? When you saw how depressed I was after Vance died, you encouraged me to join the Clinic's grief counseling group. And when I wanted to sell the fixer-upper house Vance and I bought, you convinced me to keep it and go ahead with the renovation. You said it would help me to heal... and Earl, too. And you were right. Tearing out ugly carpets, cabinets and wallpaper was like therapy. We weren't just rebuilding a house; we were rebuilding our lives. And you were there, working alongside us."

"Don't forget, Jo and Claudia helped with the demo," Kyle said.

"I knew Jo would volunteer, but Claudia surprised me. She kept on working, even though she broke all her fingernails."

Kyle released Roxy's hand when he saw his aunt approaching.

Thelma set down the takeout boxes. "I made both pie slices extra-large, Kyle."

He grinned at her. "That's why you're my favorite aunt."

They slid out of the booth and Kyle led the way to the diner's back door. He held it open, and then he followed Roxy outside, into the shock of blinding sunlight and sultry heat. She fell in step with him as they walked down the alley. "I meant to ask you about Josh at lunch. How is the church's mission trip going in Georgia?"

"They've been repairing homes for veterans, and Josh loves the construction work. Yesterday, he worked on wheelchair ramps."

Roxy nodded. "Josh is a natural carpenter, like his dad. He helped out a lot, during the house remodeling." She paused. "It's hard to believe he's sixteen, now. I remember when he was your little fishing buddy, like Sheriff Andy Taylor and Opie."

Kyle glanced at her and smiled. "After Josh gets back from the mission trip, he'll start working at the diner, just like I did when I was his age. He plans to get his driver's license this summer, and he wants to earn as much money as he can to buy a used car. I told him I'd chip in on that." He stopped at the police station's rear entrance and tapped his ID badge on the scanner. As he walked inside, his ringtone sounded. He juggled the takeout boxes as he checked his phone screen. "Rox, it's the Sheriff's Office. Will you put our pies in the break room fridge? You can pick yours up after work."

"Sure." She reached for the takeout boxes. "Thanks again for lunch."

He swiped the screen and kept his gaze on Roxy as she hurried down the hallway. "Boyd, what's the news?"

"The dentist confirmed the ID on the body."

By mid-afternoon, the humidity had risen to suffocation level. The sun's relentless heat drained Roxy's energy as she weaved her way along the crowded downtown sidewalks, towing her rolling box from building to building. The news linking Greta's car to the hit and run had spread around town, and everyone on her mail route wanted to talk about it. Each comment about Vance's death, no matter how kind or compassionate, brought back sharp, painful memories. Roxy felt as if the scar covering her grief was being ripped away, stitch by stitch, exposing the raw wound.

She let out a relieved sigh as she headed toward the entrance to Shyanne's Boutique, her last downtown delivery stop. After this, she had two remaining stops; the Senior Living Center and Riverside Bay Estates.

The bell on the boutique's entry door made a soft jingling sound as she entered. The store's owner glanced up and smiled. Shyanne Waltham was in her late fifties, but her dark brown complexion held a youthful look. She handed a garment bag to a customer and said, "I hope you'll come back and visit our little town again."

The young woman held up the bulging bag as if it was a trophy. "When I get back to Duluth, I'm going to tell everyone about River-side Bay. It's a great place to shop." The bell on the door jingled as she walked out.

Shyanne turned to Roxy. "I think you'll be happy with your dress."

"Thanks for doing the alterations so quickly. I shouldn't have waited until the last minute to buy it." Roxy handed Shyanne a stack of mail and then collected a few outgoing bills from a tray at the end of the checkout counter.

Shyanne quickly thumbed through the mail stack before setting it under the counter. "Rox, do you want to take your dress with you, now?"

She shook her head as she tucked the outgoing bills into her shoulder bag. "I'm driving an old mail truck today, and it has a disgusting moldy odor. I don't want my dress hanging inside it while I finish my route. Can I pick it up after work?"

"Sure, if you can get here by four thirty. I'm closing early so I can catch an evening flight to Savannah. We're having a big family reunion, the first one in years. The shop will be closed all weekend."

"That sounds like fun. Have a great time," Roxy said. "If I can't make it back before you close, I'll call Claudia at the realty office and ask her to pick up the dress for me." She turned to leave and then stopped when Shyanne called out her name.

"I heard about Greta's car, Rox. I'm sorry, I know this must bring back painful memories."

Roxy nodded. She read the compassion in Shyanne's eyes, and it blunted the pain. Her husband died of cancer a few weeks before Vance was killed, and they attended the Clinic's grief counseling group together. Shyanne was the one who gave Roxy the book of quotes by Epictetus.

After she took another water break, Roxy drove out of the Silva Building's parking garage and turned onto Marina Drive. She drove to the Senior Living Center, one block away and parked in her usual spot. Despite the heat, several residents were sitting in patio chairs on the shady front porch, beneath the whirling ceiling fans. She walked up the wheelchair ramp and then stopped a moment and greeted all of them.

A heavy-set man frowned at her. "It's about time you showed up."

Roxy responded with a cheery smile. Grumpy Hiram's chronic sour disposition had become a personal challenge. She hadn't given up hope that someday she might encourage him to smile back at her.

When she walked into the Center's spacious air-conditioned lobby, she saw her grandpa sitting in his usual chair, facing the entrance.

Leo Patterson's expression brightened. "There's my Roxy-girl!"

"Hi, grandpa." Roxy held his walker steady as he gripped its handles and slowly rose to his feet. Then she gave him a hug.

Leo accompanied her to the front desk and chatted with the receptionist while Roxy retrieved a luggage cart. She rolled it outside and loaded it with plastic tubs of pre-sorted mail and packages. Perspiration soaked the collar of her uniform shirt as she pushed the heavy cart up the wheelchair ramp.

Her grandpa joined her when she re-entered the cool lobby. She kept pace with his walker as she steered the cart toward the mailboxes. Residents greeted her with their typical enthusiasm. Some of them eyed her with awe as they commented on her bandaged arm. Roxy felt like a Broadway star, approaching the stage for a live performance. The afternoon mail delivery was considered a daily social event, and her sinkhole experience had obviously enhanced its appeal.

Residents had already claimed every spot on the couches and chairs in the seating area near the mailbox panel, except for the chair where Leo usually sat. It always remained open, as if an invisible 'reserved' sign had been placed on it. Latecomers clustered in small groups nearby, leaning on canes or sitting on the padded seats of their walkers.

A hush always fell as Roxy unlocked and opened the doors on the long mailbox panel. Talking resumed as soon as she began distributing the mail. Over the years, she'd developed the ability to carry on conversations with residents, while reading addresses and filling the correct mailboxes.

Dottie Becker stepped toward Roxy and leaned on her cane. "My dear, what a shock it must have been, finding Greta's car in that pond."

Roxy flinched, as the gruesome image of the damaged Mercedes flashed into her mind. She gave Dottie a polite nod and continued working.

Another resident said, "I'd love to know where Greta's been hiding. She sure went crazy after Burke threw her over."

Leo spoke up. "I think Greta was always few cards short of a full deck, even when she was married to Quint and acting like Mrs. Mayor."

Roxy smiled at her grandpa's choice of words. She retrieved a stack of pre-sorted mail from a tub, and hesitated when she read Betty Norman's name on the top envelope. The automated forwarding system had missed it. Betty's mail was now being sent to the executor of her estate, Burke Devlin.

Dottie peered over Roxy's shoulder. "There's a letter for Betty. I sure do miss her. She was a wealthy woman, but you'd never know it, the frugal way she lived. Her husband made a fortune in real estate before he died. What was the name of Ruford Norman's company?"

"EverNorm Development," Leo said.

"Betty never spent much on herself," Dottie said. "But she was generous to others. When her sister Jane fell on hard times, she set up some sort of fund for her, so she could keep on living here."

"I think it's suspicious, the way Betty died… and Jane, too," Leo said. "Both sisters managed their diabetes for years without making mistakes. What are the chances they'd both die of an insulin overdose, a few months apart?"

"Leo, you watch too many detective shows," Dottie said. "Mistakes happen, especially at our age. I could see Jane's memory was going downhill."

"Maybe so," Leo said. "But Betty's mind was still sharp as a tack."

"That's not what I heard," Grumpy Hiram said. "I talked to Betty's daughter at the funeral, and she claimed her mother's mind was failing. She said Betty threw away a lot of her money, putting it into charity funds she'd never heard of."

Dottie Becker tapped her cane on the floor. "Betty loved giving money to all kinds of charities! That doesn't mean she was losing her mind!"

"That's right," another resident chimed in. "How would Betty's daughter know anything about her state of mind? She rarely came to visit her."

"She never came to visit her," Dottie said. "If you ask me, Burke Devlin did far more for Betty Norman than her daughter ever did. He brought her flowers every week... and her sister Jane, too. Burke treated both of them just like he treated his own mother. God bless Lydia's soul."

Roxy glanced at the wall clock and quickened her pace as she distributed the last box of mail. As she closed and locked the doors on the mailbox panel, residents began pulling out their mailbox keys. She placed the empty mail tubs on the luggage cart and walked back to the front desk with her grandpa.

"I'll see you tomorrow," Leo said.

"I'm taking the day off, grandpa. My class reunion is tomorrow night, remember?"

"Oh, that's right." Leo leaned on his walker. "And then you're leaving on Sunday afternoon to go camping in the Ocala Forest with your friends."

She nodded.

"Make sure you tell your friends I worked at a CCC camp in that forest when I was a teenager during the Great Depression. Earned twenty-five dollars a month building roads and firebreaks. Sent twenty to my folks and kept five to spend. We lived in barracks and wore surplus WWI army uniforms." He frowned. "Those scratchy wool uniforms smelled like mothballs when we first put them on."

Roxy smiled. She loved listening to his stories, no matter how many times she'd already heard them. She gave him a hug. "I'll see you at church on Sunday, grandpa."

"I hope Kyle won't be too busy to join us for lunch after church," Leo said. "I want to find out how the investigation is going."

Roxy thought about Dottie Becker's comment. Her grandpa loved watching detective shows, and he never missed the chance to talk to Kyle about his work.

"Don't forget, it's Taste of Italy Sunday," Leo said. "All you can eat lasagna for lunch. We need to get to the Center's dining room when it opens at eleven thirty. I want to start eating before the locusts clean the place out. People around here bring plastic bags in their pockets and purses and stuff them with food for later, like a takeout service. It's against the rules, but nobody ever does anything about it."

"We'll get to the dining room in time, grandpa." She smiled. "I need to go. Take care of yourself, okay?"

"Don't you worry about me, Roxy-girl."

She looked at him and thought, "I can't help it, grandpa." Each time she left him, she worried it might be the last time she'd ever see him—at least, in this life. An exaggerated fear of loss had haunted her since childhood, and she assumed it originated with the death of her parents. Her two miscarriages and Vance's sudden death had only reinforced it.

Roxy carried the empty mail tubs to the truck, loaded them in the cargo area, and then she sat for a moment in the sweltering truck and drank her last bottle of cold water. After checking the time on her phone, she tapped a familiar speed dial number. When the call clicked into Claudia's voicemail, she left a message asking her to pick up her dress at Shyanne's.

She drove out of the Center's parking lot and headed down Marina Drive, bouncing in the driver's seat as the dashboard fan blew hot air at her face. The gated entrance to Riverside Bay Estates came into view. She stopped at the gate and waved to the guard sitting inside the air-conditioned guard shack. He gave her a nod, and the gate slowly opened. Roxy drove to Dolphin Lane and parked the truck well away from the sinkhole area.

Every resident in the small, upscale neighborhood wanted to chat about her sinkhole experience. When she finally completed her door-to-door deliveries, she walked over to the yellow tape barrier and surveyed the damage. The sinkhole had enlarged, claiming another chunk of Dolphin Lane's pavement. If her mail truck hadn't been towed away, it would have disappeared into the hole. The drained retention pond looked like a vast muddy depression, dotted with scattered pools of murky water. Roxy peered into the sinkhole and saw only an eerie darkness.

"Hello, Rox! I forgot to give you this when you delivered my mail." Mae Sims walked up, pushing a brand-new baby stroller. Trixie sat in the stroller seat, looking contented. The elderly woman retrieved an extra-large Cool Whip tub from the shelf beneath the stroller seat and handed it to Roxy. "I baked double fudge brownies for you, a gift to thank you for saving Trixie."

"That's really sweet, Mae. Thanks."

"Do you want to try a brownie now?"

"Ah... I'm way behind schedule, today. I'll try a brownie as soon as I get home."

Mae nodded, looking pleased.

Roxy drove back to the post office, quickly completed her route duties and then clocked out. As she headed toward the employee exit, she stopped at her supervisor's office and glanced inside the open doorway.

Cedric Macklin was sitting at his desk, filling out a report. His posture remained straight and upright even while seated, and he wore his graying hair in a short, military-style cut.

"Hey, Mack. My vacation has officially started."

He looked up and took off his reading glasses. "Rox, come in here a minute."

She stepped inside. Something in Mack's deep, growling voice sparked an uneasy feeling.

"Reporters came here this afternoon. They wanted to talk to you."

She tensed. "Are they still here?"

"No. I told them you were scheduled on vacation and you'd be gone for a week." His expression relaxed into a smile, creating tiny wrinkles in the dark brown skin around his eyes. "Somehow, they got the impression you had already left town."

She grinned, as relief washed over her. "Thanks, Mack. I owe you one."

"It was the least I could do. You've had a couple of rough days, after finding Greta's car..." A look of sadness flickered in his brown eyes. He and Earl Silva—both retired Marines—had been friends for years. After the hit and run, Mack gave a generous donation to the Community Clinic, in Vance's memory.

"See you in a week... and thanks again, Mack."

"Enjoy your vacation," he growled. "And watch out for bears on that camping trip. The Ocala Forest is full of them."

As Roxy walked toward her car, she realized she hadn't heard back from Claudia. When she pulled out her phone, she was surprised to see she'd missed a text from Kyle:

"We have new evidence in the hit and run. Can you come to my office after work? I'm texting Claudia and Earl, too."

She typed: "Leaving the post office now. Be there in a few."

The reception desk stood empty when Roxy entered the police station's lobby. The day shift receptionist had gone off duty. She didn't bother pressing the button next to the entry door to summon one of the officers. Since Kyle was expecting her, she sent him a text, asking him to let her in.

Moments later, the entry door flew open, and Melody burst into the lobby. Her dark eyes flared red hot, like smoldering coals hit by a blast of wind. "What are you doing here?" The bleached blonde scowled at Roxy, as if she was trespassing on private property. "If you came to see Kyle, you're out of luck. I just left his office. He's getting ready for a meeting."

"I know. I'm meeting with him."

Melody's fiery eyes narrowed to glowing slits. "Oh... it's a private meeting, right? How long have these meetings with Kyle been going on? Maybe they started before Vance was kil—"

"Melody!" Kyle stood at the open entry door and stared at her with eyes as cold and blue as glacial ice.

Her expression registered surprise and then regret. She shot Roxy a hostile glance, as if to say she'd find a way to get even. Then she strode out and slammed the door. The sound echoed in the small lobby.

"I'm sorry, Rox..." Kyle held the door open.

Roxy shook her head as she walked past him. Humiliation mingled with anger, sending a rush of heat to her face.

They walked up the stairs and down the long hallway to his office without speaking. Kyle couldn't think of anything to say that might ease the sting of Melody's vicious words. He walked to his desk and picked up the chilled bottle of iced tea he'd purchased in the break room. "Are you thirsty, Rox?"

"Thanks." She took the bottle from him and briefly smiled. After taking a long drink, she plopped into a guest chair and set the bottle on the coaster next to his nameplate. Then she folded her arms and stared at the floor.

Kyle sat at his desk and paged through the notes he'd prepared for the meeting. The crisp sound of rustling paper seemed to amplify the tense silence between them. As the minutes ticked by, the tension steadily grew. He finally slapped down his pen. "Rox! Don't let Melody upset you! She's just a—"

"Self-centered… Hateful… Vindictive… Liar!" Roxy sat up straight. "I'm glad Earl and Claudia didn't walk in while Melody was spewing that garbage about us!"

Kyle nodded. He hadn't thought about that.

"It's been a hot, tiring day, and her outburst was the last thing I needed." She looked at him. "Melody was already upset when she stormed into the lobby. What set her off, and why was she here, anyway?"

"She came to invite me to your class reunion. And she gave me a shoulder rub."

Roxy's eyes widened.

"Melody invited me to the reunion when I saw her at the diner today, but I didn't give her an answer. Now that I think back, I guess she said she'd stop by my office, later." He shook his head. "I was so focused on a call with the Sheriff's Office, I didn't hear Melody walk in. When she put her hands on my shoulders, I got so startled, I dropped my phone! I had to end the call, and it was important!"

Roxy clapped a hand over her mouth.

"I whirled my chair around to face her, and she tried to sit on my lap! I stood up so fast, she almost fell on the floor. That's when

I lost it. I told her to leave... I had a meeting scheduled. Then I got your text and went to the lobby."

Roxy's shoulders were shaking. She pulled her hand from her mouth, and the sound of her laughter acted like a fresh breeze, sweeping the tension from the room. "Melody almost fell on the floor?"

He nodded and grinned. His body relaxed, and he leaned back in his chair. "I guess her outburst is partly my fault. I made her mad, and you were a convenient target."

"Don't blame yourself, Kyle. Melody and I have never gotten along." She paused. "You know I'm not a violent person. But when I realized what she was saying about us, I felt a strong urge to slap her into next week. You came out just in time."

"Too bad," Kyle said. "I might have enjoyed seeing that."

Their eyes locked, and they burst out laughing.

"You two are having way too much fun in here!" Claudia strolled into the office. "Sam saw me in the lobby and buzzed me in."

"You're not the only person he's buzzed in this afternoon," Kyle said, exchanging glances with Roxy.

"Is he joining us?" Claudia asked.

"No. He and Kendra are heading out to interview a witness. There was another burglary at Riverside Bay Estates last night."

"A string of burglaries and a sinkhole. That neighborhood is jinxed." Claudia sat in the guest chair next to Roxy. "Dad's on his way. I just got off the phone with him. He said it's been crazy, ever since the Sheriff's Office released the news about Greta's car. Reporters have been calling him at the realty office, and a news crew even barged in with cameras rolling, trying to get an interview. I'm glad I went to the spa after lunch. I was there all afternoon." She pulled a mirror from her purse and smiled as she checked her reflection.

"You got your hair layered," Roxy said. "And I love that navy blue nail polish."

Claudia held out her hands. "The color is called, 'Nautical but Nice.' I had tiny white anchors painted on them. Aren't they cute?"

Kyle watched them, amused at the fuss they were making over painted fingernails. He and Vance used to tease them about their 'beauty talk.' The memory prompted a stab of grief.

"Anchors? Oh, that's right," Roxy said. "Paul's sub comes into port tomorrow."

Claudia beamed. "I can't wait to see him! These long duty tours aren't easy. Nobody understands how hard it is to be the wife of a naval officer. At least Paul and I can email each other—" She stopped, and her face took on a guilty look. "Rox, I didn't get your message about the dress. It was loud at the spa and I didn't hear my phone. Did you get to Shyanne's in time?"

"No. But that's okay. I can go back to plan A, the dress I wore to Josh's birthday dinner."

Kyle spoke up. "I like that dress—"

"Oh, no!" Claudia shook her head. "That black dress is too plain. This is your class reunion, Rox. You need to wear a dress that'll wow everyone."

"Like this one?" Earl strode into the office, carrying a Shyanne's Boutique garment bag.

"My dress!" Roxy stood and took it from him. "Thanks!"

Earl sat in the chair next to Claudia. "Shyanne brought it over to my office after she closed the shop."

"That was sweet of her." Roxy looked around. "Where can I hang—"

"Right here." Kyle had already gotten up. As he closed his office door, he pointed to the hook on the back, where his summer-weight sport coat was hanging.

Roxy was still smiling as she walked back to her chair.

Kyle glanced at Earl as he sat down. "I was hoping Burke could be with us. When will he be back in town?"

"The realty conference ends tomorrow," Earl said. "But he didn't say when he's flying back."

"Burke texted me," Roxy said. "His plane lands tomorrow afternoon."

Claudia looked at her. "Why did he tell you that? Is he still harassing you about your class reunion?"

"He's not harassing me—"

"Rox, he is har—"

"Let's drop it!" Roxy paused and softened her voice, "Okay?"

Claudia clamped her mouth shut, sat back and folded her arms.

"What's going on?" Earl asked.

"It's nothing." Roxy gave him a reassuring smile and then turned to Kyle. "I'm anxious to hear about the new evidence."

Kyle nodded and made a mental note to ask Roxy about Burke, later. He leaned forward and looked at each of them. "What I'm about to tell you needs to be kept confidential. No exceptions."

Claudia unfolded her arms and sat up. All three of them nodded.

"We found a body locked in the trunk of Greta's car. We identified her skeletal remains through dental—"

"It's Greta!" Roxy gasped.

Claudia's mouth fell open, and Earl looked pained.

"That's right," Kyle said. "The Sheriff's Office won't release the information about Greta's death to the media until family members in New Jersey have been notified." He paused. "Two years ago, we assumed Greta had left town because her car was missing, along with her passport, her phone—"

"That's why you said we can't assume Greta was the driver," Earl said.

Kyle nodded. "We haven't ruled that out. But we think the person who killed Greta was probably also involved with her in the hit and run. That's why I set up this meeting. Since all of you knew Greta well, I got permission to release this information to you, so we could start brainstorming about who might have been involved in her murder. Of course, Burke knew Greta best. But I'll have to talk with him, later." He glanced at Roxy.

She met his gaze. Her face wore a dazed expression, as if she was struggling to piece together a jigsaw puzzle without a clear picture to guide her.

Kyle opened his notebook. "Let's start by reviewing the facts. Two years ago, on a Monday morning, Vance and Burke left their condos in the Silva Building and took the alley short cut to Milo's Diner, to have breakfast before a meeting. Burke ate at the diner every weekday morning. Greta knew his routine, but she probably wasn't aware Vance would be joining him. It was early, just before dawn. Visibility was limited in the alley, and the two men bore a close family resemblance. Greta, or an accomplice, deliberately drove her Mercedes—" Kyle stopped as a surge of anger closed his throat. He paused for a long moment. "Greta had a clear motive against Burke. They had recently broken up, and she'd had a hostile confrontation with him in a restaurant parking lot on Saturday, two days before the hit and run."

"I'll never forget that night," Earl said. "We had dinner at Ozzie's Grill to celebrate my birthday. Greta was sitting at the bar, and she saw us as we were leaving. Right away, she started screaming at Burke. She was drunk, out of control. She kept on screaming as she followed Burke out into the parking lot. He held his temper, until she accused him of embezzling—"

"That's when Burke went ballistic," Claudia said. "Vance stepped in and separated them. He pulled Greta aside and finally calmed her down."

"Do you remember any other details about that night... anything Greta said, or did that might be important?" Kyle asked.

Claudia and Roxy shook their heads.

Earl cleared his throat. "Kyle, there was something."

Earl kept his focus on Kyle. "Greta told Vance she had proof Burke was embezzling."

"What kind of proof?"

"Copies of financial files," Earl said. "Greta figured out Burke's passcode just before they broke up, so she could search his social media and financial accounts and see if he was cheating on her. She claimed she found suspicious transactions and copied them on a flash drive."

"Dad, you never told me that," Claudia said.

"Why didn't you mention this in your original statement?" Kyle asked.

"It didn't seem relevant. Greta arranged to meet with Vance the next day to show him that flash drive. Then she texted him on Sunday morning and cancelled, saying she had a migraine."

"No surprise there, considering how drunk she was Saturday night," Claudia said.

"So... you never saw this flash drive?" Kyle asked.

"No." Earl shook his head. "Vance and I were convinced it was a lie... just another one of Greta's crazy accusations against Burke. Remember how vindictive she was when she was divorcing Quint? He lost his re-election bid for mayor because of the way she publicly trashed his reputation."

"I'm sure Greta got some sort of twisted pleasure from doing that," Claudia said. "The accusations she threw at Quint were outrageous, but the media ate it up."

"Her flash drive story didn't make any sense, either," Earl said. "Why would Burke embezzle money from his client trust accounts? He inherited a fortune when his wife died a few years ago, and he built up a thriving law practice here in town. Then I wondered if Greta might actually have a flash drive... one that she doctored. It would have been easy for her to copy Burke's trust account files and then alter them to make it look as if he was embezzling." He paused and briefly frowned. "That's why I asked Vance to meet with Burke on Monday morning. I wanted him to review those files, in case Greta went public with a counterfeit flash drive."

Kyle nodded. "Since Vance was a CPA, he could have easily identified any of Greta's phony transactions."

"And then we could have responded quickly, by presenting the facts," Earl said. "You know how it is in a small town like Riverside Bay. Greta could have done a lot of damage to Burke's law practice... and my realty firm, since Burke does all our legal work. I just wanted to protect the family's reputation." He blew out a sigh and bowed his head.

Claudia reached out and patted his arm.

Kyle went quiet as he scribbled notes. He looked up and said, "Let's shift our focus to Greta's murder. We're assuming her killer was also involved in the hit and run. What could have been the motive to kill her?"

"Money," Roxy said. "If Greta hired a driver for the hit and run, she could have refused to pay because Burke was still alive. Maybe the driver got angry enough to kill her."

"It's possible," Kyle said. "Greta's bank accounts were emptied on the day of the hit and run. At the time, we assumed she did that before leaving town."

"Were you able to trace that money?" Earl asked.

"It was wired to a bank in the Cayman Islands and deposited to an account in the name of a shell company. Then we hit a dead end, because of their banking privacy laws."

Roxy looked at Kyle. "I talked to Quint this morning. He said he was sure Greta's money was stashed in the Cayman Islands."

"Interesting..." Kyle jotted that down.

"What happens to Greta's half-ownership in the marina business, now that she's dead?" Earl asked.

"If it reverts back to Quint, that gives him a strong motive," Kyle said. "It depends on their divorce agreement, and the terms in her will."

"I can ask Burke," Earl said. "He'd know the terms in both—"

"I'd prefer to talk to him about that," Kyle said.

"Wait a minute," Claudia said. "I know Quint had a strong motive against Greta... and Burke, too. But I can't see him as her accomplice in the hit and run or anything, not after their bitter divorce. Greta tore his world apart. He's a beaten man."

"Don't let his shabby appearance fool you," Kyle said. "Quint has an intelligent mind."

"Maybe when he's sober," Claudia said. "Besides, if Quint wanted to reclaim full ownership of his marina, he'd want Greta's body to be found, wouldn't he? Why hide it in her car at the bottom of a pond? That makes no—"

"Kyle! I just remembered something Burke told me about that retention pond," Earl said. "Part of it borders an undeveloped tract of land owned by EverNorm Development."

Claudia looked surprised. "Alan Everley's company?"

"How does Burke know about the EverNorm tract?" Kyle asked.

"Alan hired him to do legal research on that tract a few years ago," Earl said. "Something to do with development restrictions, since it's close to the wildlife refuge."

Roxy's eyes widened. "Alan was sitting with Greta at Ozzie's Grill, the night she made that scene with Burke."

Claudia turned to Roxy. "I remember seeing Alan with Greta, too. He drove her home after Vance calmed her down."

"Greta and Alan?" Kyle shook his head. "He's old enough to be her grandfath—"

"He's male, wealthy and breathing," Claudia sniffed. "That's all Greta ever cared about."

Kyle tapped his pen on his notebook and thought about Alan Everley. Burke could have discovered something when he researched EverNorm's land holdings—something he could use as blackmail. Maybe Alan wanted Burke silenced. He turned to Earl. "You've known Alan Everley a long time. Do you think he could have been Greta's accomplice in the hit and run?"

"It's possible. Alan has a nasty temper. You wouldn't want him as an enemy. Remember his former business partner, Ruford Norman?"

"He was the 'Norm' of EverNorm Development," Kyle said.

Earl nodded. "He and Alan had a bad falling out, several years ago. A few days later, Ruford was found dead at the bottom of the stairwell at work. His wife never got over it. Shortly after his funeral, Betty Norman sold their big house and moved into the Senior Center."

"I was still with the Sheriff's Office when that happened," Kyle said. "The case was in Riverside Bay's jurisdiction, so I wasn't involved in the investigation. I'll have to ask Sam about it. He's been with Riverside Bay's police department for years." He paused and added that to his notes. "Can you think of anything else?"

They shook their heads.

"Okay. Remember... the news about Greta's murder has to remain confidential, for now. Don't tell anyone." He glanced at Earl. "Not even Burke. I want to talk to him, myself."

Earl gave Kyle a nod before he left.

Kyle glanced up from his notes when Sam walked into his office. "How did the witness interview go? Did you get anything useful?"

"We did," Sam said, as he sat in the guest chair Earl had vacated a few minutes earlier. "Looks like the same group of burglars has been targeting those fancy houses in Riverside Bay Estates. The witness saw four men, white, mid-twenties, and they were driving a van that matches the description we got from the last witness. But he didn't see the license plate."

Kyle set down his pen. "Did he get a good look at them?"

"Only one of them," Sam said. "Kendra's meeting with the witness, right now. She's using that new software program to create a digital sketch of the suspect."

"Any luck with the prints on the jewelry case?"

"We got one good thumbprint that doesn't match the family or the housecleaner. We'll run it through the databases." Sam paused as he drank from his Brew Be takeout cup. "How did your meeting go? They must have been shocked about Greta."

"They were." Kyle quickly summarized the discussion while Sam took notes. "We need to interview Alan and Quint before the news about Greta's body is released. I want to see the reactions of both men when we tell them she's been murdered."

Sam nodded as he closed his pocket-sized notebook.

"Earl mentioned the Ruford Norman case," Kyle said. "Were you involved with that?"

"I hadn't made detective yet, but I was one of the officers who responded to the call. We got there around mid-morning. An employee had discovered Ruford's body in the stairwell a few minutes earlier. Betty told the detectives Ruford left for work around six, and the coroner said he'd been dead for hours. Everyone knew he was an exercise fanatic. He always used the stairs, even into his seventies. Ruford's death was ruled an accident." A doubtful tone had entered Sam's voice.

"You didn't believe that?" Kyle asked.

"It seemed suspicious to me," Sam said. "Alan admitted he came into work early that morning, but he always used the elevator. He claimed he had no idea Ruford was even in the building."

Kyle added this to his notes.

Sam paged through his notebook. "I hadn't thought of Alan as a potential suspect. But Quint doesn't surprise me. That scruffy guy came in here today around lunchtime and asked if we knew where Greta was. When I said I couldn't release any information to him, he blew up."

"That's strange. Why would Quint be so anxious to know where Greta is?"

"I don't know." Sam shrugged. "He just asked me if we found her."

"If we found her?" Kyle stared at Sam. "Maybe Quint already knows where Greta is."

Sam startled. "You mean... he's wondering if we've been able to identify her body?"

Kyle nodded. He added that to his notes, and then he looked up and smiled. "It feels good, Sam... working on this case again."

Sam smiled back and lifted his takeout cup as if he was raising a toast. He took a long drink and then asked, "Have you talked to Burke yet?"

Kyle frowned. "He didn't pick up when I called. I left a callback message."

Sam eyed him. "You don't like him, do you?"

"Burke has his good points. He's an intelligent lawyer, and he's a generous donor to local charities." Kyle paused. "But I also think he's an arrogant, self-centered egotist."

Sam grinned. "That description fits my brother-in-law, with a few exceptions. He's an arrogant, self-centered egotist. But he's not intelligent, he's not a lawyer and he's the charity the family donates to."

Kyle laughed out loud. He stood and slipped his phone into his pocket. "Let's go talk to the chief. He wants an update on the investigation. Then we can grab a quick meal at the diner."

"Dinner at Milo's sounds great," Sam said. "I'm tired of microwave dinners. My wife's still in Cincinnati helping her mother recover from hip surgery. She won't be home for another couple of weeks." He unwrapped a peppermint and slipped it into his mouth. He held out another candy.

"No, thanks." Kyle said. "I've eaten more peppermints since you quit smoking, than I ever ate as a kid. Aren't you getting sick of them?"

"Not really," Sam said. "Right now, I need a sugar boost. This meeting might take a while. You know how Chief Thornton goes on and on, once he starts talking."

Kyle resisted the urge to say, "Just like you."

Roxy took Buddy for a walk and fed him dinner. Then she went upstairs to take a shower—a lukewarm shower. She reached for her hair dryer and then shook her head. After spending hours in front of that dashboard fan, she didn't want another appliance blowing hot air in her direction. As she towel-dried her hair, she realized the pain in her stitches had vanished. She slipped on comfortable workout shorts and a faded postal uniform shirt, too worn to wear on the job. When she walked downstairs, she saw Buddy curled up on his favorite rug in the family room. "There's my sweet guy."

The retriever lifted his head, and his wagging tail thumped hard against the floor.

Roxy went into the kitchen and made a grilled cheese and ketchup sandwich on homemade wheat bread. She sliced an apple she'd chilled in the refrigerator and then carried her plate and a glass of iced coffee to the island. Her gaze traveled around the kitchen and family room as she ate. When she and Vance drew up the renovation plans, they agreed on an open floor plan with a nautical theme, including ocean-blue walls, marble countertops and teak kitchen cabinets with brass seahorse knobs. He sketched out the design for the porthole window in the back door, the large porthole-shaped window over the sink, and the tall glass sliding doors in the family room, overlooking the Indian River. Roxy sighed. Vance would have loved this house.

She opened her high school yearbook, which she'd dug out of her closet the night before. She flipped through the pages until she reached the senior class photos. Her gaze locked on Trent Thorson's smiling face, and her stomach twisted into a tight knot. She pushed away the yearbook and wondered, "How am I going to cope with seeing him again, if I react like this to his photo?"

A knock sounded at the back door, and Claudia's face appeared in the window. Buddy trotted beside Roxy as she walked to the door and unlocked it.

Claudia entered and gave Buddy a quick pat on the head. She eyed Roxy's plate, sitting on the island. "Is that all you're having for dinner?"

"The heat took away my appetite." Roxy closed the door, walked back to the island and ate the rest of her sandwich standing up.

"At least you didn't make a casserole from one of your Aunt Nell's church cookbooks. I think every recipe includes cream of something soup or jello." Claudia wrinkled her nose.

Roxy grinned as she carried her empty plate to the sink. "Want some iced coffee?"

"Sure." Claudia strolled to the counter and peeked inside the Cool Whip tub. "I see you baked some brownies."

"No... Mae Sims baked them for me as a thank-you gift."

Claudia looked alarmed. "You didn't eat any, did you?"

"I bit into one. It tasted strange." Roxy inserted a coffee pod into the brewer and hit start.

"Rox! Do you have a death wish? Yesterday you leaped into a sinkhole to rescue Mae's dog, and now you're eating her brownies!"

"I didn't eat one. I told Mae I'd try one when I got home, and I took a small bite so it wouldn't be a lie."

"Even a small bite could send you to the ER! Remember Mae's banana bread at the church bake sale?"

"That mistake was probably a one-off," Roxy said. "You have to admit, Lestoil is the same amber color as vegetable oil. The bottles look similar, and the label says oil."

"That's no excuse! It's a household cleaner with a distinct odor." Claudia sniffed the brownies. "I smell pine! These have to go!" She carried the plastic tub to the garbage can.

"Don't toss the tub, I'll recycle it." Roxy set a glass of freshly-brewed iced coffee on the island. "Come and sit down. I assume you've already had dinner."

Claudia nodded as she sat on a barstool. "Dad and I just finished. I made a shrimp stir-fry, seasoned with fresh herbs from my rooftop garden." She reached for the open yearbook and used her finger to scan the individual photos. "You wore your hair long in high school, Rox."

"I did, but I had it cut short after graduation, when I moved to Orlando to help my grandparents. Since Grandma Anna was battling cancer, I donated my hair to an organization that makes wigs for cancer patients."

Claudia pointed to a candid photo of the senior prom. "Look, you're dancing with one of the Thorson brothers. He's every bit as good-looking as his brother, Seth." Her face took on a dreamy look, as if she'd instantly regressed to the age of sixteen, and she envied Roxy for attracting the best-looking guy in the class. "He's holding you awfully close. What's the story with you two?"

"We dated a while..." Roxy kept her tone casual. She knew if she mentioned anything about her broken engagement, Claudia would begin a grueling interrogation.

"I never knew you dated Seth's younger brother. But then, I was away at college when you started high school." She paused. "Looks like he was quite a catch!"

Roxy kept quiet and thought, "Looks can be deceiving, Claudia-girl."

"I had a huge crush on Seth before I started dating Duke. I think every girl in my class had a crush on Seth. I'll bet it was like that in your class, with... what's his name? Troy?"

"It's Trent. And yes, it was like that in my class, too."

"Looks like Bri Thorson was also in your class. Wasn't Troy a year or two older?"

"Trent was a year older, but he had to repeat the fifth grade because he broke both legs in a bike accident and missed so much school."

"What a bad break... no pun intended." Claudia grinned. "I remember Seth worked at his dad's auto repair shop during high school."

"Trent worked there, too," Roxy said.

"When did their dad close his repair shop and move away?"

"The year after we graduated from high school... shortly after his wife died. Her death hit the whole family hard. He opened another repair shop in New Smyrna Beach. Seth's now a partner in the business. I've kept in touch with Bri. She lives in a townhouse near her dad, and she works at a beachfront spa in New Smyrna."

"What about Troy?"

"He lives in Minnesota." Roxy reached for the yearbook and closed it, hoping this would put an end to her questions.

Claudia stared at the white anchor on the yearbook's navy blue cover. "Look, my manicure matches the cover." She smiled. "The Riverside Bay High School Sailors. Our mascot was a sailor, and now I'm married to one."

"I liked our mascot, but I hated our majorette uniforms," Roxy said. "Those white pleated skirts and sailor shirts made everyone look twenty pounds heavier."

Claudia pointed to the Shyanne's Boutique garment bag, hanging on the coat rack by the back door. "Haven't you tried on your new dress?"

"No... you said you'd stop by on your way out of town, so I waited. Since you convinced me to buy the dress, I thought you might want to see how the alterations turned out."

Claudia smiled.

Roxy lifted the bag off the coat rack and carried it upstairs to her bedroom. She slipped on the jade green dress and a pair of dressy sandals and then eyed her reflection in the full-length mirror. The satin fabric skimmed her curves just right, the hem fell just above her knees, and the lace sleeves covered her arm bandage. She ran a comb through her hair, letting it fall in waves to her shoulders. Roxy smiled, feeling a bit like Cinderella, wearing a beautiful dress instead of her frumpy postal uniform. Claudia had played the role of her fairy godmother—a bossy, irritating fairy godmother. Instead of waving a magic wand, she'd used her relentless nagging skills to persuade Roxy to splurge on a new dress for the reunion.

When she started down the stairs, she heard Claudia talking and assumed she was on the phone. Roxy didn't hear Kyle's deep voice until she reached the last step. She swept through the family room like a fashion model and adopted a stylish pose. "Ta da! How do I look?"

Claudia and Kyle stared at her. They sat next to each other at the kitchen island, like a mini-panel of fashion judges. Roxy half-expected them to lift up a sign with a numbered score. Buddy stood next to Kyle's barstool and gazed at her, as if he was the furry, tie-breaking judge. His tail thumped against the barstool legs. Buddy's vote was clearly a ten.

"Well?" Roxy extended her arms.

Claudia smiled. "The dress fits perfectly, and the color brings out the green in your eyes."

Roxy shifted her glance toward Kyle. The Milo's Diner takeout box caught her attention. "My apple pie! I forgot all about it."

Kyle visibly startled. "I… ah, saw it in the break room fridge, so I thought I'd drop it off on my way home." He stood and gave Claudia a brotherly kiss on the cheek. "Drive safely. Send me a text as soon as you get to Amelia Island tonight."

"I will."

"Say Hi to Paul for me. Do you know when his sub is docking tomorrow?"

"They never give out the exact time, but it's usually in the afternoon. I'll spend the morning at our condo getting everything ready, and then I'll drive to King's Bay."

Kyle nodded, and then he turned toward Roxy. "I forgot to tell you at lunch... I plan to use the boat early tomorrow morning. I want to do a little fishing before I go in to work. Helps to clear my mind. Want to come with me?"

"You know I love going out in the boat, but I can't tomorrow. Jo and I are going to pack for our camping trip." She paused. "Buddy always gets me up early. Why don't you have breakfast with me before you go? I baked cinnamon rolls this week and there are plenty left."

"Sounds great." He moved to the door, and Buddy trotted beside him. He leaned down and stroked the dog's head. As he straightened up, he looked at Roxy and smiled. "Your dress looks good, Rox. Really good."

CHAPTER 10

Kyle made the short drive to his house, located a few blocks away from the Indian River. When he parked his truck, his thoughts abruptly flashed back seven years, to the moment he pulled into this driveway, after spending twenty-two straight hours at the hospital. He'd spent the first several hours with April, as she struggled through a difficult labor. When the baby showed signs of distress, a C-section was performed. But complications arose. April sank into a coma after suffering a massive stroke, and their baby girl was stillborn.

He moved through the next nightmarish hours in a daze. Vance rushed to the hospital and stayed by his side, while Rox continued taking care of Josh at their condo. After April died, they offered to keep Josh a few more hours, so he could go home and rest. He knew he wouldn't sleep, but he was still in shock, stunned by the staggering impact of losing her and the daughter they had planned to welcome into the world together. He needed time to figure out how to break the terrible news to his nine-year-old son.

When he entered his kitchen and placed his keys on the counter, he thought he heard April call out a greeting. That's when he realized he was never going to hear her sweet voice, see her lovely face, or hold her in his arms again. The crushing weight of grief sent him to his knees.

Kyle's thoughts snapped back. He sat in his truck and wondered what had triggered the memory of April's death. Maybe it was the grisly sight of that damaged Mercedes. It had dredged up his grief at losing Vance, why not April, too? Her loss always seemed more intense whenever he celebrated a milestone in their son's life, and Josh had recently turned sixteen.

He recalled the support Rox and Vance had given him as he struggled to cope with April's death and his new role as a single father. He and Josh ate countless home-cooked meals at their condo. Rox took care of Josh whenever he had to work late hours, and Vance was the one who convinced him to admit his drinking had become a problem and encouraged him to attend his first AA meeting.

After Vance died, he'd felt an obligation to offer the same kind of support to Rox, by treating her to lunches and helping her with the house remodeling. But as the months passed, he became aware of how much he looked forward to the times they spent together. Her quirky personality had brought the sunshine back into his life, radiating the light and warmth that had been missing for too long. It seemed strange, at first, when he realized how much his feelings had deepened for her. But April had been gone for years, and Vance was gone, too.

Kyle let out a long sigh as he stepped out of his truck. When he entered his kitchen, his black lab bounded toward him. He leaned down and stroked the smooth fur on the dog's head. "Come on, Clyde. Let's go for a walk."

After Roxy changed back into casual clothes, she sat at the kitchen island and thumbed a text to Shyanne, thanking her for dropping off the dress with Earl and for doing a great job on the alterations. She attached a photo Claudia had taken of her wearing the dress and then sent the text. The coffee brewer began humming and Roxy glanced up at Claudia, who was standing at the counter.

"I'm making myself another iced coffee before I start driving to Amelia Island. Want a refill, Rox?"

"Sure, thanks." She handed her empty glass to Claudia. Her phone chimed and she glanced at the screen.

"Did Shyanne text back already?" Claudia stood with her back toward her as she slid a fresh coffee pod in the brewer.

"No, it's another text from Burke." Roxy scanned it and then sighed as she pushed her phone away. "When he stopped asking me out a few weeks ago, I thought I finally convinced him I'm not interested. Why has he started again?"

"Rox, you always look for the why in everything! The fact is, he's harassing you!"

She caught the injured tone in Claudia's voice. "I'm sorry I cut you off today, when you were talking about Burke."

Claudia turned and smiled.

"What more can I do? I keep telling Burke I'm not interested, in a nice way—"

"Rox! There's the problem." Claudia paused as she added cream to both iced coffees. "You're being too nice about it."

"Well, I don't want to cause any hard feelings. I'm grateful to Burke for helping me so much after Vance died. There were legal issues with the will, financial decisions to make. And I was so depressed... I couldn't think straight. Maybe I leaned on Burke too much and gave him the wrong idea—"

"Now you're blaming yourself!" Claudia set the iced coffees on the island and sat down. "Rox, if you want to get your message across, you have to be firm with Burke. I know him better than you do. I practically grew up with him."

Roxy nodded. "When did Burke and Aunt Lydia come to live with you?"

"I was eight. No, I had just turned nine. Burke was eleven, Vance's age. Uncle Red was in prison, and we drove up to Atlanta to see how they were doing. Dad saw Aunt Lydia was struggling, so he took them in. Mom had died a few months earlier, and Aunt Lydia became like a second mom to us. But Burke..." She shook her head.

"I don't understand why you and Vance never felt close to him. I grew up with Jo, and I love her like a sister."

Claudia's expressive brown eyes took on a faraway look, as if she was visualizing an old home video. "To tell the truth, I think we were jealous of the extra attention dad gave Burke. Vance had a harder time with that, since they were in the same grade. He always did well in school, but Burke excelled, like some kind of genius. Both of them earned scholarships to FSU. Vance started working at the realty firm after he got his accounting degree. But Burke went on to get his law degree at a private college in Atlanta. Dad paid all his expenses, and I think he did that to please Aunt Lydia." She paused. "Personally, I was glad when Burke moved to Atlanta to get his law degree. And I was even happier when he stayed there to work for that big law firm."

"That's where he met Erika," Roxy said.

"Yeah... I really liked her. I was a bridesmaid in their wedding." Claudia's face took on a sad expression.

"It was an awful shock when Erika died in that car accident," Roxy said. "That's why Burke moved back here. He said there were too many memories of her in Atlanta."

Anger sparked in Claudia's eyes. "I wish he'd never left Atlanta! If Burke had stayed there, Vance might still be alive!"

Roxy stared at her.

"As soon as he moved back to town, he got involved in that toxic relationship with Greta! Burke is the reason she planned that hit and run! It's his fault that Vance is dead, and I'll never forgive him for it!"

The intensity of Claudia's anger stunned her. Roxy sat for a moment, absorbing the impact. "I had no idea you felt this way."

"I have to work with Burke every day, so I hide it well." Claudia turned and gazed out the sliding glass doors overlooking the Indian River.

Roxy followed her gaze. The river's calm surface acted like a mirror, reflecting the vivid pink glow of sunset.

Claudia blew out a shaky sigh. "Rox, I'm sorry I got so emotional. I've been this way ever since Greta's car was found. It's triggered a lot of painful feelings."

"I know. It's brought back my grief, too."

Tears formed in Claudia's eyes. "I miss him, Rox."

"I do, too..." Roxy's eyes stung. As she blinked back hot tears, she felt the brush of soft fur against her leg. She reached down and stroked Buddy's head. "You're my sweet guy, aren't you?" She glanced at the takeout box from Milo's Diner sitting on the island. When she opened it, she breathed in the sweet aromas of apples and cinnamon. Her mouth watered as she eyed the thick golden filling between the flaky crusts. "Want to split this pie with me?"

Claudia wiped her eyes and stared at the generous slice.

Roxy could almost hear the computer clicking in Claudia's brain, estimating the calories and fat grams in a half slice. "Apples are a healthy fruit, and the sugar in the pie will keep you energized while you're driving to Amelia Island tonight."

"The sugar rush is only temporary, Rox."

"I'll send you off with a travel mug of fresh coffee."

Claudia's eyes registered surrender.

Roxy got out two forks and two plates and split the pie slice in half. They both went quiet as they dug in.

Claudia pushed away her empty plate. "I'm on a big sugar-high, now. I had key lime pie at the marina's restaurant, when I took that creepy Harmon Doyle and his ditzy partner to lunch. That man must be filthy rich. Did you see the gold jewelry they were wearing? I'm sure it was the real thing. Izzy's bracelets clanked together like jingle bells. And he drove—"

"A red Ferrari convertible. I saw it in the parking garage," Roxy said. "I knew his name sounded familiar, and then I remembered seeing it on return address labels when I delivered Burke's mail."

"That's your photogenic memory."

"Photographic memory," Roxy said. "Photogenic means you look good in photos."

"Oh." Claudia ran a hand through her layered hair, as if to say, "of course I do."

"Did Harmon Doyle decide to rent that condo at Marina View?"

"No... he seemed distracted when I showed it to him," Claudia said. "I got the feeling he wasn't really interested in renting anything in town."

"Then why was he so interested in my old condo?"

"I don't know." Claudia looked puzzled. "At lunch, he kept asking me questions about the hit and run. He seemed fixated on Burke's relationship with Greta."

"Well... the news about Greta's car was all over town," Roxy said.

"But he had a strange, morbid interest in the details."

"Claudia, everything about Harmon Doyle was strange."

"You got that right. He's creepy strange, like Uncle Red was. Do you know what dad used to call Red Devlin in private? The Red Devil."

"He died in prison, didn't he?"

Claudia nodded. "It really upset Aunt Lydia. She still had feelings for Uncle Red, even after all those years of abuse. But Burke showed no emotion at all."

Roxy thought about that. She wondered what kind of abuse Burke had witnessed, or even endured in his childhood.

"It's getting late, Rox. I need to get on the road." Claudia carried her plate to the sink and headed for the half bath, off the family room.

Roxy poured fresh coffee into a travel mug and put cinnamon rolls in a bag. She glanced up as Claudia returned. "Are you and Paul going anywhere special during his leave?"

"No, we plan to stay at our condo on Amelia Island and spend time getting to know each other again. Sometimes, after these long separations, I worry that maybe we've drifted apart." She paused. "I just realized how funny that sounds... drifting apart, when Paul's been away on a submarine."

Roxy smiled. "I've prayed for Paul's safety while he's been on sea duty. Now I'll pray for his homecoming."

Claudia gave her a hug. "Have fun at the reunion, Rox. You'll look gorgeous in that dress. Did you see Kyle's reaction when he first saw you?"

"What reaction? He just sat there and looked at me."

"Are you blind? Haven't you noticed the change in him?"

"What change?"

"Rox... Kyle is in love with you."

Her heartbeat quickened. "Did he tell you that?"

"He didn't have to. Kyle is like my second brother. I can tell, by the way he's been acting around you." Claudia looked at her. "You're smiling, Rox. Does that mean you feel the same way about him?"

"Well, I do love him... as a friend. He's one of the best friends I've ever had."

"A friend." Claudia tilted her head. "Seriously? When Kyle dated that blonde receptionist at the police station, it bothered you."

"She didn't seem right for him."

Claudia smirked. "And when he dated Melody, it really bothered you."

"She's totally wrong for—"

"I agree, Rox. Melody's a troublemaker. If she wasn't one of the top realtors in our office, dad would let her go." She paused. "I couldn't figure out why Kyle would date either one of them... and then it hit me. They're petite, with long blonde hair—"

"They resemble April!"

Claudia nodded. "You don't look anything like April, but it's obvious Kyle's in love with you. And I think you're in love with him, too."

Roxy blinked. "Tell me, have you set the date for our wedding?"

Claudia shot her a look. "Dad agrees with me. We've seen how lonely you and Kyle—"

"You've been talking to dad about Kyle and me?" Heat rose to her face. "Claudia, it's only been two years since Vance—"

"There's no law about how long you have to wait before moving on with your life."

An image of Melody's angry face flashed into Roxy's mind.

"Sorry, Rox... I didn't mean to upset you."

"No. It's not you, Claudia. It's Melody. She said something today..."

"What?"

"She accused me... Kyle and me... of being involved, even before Vance died."

"That vicious little...!" Claudia mumbled the last word.

"You should have seen Kyle's face—"

"Melody said that in front of him?"

Roxy gave her a quick summary of what happened, and they both laughed out loud when she described how Melody almost fell on the floor.

Claudia glanced at her watch. "Rox, I really need to start driving."

Buddy trotted out the back door ahead of them and began sniffing the dew-covered lawn. An oppressive amount of humidity lingered in the warm evening air. The floodlight on the garage clicked on, lighting up the driveway. Claudia slid into the driver's seat of her silver Lexus sedan, one of the Riverside Bay Realty cars awarded to the top realtors. She closed the door and lowered the side window.

"Drive safe," Roxy said.

Claudia pointed to the travel mug and the bag of rolls. "I'll be the most alert, energized driver on the road." She started the engine.

"Don't forget to check out the photos on my class reunion website."

Claudia nodded as she raised the window.

Roxy watched her drive away and whispered a prayer for her safety. She called Buddy inside, secured the deadbolt, and then stood for a moment, thinking about Kyle. She wondered if Claudia was right about his feelings. Hope stirred, followed by a rush of anxiety. She sighed, feeling too exhausted to think about it now.

Buddy's paws clicked on the wooden stairway as he raced upstairs ahead of her. When he reached the top, he turned and wagged his tail, as if he was saying, "Hurry up, slowpoke."

It was almost midnight when Roxy finished getting ready for bed. As she set her phone on the nightstand charger, she realized she hadn't answered any of Burke's texts today. She recalled what Claudia had said about being too nice. Maybe she'd get her message across if she continued ignoring his texts and calls. She turned out her bedside lamp and snuggled under the covers. Moonlight streamed in through the window blinds, sending thin strips of light across the wall. She yawned as her body relaxed. Drinking coffee in the evening rarely kept her awake.

Buddy jumped up on the bed. The mattress convulsed as he turned around in a full circle and stretched his warm furry mass beside her.

Roxy closed her eyes. Sleep rushed toward her like tumbling ocean waves, rocking her as they advanced and receded. She floated out on the rolling surf, and then she slipped below the surface, sinking deeper and deeper, until she reached the dark silent place where dreams are born.

Saturday morning

Roxy startled awake. Fragments of a dream came into sharp focus. Her dad in the driver's seat... A bright light... Dark shapes looming around her, shrouded in fog.

Her mind tried to capture the images, but they quickly receded into her subconscious. She'd had The Dream again, and it had left her shivering.

Buddy yawned and rose to his feet. Before Roxy could shield her face, he was giving her sloppy dog kisses. She rolled onto her stomach and buried her face in her pillow. "Buddy, stop!" Her voice came out muffled, but it didn't matter. He continued nudging and kissing her. She rolled out of bed, switched on the lamp and read the time on her phone: 3:36 a.m. She stretched her arms, feeling wide awake. Three and a half hours of sleep would have to do.

She dressed in workout clothes and took Buddy for a walk in the sultry night air. A full moon hovered in the black sky, surrounded by dim stars. Streetlights cast long oval pools on the sidewalk. Buddy tugged on his leash, pulling her from one light pool to another. When they returned home, she fixed his breakfast and then went upstairs and showered.

Roxy swept her damp hair into a topknot and applied light make-up. She slipped on a pair of denim shorts with a glittery design on the back pockets, and a yellow peasant-style blouse with sleeves long enough to cover most of the scratches on her arm. Roxy opened the black velvet box sitting on her dresser. She smiled as she gazed into the mirror and put on the pearl and alexandrite pierced earrings—June's birthstones. Aunt Nell and Uncle Cal had given her these earrings as a high school graduation gift. Jo had received identical earrings at graduation, since she was also born in June. Her birthday fell on the first day of the month, and Roxy's fell on the last day.

Buddy gave her an enthusiastic greeting as she walked into the kitchen. Roxy grinned as she stroked his furry, bobbing head. "How can you have so much energy, after waking me up so early?" She brewed a mug of coffee, carried it to the island and pushed aside her high school yearbook as she sat down. After opening the Bible app on her phone, she spent time praying and writing in her gratitude journal.

A familiar knock sounded at the back door. Roxy waved to Kyle as she set a basket of warm cinnamon rolls on the island, next to a bowl of fresh fruit. Buddy stood by her side as she opened the door.

Kyle walked in, wearing black cargo shorts and a tan fishing shirt that stretched across his muscular chest. "Good morning, sunshine."

Sunshine... He'd been calling her that for a while, but this morning Roxy heard the tone of endearment in his voice. She caught the masculine scent of his spice aftershave as she closed the door. "Where's Clyde? He usually goes fishing with you."

"I left him at home. It'll only take five minutes to drive back and pick him up, along with my fishing gear." He looked at her. "You really are a ray of sunshine in that yellow shirt."

Roxy met his blue-eyed gaze and her heartbeat skipped. She disguised it with a smile. "Have a seat, I'll make your coffee." She stood with her back to him and started the brewer. While she waited for his mug to fill, she listened to the sound of his deep voice as he talked to Buddy in affectionate guy-to-dog language. When she set his steaming mug on the island, she saw he was paging through her high school yearbook.

He pointed to her graduation photo. "Roxelle Anna Rode. Look at your long hair." He slid his finger down the page and stopped briefly on Trent's photo. Then he turned back a few pages, to her cousin's photo. "Joelle Lyn Dowling. It's interesting, Rox. You two are closely related, but you don't look anything alike."

"Jo inherited the Patterson's Scandinavian traits. If you put her graduation photo next to Aunt Nell's, it's amazing how much they look alike. I take after my dad, the Rode family's Scottish heritage." She paused. "It's weird that Jo and I don't resemble each other more, because our moms were twins."

"They were?"

She nodded. "I think that made it easier for me to adjust after my parents died. Aunt Nell looked so much like my mom."

Kyle looked up. "What was your mother's name? Did it begin with an N, since she and Nell were twins?"

"No. Well, yes. Their names began with the same letter, but it's L, not N. My mom's name was Lorelle Anna, and she went by Lori. Aunt Nell's name is Lynelle Anna, but she's always been Nell, not Lyn."

Kyle kept his gaze on her. "Your parents died in a car accident, right?"

She nodded. "It happened a few days after my sixth birthday, so I don't remember much about it. We were driving back to Orlando on a foggy night, after spending the Fourth of July at the beach with Aunt Nell and Uncle Cal. There was a head-on collision, and I was thrown from the car. A state trooper found me, nestled in a bed of leaves between a stand of trees. It was a miracle I wasn't thrown against one of them. At least, that's what Aunt Nell said. All I remember are bits and pieces. I dream about it, sometimes—" She stopped, as a shiver slid through her.

"You okay?"

She nodded. Something stirred in her heart when she read the genuine concern in his eyes.

"Rox, do you realize how similar our backgrounds are? We both lost our parents at an early age, and we were raised by an aunt and uncle. I was only three, too young to remember anything about my parents."

"What happened... was it a car accident, too?"

"No. They were mugged and killed in a parking lot. They had gone away for the weekend to celebrate their anniversary. Uncle Milo and Aunt Thelma were babysitting me." He paused and shook his head. "The police never made an arrest."

Roxy wondered if the unsolved murder of his parents had influenced his decision to go into law enforcement.

"I want to see a photo of you in your majorette uniform." Kyle quickly turned the pages until he found it. "Look at that sailor suit. I like the short skirt." He laughed when she gave him a playful nudge. "Let's see, there are eight majorettes on the squad and six are going on your camping trip. There's you and Jo, and you mentioned Bri Thorson yesterday at lunch, that makes three. And Sal Whitlock was the one who had the idea for the trip, that's four." He pointed to the shortest majorette. "Leeann must be going, since she and Sal are part of the same family."

Roxy nodded. "They married the Whitlock brothers the summer after high school. Sal and Matt got married in June. Leeann and Greg, in July." She paused. "When Matt and Greg opened up the Pet Wellness Center, Jo and I thought it was kind of funny. The Whitlock brothers used to fight like cats and dogs growing up, and now they're working together as vets, healing cats and dogs."

Kyle grinned.

Roxy pointed to the next majorette. "Tara is the last member of our group."

He nodded. "I got to know her and Leeann quite well last year. Tara was Josh's History teacher, and Leeann was his English teacher." He moved his finger to the seventh majorette. "There's

Tara's sister Nikki. They sure look like they're related, with that curly red hair."

"Nikki was the only junior on our squad." Roxy let out a sigh. "It's still hard to believe she passed away last year."

He looked up. "Tara and her husband adopted Nikki's son. How's that going?"

"Ian's been through a lot, but Tara said he's finally starting to adjust to all the changes in his life."

Kyle nodded. He turned back to the yearbook and pointed to the eighth majorette. "There's Melody."

Roxy frowned. "Little miss shoulder rub…"

He chuckled as he closed the yearbook, and then he pulled out the neighboring barstool for her.

As soon as Roxy sat down, she became acutely aware of Kyle's closeness. She could almost hear the hum of electrons as a current of attraction passed between them. They often brushed arms as they ate, since she was right-handed, and Kyle was left-handed. The current sparked each time they touched, setting off a fluttering in her stomach. Roxy found it hard to concentrate as they exchanged small talk, and she only picked at her food.

After breakfast, Kyle loaded the dishwasher, while she placed leftover rolls in a brown paper bag for him.

"Thanks, Rox." He carried the bag to the back door. "I'll go pick up Clyde and my fishing gear. I'll be happy to take Buddy fishing, too."

"You'd take both dogs, without me along to help? You're a brave soul."

He shrugged. "They usually settle down after the boat starts moving. Be back in a few minutes."

As Roxy closed the back door, she heard a sharp yelp, followed by a high-pitched whimpering. "Hey, Bud. What's the matter?" She walked around the island and found Buddy crouched in an odd position under one of the wooden barstools. "What in the world?" She went down on her knees and crawled next to him.

Buddy's tail thumped against the tile floor. He tried turning her way, but something jerked his head and he yelped again.

She leaned close, gently pushing his thick blond fur out of the way until she discovered the problem. Long crooked nails protruded from a barstool leg, and they had snagged the tag ring on his collar. "How did this happen, Bud?" She glanced at the barstool's other legs and saw long nails protruding from all of them, at the point where they attached to the seat bottom. She muttered, "That's why I got such a great deal on these barstools at that estate sale."

Roxy freed the tag ring, and Buddy leaped away. He let out a joyful bark and then dashed back and showered her with sloppy kisses. She turned to avoid his dog breath, and her head hit the bottom of the seat. She twisted her neck back and forth, as Buddy continued altering the angle of his love attacks. When she tried backing out from under the stool, something yanked her hair and she let out a sharp cry. The pain shot down to the roots.

She crawled back under the seat and used her elbows to keep Buddy at bay as she probed her hair. Nails had snagged the elastic band around her topknot, and they were now embedded in the thick tangled mass. Every head movement triggered a sharp pain. She thought, "I can't believe this! I'm trapped by my hair under a barstool, and my sweet Buddy is torturing me with his slobbering affection. I can't even turn my head to get a view of the tangle, without yanking my hair out by the roots." Roxy heard a knock on the back door and shouted, "Come in, Kyle! I need help!"

The door flew open and Clyde started barking. "Rox! Where are you?"

"Over here!" She dodged another one of Buddy's kisses. "Ouch! I'm under a barstool."

He laughed. "That's quite a view. I like the sparkles on your back pockets."

"Stop laughing! Ouch! My hair is caught on this stool and Buddy is having a love fest."

Kyle laughed even harder. "Come here, Bud." He whistled, and Buddy left Roxy's side.

A black furry head came into view.

"Clyde, get back here!" Kyle whistled again. "I'll put both dogs in the back yard, Rox. Wait there."

She groaned. "I'm not going anywhere."

Moments later, Kyle slid the neighboring barstool out of the way and kneeled beside her. His grinning face appeared in her peripheral vision. "I'm guessing this isn't the right time to ask what you're doing under here."

"No, it's not! Just get my hair untangled... please. I think the band around my topknot is snagged on the nails attaching the legs to the seat."

His fingers yanked her hair as he probed the tangle.

"Ouch! Ow, that hurts!"

"Sorry, Rox. This is a real mess. I might have to get the scissors."

"No! Don't cut off chunks of my hair! Think how that will look."

He chuckled.

"Stop laughing! Just get me untangled. I don't care how much it hurts." She clenched her teeth together to keep from crying out each time Kyle tugged her hair.

"I've almost got it. Okay, that's it. You're free."

"Thanks." Roxy backed out, feeling a surge of relief. She now understood why Buddy had been so enthusiastic in showing his gratitude. She remained on her knees as she rubbed the sore spots on her scalp.

Kyle was on his knees facing her, and he was struggling to maintain a straight face.

Roxy realized how ridiculous it was, getting trapped under a barstool by her elastic band, and she cracked a smile. "That was a hair-raising experience. I'm glad you didn't have to amputate anything."

He burst out laughing, and she joined him. Then he reached for her and swept her to her feet in one smooth motion.

"Kyle, I must look a mess."

He pulled her close and his gaze intensified. "You're the most beautiful mess I've ever seen."

She looked straight into his mesmerizing blue eyes. The air between them thrummed with a powerful magnetism that kept her gaze riveted to his. She felt lightheaded, as if she was sitting in a car at the top of a roller coaster, suspended in that breathtaking moment before rushing headlong down the steep incline.

A question formed in his eyes, and she gave a nod. He leaned down and touched his lips to hers, sending a shock wave through her body. He slid his arms around her as he intensified his kiss. Her heartbeat accelerated, as if the car was racing full speed down the steep roller coaster tracks.

When he broke off the kiss, he brushed his lips against her cheek and whispered, "I love you, Rox."

She leaned her head against his muscular chest and felt the vibration of his heartbeat beneath the fabric of his shirt. "I know," she whispered.

After a moment, he stepped back and looked at her. "You know?"

She nodded. "Claudia told me. She figured it out, when she saw how you were acting around me."

"I must have given myself away last night. My heart nearly stopped when I saw you in that beautiful green dress." He leaned down and gave her another kiss, this one sweet and soft. He pulled back and searched her eyes. "What about you?"

She hesitated. "I love you, Kyle... but..."

A look of apprehension flickered in his eyes.

"This is so sudden. I need time to sort out my feelings."

"Okay..." He gazed at her and nodded. Then he smiled and patted her topknot. "Rox, what were you doing under that barstool?"

"Those nails snagged Buddy's collar tag. After I freed him, my hair got tangled."

Kyle's gaze slid behind her. "I'll bring over my tools and fix that barstool. I should check the other barstools, too."

She turned and saw a colorful gift bag sitting on the island. "Is that for me? My birthday isn't until Tuesday."

"I know. This is something for your camping trip."

Roxy smiled. She opened the bag and pulled out a pair of black nylon gloves with the fingertips missing. "Fishing gloves?"

"They'll protect your hands and give you a better grip on canoe paddles."

She put them on. The fabric felt stretchy and strong, and they fit perfectly. "These are cool, Kyle. Thanks." She startled, as the sound of barking rang out.

"I guess I'd better let the guys in." Kyle walked into her laundry room and unlocked the doggy door he'd built, which opened to her fenced back yard. Both dogs darted inside.

"Hey, Bud. You deserve a treat after your trauma." Roxy opened his treat jar and tossed up a biscuit. Buddy caught it in mid-air. Clyde trotted over and she tossed him a biscuit. Seconds later, both dogs were looking up at her, licking their lips.

Kyle grinned. "They'll keep begging until that jar is empty."

She tossed each of them another biscuit and set down the jar. "That's all for now, guys." As she turned, she caught her reflection in the mirror mounted on the wall near the back door. She let out a shriek. "Look at my hair!" Her topknot tilted on her head like a lopsided bird's nest, and spikes of tangled hair protruded from it. Roxy tugged at the elastic band, but her hair was wound in knots around it. She walked over to her purse, hanging on the coat rack and pulled out a comb. She gazed into the mirror and Kyle walked up behind her. She turned and pointed the comb at her head. "How could you kiss me, with my hair looking like this?"

"I closed my eyes."

She pretended to throw her comb at him, and he pretended to duck.

Kyle held up two dog biscuits. "Want a treat? You were traumatized, too."

She grinned. "They might be kind of tasty, with a little ketchup."

He laughed as he tossed a biscuit to Buddy and then to Clyde. "Rox, since I'm taking Buddy fishing, why don't I keep him at my house tonight, while you're at the reunion? I'll be glad to take care of him while you're on your camping trip, too. Don't trouble your Aunt Nell. I already have Clyde, and our two dogs get along great."

"Okay... I think Buddy would like that. Thanks." She paused. "Kyle, I know it's last minute, but would you like to come with me tonight, as my date?"

"I'd love to." He reached for her gloved hand and planted a kiss on each exposed fingertip.

She smiled as a flush of pleasure traveled down her arm.

"I can still take Buddy back to my house after I'm done fishing," Kyle said. "That way, you'll have more time to get ready for tonight... and you're going to need it, to fix that tangled mess on your head."

This time, she didn't pretend to throw her comb.

Roxy covered her lopsided topknot with a baseball cap and took Buddy and Clyde for a walk in the steamy heat, while Kyle loaded his fishing gear on the boat. For years, he and Vance kept their boat at the marina and split the monthly fee, which Quint generously discounted. But after Greta filed for divorce, Quint ended their fee discount, presumably because Vance was related to Burke. Shortly after purchasing the fixer-upper house on the river, Vance split the cost of building a dock and a boat lift with Kyle, so they could move their fishing boat out of the marina.

When she returned with the dogs, she waved at Kyle, who was sitting on the built-in bench at the end of the dock. Buddy and Clyde squirmed as Roxy unclipped their leashes. They raced down her sloping back yard and bounded onto the dock. Kyle leaned down and stroked their bobbing heads.

Roxy walked out on the dock and glanced at the fishing boat, which had been released from the lift. It bobbed in the rippled water, tied to the dock pillars. Kyle's fishing gear and cooler sat on its sunlit deck. "Looks like you're ready to go."

"Almost." He glanced up and patted the spot on the bench next to him. "Can we sit and talk a minute?"

Kyle's serious expression sparked her curiosity. She sat down and lifted the brim of her baseball cap as she gazed at an osprey hovering high above the river, riding the sultry breeze.

"Rox, in the meeting yesterday, Claudia said something about Burke harassing—"

"That reminds me," Roxy said. "Did you hear from Claudia last night?"

He paused and then nodded. "She texted me when she got to Amelia Island, but it was late. You two must have talked a long time."

"We did... mostly about you." She smiled at him.

He gave her a look. "You don't want to talk about Burke, do you?"

Roxy blew out a sigh. "He's not harassing me, Kyle. He's just been asking me out a lot."

"Does that make you feel uncomfortable?"

"No. Well... his persistence bothers me. I think I leaned on him too much after Vance died. Burke took me out to dinner a few times while he was helping me sort out legal issues. After everything was resolved, he kept asking me out. I told him I wasn't interested in a relationship, but—"

"This been going on for two years?"

"He stopped for a while. Then he started again."

"And you've made it clear you're not interested?"

She nodded.

"That sounds like harassment, Rox. Do you think it would help if I talked to him?"

"No!" She saw his surprised reaction and softened her voice. "There's no need for you to confront him. I can handle it."

Kyle glanced away and flexed the muscles in his jaw.

Sensing an argument, she shifted the topic. "Have you ever heard Burke talk about his uncle, Harmon Doyle?"

"Never heard of him."

"Earl and Claudia hadn't heard of him, either. He's Red Devlin's half-brother. He met with Claudia yesterday, to look at rental condos." Roxy stopped as a fishing boat with a loud, sputtering engine cruised past the dock. She exchanged waves with the lone fisherman and waited until the noise subsided. "Burke's uncle drove a Ferrari convertible, and he and his ditzy woman partner were wearing gaudy, expensive jewelry."

"You met him?"

"Unfortunately." Roxy repeated the lewd comments Doyle made to her.

Kyle frowned. "Is he planning to move here?"

"That's the weird thing. Claudia said he didn't really seem interested in renting anything. He kept asking her questions about Burke's relationship with Greta. I know everyone in town was talking about the hit and run yesterday, but Claudia thought he was strange, and so did I. He had cold, dark eyes... scary eyes."

"Red Devlin had eyes like that," Kyle said. "Vance and I weren't surprised when we heard he went to prison. I wonder if Red's half-brother has a criminal history."

"If you want to check Doyle out, I can text you his full name and Miami address."

"How do you know—"

"His return address labels on Burke's mail."

Kyle shook his head. "You'd make a good detective, with your snapshot memory."

She smiled. "I learn a lot about people from the mail I deliver— their magazines and newsletters, the timing of their greeting cards and the return addresses on their packages and bills."

"I never thought about that."

"I can also give you information about Doyle's Ferrari... the license number, and the name and phone number of the car dealership in Miami. I saw it parked in the garage." She pulled out her phone and began thumbing the text. Kyle rested his hand on her arm, and she looked up.

"Rox, if Burke keeps bothering you—"

"I'll let you know. Don't worry, okay?"

His gaze grew intense, and he leaned toward her.

"Hey, Rox!"

They startled and turned.

Jo waved as she walked toward them.

Buddy and Clyde paced the deck of the fishing boat, their tails wagging. As the boat pulled away from the dock, both dogs curled up next to each other behind the cockpit. Kyle turned and waved.

Roxy and Jo stood on the dock and waved back.

"Hey, Rox. What were you and Kyle talking about when I walked up?"

"It's a long story."

Jo raised an eyebrow, and then her gaze shifted. "You're wearing our graduation earrings."

"I was going to wear them tonight at the reunion, and then I decided to put them on this morning." Roxy turned and started walking toward the house.

Jo walked beside her. "I'll wear my graduation earrings tonight, too." She paused. "So... what's the long story?"

Roxy turned to her and smiled. "You're not going to believe what happened this morning."

"Try me." Jo's eyes sparked with interest.

When Roxy entered her kitchen, she glanced over her shoulder. "Want some coffee, Jo?"

"Is the earth round?"

"I'll have to give that some thought." Roxy inserted a fresh coffee pod in the brewer.

"I like your yellow blouse, Rox. Is it new?"

Roxy shook her head. "It's a Salvadore Armani."

"You got it at Salvation Army?"

"No. I bought it at Clinic Thrift, during my volunteer shift. You know that fake designer name applies to all thrift shops."

"Except Gucciwill." Jo shot Roxy a grin as she sat at the island.

Roxy brewed two coffees and added cream to both mugs. She carried them to the island and sat across from Jo.

"Okay, what happened this morning that I'm not going to believe?" Jo leaned against the padded back of the barstool. She wore an expression of eager anticipation, as if she was waiting for a movie to start.

Roxy took a quick sip, savoring the coffee's creamy hazelnut flavor.

"Well...?" A look of impatience crossed Jo's face.

"It all started when Buddy's collar got hung up under the barstool..." When Roxy explained how her topknot got tangled on the nails, Jo started giggling. When she told her Kyle almost got out the scissors, Jo giggled harder. And when Roxy took off her baseball cap and revealed her lopsided tangled topknot, Jo laughed so hard she knocked over her mug. Coffee splashed across the island and dripped onto the floor.

They both giggled as they grabbed dishtowels and mopped it up. Jo started brewing another coffee and glanced down at her outfit. "I got lucky. No coffee stains on my white shirt, and the stains won't show on my black shorts."

Roxy's text chime sounded. "It's Kyle." She laughed as she enlarged the image on the screen.

"What did he send?" Jo carried a fresh mug of coffee to the island and sat down.

"A funny photo of the dogs. They have their noses close to the camera, like they took a selfie." She handed the phone to Jo.

"Rox, your screen is a mess. Did that happen when you rescued Trixie?"

She nodded.

"Buddy and Clyde. They look like a goofy team of doggy bank robbers." Jo glanced up and refocused on Roxy. "You haven't told me the whole story about Kyle, have you?"

Roxy grinned. She described Kyle's stunned reaction when she modeled her new dress, and then she summarized her conversation with Claudia.

"I knew it! When I saw you and Kyle on the dock, I was sure he was about to kiss you."

"It wouldn't be the first time," Roxy said. "He kissed me after he untangled me from that barstool."

"With your hair looking like that?" Jo let out a howling laugh and grabbed her coffee mug. "I didn't knock it over this time." She took a sip of coffee and then eyed Roxy over the rim of the mug. "Claudia's not the only one who noticed a change in Kyle."

"You saw it, too? Why didn't you tell me?"

"It was just an impression, Rox. I could have been wrong about him. I'm not like Claudia. I know how to mind my own business."

Roxy laughed. "I can't believe you said that!"

"Why? When have I meddled in your life?"

"I'm not sure I can count that high."

Jo waved away the subject. "Rox, I haven't seen the new dress you bought for the reunion. What does it look like?"

"Claudia took a photo last night." She reached for her phone and began scrolling.

"Too bad you didn't ask me to go shopping with you," Jo said. "It would have been fun, helping you find a reunion dress."

Roxy looked up. "Jo, I went to Shyanne's with Claudia on the spur of the moment, after I got fed up with her nagging. You know you're always the first person I call, when I want to go shopping."

Jo shrugged and nodded.

"Here it is." Roxy held out the phone.

"I love that shade of green, Rox. The dress is perfect for the reunion. Too bad Kyle isn't going as your date."

"He is... I asked him this morning."

"Good." Jo gave an approving nod. "We can all ride together, like a double date."

Roxy glanced down, as anxiety rolled through her stomach.

"What's wrong?"

She sighed. "One minute I'm happy Kyle loves me, and the next minute I'm nervous. When I was writing in my journal this morning, I realized how deep my feelings are for him. And that scares me, Jo. You saw how I fell apart after Vance died. I'm not sure I want to risk loving someone that much, again. Kyle's a detective, and that's a dangerous job. What if I lose him, too?"

"I wish you didn't have such a huge fear of loss, Rox." Jo paused and studied her face. "I have a feeling there might be something else about Kyle that's holding you back."

Roxy took a moment. "It bothers me that he was Vance's best friend."

Jo nodded. "Do you think you'd be cheating on Vance somehow, if you got involved with Kyle? I can understand how you might feel that way, even though it's kind of... irrational."

"It probably is irrational. But it's hard to think of Kyle as—"

"Rox, you need to give it time. Just enjoy being with him tonight. I'm glad you decided to take a date to the reunion. When you show up with Kyle, Trent will probably keep his distance."

Roxy blinked. She'd been thinking so much about Kyle; she'd forgotten about Trent. She read the look on Jo's face and frowned. "You're convinced Trent's interested in getting back together with me, aren't you?"

"He asked me a lot of questions about you," Jo said. "So I called Bri. You know how close she and Trent are. She said he's always regretted his fling with—"

"No. Don't go there, Jo." Roxy turned away.

"... the family pressured Trent to marry Celia when she got pregnant—"

"Jo! I don't want to rehash this! Trent didn't even bother to break off our engagement before he eloped with her!"

"I know." Jo sighed. "All I'm trying to say is... Bri told me Trent still loves you, and he always has."

Roxy's stomach went queasy. "If that's true, it adds a whole new layer of weirdness to everything."

They went quiet for a long moment.

"Rox..."

"What?"

"When are you going to tell Trent about his daughter?"

Roxy had been wrestling with that question ever since she heard Trent was coming to the reunion.

"I never understood why you didn't tell him—"

"I tried to, Jo. But he wouldn't listen to me."

A look of surprise crossed Jo's face, but she remained quiet, waiting.

Roxy drank the last of the coffee in her mug and sighed as she set it down. "You know how upset I was when I found out I was pregnant. It took a while to work up my courage, but I finally called Trent. He and Celia had moved to St. Paul by then, to live with her father. My hands were shaking so hard, I had trouble holding onto my phone. Celia answered the call, and she blew up right away. She said something like, 'He's my husband, not yours!' Then Trent grabbed his phone and started shouting, telling me to stay out of his life. He was sloppy drunk and slurring his words. He got so abusive, I hung up on him. Then I completely broke down. He had already humiliated me by running off with Celia. This was just too much."

"Oh, Rox. Why didn't you tell me?"

"I didn't want any more sympathy from you, or anyone else. I was tired of feeling like an object of pity."

"You weren't an object—"

"That's how I felt, Jo. I needed to get away from Riverside Bay, and it made sense for me to move to Orlando to help grandpa and grandma. I think they enjoyed having me with them while I was pregnant." She paused. "I knew I wanted to have the baby, but I wasn't sure I was ready to be a single mom, so met with a counselor and decided adoption was the right choice."

Jo nodded.

Roxy's mind brought up an image of her newborn daughter, an image she treasured. "They let me hold her for a few minutes, Jo. She had blue eyes, silky blonde hair, and tiny perfect hands." Her eyes welled up as the pain rushed back; the pain of giving up the only child she had carried to full term.

Jo grabbed the tissue box and set it near her.

"I've been so emotional, lately." Roxy hiccupped as she dabbed her eyes. "My daughter turned fourteen in January, and I don't even know her name. I pray for her every day. I often wonder... does she live in Florida? Is she healthy... happy?"

"Have you ever thought about looking for her?"

"I did, after Vance died. But you know how depressed I was. For a while, I could barely function. And what would I say to Earl and Claudia? I never told Vance about her."

"Why not?"

She shrugged. "I think it was too painful to talk about while we dated. And then, after our first miscarriage, I didn't know how to tell Vance I'd given up a child."

"Rox, what if she looks up her birth parents and contacts Trent—"

"Trent's name isn't on her birth certificate. I had them list the father's name as unknown."

"Why did—"

"Trent made it clear he wanted me out of his life!"

Jo nodded. "I guess I understand why you kept him out of the loop back then, but what about now? He has a right to know about her."

"He does, but I can't tell him tonight at our class reunion. I mean, how weird would that be?" Roxy paused. "I've been thinking a lot about my daughter lately, even before I found out Trent was coming to the reunion. I think I'm ready to start looking for her.

Maybe I should find out more about her situation, before I tell Trent about her."

Jo reached out and squeezed her hand. "I'll be glad to help."

Roxy smiled, as a feeling of nervous excitement stirred.

Jo glanced at her smartwatch. "It's almost ten-thirty. We're meeting the rest of the group for lunch in New Smyrna at noon. There's no time to start packing today. We can pack for the camping trip at my house tomorrow, after church."

"I've already put some camping clothes in an old suitcase," Roxy said. "I'll load it into your truck right now. We can drop it off at your house after we get back from lunch, and then I won't have so much to bring over tomorrow." She patted her tangled topknot. "What should I do about my hair?"

"You can try combing it out while I'm driving to New Smyrna," Jo said. "But you'd better bring your baseball cap, just in case."

Roxy glanced out the windshield and realized they were nearing the exit to New Smyrna Beach. She refocused on the visor mirror and used her comb to free the last tangled knot. The pain traveled down to the roots. When she freed the elastic band, she breathed out a relieved sigh. She turned to Jo. "Do we have time to make a quick stop at the Ponce Inlet Lighthouse? You know I love the view of the coastline from the top."

Jo kept her focus on the traffic ahead. "I think so. We left early, and it's not too far out of our way." She switched on the turn signal as she approached the exit. "By the way, I've planned a birthday surprise for you, after lunch."

"What kind of surprise?" Roxy glanced into the mirror as she finished combing out the remaining tangles.

"I'm treating you to a manicure and pedicure at the spa where Bri works. I thought it might be fun, having a spa afternoon before our reunion. I got the idea when I saw your broken fingernails after your sinkhole dog rescue."

Roxy smiled as she put away her comb. "Thanks, Jo. My nails are a mess, and I haven't had time to do anything about it." She gathered her hair into a ponytail and secured it with the elastic band. "I'm finally tangle-free!"

"That's nothing short of a miracle, Rox." Jo turned into the Ponce Inlet Lighthouse parking lot and took the first open spot. "Let's just take our phones. We can lock our purses in the truck. We won't be long."

"That works for me. It's over two hundred steps to the top." Roxy slipped her phone in her pocket as she stepped out of Jo's pickup truck. The strong breeze off the Atlantic held a fresh, salty taste. "I'll take care of both admission charges, since this was my idea."

"I'm not making that crazy climb," Jo said. "I'll stay in the museum and check out the exhibits." She pointed to the circular red brick lighthouse and grinned. "Rox, when you get to the top, try not to drop your phone from the viewing platform."

Roxy entered the lighthouse and then stood on the black and white tiled floor for a moment, gazing up at the tall winding spiral stairway. A few people leaned over the railing and looked down at her. As she began climbing in tight circles, her thumping footsteps mingled with the thumps of other footsteps echoing against the curved white brick wall. Each time she met people descending the narrow stairway, she turned slightly to let them pass. Her heartbeat rose with each step, and when she finally reached the top, she paused to catch her breath. Roxy kept a tight grip on the black metal railing as she looked down at the dizzying spirals leading to the checkerboard floor, far below.

She stepped outside onto the circular viewing platform and gazed at the breathtaking sight. The ocean's vast turquoise surface stretched to the horizon, where it merged with the hazy blue sky. The strong breeze made a loud whistling sound as it rushed through the tall wire safety cage fastened to the waist-high railing. Roxy turned her head, and the wind whipped her ponytail against her face. She held back her hair as she moved slowly around the platform, taking in the panoramic view. After walking full circle, she realized she was alone at the top.

Moments later, she became aware of thumping footsteps echoing inside the lighthouse. Someone walked out onto the viewing platform behind her, breathing heavily. The person stood next to her, close enough to brush against the sleeve of her yellow blouse. In her peripheral vision, Roxy saw a man around Kyle's height, with blond hair. She bristled, thinking, "We're alone up here. Why is he crowding me?" Roxy moved a half-step away and deliberately ignored him as her gaze wandered down the ocean's long shoreline.

"Rox… it's been a long time."

With a jolt, she recognized his voice—a voice she hadn't heard for fifteen years.

CHAPTER 15

Trent was looking at her, his pale blue eyes taking in every detail of her face. As she met his gaze, he smiled. It was the same smile she'd fallen in love with, set in an older face. The faint lines etched around his eyes and traces of gray in his beard stubble added a depth of maturity to his striking good looks.

"Rox, you look... amazing." His gaze swept over her body.

Seeing him again had unleashed an overwhelming flood of memories. Roxy stared at his face, stunned, unable to break eye contact or even speak. The ocean breeze slid down the collar of her blouse, and she shivered.

"Let's get away from this wind." Trent placed his hand at the small of her back as he guided her around the circular platform. He used to guide her like this years ago, whenever they walked together. Back then, she viewed this placement of his hand as a sweet, protective gesture. Now it struck her as manipulative. He stopped when they reached a spot sheltered from the wind.

Roxy turned to face him and stepped back, making sure she stood out of his immediate reach.

"Is this better?"

She nodded, even though she was still shivering. Her heartbeat had accelerated, as if it sensed an enemy and saw the need to pump extra adrenaline into her bloodstream.

"When I saw you walking into the lighthouse, I thought I was imagining things. Then I spotted Jo in the museum, and I knew it was you." Trent extended his hand. When she didn't respond, he pulled it back and gave her an awkward smile. "I flew in from St. Paul yesterday..."

A cold sweat washed over her, triggering a dizzy, lightheaded feeling. She found it hard to concentrate on his words.

"...I'm staying in New Smyrna with Seth..."

The platform shifted beneath her feet, and she gripped the railing to keep her balance. She realized Trent had stopped talking. He stared at her, as if he was waiting for a response. Floating pinpoints of light distracted her. "Ah… what were you saying?"

"I said, I'm sorry about what happened to your husband."

An icy chill gripped her as the platform tilted.

Roxy became aware of leaning against something... someone? She pushed away and wobbled on her feet, as twinkling stars danced in her field of vision. The stars vanished slowly, one by one. Her dizziness eased as strength returned to her legs. "I… ah. What happened?"

"You fainted." Trent held her upper arms in a light steadying grip.

"I did?" She straightened her shoulders, shrugging off his hands. "I... ah... didn't sleep well last night. And I haven't had much to eat today."

He kept his gaze on her. It was a clinical gaze, like a doctor assessing a patient. Then she remembered he worked as an EMT for a suburban St. Paul fire department. "You still look pale, Rox. Are you feeling okay?"

"I'll be fine." She suppressed the urge to say, "As soon as I get away from you."

"You had me worried, for a minute."

Roxy eyed him, thinking, "Oh, really? You care about me? You ordered me to stay out of your life, remember?"

The sound of voices broke into her thoughts. A young couple strolled into view. The man was holding a baby girl in a pink outfit.

An image flashed into Roxy's mind. Her newborn baby... Trent's baby. Emotions surged. She cleared her throat and glanced at Trent. "I have to go. Jo's waiting for me."

"Okay, see you tonight." Trent smiled.

Roxy turned away and bumped into Seth, who had just made the climb. She apologized and then hurried down the spiral stairway. Hot, angry tears filled her eyes. With each downward step, her anger grew. She thought of all the things she wished she'd said: "Trent Thorson, you jerk! How can you smile and make small talk? Don't you realize the pain you put me through? I was in love with you, and you threw me away like yesterday's garbage!"

She was still shaking with anger when she left the lighthouse. As she approached Jo's bright red pickup truck, she sensed she was being watched. But she resisted the temptation to glance up at the viewing platform. Roxy climbed into the passenger seat and shut the door. "Sorry I took so long."

"I was starting to get worried." Jo had already started the truck's engine. Cool air poured out of the dashboard vents. "I called you when I spotted Trent in the museum, but you didn't pick up. Did you get my warning?"

"No. I didn't hear my phone. The wind was loud up there."

"It must have been a shock, seeing Trent."

Roxy stared at her hands and realized she was still trembling. "I fainted, Jo!"

"What?"

"Trent absolutely blindsided me. I was expecting to see him at the reunion tonight, not at the top of the lighthouse." She paused. "When I saw a couple with a baby girl, I thought about our baby, and I almost fainted again."

"Rox... that's not like you." Jo wore a sympathetic look.

"Seeing Trent again was a lot harder than I thought it would be." She blew out a long sigh. "I sure hope you're right."

"About what?" Jo checked for traffic as she backed out of the parking spot.

"That Trent will keep his distance tonight, if I show up with Kyle." She looked at Jo. "Did you make sure he wouldn't be seated near us during dinner?"

"I assigned him to a table clear across the ballroom." Jo glanced at Roxy. "I seated Melody there, too."

Every parking spot on Canal Street in New Smyrna Beach's historic district was taken, so Jo dropped Roxy off at the Beach Thyme Café and drove away to find parking on a side street.

Roxy's phone chimed as she got out of the truck. When she saw it was another text from Burke, she slipped her phone back into her pocket. As she entered the café, she saw Tara and Leeann standing in the waiting area. Both of them were dressed like Jo, in white t-shirts, dark shorts and sandals.

"Rox! Great to see you." Tara's hazel eyes held a vivacious spark. Tiny freckles, faintly visible beneath her make-up, dotted her attractive face, and a surprising number of gray streaks ran through her frizzy red hair. Her curvy, full-figured body stood five ten, slightly taller than Roxy, making her the tallest woman in the group.

"We heard about the sinkhole, Rox. We're glad you're okay." Leeann's wide sweet smile revealed part of her upper gum line. Chin-length black hair framed her oval face, with its delicate Asian features and dark brown eyes. Her slender frame stood just under five feet, which made her the shortest woman in the group.

"Rox, is the rumor true?" Tara asked. "Did you really jump into that sinkhole to rescue Mae's poodle? We heard you barely got out alive."

Roxy shook her head and slid a glance toward Leeann. "Reports of my near-death have been greatly exaggerated."

Leeann laughed out loud. "My favorite Samuel Clemens quote!"

"Didn't he also say something about getting the facts straight?" Roxy asked.

She nodded. "Get your facts first, and then you can distort them as much as you please." Leeann's soft voice held a melodic tone.

Tara did an eye roll. "English teachers... you have a literary quote for everything."

Jo opened the café door, letting in a burst of humid air. She was carrying a canvas tote bag, along with her purse. "I finally found a parking spot—"

"I'm the hostess! I'll seat you now!" A tall slender woman stared at them with a stern, unsmiling expression. Her green ankle-length dress matched her green spiked hair, and she held a stack of menus in the crook of her left arm. If she'd raised a torch in her right hand, she'd have looked like the Statue of Liberty.

They followed Lady Liberty single file through the noisy café. She frowned as she pointed to an oversized booth next to a window. Leeann and Tara slid into a bench seat, and Roxy and Jo slid into the opposite bench. The hostess slapped their menus on the table. She scowled as she took their beverage orders, and then she strode away.

"What's with her?" Tara asked. "She never cracked a smile."

"At least she didn't snarl at us and gnash her teeth," Leeann said.

Jo grinned. "She'll probably do that the next time we see her."

Roxy looked at Tara. "How is Ian doing this summer, now that he's out of school?"

"Pretty well. He has a hard time adjusting to any changes in his life, just like a lot of children with Asperger's. But Ian is very bright, and we're learning how to help him cope." Tara paused. "I never thought I'd say this, but it's a blessing Cole and I don't have any other children. We can give Ian our full attention."

"He turned seven last week, right?" Roxy asked.

Tara smiled. "I can show you some photos from his birthday party."

Jo spoke up. "Rachel was there, to help out. And so were Leeann's twins."

"Ian loves those three girls," Tara said, as she scrolled through her photos. "They've been taking turns babysitting him. I don't think I could have continued teaching last year without their help. Every day after school, one of them would come over and look after him, while I graded papers and got dinner started." Tara used her fingers to enlarge a photo, and then she handed her phone to Roxy.

"Look at his curly red hair," Roxy said.

"Ian is the image of Nikki." Tara was smiling, but her eyes held a look of sadness. "Scroll to the next photo and you'll see his birthday cake. Leeann made it. It's decorated like a racetrack, because Ian loves cars so much."

"Emma and Ella helped me decorate it." Leeann turned to Jo. "Greg and I called the twins this morning. The church mission team finished building all the wheelchair ramps, and today they're going to start painting houses."

Jo smiled. "I know. Charlie and I talked to Rachel last night."

A young man dressed in a Beach Thyme Café t-shirt and jeans walked up, holding a tray with four glasses of iced tea. A mixture of pimples and beard stubble covered his face. He set down the glasses and tucked the tray under his arm. "Ready to order?"

"Two people will be joining us," Roxy said.

"Oh…" Tara said, "We forgot to tell you. Sal and Bri aren't coming."

The server described the lunch specials and asked if they had questions about the menu.

"I do," Leeann said. "One of the Cobb salad ingredients is crispy lavash. What's that?"

"It's a cracker-like topping."

"That sounds good. I'll order that."

The others ordered the same salad. As he collected the menus, he asked, "Can I get you anything else?"

"A bottle of ketchup, please," Roxy said.

He looked puzzled, but he gave her a nod.

Leeann turned to the others. "Have you ever heard of crispy lavash?"

Jo grinned. "It sounds like the name of an exotic dancer in Key West."

That prompted a round of giggles.

Roxy looked at Tara. "What happened to Sal and Bri?"

"Bri is fitting in extra clients today, since she'll be away from the spa until Thursday," Tara said. "Sal is one of them. She made a noon appointment to get her hair done. I'm going there after lunch, so Bri can style my hair for tonight."

Leeann's face took on a worried look. "I hope this camping trip won't be too much for Bri to handle."

"Her MS has been in remission," Jo said. "Her new medication has really helped, and Bri is doing all the right things... exercising and eating right."

Roxy glanced at the canvas tote sitting on the bench seat. "What's in the bag, Jo?"

"It's a surprise, for our camping trip." Jo's smile conveyed excitement, as if she was a game show host getting ready to reveal the prize behind Door Number One.

Tara and Leeann leaned forward.

"I designed matching t-shirts for our group. Charlie's sister Ava works for a business that makes items with company logos. She offered to make the t-shirts for free." Jo pulled out a short-sleeved, powder blue shirt and held it up. Its colorful graphic depicted two people paddling a canoe, silhouetted in black against a bright orange setting sun. The water's calm surface reflected the orange sunset. Above the graphic, in large words: Ocala Forest Wilderness Women. Below the graphic, a website address that included the same words.

"What a cool shirt!" Tara and Leeann said, in unison.

"Did you really set up a Wilderness Women website?" Roxy asked.

Jo shook her head. "I made it up, for fun. I went online first, to make sure there wasn't already a website with this address." She handed a large t-shirt to Tara, a medium to Roxy and an extra-small to Leeann.

"It'll be fun having matching shirts," Tara said.

"Ah... one of them doesn't quite match." Jo rummaged through the bag and held up another shirt. The wording was the same, but the graphic had been flipped. It looked as if the canoe had over-turned, both people had their heads underwater, and the bright orange sun had sunk beneath the water's surface and continued glowing.

Tara and Leeann giggled.

Roxy laughed out loud.

Jo shrugged. "It's one of the mediums. Since that's my size, I'll wear it. I guess I can't complain, since it's a freebie."

The server appeared with a large tray. He set down their salad bowls and a bottle of ketchup. Leeann passed around a small bottle of hand sanitizer. Before they began eating, they bowed their heads as Jo said grace. Then Roxy reached for the ketchup bottle and put a large dollop on each of the hard-boiled egg slices in her salad.

When they finished eating, they headed to the checkout counter. Tara was last in line, and the others waited while Lady Liberty rang up her order.

Tara pointed to the register's display. "I think you undercharged me for the Cobb—"

"It's Saturday, senior discount day," Lady Liberty said, looking bored.

"You gave me the senior discount? What age does that start?"

"Fifty."

"I'm thirty-three!"

A plump man wearing a name badge walked past the counter and said, "I'm the manager, and I'll be happy to give you the senior discount."

"But I didn't ask for the discount," Tara said.

The manager had already walked away.

Lady Liberty sneered, "I guess this is your lucky day."

Tara finished paying and shoved her wallet in her purse. Her face glowed bright pink, and she looked as if she wanted to kick someone. She waited to speak until they walked outside. "Bri's been telling me I should cover up this gray! Today, I'm going to let her do it!"

Jo followed Tara's car on the short drive to the spa. When they entered the spa's reception area, they greeted Bri, who was leaning on the counter, talking to the receptionist.

Bri turned and broke into a smile. She was wearing a blue spa vest over the day's apparent uniform, a white shirt and dark shorts. Her petite frame stood slightly taller than Leeann, and she'd been blessed with extremely attractive features, like the rest of the Thorson family. Her pink lipstick matched the pink highlights in her blonde hair, and a dusting of smoky eye shadow added depth to her pale blue eyes.

Roxy's smile dimmed when she saw Bri's thin arms.

"I've lost a little weight recently," Bri said, obviously noting Roxy's reaction. "But I've been doing yoga and exercising with resistance bands."

An awkward silence followed. The two of them had preserved their friendship by avoiding any mention of Trent when they were together. Roxy decided it didn't make sense today, since they'd all be attending the reunion tonight. "I ran into Trent at the Ponce Inlet Lighthouse—"

"I know," Bri smiled. "He called me right after he saw you."

"Where's Sal?" Jo asked.

"You just missed her. She got a call from Matt right after I finished styling her hair. They've had a string of emergencies at Pet Wellness, and she needed to get back to the office and clear up the paperwork."

"I'll have to give her the group t-shirt tomorrow," Jo said.

"What group t-shirt?" Bri asked.

Jo put on her game show host smile as she pulled an extra-small shirt from her tote bag and handed it to Bri.

Roxy and Jo stopped by Bri's workstation before leaving the spa. Tara swiveled around in the chair and grinned at them. Dark red foam covered her head.

Thunder rumbled as they walked outside. Roxy glanced up at the line of black clouds blowing in from the Atlantic. "There's the summer afternoon rainstorm, right on schedule."

As soon as they climbed inside the sweltering truck, Jo started the engine and cranked down the air conditioning. "It's not raining yet, Rox. Let's sit a minute with the doors cracked open, to let the hot air escape."

Roxy admired her fingernails. "Thanks again, Jo. I usually don't like surprises, but this was a great one."

Jo smiled. "I love this nail design. White anchors on navy polish. Did you get the idea from our yearbook cover?"

"Ah... kind of..." Roxy knew better than to tell Jo it was Claudia's design.

Raindrops spattered the windshield as Jo left the parking lot. The rain continued as the truck sped down the freeway and finally subsided when they reached the Riverside Bay exit. By the time they turned onto Main Street, the dark clouds had parted, revealing patches of blue sky. Sunlight sparkled on the wet grass in the town's community park. Roxy recalled all the hours she and Jo had spent there, perfecting their baton twirling routines. As they drove past their church, she turned to Jo and asked, "When is the church's mission team coming back?"

"On Friday afternoon. Ava is one of the chaperones. She'll call Charlie as they're driving back, to let him know what time the van will arrive at church. He plans to pick up Rachel and Josh, too. Charlie knows how busy Kyle is, right now."

"It had to be hard for Ava and Charlie, growing up as the pastor's kids," Roxy said.

Jo nodded. "Charlie said they felt like people were always watching them and wondering when they were going to mess up." She turned left and drove slowly past their childhood home.

Roxy gazed at the beige and brown craftsman-style house, where her Aunt Nell still lived. A colorful flower garden bordered its front porch, and a sign posted in the yard read: Garden Club Tour stop # 8. "Hey Jo, why are the signs up already? The garden tour isn't until next Saturday, the Fourth of July."

"The club's new president wanted them up a week ahead of time," Jo said. "Rox, why don't you join the town's garden club? You own a house with a nice yard, now."

"You and Aunt Nell are the Master Gardeners. I'm not."

Jo parked in the driveway of her craftsman house, painted in shades of green and gray. The terraced front yard garden held vibrant groupings of flowers and tropical shrubs. A sign posted near the front porch read: Garden Club Tour, stop # 9.

Roxy shifted her gaze to the dilapidated house that sat between Jo's house and Nell's. Its garish purple paint had peeled off in long sections, revealing layers of orange, blue and burgundy, the 'tree rings' of its color history. Tall patches of green weeds had sprouted up in the dead lawn. A Riverside Bay Realty sign stood near the curb, with Melody Manor listed as the realtor to call. "When did the rental-wreck go up for sale?"

"The sign went up yesterday," Jo said. "I hope Melody sells it to someone who'll fix it up. You know what a nightmare the renters have been."

Roxy nodded. "The rental-wreck has been the black eye on the block for years."

"More like the purple eye," Jo said, as she opened the driver's door.

As Roxy got out of the truck, she heard her aunt's voice.

"How was your spa afternoon?" Nell hurried up the driveway.

"Come and see our manicures. They match our yearbook cover," Jo said, as she walked around the truck. She stood next to Roxy, and they both held out her hands.

Nell smiled. "I like those cute little anchors."

Jo's text chime sounded, and she pulled out her phone. "Charlie's on his way home from the Clinic. I want to point out the wobbly pavers in the back garden walkway before I drive you home, Rox. He promised to fix them while we're on our camping trip. I don't want visitors toppling over next weekend, during the garden tour."

"Rox, come over to my house," Nell said. "We haven't had a good long chat for a while."

Roxy smiled. "Okay. But first, I need to unload the suitcase with my camping clothes."

"You go with mom," Jo said. "Charlie can unload it."

Roxy stepped into Aunt Nell's compact kitchen, which always seemed larger in her memories. The room hadn't changed much over the years, with the exception of a massive new stainless-steel French door refrigerator. Her gaze strayed to the old chalkboard hanging on the wall. Deep scratches marred its surface. She read the Bible verse, written in Nell's distinctive left-handed slant:

"Love the Lord your God with all your heart, and with all your soul, and with all your strength, and with all your mind; and Love your neighbor as yourself." Luke 10:27.

Ever since Roxy could remember, her aunt had written Bible verses on that chalkboard, changing the verse every Sunday, before church.

"I see you're wearing your graduation earrings." Nell smiled. "Sit down, I'll have the coffee ready in no time. Want it over ice?"

"Sounds good." Roxy sank into a chair at the oak kitchen table Grandpa Leo had made. She used her fingers to trace the distinctive wood grain in its polished surface.

"What do you think of my new fridge? It's a lot bigger than my old one. I got a great deal on it... fifty percent off. I'd have been a fool not to buy it."

Roxy grinned. She sat back and looked around the cozy room, taking note of the faded flowered wallpaper, the speckled Formica countertop, and the white porcelain gas range. She had spent countless hours in this kitchen, helping Aunt Nell make dinner and washing dishes with Jo. She and Jo had done their homework at this oak table. And she had answered the phone in this kitchen, when Bri called to tell her that Trent had eloped with Celia. The memory stung, triggering an unexpected surge of emotions. She struggled to hold them back.

Nell set plates, napkins and a basket of homemade chocolate chip cookies on the table, along with a small cow cream pitcher—a birthday gift Roxy and Jo had bought for her years ago, by pooling their weekly allowance. Nell set down two glasses of iced coffee, added cream to Roxy's, and then she sat in her usual chair, near the window. "What's going on, Rox? I can see something's bothering you." Her blue eyes radiated caring.

Roxy met her aunt's gaze, and her emotions tumbled out in a burst of words. She described how seeing Greta's damaged car had brought back her grief for Vance... how confused she was about her relationship with Kyle... how painful it was to see Trent again... and how guilty she felt about keeping their daughter a secret. When she finished, she sat back in the chair, feeling suddenly hungry. Roxy reached for a cookie and took a large bite, savoring the chocolate bits and the hint of orange zest. "I thought about skipping the reunion, after I found out Trent was coming," she said, chewing. "But now that Kyle is my date, I'm looking forward to it."

Nell nodded. "Kyle's a handsome man. I hope Trent's dark heart seizes up with jealousy when you walk in with him." She took a sip of coffee and her expression shifted. "I'm glad you're going to search for your daughter when you get back from the camping trip. She'd be my great-niece, but I'd think of her as my granddaughter."

Roxy caught the wistful look in her aunt's eyes, and it struck her that this wasn't simply a matter between her and Trent. Finding their daughter would impact Aunt Nell and everyone else in both families. Jo and Charlie would meet their niece, and Rachel would meet her cousin. Trent's dad would meet his granddaughter. Bri and Seth would meet their niece. And TJ, the son Trent had with Celia, would meet a slightly younger half-sister.

The grandfather clock in the adjoining family room began chiming. Roxy glanced at the wall clock. "Oh! The reunion is set to begin in an hour and a half."

"I'll drive you home, right now," Nell said. "I can take Buddy a day early—"

"There's been a change of plans," Roxy said. "Kyle already took Buddy to his house, and he's going to take care of him while I'm on the camping trip."

Nell smiled.

Kyle sat at his desk and paged through the notes he had taken during separate interviews with Quint Wilder and Alan Everley. He took a sip of coffee, and then he pulled a cinnamon roll out of the bag on his desk.

Sam strolled into his office. "That roll looks good. Where did you get it?"

"Rox baked it." Kyle bit into the sweet buttery roll and nodded toward the paper bag.

"Any rolls left?" Sam asked, as he sat in a guest chair.

Kyle mentally kicked himself for pointing out the bag. "There's one... you want it?"

Sam nodded as he set down his coffee mug. He pulled out the roll, bit into it and made contented humming sounds as he chewed. When he finished, he crumpled the empty paper bag and tossed it high in the air. It hit the rim of the trash can and bounced inside. "Three points!"

"Sam, you're practically sitting next to the can. That was an easy two-point layup."

"I deserve an extra point for my perfect form."

Kyle shook his head. "Let's get to work. What are your thoughts about the interviews? Both Quint and Alan seemed shocked when we told them about Greta."

Sam nodded. "They also denied any involvement in her murder or the hit and run. I arranged for Kendra to give each of them a voice stress analysis test on Monday morning. That test has its limitations, but it should give us a good idea if they're being truthful."

He paused and took a long drink from his mug. "Both men claimed they were at home, getting ready for work on the morning of the hit and run. Since they live alone, all we have is their word on that."

"True," Kyle said. "But unless they're great actors, I don't think they had any idea Greta's body was in the trunk of her Mercedes."

"Quint could have given an Oscar-winning performance," Sam said. "That scruffy guy is hard to read. He admitted Greta's ownership in the marina reverts back to him after her death."

Kyle nodded. "His comment to Rox also bothers me. How did he know Greta's money was in the Caymans?" He paused and glanced down at his notes. "He had a clear motive against Burke. But if he killed Greta to regain full ownership of his marina, why hide her body?"

"You could argue Quint has had full ownership for the past two years, without Greta around to control things," Sam said. "Maybe his motive goes deeper. Quint could have killed her out of hate or revenge, for the way she destroyed his reputation."

"That's possible," Kyle said. "Okay, let's turn to Alan. He was romantically involved with Greta before the hit and run, and the pond borders a tract of land he owns. But I can't see him risking his reputation to help Greta in the hit and run. We know Burke did legal work for Alan. But the blackmail theory is a stretch, and we have no proof. And in Greta's murder, I can't figure out a motive for Alan that makes sense."

Sam let out a cynical laugh. "Motives don't have to make sense. People kill for all sorts of trivial reasons. Someone gets cut off in traffic—"

"I know, I know..." Kyle sighed.

"Have you talked to Burke, yet?"

"He hasn't returned my calls."

"Maybe he's busy at that conference, Kyle. Or maybe he's just jerking your chain. He knows you don't like him, and the feeling's probably mutual."

Kyle glanced at the time on his phone. "Sam, I need to get going. I'm taking Rox to her class reunion tonight."

Sam nodded. He stood and picked up his mug. "What time are you coming in tomorrow?"

"In the afternoon. I'm having lunch with Rox and the rest of her family, after church. Want to join us? We'll meet in the Senior Center's dining room at eleven thirty."

"Lunch with all the old folks? No, thanks."

"It's Taste of Italy Sunday. All you can eat lasagna."

"All you can eat?" Sam looked hungry already. "Okay, count me in. With my wife gone, there's not much to eat at home."

As soon as Sam left, Kyle began straightening the papers on his desk. His thoughts turned to Roxy, and his heart beat a little faster when he pictured how beautiful she had looked in that green dress. Then he recalled how upset she appeared at lunch yesterday, when she heard Trent was coming to the reunion. He wondered, "Does she still have feelings for him? First loves are often the hardest to get over."

Sam rushed into his office. "Kyle! There's been a shooting at Riverside Bay Estates!"

Roxy unlocked her back door and then turned and waved as Nell backed out of her driveway. The kitchen seemed lonely and quiet without Buddy rushing up to greet her. As she set her purse and her phone on the island, a knock sounded at the back door. She suppressed a groan when she saw Burke's face in the window. He had already seen her, so she couldn't ignore him.

He flashed her a wide smile as she opened the door. "I just came from the airport, and I wanted to see if you changed your mind about tonight. I haven't heard from you in a couple of days."

"I'm sorry, it's been a bit hectic." She paused, searching for the best way to break the news. "Burke... I decided to take a date at the last minute... and Kyle was here, so I asked him."

His face registered surprise.

Her ringtone sounded. Roxy hurried toward the island, leaving the door open. She saw Kyle's name on the cracked screen and quickly answered.

"Rox, I can't make it tonight. We just got an urgent call. I'm sorry..."

"I understand, Kyle. I know this comes with your job."

"I have to go. I'll call you tomorrow."

"Okay, talk to you then. Stay safe." She turned toward Burke, who was standing inside the kitchen.

He grinned. "Looks like you need a date, after all."

After drying her hair, Roxy ran a brush through the waves and quickly applied her make-up. As she slipped on her green dress and a pair of silver sandals, a queasy feeling rolled through her stomach. She dreaded seeing Trent again, and she felt a vague uneasiness about Burke. She had already called Jo and explained the situation. They still planned to ride to the reunion together, like a double date.

Roxy put on an alexandrite necklace that coordinated with her graduation earrings and then picked up her phone. Before tucking it inside her silver evening bag, she checked the time on its screen: 6:15 p.m. The reunion's social hour was set to begin in fifteen minutes, and the event center at the beach was only a ten-minute drive from her house. Burke would be arriving at any moment.

Her queasiness increased as she headed downstairs. She sat on the couch, closed her eyes and took slow deep breaths as she prayed for calm nerves and wisdom in handling whatever came her way tonight. A knock sounded, and she jumped as if she'd been shocked. Roxy sighed as she walked toward the back door.

Burke stepped inside and gave her a hug. His dark brown eyes radiated a disturbing eagerness. "You look stunning in that dress, Rox."

She forced a smile. "Thanks. You look nice, too."

He smirked, as if he viewed her compliment as a vast understatement.

Roxy heard the sound of car doors closing and peered outside. "Charlie and Jo are here."

Burke frowned.

Jo breezed through the open doorway, wearing a navy and white chiffon dress that flowed in silky layers to her knees. She had added volume to the layers in her blonde hair, and she was wearing bright red lipstick.

Burke's smile returned as he gave Jo a quick hug. He shook hands with Charlie, who had followed her inside.

Roxy watched the two men as they exchanged small talk. Charlie was wearing a navy blazer over a light blue shirt. His belted khaki trousers emphasized his trim waistline. Dark-rimmed glasses and a receding hairline gave his face a scholarly look, but Charlie's engaging smile instantly transformed his appearance from brainy to good-looking. Burke stood slightly taller and his outfit looked more polished—a crisp white shirt, creased black trousers and an expensive-looking charcoal blazer, tailored to fit his broad shoulders.

"It's getting late, we should get going," Jo said.

"I'm taking Rox in my car," Burke said, his tone firm.

After a brief silence, Charlie nodded. "Okay, fine with us."

Burke escorted Roxy to his black sports car and opened the passenger door for her. As she got seated, she noticed he was standing close by. He kept his hand on the open door, as if he was trying to prevent her from making a quick getaway.

The BMW's engine purred as Burke pulled away from the curb. "I like the anchors on your blue fingernails, Rox. Clever design for the reunion."

"You noticed them?"

"I don't miss much."

Roxy looked at him and thought, "I'm sure you don't."

"High school reunions can be interesting," Burke slid a glance at her and smiled. "I'll bet you were the homecoming queen."

"No, that was Sal."

"Sal Whitlock, from Pet Wellness?"

Roxy nodded.

"Okay, let me try again. I'll bet you were a cheerleader."

"You're close. I was a majorette."

"That fits," Burke said. "I can see you twirling a baton. When I was in high school, the Riverside Bay majorettes wore sailor uniforms with short skirts."

"We did too, unfortunately."

A brief silence followed. Burke cleared his throat and said, "I was sorry I missed the meeting with Kyle yesterday afternoon. It had something to do with new evidence in Greta's car, right?"

"In the trunk—" She stopped, regretting the slip. Kyle had made it clear he wanted to talk to Burke, himself.

"Unbelievable... finding Greta's body, like that."

"You know?"

"Oh, sure. Kyle called me."

Roxy nodded. "We were shocked. It's hard to believe she was murdered."

"It's a terrible shame, isn't it?"

She glanced at Burke and went quiet. His voice held a strange flat tone. He and Greta had been involved in an intense relationship for months. But then, they'd had a bitter break-up, and he'd had two full years to get over her. She wondered if he was holding back his emotions. Roxy recalled how stoic Burke had remained during his mother's funeral, until they stood at her gravesite. When family members began dropping long-stemmed red roses onto Lydia's lowered coffin, Burke abruptly doubled over and crushed the rose to his chest. His shoulders heaved as he sobbed, and tiny red petals slipped through his fingers, falling softly into his mother's grave.

Roxy's focus snapped back when Burke's ringtone sounded. He slowed to a stop at a red light and pulled his phone from the side pocket of his blazer. Roxy watched as he punched in his numbered passcode. He frowned at the screen and then slipped the phone back into his pocket. "Nothing urgent. I ran into an old law school friend at the conference. I'll call him tomorrow." His voice sounded casual, but his face wore a troubled expression.

"Is that a new phone?"

He nodded. "I bought it yesterday, in Tallahassee."

"You unlocked it with a code. Doesn't it have facial recognition?"

"I haven't taken the time to set it up, yet."

Burke came to a stop behind Charlie's SUV and joined the long line of vehicles waiting for valet parking at the event center. Jo stepped out and headed toward them. Roxy lowered her window as Jo walked up. "Hey Rox, let's go inside and check-in while the guys wait to park."

Roxy turned to Burke. "Okay with you?"

He nodded.

The moment they entered the event center, Jo said, "You looked really uncomfortable with Burke at the house."

Roxy shrugged. "It's going okay."

"You've only been with him ten minutes, Rox."

"And it hasn't been terrible. Besides, I'm hoping Burke will help me keep my distance from Trent."

"Hey, Rox! You look great!" Duke Murphy walked up, looking trim in a tan polo shirt and dark trousers. He gave her a quick hug.

Roxy smiled. "I almost didn't recognize you without your white baker's apron. Who are you with—"

Melody strode toward them, wearing a tight black dress and a scowl on her face. She handed Duke his name tag, linked her arm with his, and glared at Roxy before pulling him away.

"I'm glad I seated Melody across the ballroom from us," Jo said. She turned toward the registration table. "Rox, look at that thin bald guy over there. Something about him looks familiar, but he seems way too old to be in our class."

Roxy studied him. His shaved head and skeletal build gave him an elderly, frail appearance. A flash of recognition hit. "That's Zane Grayson!"

Jo's eyes grew large. "That's 'In-Zane,' the wild and crazy hunk who had the coolest rock band in high school?"

Roxy nodded. "Hard to believe, but I'm sure that's him."

Jo nudged her. "Remember what Zane said to you back in eighth grade, after you got that horrible haircut?"

"How could I forget? It was such a trauma; I didn't get another haircut for years."

Jo started giggling. "You broke your wrist that same weekend."

Roxy grinned. "I left school on Friday with long hair. And I came back on Monday with my hair chopped off and a cast up to my elbow."

"And Zane said..." Jo's giggling grew louder. "He said... 'What happened to you, did you get caught in a fan?'" She laughed out loud and then clapped a hand over her mouth.

Roxy giggled. "He used to tease me about my name, too. Roxy Rode... rocky road." She glanced at the registration table. Zane had disappeared in the growing crowd of people.

Jo's expression turned serious. "Zane doesn't look healthy, Rox. I hear he's been in and out of drug rehab."

Bri headed toward them, wearing a silky pink dress and a matching cropped jacket. Her blonde hair held additional pink highlights that framed her pretty face. "My date canceled at the last minute, so I'm declaring myself the official photographer for our reunion website." She stepped back and snapped a photo of them.

"Will you take one with my phone?" Roxy pulled it out and handed it to Bri.

"Rox, your screen is all cracked. But I love the little blue dolphins on your case." She took a quick photo and handed back the phone. As they headed toward the registration table, Bri turned to Jo. "There have been some last-minute dinner cancellations. Can you help us rearrange the table seating?"

Roxy picked up her pre-printed name badge. Burke had already paid for his dinner online, so she filled out a name tag for him. While Jo and Bri looked over the seating chart, she wandered toward the ballroom doors and peeked inside. Huge crystal chandeliers sprayed sparkling patterns of light across the mirrored ceiling. Each round dining table held a floral centerpiece, topped with a glittering navy and white sign: Riverside Bay HS 15th Reunion. A man stood on the raised platform set up for the live band. His voice echoed in the cavernous room as he tested the microphones.

A hand touched the small of her back. Roxy turned, expecting to see Burke. Her eyes locked with Trent's, and her body flinched.

"Hey, you two. Look over here and give me smiles." Bri's voice.

Roxy turned. The flash went off as Trent kissed her on the cheek.

"Roxy Rode! I can't believe it!" A man with thick brown hair strode toward her. His muscular arms gave him the look of a weightlifter. He was wearing dark trousers, a blue polo shirt, and no name tag.

Roxy gazed at his face and searched her memory, but her mind seemed unable to focus. Trent was standing so close; she could feel the heat radiating from his body.

The man gave her an enthusiastic hug. When he looked at her, he realized she was struggling. "I'm Owen."

"Owen Dalczak? Wow! It's been a long time. You look so… good." Roxy was about to say different, but she stopped herself, thinking he might be offended. Owen had been the stereotypical weak-looking nerd in high school. Back then, he wore glasses with thick lenses. But he wasn't wearing glasses tonight, and his brown eyes looked dreamy.

Owen shook Trent's hand, and then he introduced them to his wife, Jodilyn. The pretty, dark-haired woman was wearing a sleeveless black and white dress.

Trent had stepped away from Roxy when Owen gave her a hug. But as they began talking, he stepped back.

Trent's closeness ignited a spark of irritation, and Roxy moved a half-step away.

He smoothly closed the gap.

"There you are, Rox." Burke walked up and shot a cold glance at Trent.

Roxy handed Burke his name tag and introduced him to the others. Trent and Burke eyed each other as they exchanged polite 'nice-to-meet-you' comments. The two men were wearing similar outfits, but Trent's charcoal blazer didn't look as tailored as Burke's.

Owen smiled at Roxy. "Do you remember our one and only date, back in tenth grade?"

She nodded. "It was unforgettable."

"Owen Dalczak!" Jo walked up. "You look so different!"

He gave Jo a hug, shook Charlie's hand and then introduced them to Jodilyn.

"Owen, I heard you mention your date with Rox." Jo grinned and turned to Burke. "I set it up. It was a double date with Charlie and me. What a disaster!"

Owen let out a good-natured laugh. "I was a real klutz that night."

"I was just as klutzy as you," Roxy said. "We had a great time at the movie, but when we went to the diner—"

"I knocked over a full glass of Pepsi, and it spilled all over you," Owen said.

Roxy giggled. "I jumped up to wipe off my jeans at the exact time the server arrived. My head hit her tray and food flew every-where. Burgers, fries, ketchup... I'm afraid you got the worst of it, since you were sitting next to me."

Owen laughed. "Rox, as crazy as that night was, I would have gladly asked you out again. But this guy beat me to it." He nodded at Trent. "After that, you two were a couple."

Roxy glanced away, feeling awkward.

"Rox! I love your green dress!" Sally Whitlock walked up and gave her a hug. She was wearing a clingy lavender dress that skimmed her slender, fit body. Layered light brown hair framed her attractive face, and her eye shadow brought out the violet hue in her eyes. Sally's gaze slid to Burke. "I haven't seen you for a while. You used to bring in your mother's cat for check-ups."

Burke smiled. "My mother loved that little tuxedo cat."

"Hey, Sal." Jo pointed toward the registration table. "Matt's waving at you. I think there might be more problems with the seating chart."

Sally headed toward the registration table, and Owen and Jodilyn walked with her to pick up their name tags. Charlie and Jo began chatting with a nearby group.

"I'm going to the bar," Burke said. "Do you want anything, Rox?"

"Not right now." As Burke walked away, Roxy stepped toward the group Jo and Charlie had joined.

Trent placed his hand on her arm, holding her back. "I thought you weren't bringing a date tonight."

"It was a last-minute thing." Roxy shook off his hand.

Tara and her husband Cole walked up. She looked radiant in a silky black dress that flattered her curvy figure. With her copper hair color restored, Tara looked years younger. Bri had done a beautiful job of erasing the gray streaks that had appeared during Nikki's long illness.

When Trent and Cole began talking about sports, Tara pulled Roxy aside. She kept her voice hushed as she said, "It was a shock, at first, when I saw you with Burke. I forgot how much he looks like Vance."

Bri walked up while Tara was speaking. "Burke's got a real James Bond look going tonight, with his dark good looks and that sharp outfit. I didn't realize you two were involved—"

"We're not involved!" Roxy glanced around and lowered her voice. "He's just my date."

"So... if someone else is interested...?"

Roxy smiled. "Go for it, Bri."

Burke rejoined them, carrying a glass of red wine. He caught the flirty smile Bri tossed him, and he smiled back. His gaze lingered on her for a long moment.

The ballroom doors opened, and Burke escorted Roxy to their assigned table. He pulled out her chair and then took the seat to her left. Trent surprised her by sitting across the table. Bri sat next to her brother and explained that he'd volunteered to take the seat reserved for her date.

Sally and Matt sat next to Bri, and Jo and Charlie sat next to Trent. Two seats remained empty.

"Greg and Leeann will be a little late," Matt said. "Greg's taking care of an emergency, an injured terrier."

Sally introduced the topic of the sinkhole. She recounted the details Mae had given her about Trixie's rescue, moments before the sinkhole grew larger. Roxy tensed, feeling uncomfortable as the center of attention. In her peripheral vision, she caught Trent staring at her. When Matt began talking about his humorous experiences working with animals, Trent shifted his gaze, and she relaxed.

"Here we are, at last!" Leeann walked up, wearing a sleek navy blue satin dress, a sparkling anchor necklace and matching drop earrings. Her thick black hair held a lustrous shine.

Greg wore navy slacks and a white polo shirt with the words, Whitlock Pet Wellness stitched over the pocket. He sat next to Matt, who was wearing an identical polo shirt.

"How's that terrier?" Matt asked.

Greg smiled. "He's one lucky pup. He ran under a car as it was backing out of a garage and came through without a fracture. The ligaments on his back legs needed stitching, that's all."

The servers arrived with their pre-selected meals; steak, chicken or vegetarian. When they started filling the wineglasses, Roxy ordered coffee instead, since she was still on antidepressant medication. Trent also ordered coffee, which caught her attention. She recalled how concerned she had been about his heavy drinking during their senior year.

After everyone was served, Burke smoothly took over the conversation and described the challenges of setting up a private law practice after working at a large Atlanta law firm. As he spoke, he made frequent eye contact with Bri. She responded each time with a nod and a smile.

Greg announced their new side business: Scoop Troops — teams who make home visits to clean up back yard pet messes. Leeann put a quick end to that discussion, saying the scooping details could wait until everyone had finished eating.

Trent began describing his bizarre experiences as an EMT in St. Paul. He spoke with enthusiasm, using his hands as if he was directing traffic. Roxy watched him and thought, "He used those same charming storytelling skills every time he lied to me."

Dessert was served, white cheesecake topped with blueberries. Everyone switched to coffee, except Burke. He continued drinking wine, and he made sure the servers topped his glass each time they came around.

Leeann glanced at the stage, set up for the band. "When will the dancing start?"

"In a few minutes," Sally said. "But if you don't feel like dancing, you can go into the casino room we've set up."

"Casino?" Leeann looked surprised.

"It was Melody's idea," Sally said. "Her uncle owns a party rental store, and he donated the roulette tables and fake gambling chips."

Burke leaned close to Roxy and whispered, "Let's check out the casino room after dinner." He surprised her by nuzzling her ear.

Roxy cringed and leaned away from him. She refocused on the table conversation and realized Sally was talking about their camping trip.

"…Sunday night we'll stay at a lodge called Dusty's Last Resort on the Ocklawaha River," Sally said. "We'll rent our canoes from Dusty and set out on the river Monday morning."

Bri stood and excused herself, saying she wanted to take photos of the people seated at each table. She offered her untouched cheesecake to Trent, who eagerly accepted it.

Sally waited until Bri had walked away, and then she turned to Trent. "When do you and Seth plan to join us?"

"On Monday. We'll put into the river at Gore's Landing in the early morning and do some fishing while we float downstream with the current. After lunch, we plan to paddle upstream and meet you as you reach your campsite. Matt told us where it's located."

Sally shot her husband an icy frown.

Roxy glanced at Jo, who shrugged her shoulders. "What's going on, Sal?"

"The Thorson brothers plan to camp near us on Monday night." Sally's frown deepened. "I didn't know anything about it, until I talked to Trent just before we entered the ballroom."

"Seth and I planned it as a surprise for Bri," Trent said.

Roxy clenched her teeth and thought, "No wonder I hate surprises."

Trent glanced at Bri's empty chair. "We're concerned about her MS. I thought it might be good if we tagged along on the camping trip, especially since I'm an EMT—"

"Don't you think women are capable of taking care of themselves?" Sally asked.

Trent looked surprised, as if he hadn't realized anyone would view his presence as patronizing. "Ah… no. I mean, yes. Ah… it's because of Bri—"

"Sal knows that." Matt nudged his wife.

"Of course." She gave Trent a tight-lipped smile.

The band started playing, and people around the room stood up. Roxy left the ballroom with Burke, feeling relieved to get away from Trent.

Inside the casino room, members of the event center staff sat at a table, handing out plastic bags filled with fake gambling chips. Zane Grayson stood on a raised platform nearby, playing his guitar along with pre-recorded rock music. He took a break as Roxy and Burke entered. "Hey, Ms. Rocky Road! Looking good, girl!" He gave her an enthusiastic hug.

"Zane! Great to see you!" Roxy smiled a little wider to disguise the shock of seeing his pale, thin face up close. His health and good looks had faded, like an image on a sun-bleached photo. When she brought up his eighth-grade comment about her hair being caught in a fan, he laughed out loud. But Zane admitted he had no recollection of it.

Burke grabbed Roxy's arm and pulled her toward a roulette table.

She shrugged off his grip. "What's your hurry? I wasn't through talking to Zane! If you want to start gambling, go knock yourself out!" She handed her fake chips to him and turned toward the bandstand.

Burke blocked her way. "Wait. I'm sorry, I didn't mean to be rude. Stay and be my good luck charm?"

She read his penitent expression and her irritation eased. After all, he was her date.

Burke took a spot at the roulette table. He moved his chips from number to number and focused on every spin of the wheel, like a man possessed. His winnings quickly mounted, and people around the table began cheering him on. Roxy stood beside him, feeling like a second-rate actress in the casino scene of a 007 movie. Burke handed her his credit card and sent her to the bar each time he needed a drink refill.

"There you are!" Jo intercepted Roxy as she was returning from the bar. "I was looking for you in the casino room. Burke's on a big winning streak. He looks just like James—"

"Bond, I know," Roxy said. "And I've been his Bond slave, fetching his drinks." She held up the full glass in her hand. "He's switched from wine to rum and coke."

"Burke must be able to hold his liquor."

Roxy shook her head. "I've never seen him drink this heavily before. He got a phone call in the car on the way to the reunion, and I think it upset him."

"You're not having a good time, are you?"

Roxy shrugged.

Jo gave her a sympathetic smile. "After you finish your drink delivery, come and join our group in the ballroom. We pushed two dining tables together, and we're having fun talking about old times."

"Maybe I'll do that." Roxy turned and ran into Trent, who had been standing nearby.

"Rox, I heard you talking to Jo. Don't go back to the casino. I know you love dancing, and the band is great. Come and dance with me?"

She shook her head and hurried inside the casino room. Bri was standing next to Burke at the crowded roulette table. The loud music, shouting and cheering made talking difficult. Roxy tapped Bri's shoulder and pointed to Burke as she handed her the rum and coke. Then she mouthed the word "ballroom" and pointed toward the exit.

Bri mouthed, "ballroom" and nodded.

Burke kept his focus on the roulette wheel as Bri handed him the drink.

When Roxy entered the ballroom, she heard laughter coming from the area where the two tables had been joined together. Every seat had been taken. Charlie caught sight of her and waved. He pulled a chair from a neighboring table and slid it between him and Jo. Roxy sat down and leaned against the back of the chair as the tension drained from her body. She smiled as she entered into the lively conversation.

Minutes later, someone tapped her shoulder. "Want to dance?"

She looked up into Trent's eyes.

Roxy held back the urge to shout, "No!" She sensed people around the table were watching them. If she refused to dance with Trent, she might give the impression she was still bitter, and she didn't want to trigger a wave of gossip about her humiliating past with him. She forced a smile and nodded. As she walked toward the dance floor, she promised herself she'd stay for only one dance. And she comforted herself with the prospect of stepping on Trent's foot.

The band was playing a slow romantic song. Roxy stiffened as Trent drew her into his arms. She matched his steps and avoided eye contact with him by focusing on the other dancers. When the slow song finally ended, the band started playing a classic rock song—one of her favorites. Roxy hesitated. She did love to dance, and Trent's presence didn't feel as oppressive on the crowded dance floor. She decided to stay. They danced to a long series of rock songs, until the band announced a break.

Roxy gave Trent a brief smile. "That was fun."

He eyed her. "Sounds like you didn't expect it to be fun."

"Your words, not mine." She started turning away.

"Rox, don't go back to the table. I really want to talk to you. There's a balcony with a great view of the ocean." Trent nodded toward a set of French doors.

She let out a sigh. "Okay, but only for a minute or two."

Other couples had wandered onto the wide balcony, and they stood in small groups, chatting. Roxy walked to the railing, and Trent stood beside her. The full moon glowed like a luminous white ball in the night sky, casting a silvery ribbon of light on the ocean's dark surface. Rows of waves rushed forward, crashing against the sand with a soothing rhythm. The damp salty breeze swirled through Roxy's hair, and she shivered.

Trent took off his blazer and gently draped it over her shoulders.

She turned toward him, startled by how handsome he looked in the moonlight. "This feels like a replay of today, at the lighthouse. We look at the view, and I start shivering."

He smiled. "Like déjà vu, all over again. That's the way I felt, dancing with you tonight... like it's a replay of our senior prom." He paused. "Seeing Owen again reminded me of something. Do you know when I first realized I was attracted to you?"

She looked up at him, curious.

"It was the start of football season in tenth grade. You were performing with the majorettes in that short skirt, and you looked different, somehow. You weren't my sister's silly giggling friend anymore. You looked grown up and beautiful, and you had curves in all the right places." He paused and met her gaze. "I tried to stay cool on our first date. But right away, I felt myself falling for you. And I wasn't sure I was ready to feel that way about you, or anyone. So, after a few dates, I broke up with you. Remember?"

She nodded.

"And then I saw you sitting with Owen Dalczak in the movie theater. He was a nerd, but that nerd had his arm around you, and I didn't like it. I knew I had to have you back, so I asked you out again, the next day—"

"What are you doing out here?" Burke strode out onto the balcony.

"Just enjoying the view," Trent said, his voice casual.

Burke turned to Roxy. "You're coming with me!"

"You can't order her around—"

"Stay out of this!" Burke stepped toward Trent.

Heads turned and conversations stopped.

"Calm down, Burke. I'll come with you." Roxy slipped off the blazer. She gave Trent an apologetic smile as she handed it to him.

Burke linked arms with her as they walked back into the ball-room. "What's going on between you and him?"

"Nothing." She caught the sour smell of alcohol on his breath and turned her head away. "How did you do at the casino?"

"I lost everything on that stinkin' black twenty-two! Then I saw I lost you, too." He tripped and staggered but recovered quickly. "Let's get something from the bar."

"You go ahead. I'm heading to the restroom."

"I'll wait for you in the hallway. I'm not going to lose you again."

Roxy pushed open the restroom door and smiled when she saw the long line waiting for an open stall. She wasn't in any hurry to rejoin Burke. Several minutes later, she stood at the sink and took her time washing her hands. She pulled a comb from her purse and ran it through her hair as slowly as she could manage. The restroom gradually emptied, until Roxy stood alone at the mirror. She turned and greeted Leeann and Tara as they entered. When they emerged from the stalls, Roxy was still combing her hair. They stood on either side of her as they washed up.

"Wasn't the band great? They just played their last song," Leeann said.

Tara reapplied her lipstick and closed the tube. "It's been a long time since Cole's been so eager to dance with me. I'm sorry to see this evening end."

Roxy thought, "I'm not."

Melody entered the restroom. She wobbled on her feet and leaned against the door as it closed. She wore a sloppy grin. "Hey, Rokshy. Burke's ashking about you—"

A thump sounded and the door flew open, flinging Melody against the back wall. Roxy caught a glimpse of Trent's longish hair before the door closed. Shouts erupted in the hallway.

"Wha' happened?" Melody leaned against the wall and rubbed her head.

Roxy slowly opened the door and ventured out of the restroom. Tara and Leeann followed close behind.

Burke was standing across the hallway. Blood leaked from his mouth, and red splotches covered his white shirt. Duke Murphy gripped Burke's shoulder, as if he was restraining him. Trent stood a few feet away and glared at Burke as he rubbed his jaw. Charlie walked between them and said, "Let's all settle down."

Melody stumbled out of the restroom and held up a silver bag. "Shomeone left thish—"

"Oh! It's mine, Melody. Thanks." Roxy retrieved it and then hurried over to Burke. "You're bleeding."

Burke shrugged off Duke's grip and dabbed his bloody mouth with his fingers. "I'm okay. No thanks to him." He shot a dark look at Trent. Then he slipped off his blazer and handed it to Roxy. "Hold this for me. I need to get cleaned up." He walked into the men's restroom.

The hallway emptied as the crowd dispersed. Jo walked up and said, "Burke's in no shape to drive, Rox. We'll give you both a ride home. Charlie's on his way to the valet stand."

"Thanks." Roxy draped Burke's blazer over her arm and felt the outline of his phone in the side pocket. She glanced at the restroom door, and then she pulled out his phone.

"Rox! What are you doing?"

"I'm curious about that phone call Burke got on the way here. He passed it off as nothing, but I think it's been bothering him all evening." Roxy visualized his passcode and tapped it in.

"You know his passcode?"

"I memorized it." She scrolled through Burke's call log. An unanswered call from Kyle was at the top, received at 9:25 p.m. The next call on the list had no name attached. The number appeared twice. First, as an incoming call at 6:26 p.m., while they were driving to the reunion. And then, as an outgoing call at 6:40 p.m., while Burke was alone in the valet parking line. The call lasted nearly ten minutes. Roxy focused on the number while her mind photographed it. She quickly scrolled through his earlier calls. She found several unanswered calls from Kyle, but she didn't spot a return call.

Jo nudged her. "Hurry up! Burke's drunk. He won't be happy if he finds you snooping on his phone."

As she closed the screen, the men's restroom door opened. Jo quickly moved, blocking Burke's view as Roxy slipped his phone back into the pocket.

Burke's eyes narrowed as he stepped around Jo. He took his blazer from Roxy. "Let's go, Rox. I'll get the car."

"We should ride with Charlie and Jo. You've had a lot to drink—"

"I'm not drunk! Come on!" He grabbed her arm.

"No!" Roxy pulled away. "I'm leaving with them!" She read the surprised look in Burke's eyes, and then she turned and walked away with Jo.

The floodlight clicked on as Charlie pulled into her driveway. Roxy thanked them for the ride as she got out. When she entered her kitchen, she switched on the light and locked the back door. She sat on a barstool at the island, set down her purse and then slumped forward, exhausted.

Roxy glanced at her purse and saw it was unzipped. A cold sweat broke out when she reached inside and realized her phone was missing. She pictured the last time she opened it. The restroom! Did her phone slip out when Melody found her purse? Did it fall out when she was walking with Jo to the valet stand? While she was riding home with Charlie and Jo? Roxy decided to call Jo, and then she remembered she didn't have a phone. For the first time, she regretted her decision not to install a landline phone when she remodeled her house.

She startled when she heard knocking at the back door. Burke's face appeared in the porthole window, illuminated by the porch light. Roxy let out a groan. She walked to the door and unlocked it, but she kept the chain slide secured. She peered outside. "Burke, I'm tired—"

"I know. I just came over to apologize for the way I behaved tonight." He paused and looked through the narrow door opening. "Are you going to make me stand outside? It'll only take a minute."

Roxy realized she could use Burke's phone to call Jo and ask her to search Charlie's car. If her phone wasn't there, maybe she could call the event center and ask someone to look for it tonight. She slid off the chain.

Burke entered and closed the door. "Where's Buddy? He's usually right by your side."

"Kyle's taking care of him tonight." Roxy yawned, a large yawn that made her eyes water. She blinked to clear away the moisture. "Can I use your phone to make a quick call to Jo?" She heard the click of the deadbolt and looked at Burke.

His dark eyes were focused on her. "I'm sorry you didn't have fun at the reunion." He took off his blazer and tossed it on the kitchen island.

Roxy stared at him and froze, as if blinded by the headlights of an oncoming car.

Burke walked toward her, and his lips curved into a vicious smile.

Comprehension kicked in, sending a shock to her heart. She backed away and thought, "He's blocking the door, and I don't have a phone!" She glanced at his crumpled blazer on the island and lunged toward it. She pulled his phone from the side pocket.

Burke grabbed her wrist. He wrestled his phone out of her hand and threw it across the room. It hit something hard.

Roxy recognized the sound of a phone screen shattering as she jerked her wrist out of his grasp. She ran to the back door and gripped the deadbolt knob.

He yanked her hand away and wrapped his arms around her body, pulling her close.

"Burke! Stop! Let me go!" She squirmed, but he kept her arms pinned to her side.

"You want this, Rox. I know you do." The sour smell of his hot breath sickened her. "Every time you look at me you see Vance, don't you? I've seen the passion in your eyes—"

"No!" Panic surged and she wrenched an arm free. She raised her hand and dug her fingernails into the side of his face, scraping hard.

He cried out and his grip loosened. She ran into the family room, toward the front door. Burke reached her before she could unlock it. He twisted her arm as he whirled her around. Then he slapped her face and threw her onto the couch.

Roxy landed face down. She felt the weight of Burke's knee on her lower back as he tugged the zipper on her dress. Fear twisted her stomach into a knot. She screamed, "Burke! Don't do this!"

"Shut up!" He put his hand on the back of her head and pressed down hard.

Her face sank into the soft suede cushion, cutting off her air. As she fought to breathe, the knot in her stomach twisted tighter. She needed air soon, or she'd pass out. She sent up a silent prayer, "Help me, God..."

The front door shook as the pounding started. "Open up! I know you're in there, Burke!" Trent's voice.

Burke's weight shifted, and the pressure on her head eased. Roxy took a gasping breath and screamed, "Trent! Help me!"

The door shuddered as if it was being kicked. "Let me in! Now! I'm calling 911!"

Burke rolled his knee off her back.

Roxy struggled to her feet. She clutched her dress to keep it from sliding off her shoulders as she ran to the front door and unlocked it.

Trent rushed inside; his eyes wild. "You okay?"

She nodded, trembling violently. Her heartbeat thundered in her chest.

A noise came from the kitchen. The click of the back door deadbolt.

Trent whirled around. "Burke! You're not getting away —"

"No!" Roxy grabbed Trent's upper arm. She felt the hard tensed muscle through the fabric of his blazer. "Don't leave me!"

He turned to her, and his expression wavered between rage and compassion. He glanced into the kitchen as the back door slammed shut.

"Let him go, Trent! Lock the door behind him!"

He ran toward the kitchen.

Roxy secured the deadbolt on the front door and then leaned against it, feeling woozy. She'd read the look in Trent's eyes, and her trembling intensified. She recalled how he and Seth had taken their revenge on Bri's former husband years ago, when his savage abuse put her in the hospital on Christmas Eve. Their beating sent him to the ER on the same night.

She closed her eyes and prayed that Trent wouldn't run after Burke. She didn't want to be left alone.

"Rox, are you okay?"

She turned and saw Trent hurrying toward her. When they made eye contact, his expression softened.

"Let me help you." He quickly zipped up her dress.

Roxy's knees went weak. A deep numbing cold had penetrated her body, as if her blood had frozen into an icy sludge.

Trent wrapped his blazer around her and held her tight. "It's okay now, Rox. It's okay." He walked her to the couch, sat next to her and wrapped his arms around her. She leaned her head against his chest and continued shaking as she whispered, "How could this happen? Burke's part of my family. He was a groomsman in my wedding—" Knocking sounded at the front door, and she let out a startled cry.

"It's okay, Rox. It's probably Bri. She rode here with me." Trent moved to the door and looked through the peephole before unlocking it.

Bri stepped inside. "I got tired of waiting for you in the truck. What's going on? I saw Burke rush out the back door and drive away. Did that creepy drunk pick another fight with you?" She glanced at Roxy. "What happened to your face?"

She touched the sore spot on her cheek and sank back against the cushion.

Roxy heard familiar voices, talking softly. She opened her eyes and realized she was lying on the couch, covered with a handknit throw blanket Aunt Nell had made for her. Trent, Bri, Jo and Charlie were sitting in her family room. She pushed aside the blanket and sat up. The fog cleared from her brain and images of Burke's attack flashed, prompting a violent shiver.

Trent moved to the couch and sat beside her. "How do you feel?"

"I'm... okay..." She looked into his eyes, and gratitude overwhelmed her. "Thank you, Trent..."

He smiled.

A question surfaced. "Why did you come to my house?"

He reached into the pocket of his blazer and pulled out her phone. "Bri found it on the floor in the restroom, and she recognized the cracked screen and the blue dolphin case. We rode to the reunion together, and we wanted to return your phone before driving back to New Smyrna."

Roxy nodded as she set her phone on her lap. She glanced at the throw blanket. "I don't remember putting this on."

"I wrapped it around you," Trent said. "I was afraid you were going into shock."

"Rox..." Charlie said. "I'm getting ready to call Kyle."

She tensed. "Why?"

"You need to report Burke's assault."

She shook her head. "I can't do that. I let him in. I knew Burke was drunk, but he said he wanted to apologize. How could I have been so stupid?"

"It's not your fault," Trent said. "I've responded to domestic violence calls, and I've seen the injured victims blame themselves. Don't do that, Rox."

"He's right," Charlie said. "You have to report this. What if Burke tries to assault someone else?"

Roxy sighed and looked down at her hands. Every fingernail on her right hand had broken off, the white anchors sheared in half. She shuddered, recalling the feel of Burke's perspiring skin as she raked her nails down the side of his face.

"I'm going to call Kyle now," Charlie said.

She nodded.

Kyle stared at a page of scribbled notes sitting on the desk in his home office. He blinked and then rubbed his tired eyes as he leaned back in his desk chair. He'd left the police station around midnight, and then he took the dogs for a brisk walk. An uneasy feeling had kept him wide awake and edgy. He swiveled his chair around and smiled when he saw the dogs. They were both asleep, sprawled on the floor in front of the doorway, so he couldn't leave the room without tripping over them.

He thought about Roxy and checked the time on his phone: 2:23 a.m. He wondered if any of tonight's photos had been posted on her class reunion website. He moved his chair close to the desk and pulled up the website on his laptop screen. He scrolled past the section of old yearbook photos and began searching through the reunion photos. Roxy's vivid green dress made her easy to spot. He blinked when he saw the first photo of her with Burke. He found several more photos of them, seated at dinner and standing by a roulette table. Burke must have stepped in as her date! When he saw a photo of Trent kissing Roxy on the cheek, his body tensed. He scrolled through a few more photos of them dancing together.

His ringtone sounded, and Charlie's name flashed on the screen. A feeling of dread surged. Calls at this time of night always signaled bad news. He held his phone in his right hand as he answered the call. Out of habit, he gripped his pen in his left hand and pulled a blank notepad close.

"Kyle, I'm sorry it's late..."

He heard the stress in Charlie's voice. "No problem. What's wrong?"

"It's Rox... Burke attacked her tonight!"

Kyle recoiled, as if he'd been gut punched. "How is—"

"She's okay..."

"Thank God," he whispered.

"...Trent got there in time."

Kyle's pulse sped up.

Charlie briefly summarized the attack and said, "Rox wants to file a report. Can you come over to her house?"

"I'll be there as soon as I can." Kyle ended the call and then sat, grinding his teeth together. If Burke had walked into the room at that moment, he wouldn't have been able to stop himself from beating the man senseless.

A searing pain in his left hand caught his attention. He looked down, surprised to see he'd snapped his plastic pen in half. Black ink leaked from the jagged break and mingled with the blood leaking from the deep gash on his index finger.

Kyle spotted an extended-cab pickup truck parked at the curb in front of Roxy's house. The cruiser's headlights illuminated the words on the driver's door: Thorson's Auto Repair, New Smyrna Beach. He parked the cruiser in Roxy's driveway, behind Charlie's SUV. Then he turned to Sergeant Kendra Nichols, who was sitting in the passenger seat. "Charlie said her face is bruised. After you take her statement, make sure you take photos."

Kendra nodded. "I will, Lieutenant."

A burning pain smoldered inside Kyle's gut as he knocked on the back door. Charlie opened it and led them into the family room. Jo stood near the couch, with her arms tightly folded. She gave them a nod as they entered. Her face wore a stricken expression, and she was biting her lower lip, as if she was holding back strong emotions.

Roxy was sitting on the couch with her head bowed. The lace sleeve on her dress had been torn. Kyle saw the reddish bruise on her face, and the burning pain in his gut intensified.

Trent sat on the couch next to Roxy, and his sister Bri sat next to him, looking fatigued and pale. She remained seated and simply glanced up and nodded as Charlie introduced Kyle and Kendra. Trent stood and shook their hands.

Kendra escorted Roxy to the kitchen and began taking her statement. Kyle interviewed Trent on the back porch. He found it painful to hold a pen in his injured left hand, and his writing looked like a child's scrawl.

Trent eyed Kyle's index finger. "That's a deep cut. It's an infection waiting to happen. You need to get it treated."

Kyle nodded as irritation surged. Trent seemed overly-eager to help everyone tonight. He recognized the ugly emotion behind that thought. He quickly suppressed it and focused on completing Trent's statement. When they returned to the family room, Roxy and Bri were sitting on the couch and Charlie stood nearby. Kendra was standing at the kitchen island, talking on her phone.

Jo walked downstairs, carrying an overnight bag. She set it near the front door. "I packed this for you, Rox. You're coming home with us tonight."

"I was going to suggest that," Kyle said.

Jo looked at him. She held up a tube of antibiotic cream and a box of bandages. "I got these from the medicine cabinet upstairs. I'm going to take care of that nasty cut on your finger."

Kendra lowered her phone as they entered the kitchen. "Lieutenant, the officers tried Burke's condo again. He's still not there, and his car isn't in the parking garage or anywhere near the Silva Building."

"Tell them to keep that building under surveillance."

She nodded as she lifted her phone and resumed the call.

After Jo bandaged his cut, Kyle went back into the family room and briefly explained the procedures involved in filing charges.

Chapter 22

Roxy kept her head bowed as he spoke. When he asked her if she had any questions, she glanced up and shook her head.

When Kyle read the misery in her eyes, he longed to reach out and comfort her.

She glanced away.

He followed Kendra out the back door, into the humid darkness. The floodlight mounted on the garage clicked on as they walked down the driveway.

"Did you get a good photo of that bruise on her face?" Kyle asked.

"I did," Kendra said. "Bruises are forming on her arms, too. I told Rox to come into the station tomorrow, so I can take more photos as the areas darken."

When they reached the cruiser, Kyle stopped and punched the driver's door with his fist. Then he flinched at the pain in his bandaged finger.

Roxy followed Jo as they entered her kitchen. She squinted when Jo switched on the overhead lights. The throbbing pain behind her eyes increased as the harsh glare bounced off the white cabinets, the polished granite countertop and the red accent wall. Roxy set her purse on the kitchen counter. She swayed on her feet and gripped the counter's smooth edge for support.

The back door opened, amplifying the grinding sound of the garage door closing. Charlie carried her overnight bag through the kitchen and into the hallway leading to the guest bedroom.

Jo sat at her kitchen table and leaned on her elbows as she massaged her forehead. "Bri told me she uploaded all her photos to the reunion website on the drive to your house. And I uploaded my photos, before we got Trent's call." Her voice quivered. "I wish we hadn't done that! I don't want any photos of Burke on that website!" She pounded her fist on the table. "How could he do this to you?"

"I don't know..." Roxy let out a loud choking sob. Jo's outburst had acted like a key, unlocking her pent-up emotions. She leaned against the counter as the tears flowed.

"Oh, Rox..." Jo stood and wrapped an arm around her shoulders.

Charlie walked back into the kitchen and wrapped his arms around both of them.

Roxy stepped into the guest bathroom shower and turned the faucet handle until the water temperature was as hot as she could stand it. Steamy water jets drummed against her back as she soaped a washcloth. Vivid images of Burke's attack flashed into her mind, and she scrubbed hard to remove the repulsive feel of his hands on her skin. Without warning, she let out a strangled cry, as more tears poured out in powerful, choking bursts. Tears of anger... humiliation... revulsion. They streamed down her face and mingled with the hot soapy water flowing over her body and into the drain. When she shut off the water, she leaned against the smooth subway tiles, dripping wet and hiccupping, until her heartbeat slowed to normal.

She quickly toweled off, dried her hair and put on her nightgown. As she climbed into bed and turned out the light, another image flashed—Burke walking toward her in the kitchen, wearing that sinister smile. At that moment, his handsome shell broke away, revealing the ugly, violent creature within.

Roxy said a prayer to suppress the image, and then she rolled onto her side, grabbed her pillow and hugged it tight. Each time another violent image surfaced, she prayed... until the overpowering weight of exhaustion pulled her into the healing realm of sleep.

Sunday morning

Sunlight streamed in through a gap between the curtains. Roxy sat up in bed, feeling groggy. She headed into the adjoining bathroom. As she washed her hands, she gazed at her reflection in the mirror. The skin around her eyes appeared puffy, and the swollen bruise on her cheek had darkened.

She sat on the bed and checked the time on her phone. It was nearly ten thirty. Even though she had slept a few hours, her nerves sparked like frayed electrical wires. She closed her eyes and breathed deeply as she prayed. A peaceful feeling settled over her, calming her nerves. She unlocked her phone, opened her gratitude journal and began typing.

Her phone chimed, and she read Kyle's text: "How are you feeling?"

She typed: "I'm okay. I need to come into the station today, so Kendra can take more photos. Will you be around?"

Moments later, her ringtone sounded. Kyle's name appeared.

"I'm in the office now, Rox. I'll be here most of the day." He paused. "Did you get any sleep?" His deep voice held a gentle tone.

"I did. I just woke up a few minutes ago."

"Good."

"Have you found Burke?"

"Not yet." Another pause. "Rox, Earl knows about the attack. He heard the officers last night when they were knocking on Burke's door, across the hall."

"How did he take the news?" Roxy asked.

"He's furious with Burke. I've never seen Earl this angry. He came into my office this morning to find out more about the attack. He said he'd tell Claudia about it later today. I advised him to call me if he has any contact with Burke, and to avoid confronting him. But Earl is so upset, I doubt he'll follow my advice."

Roxy let out a long sigh.

"You sure you're all right?"

"I am, Kyle."

"Okay... I'll let Kendra know you'll be coming in today." He paused again, as if he was reluctant to end the call. "See you later, Rox."

She sat for a few more minutes and added thoughts about Kyle to her journal. Then she dressed in a t-shirt, workout shorts and sandals. After making the bed, she moved to the window facing Jo's front yard and opened the curtains. Warm sunlight flooded the guest room. As she looked up at the cloudless blue sky, an image of Burke's attack flashed, and she blocked it with a prayer.

A silver Lexus SUV came into view, driving slowly past the house. It looked like one of the Riverside Bay Realty company cars, but its dark tinted windows made it difficult to see the driver. Melody drove a car like that, and Roxy wondered if she had sobered up enough to drive potential buyers past the rental-wreck, next door. She read the SUV's rear license as it drove away. It wasn't Melody's personalized plate. Maybe a potential buyer was checking out the rental-wreck before making an appointment to see it.

Roxy headed to the kitchen and brewed a mug of coffee. She poured it over ice and added cream. Then she spooned in a generous amount of sugar, something she only did when she felt stressed. She took a sip of the sweet icy brew as she stood at the kitchen window and gazed at Jo's enormous back yard garden. A paved walkway wound through lush groupings of flowers, palms and tropical plants. It led to a large patio at the far corner of the garden, where lounge chairs surrounded a tall palm tree fountain.

She glanced to her left and caught movement on the deck built off the kitchen. Jo was standing at the railing, dressed in denim shorts and a gray t-shirt. Roxy opened the sliding door leading to the deck and stepped out into the oppressive heat. The musical chirping of songbirds mingled with the peaceful sound of water cascading into the palm tree fountain's circular pool.

Jo turned, and her eyes widened. "Look at that bruise on your face!"

"I know. I need to borrow cover-up cream." She stood next to Jo and set her iced coffee on the railing's flat top. "How long have you been up?"

"About an hour." Jo's voice held a weary tone. "Charlie's at church right now. He always gets up at dawn. I was so tired; I didn't hear him at all."

"Buddy usually wakes me up early. I never sleep this late." She took a long drink of the sweetened iced coffee.

"I'm glad you slept in, Rox. I texted mom and told her we over-slept for church, and we'd skip lunch at the Senior Center. I said we got home late and we're tired. It's a good excuse, and it's the truth." Jo tucked a stray lock of blonde hair behind her ear. "I thought it might be too hard on you today, having lunch with the family..."

"Thanks." Roxy leaned against the railing and shook her head. "I have no idea how I'm going to tell them about what happened."

"Rox, do you still want to go on the camping trip?"

"Of course! I'm not going to stop living my life because of Burke. Besides, I've taken a whole week of vacation. I think it'll be good for me to get away and enjoy the peace and beauty of nature."

Jo gave her a smile, but it quickly faded. "Your arms are bruised, too. I should check out your stitches."

Roxy glanced down at her arm. "It's amazing the bandage stayed on. I took a long shower last night." She went quiet as she gazed at the garden. The sun's heat penetrated the fabric of her t-shirt, warming her back. She caught sight of a red cardinal perched in a live oak and watched as the bird flew from branch to branch. A disturbing image of Burke flashed into her mind. She flinched and blocked it with another prayer.

Jo looked at her. "Rox, you can't stop thinking about what happened last night, can you?"

"It keeps replaying in my mind, like a horror movie." She paused. "Maybe it'll help if I eat something."

"I haven't had breakfast, either," Jo said. "I'm too tired to cook, but there are plenty of oatmeal raisin cookies."

Roxy grinned. "That sounds like breakfast."

Jo gave her a nod. "We still need to pack for the camping trip. Sal wants everyone to meet at her house around three thirty."

"Most of my camping clothes are in that old suitcase I brought over, but you'll have to drive me to my house, so I can pack my overnight bag for the lodge. Then I need to meet with Kendra at the police station."

"Okay," Jo said. "But first... cookies."

They went inside, and Roxy made two fresh iced coffees while Jo poured the orange juice and stacked cookies on a serving plate. They sat at the table across from each other and dug in.

"Jo, I realized something that surprised me when I was writing in my journal this morning." Roxy took another cookie bite and paused as she chewed. "I don't feel bitter or angry at Trent, anymore. I know he caused me a world of grief, fifteen years ago. But last night, he saved me a world of grief. And all I feel now, is gratitude. When I was writing about that, my spirit felt lighter somehow... as if a heavy weight had been lifted. I think the bitterness I held onto all these years acted like an anchor, keeping me stuck. Now I feel like I can finally let go of the past and move forward." She sat back in her chair and looked at Jo. "Do you think gratitude is a type of forgiveness?"

Jo nodded as she set down her juice glass. "It could be, Rox."

"I've been thinking about how everything in life can change in an instant; from safety to danger... joy to grief... life to death. There I was last night, standing in my kitchen, feeling safe with

Burke—" Roxy stopped and blocked another violent image with a silent prayer.

"I'm really glad Trent showed up when he did, Rox."

"He came to my front door, right after I prayed for help." She paused, as chill bumps rose on her skin. "My feelings for Trent and Burke have totally reversed. Now I feel angry at Burke. Really angry! He was so vicious last night; he could have killed me!" Roxy made a fist, and then she glanced down at the crumbled cookie in her hand.

"I thought about that, and it scared me," Jo said. "I didn't fall asleep for a long time."

Roxy ate a few cookie crumbles and then asked, "Do you remember the book we read a few months ago in book club, The Hiding Place?"

"The one by Corrie ten Boom, who survived a Nazi concentration camp?"

Roxy nodded. "She was part of a Dutch Christian family, and the Gestapo arrested them for sheltering Jews and helping them escape. Corrie and her sister Betsie were sent to Ravensbruck, and Betsie died there. Corrie went on to write books after the war, and she also gave talks, spreading the gospel message." Roxy paused and ate the rest of the cookie crumbles. "I thought about Corrie this morning, and how she came face to face with a former SS guard from Ravensbruck after one of her talks. He walked up to her and said he was grateful to hear that Jesus had died for his sins. When he held out his hand to shake hers, Corrie just stood there. She couldn't respond, even though she'd just given a talk about God's love and forgiveness. Seeing that Nazi guard again brought back horrible memories of the concentration camp, especially Betsie's death. And all Corrie could feel was anger." Roxy sighed. "Now I know how she felt."

"But she forgave that Nazi guard," Jo said.

"Only after she said a silent prayer, right then, for God's help to forgive him. And then, as she shook his hand, something amazing happened. A feeling of love welled up inside her. Not her love, but God's love, flowing through her. Corrie said she learned that forgiveness can only begin when we surrender our anger and open ourselves to God's love." Roxy paused and shook her head. "For Corrie, it took one heartfelt prayer. For me... I don't know how I'm ever going to forgive Burke."

"Rox, you used to say you could never forgive Trent."

"That's different, Jo. Trent helped me last night, and he comforted me. What he did made up for the way he hurt me all those years ago, and I'm grateful."

"So... it's like he atoned for his sin?"

"I guess so... maybe that's why I can forgive him," Roxy said. "But how can I forgive someone as brutal as Burke? I'm sure he'll never do anything to make up for what he did last night."

"That brutal Nazi guard didn't do anything to make up for what he did to Betsie and Corrie," Jo said. "But she was able to forgive him through the love of Jesus, who atoned for all sins."

Roxy sat very still as she thought about that.

Roxy's stomach went queasy as she fit her key into the lock on the back door. She went upstairs and quickly packed clothes for the lodge in a lightweight backpack. She slipped on her powder blue group t-shirt, black cargo shorts and hiking sandals, and then she carried the backpack downstairs.

Jo was sitting at the kitchen island, reading her phone screen. "I'm looking at the weather forecast. A tropical storm is heading into the Gulf, but they predict it'll stay away from Florida's Gulf coast."

Roxy set her backpack on the island. "You know what Grandpa Leo says about weather forecasting. It's the only career where you can be wrong most of the time and still keep your job."

"That's our grandpa." Jo glanced at Roxy and hesitated, as if she was reluctant to admit something. "I called Sal while you were upstairs, and I told her about Burke. I asked her to tell Tara and Leeann, too."

"What? Why did you—"

"Rox, think about it. Bri already knows what happened, and the others would have seen your bruises and asked a lot of questions. I saw how upset you were last night, when you were giving Kendra your statement. I thought it might be easier on you if everyone already knew about it." Jo paused. "I also told Sal it would be best if we didn't talk about it during the trip, and she agreed."

Roxy took a moment and then sighed. "I guess it will be easier, not having to tell everyone about it."

Jo's expression relaxed. She slid off the barstool and picked up Roxy's backpack. "I'll take this to the truck."

"I'll come out in a minute. I have one more thing to do." Roxy opened a zip-top sandwich bag and slipped her phone inside, along with a thin wallet containing a credit card, her driver's license, her health insurance card, and money. She slid the waterproof camping purse into the side pocket of her cargo shorts, and then she picked up a grocery bag she'd already packed with coffee items for the camping trip. After locking the house, she climbed into Jo's truck. Her ringtone sounded. She retrieved the sandwich bag purse and pulled out her phone. "It's Claudia."

Jo frowned as she backed out of the driveway.

"Rox! I'm looking at your class reunion website, and I just saw Burke in the photos! He was your date, wasn't he? How did that happen?"

She cringed. Earl obviously hadn't talked to Claudia, yet. Roxy decided she didn't have the emotional energy to tell her what happened and endure the drama of her shock and anger. "Claudia, I can't explain, right now. I'm leaving on my camping trip this afternoon, and I need to finish packing."

"Okay." Claudia let out a frustrated sigh. "Now I'm scrolling through photos of you dancing with that Thorson hunk. There's even a photo of Troy kissing you!"

"It's Trent," Roxy said.

Jo glanced over and raised an eyebrow as she turned onto Main Street.

"Whatever," Claudia said. "I see photos of you and Burke at a roulette table. He had a real James Bond look going."

Roxy's stomach went queasy again. "How is Paul? I'll bet he's glad to be home."

Claudia went quiet a moment, and then she began gushing about how wonderful it was to be with Paul again.

Roxy sat back, feeling relieved she'd managed to steer the conversation away from the reunion. She smiled as she listened to Claudia. Someone who didn't know her well might dismiss her bubbly enthusiasm as phony, but Roxy could hear the genuine tone of joy in her voice. An image suddenly flashed into her mind—the number she'd memorized from Burke's call log. "Oh! Can you look up a phone number for me, Claudia?"

She stopped in mid-sentence. "What phone number?"

"Burke got a call that upset him, and when I checked the call log on his phone—"

"You were snooping on Burke's phone?"

"I'll explain, later. I just want to know if you have Harmon Doyle's phone number in your contacts list."

"Why do you want—"

"Claudia, please. Just tell me."

"Okay! Give me a minute!"

Jo turned toward Roxy. Her eyes radiated an intense curiosity.

"Rox, I have the number Doyle used when he set up the appointment to look at condos."

"Is this it?" Roxy read the number from the snapshot in her memory.

"That's it. What's going on?"

"I knew Burke was lying! He said the call was from an old college friend." Roxy glanced up as Jo pulled into a visitor parking spot at the police station. "Thanks for looking up the number, Claudia. I have to go, now."

"Wait! You need to tell me what's going on!"

"I don't have time, right now. Say Hi to Paul for me."

"Okay! Bye!"

Jo turned to Roxy. "Who is Harmon Doyle?"

Roxy briefly described meeting Doyle, and his relationship to Burke.

"Why do you think Burke got so upset when his uncle called?"

"I have no idea." Roxy visualized Burke's call log again. Something about it bothered her, as if she'd overlooked an important fact. She mentally reviewed the list of calls, and then she let it go, hoping the fact would eventually surface on its own.

Kyle sat at his desk and read the report he'd just downloaded to his laptop. A few minutes earlier, he'd entered Burke's name and identifying information into a law enforcement database.

Sam briefly knocked before walking inside the open doorway. He stopped and stared at Kyle. "Man, you look rough. Did you get any sleep last night?"

Kyle rubbed his face and realized he'd forgotten to shave.

"What happened to your hand?"

"I broke a pen..." He fixed a dead-eyed gaze on Sam, feeling too tired for small talk.

"I have something for you." Sam set a large Brew Be takeout bag on Kyle's desk, along with an extra-large Brew Be takeout coffee. He opened the bag and pulled out a zip-top plastic bag of lasagna, a set of plastic utensils and a Brew Be cookie shaped like Toto the dog. "You should have come to the Taste of Italy lunch. They sure make great food at that Senior Center."

Kyle couldn't help smiling. "Did you bring a plastic bag for leftovers?"

"Leo brought the plastic bag," Sam said. "He says everyone takes leftovers. Besides, it was all you can eat. The buffet had pans and pans of lasagna."

Kyle opened the zip-top. He hadn't eaten any breakfast, and his mouth watered as he breathed in the warm aromas of meat sauce and melted cheese. "I should get a plate from the break room."

"Why bother? Just eat it out of the bag," Sam said.

He plunged the plastic fork into the lasagna and took a large bite.

Sam sat in a guest chair and leaned back. "I ate with Nell, Charlie and Leo. They missed you at lunch. That Leo is a sharp old guy. He asked a lot of questions about the hit and run investigation. Nobody mentioned Burke's attack. I assumed Charlie stayed quiet, so Rox could tell them about it later."

Kyle nodded as he chewed.

"Kendra went over to the hospital this morning," Sam said. "The homeowners are both in stable condition, recovering from their gunshot wounds. She was able to question them, but they couldn't tell her much about yesterday's burglary. They came home from vacation a couple days early and surprised three, maybe four young guys inside the house—white, average height and weight. That matches the other descriptions we've gotten. They said the tallest guy had a gun. After he fired the shots, they all ran off."

"So, they came back early from vacation," Kyle said. "Every one of the burglaries in Riverside Bay Estates has happened while the homeowners were out of town."

"That gang must be checking social media or observing the neighborhood," Sam said. "We've got extra officers on patrol, and we've advised the homeowners not to post any vacation plans." He leaned forward, and his expression shifted. "We put out a BOLO on Burke, and officers are watching his condo and that fancy yacht of his at the marina. Quint even volunteered to help us keep an eye on it. What about you? Any luck, tracking him down?"

Kyle shook his head as he finished chewing a large bite. "I checked with the airlines, and even Amtrak and the bus lines. No reservations in Burke's name. He's not answering his phone, but Rox said in her statement he could have broken it last night." He paused and took a long drink of coffee. "Earl came into my office this morning. He has a key to Burke's condo, and he's going to let us in this afternoon. Maybe we can get a clue about where he's gone." He glanced up and read Sam's expression. "It's okay. Earl owns all those condos, and he's given us permission to search."

Sam nodded. "Burke could have gone back to Atlanta. He must have contacts there."

"I plan to call the law firm where he worked, first thing tomorrow," Kyle said.

"Have you started doing a background check on that scumbag?"

"I'm working on it, now."

Sam stood and pulled out a peppermint. He stared at the candy and shoved it back into his pocket. He started for the door, and then he stopped and turned to Kyle. "It's gotta be tough on you and Rox... what happened last night."

Kyle gave him a nod. "Thanks for the lasagna... and everything."

Sam briefly smiled before he walked out.

After finishing the last bite of lasagna, Kyle refreshed his laptop screen and continued reading the report he'd downloaded. Minutes later, he heard a knock on his open door.

"Hi, Kyle..."

He looked up at her beautiful face, and his gaze locked on the dark bruise covering her cheek.

Roxy touched her face, as if she'd read his expression. "I just came from Kendra's office. I had to clean off my make-up before she took photos."

He shook his head and groaned. "I should have been with you last night. If I hadn't cancelled our date, it wouldn't have hap—"

"Kyle, don't. It's not your fault." She stepped closer. "You look tired."

He shrugged off her concern. Then he noticed her t-shirt graphic, people paddling a canoe at sunset. "Ocala Forest Wilderness Women. Did you design that shirt for your camping trip?"

"Jo designed it. She had shirts made for all of us."

"Does that mean you're still leaving on your trip this afternoon?"

"Why not? I won't stop living my life because of... ah... last night."

"Do you think it's wise, Rox? We still don't know where Burke is."

"I think I'll feel safer being away from town. I can't see Burke going anywhere near the Ocala Forest. The wild outdoors isn't his kind of thing." She glanced at the empty zip-top bag. "It smells great in here. Did you go to the Taste of Italy lunch?"

"No, but Sam did. Leo gave him this bag to take leftovers."

"Grandpa gave him that bag?" Roxy grinned. "He always complains about people who do that." She paused and said, "I should get going. Jo and I still need to pack for the trip."

Kyle stood. "I need more coffee. I'll walk with you to the break room." As he stepped around his desk, he met her gaze, and his pulse quickened.

She moved toward him.

Kyle gently drew her into his arms. "Last night, I wanted to hold you, so much..."

"I know..." Roxy let out a sigh as she rested her head against his chest.

Jo saw the note on her refrigerator as soon as she got home. "Mom came over while we were gone. She left something for us in the fridge, in case we haven't eaten lunch."

"Good. I'm starved," Roxy said. "Kyle's office smelled like an Italian restaurant. Sam ate lunch at the Senior Center, and grandpa gave him a plastic bag so he could bring leftover lasagna to Kyle."

"Grandpa did that? I can't believe it." Jo opened the refrigerator and pulled out two zip-top bags of lasagna. "Looks like grandpa brought more than one bag."

Roxy grinned. "Maybe he brought enough bags to fill his freezer. You know how he loves lasagna."

They heated the lasagna on plates in the microwave and then ate standing at the counter. After they cleaned the kitchen, Roxy went to the guest room and reapplied the cover-up cream and make-up, while Jo went into her bedroom and changed into her group t-shirt with the upside-down graphic, cargo shorts and hiking sandals.

They met in Jo's laundry room and began filling a large Duluth pack with their camping clothes and personal items. Sally had organized them into three packing teams—Roxy with Jo; Tara with Leeann; and herself with Bri. They'd save space in the canoes by taking three shared personal packs, rather than six separate ones. To keep the clothing separated, Sally advised them to place each item in a zip-top bag and press out the excess air before sealing it. As an extra layer of waterproofing, she instructed them to line every pack with a garbage bag before filling it.

After they placed all their personal items in the shared pack, Jo closed it up and set it aside. She inserted a garbage bag liner into a second Duluth pack and placed a bright orange tent sack inside. "This pack will carry all the group's equipment. Sal has the rest of our camping equipment at her house." Jo opened a Rubbermaid tub in the laundry room and pulled out an old-fashioned extra-large canvas Duluth pack. "I found this huge pack at a garage sale. Sal wants to use it as our food pack."

"Why does she want to use that old canvas pack for our food?"

"It's the largest one we have," Jo said.

As Roxy inserted the garbage bag liner, she took a closer look at the pack. "Jo, the metal buckles are rusty, and the canvas shoulder straps look frayed."

"I think it's sturdy enough for our trip."

Roxy shrugged. "Sal asked me to bring the coffee items for the trip." She opened the grocery bag she brought over and slipped three zip-top plastic bags inside the food pack. One contained a package of regular coffee, another held a decaf package, and the third one held a plastic box of creamer pods.

"Sal assigned me desserts," Jo said. "I baked cookies and caramel bars and froze them." She pulled three half-gallon milk cartons from her freezer and set them inside the food pack.

"Why did you freeze everything in milk cartons?"

"They're cardboard, and they burn well. It's primitive camping, Rox. No trash bins. Whatever we pack in we have to pack out, unless it can be burned to ashes in a campfire. These sturdy cartons will also keep the cookies from being mashed into crumbs."

They loaded the three Duluth packs in the bed of Jo's red truck and then secured the rigid truck bed cover. Jo went back to double-check the house before she locked up.

Roxy's nerves tingled with excitement as she slid into the passenger seat. She glanced at the rental-wreck next door and thought about the silver Lexus SUV she'd seen driving by this morning. She said a prayer the house would sell soon.

The truck rocked as Jo climbed into the driver's seat. She held out a paper lunch bag. Roxy smiled when she peeked inside and saw the single-serve ketchup packets. "Thanks! I'm glad you thought of this."

Jo grinned. "I didn't want you to go into ketchup withdrawal in the middle of the forest." She made the short drive to her mother's house and parked in the driveway. They both got out and walked toward Nell, who was working in the flower garden bordering her porch.

Her expression brightened when she saw them. She stood and brushed the dirt off her denim capris. "It's about time you girls came over. Did you see the lasagna I left for you?"

Roxy nodded. "We ate all of it."

Nell smiled. She took off her gardening gloves and eyed their t-shirts. Her gaze lingered on the upside-down graphic. "Jo, I hope Ava didn't make you pay full price for that shirt."

"She did the job for free. So, I'll live with it."

"Do you girls have time for an iced coffee?" Nell removed her sun hat and fluffed her gray-streaked blonde waves.

"We need to be at Sal's in about an hour," Jo said.

"Plenty of time." Nell led the way into her house. She left her gardening clogs in her mudroom and entered her kitchen in sock feet. As she started the coffee brewer, she said, "I baked ginger snaps last night. Can you girls put them in a basket?"

They turned to each other and smiled as they mouthed, "you girls."

Jo reached for the old ceramic pig cookie jar. A glued crack ran through the pig's fat mid-section. She lifted the chipped lid and placed a few ginger snaps in a serving basket. Before replacing the lid, she snagged a cookie for herself.

Roxy set the basket on the table and plucked out a ginger snap. As she bit into the crispy cookie, she glanced up at the chalkboard. Aunt Nell had chosen a verse on forgiveness this morning. She marveled at how often the Bible verses related to what was going on in her life.

"Be kind to one another, tenderhearted, forgiving one another, as God in Christ forgave you." Ephesians 4:32

Nell placed the glasses of iced coffee on the table and glanced at Roxy. "I checked out the photos on your class reunion website after lunch. I saw Trent kissing you! What's going on?"

Roxy and Jo exchanged glances.

Nell looked from one to the other. "Something happened last night. It's written all over your faces."

A look of anguish crossed Nell's face as she reached for Roxy's hand. "Oh, my sweet girl. How awful…"

The warm touch of her aunt's hand soothed Roxy's quivering nerves. "Every time I describe what happened, it feels like I'm living through it again."

They went quiet. The grandfather clock in the adjoining room registered the passing time with each click of its swinging pendulum.

Roxy looked at her aunt. "It's hard to believe that Trent, the person who shattered my life all those years ago, is the same person who helped and comforted me last night. I told Jo this morning, I'm not bitter or angry at Trent, anymore. I just feel grateful."

Nell gave Roxy's hand a gentle squeeze and then released it. "I'm grateful for what he did, too. Very grateful. But you need to be careful, Rox. Your gratitude might open the door to other feelings."

"What do you mean?"

"You were head over heels in love with Trent. Feelings that strong can roar back to life." She paused. "Don't forget what he was like when you were together. He lied to you and cheated… and I'll bet Celia wasn't the only one. Trent might be older and more mature, but a leopard can't change its spots."

Roxy nodded. Grandpa Leo often used that old phrase.

Nell kept her gaze on Roxy. "You have someone else in your life, now… and he's in love with you."

"I know…" Roxy sighed. "I saw Kyle today. He feels responsible for what happened last night, because he had to cancel our date. I told him not to blame himself." She looked down and touched the rough edges of her sheared fingernails. "Why did I let Burke inside my house? It was so stupid!"

"Rox, you need to stop blaming yourself," Jo said. "You're not responsible for Burke's actions."

Nell let out a sigh. "Sometimes I think it's harder for us to forgive ourselves, than it is to forgive others."

Roxy heard the trembling in her aunt's voice. She looked up and saw a profound look of sadness in her eyes.

"I still haven't forgiven myself for letting Lori and Hugh drive home that night, it was so foggy—"

"That wasn't your fault. A drunk driver killed my parents," Roxy said.

Nell shook her head. "I should have persuaded them to stay at our beach house and drive home in the morning."

Roxy wanted to say something to lift the heavy weight of guilt and regret off her aunt's shoulders, but she couldn't find the words. She tried to imagine how hard it must have been for Nell to lose her twin sister. It would be like losing Jo. When she looked across the table and met Jo's gaze, she realized they had been thinking the same thing.

The grandfather clock rang its half-hour chime. "We need to get to Sal's," Jo said.

As they walked outside, Charlie parked his SUV in Nell's driveway, behind Jo's red truck. He got out and left the driver's door open. "I just finished my hospital rounds. I'm glad I caught you before you left." He kissed Jo and pulled her into a hug. "You be careful on the trip. Stay safe, okay?" He looked at Roxy. "Both of you."

As he walked away, Jo called out, "Don't forget to fix those walkway pavers."

"I will." Charlie tossed the reply over his shoulder as he closed the driver's door.

Roxy smiled and thought, "Does he mean he will fix them, or he will forget?"

Nell gave each of them a hug. "My two sweet girls. Take good care of each other." She glanced at Jo's t-shirt. "That overturned canoe worries me."

"Mom, it's not a bad omen," Jo said. "Besides, the Thorson brothers will be camping near us, and Trent's an EMT."

"Trent is going on the trip?"

"He and Seth are worried about Bri," Jo said.

Nell turned to Roxy.

She read the warning look in her aunt's eyes.

Sally was standing on her driveway, talking to Tara and Leeann. They were dressed in t-shirts, shorts and hiking sandals. Tara and Leeann were wearing their matching group t-shirts, and Sally wore a faded Pet Wellness shirt. They all turned as Jo parked at the curb.

Roxy glanced out the passenger window and sighed when she read their sympathetic expressions. She prayed that something would distract their minds from Burke's attack.

"Hey, Rox. Let's see how long it takes Sal to notice my upside-down t-shirt graphic. I told Tara and Leeann not to tell her anything about it." Jo retrieved Sally's t-shirt from her tote bag and draped it over her arm. They both got out of the truck and walked up the driveway.

Sally laughed. "You should have a red circle with a slash on that overturned canoe."

"That didn't take long," Jo said.

Roxy nodded and offered up a prayer of thanks for the distraction.

Sally smiled as she took her shirt from Jo. "I love your website idea. Maybe we should set one up and start a wilderness women blog." She carried the shirt into her house and returned moments later, wearing it. She walked to the garage workbench and picked up a clipboard. "Okay, group. I have our packing list. Let's get this done."

Roxy and Jo unloaded the equipment pack and the food pack from Jo's truck bed. They set them inside Sally's garage, near a pile of food items and camping equipment sitting on a blue tarp. Sally began calling out items on her list, and the women took turns placing each item them into the proper pack.

Tara stared at the bulging, extra-large food pack. "Sal, we're only camping out one night. This is too much food."

"Matt and I spent a night in the forest without food," Sally said. "Believe me, you don't ever want that to happen."

A blue extended-cab pickup drove up and parked behind Jo's red truck. The driver's door bore the name and phone number of the Thorson family's auto repair business. As Trent got out, his gaze locked on Roxy.

She smiled, and then she realized how much she'd been looking forward to seeing him. Nell's warning look flashed into her mind.

Bri called out a greeting as she walked up the driveway. Her blonde hair still held pink highlights, and she was wearing the group's t-shirt, frayed denim shorts and hiking sandals.

Trent walked beside her, looking fit in workout shorts and a black t-shirt. He was carrying Bri's pink overnight bag and a large spa shopping bag. He looked at Jo and laughed out loud. "That shirt reminds me of an emergency call I responded to."

Bri pointed to the shirt and giggled.

Jo grinned, clearly enjoying the attention.

Trent looked at Sally. "Where should I put Bri's things?"

"You can set her overnight bag next to my car. Her camping clothes go in our shared pack, over there." She pointed to a partially-filled Duluth pack on the driveway. "When you're finished, you can close up the pack."

Trent quickly shifted Bri's clothes from the shopping bag into the pack. He secured the pack flap and slipped one of the straps over his shoulder. "I can help you load up—"

"Thanks, but we can handle it." Sally's voice held a dismissive tone.

Trent shrugged. He set down the pack and gave Bri a hug. "See you on the river tomorrow." He walked over to Roxy and lowered his voice as he asked, "How are you feeling?"

"I'm okay..."

"Have they found Burke?"

She looked up at Trent and shook her head. The sunlight on his face triggered the long-buried memory of a sunny day at the beach—the day he proposed to her. She pictured the foam-capped turquoise waves rushing toward shore, and how they laughed and held hands as they splashed through them. Emotions stirred deep inside, as if awakening from a long sleep.

"Babe... see you tomorrow." Trent's smile told her he had read her emotions.

Jo walked up and said, "Babe? Isn't that what he used to call you?"

Roxy nodded as she watched Trent stroll to his truck.

"Look at him," Jo said. "He still walks with a swagger."

"Okay, group. Let's load up," Sally said.

Roxy counted the packs; one extra-large food pack, a large equipment pack, three personal packs, and a small day pack containing a first aid kit. She wondered how they were going to squeeze five large packs, a day pack and six women inside three canoes. She glanced at the upside-down graphic on Jo's t-shirt and felt a twinge of apprehension.

They loaded the day pack and the overnight bags into Sally's SUV, and then they worked in two-person teams, loading the heavier Duluth packs inside Jo's truck bed. The loading stopped when it was time to lift the last pack, the extra-large food pack. They stood and eyed each other, as if waiting for someone to volunteer.

"It'll take more than two people to lift that monster," Tara said.

"A lot more," Jo said.

A Pet Wellness van parked at the end of the driveway, with its engine running. The back door opened, and Sally's thirteen-year-old son Nolan got out. He stood tall for his age, and his facial features resembled Matt. He thanked the driver as he shut the door, and the van pulled away.

"Nolan, where's your dad?" Sally asked.

"He's taking care of an emergency, an injured cat. I got a ride home with a Scoop Troop team."

"Hey, Nolan. I hear you volunteered to help out in the boarding kennel this summer," Jo said. "How's it going?"

He smiled, revealing the clear braces on his teeth. "I'd rather help out in the kennel, than on a Scoop Troop team."

"Nolan volunteered to help Greg design t-shirts for the Scoop Troops," Leeann said.

Sally did an eye roll. "That's been a crazy process."

"It's been fun." Nolan said, glancing at his Aunt Leeann. "Uncle Greg has thought up some great slogans."

"Let's not get into that right now," Sally said.

"Nolan, would you like to volunteer to help us load this food pack?" Tara asked.

He pitched in, along with his mom, Tara and Jo. After they loaded heavy pack, Roxy helped Jo secure the truck bed cover.

"I have one last thing on my list." Sally walked into the house with Nolan and rejoined the group a few minutes later, wearing a pink bandana tied western-style around her neck. She handed an identical bandana with the breast cancer logo to each of them. "I wanted us to wear these in memory of Nikki."

Tears formed in Tara's eyes. She gave Sally a hug.

A rumble of thunder sounded. Roxy glanced up at the overcast sky. She'd been so focused on packing; she hadn't noticed the afternoon storm clouds rolling in.

"Okay, group. Are you ready to go out into the forest?" Sally held up her hand.

They gave her high fives as raindrops began falling. Tara, Leeann and Bri piled into Sally's SUV, and Roxy climbed into Jo's truck. As they drove off, thunder rumbled again.

Traffic moved slowly as the rainstorm continued. The windshield wipers on Jo's truck made a repetitive squeak as they moved back and forth, creating brief arcs of clear visibility. The red tail lights of Sally's SUV were barely visible through the thick watery curtain. They reached Ocala an hour later than they had planned. Black clouds hovered low overhead, triggering the city's light-sensitive streetlights and storefront signs.

Roxy's text chime sounded. "It's Tara. Sal is stopping for gas at the station up ahead. She wants us to pull in and wait for her." She texted 'OK' and kept the phone in her hand.

Jo parked in front of the station's convenience store and left the engine running. The wind-driven rain made a loud drumming sound as it hit the truck's roof.

Roxy's phone chimed again, and she assumed it was Tara. She blinked when she recognized the phone number, and then she let out a surprised cry when she read the text.

"What's wrong?"

"I got a text from Harmon Doyle's number." Roxy tensed as she read it out loud: "You won't get away from me next time."

"What? Let me see it!" Jo grabbed the phone and her eyes widened. "This is crazy! Why would Burke's uncle send you a text like this?"

"Burke could be using his uncle's phone," Roxy said. "I think he broke his phone last night. He threw it after he took it away from me, and I heard the sound of a phone screen shattering."

"Well... you'd know that sound, Rox." Jo handed the phone back.

The phone chimed again, and they both startled. Roxy read the cracked screen and breathed out a sigh. "It's Tara. Sal's pulling out, and she wants us to drive to the Minnie Moose Café for dinner. It's two blocks away, on the right."

Roxy re-read the threatening text on the way to the café, and her anger surged. "I need to tell Kyle about this. I'm not going to let Burke scare me!"

"He's already scared me," Jo said, as she parked the truck in a spot near the café.

"I'll stay here in the truck while I talk to Kyle," Roxy said. "I don't want to worry the others. You go inside and save a place for me."

Jo reached under her seat and pulled out an umbrella. "I only have one of these."

"You take it. I'll pull up the hood on my rain jacket."

"Okay." As Jo got out of the truck, the wind nearly snatched the umbrella from her hands. A heavy spray of rain blew inside before the door closed.

Roxy wiped the moisture off her face and then pressed speed dial. Frustration surged when her call clicked into Kyle's voice mail. She left a message and waited. The rain's drumming grew louder, as if the angry clouds were hurling pebbles at the truck. Her ringtone sounded, and Kyle's name appeared.

"Sorry I couldn't pick up right away, Rox. I had to finish a call. Where are you now?"

"We just drove into Ocala. We're going to have dinner at the Minnie Moose Café."

Kyle chuckled. "Minnie Moose? That's great." He paused. "We've had a lot of rain. Is it raining there?"

"It's raining cats, dogs and elephants. Can't you hear it? I'm sitting in Jo's truck, and it's pounding on the roof. I feel like I'm shouting into the phone. I hope I'm not talking too loud."

"I have a set of earplugs in my desk drawer, if I need them."

She briefly smiled. "Kyle... I got a scary text a few minutes ago. I think Burke sent it." She glanced at the screen as she read it out loud.

"Why did you say, you think he sent it?"

"It came from Harmon Doyle's number, and I can't imagine Burke's uncle sending me a text like that."

"How do you know Doyle's number?"

She explained how she memorized Burke's passcode, accessed his call log, took a mental snapshot of the number and then confirmed it with Claudia.

"You and your snapshot memory."

An image of Burke's call log flashed into her mind, and she suddenly realized the fact she'd overlooked. "Kyle! When did they release the news about Greta's murder?"

"The Sheriff's Office released it this morning."

"Sunday morning... okay." Her heart beat a little faster. "You made several calls to Burke, but he never called you back, right?"

"That's right."

"And Claudia and Earl haven't talked to him, since our meeting on Friday?"

"None of us have had any contact with him, Rox."

Her heartbeat accelerated. "Kyle, do you know what this means?"

"How can I? You haven't told me anything yet."

Roxy paused, trembling. "Burke knew Greta's body was in the trunk of her car. He knew it last night, Kyle."

"What?"

"While he was driving me to the reunion, Burke said something like, 'There's new evidence from Greta's car, right?' And I said, 'In the trunk.' Then Burke made a comment about finding Greta's body there. When I was surprised he knew about it, he said he talked to you."

"Are you sure you didn't say something about a body in the trunk?"

"No! I stopped at the word trunk. I'm absolutely sure I never said what was in it. And I never mentioned Greta's name! Burke didn't phrase it like a guess or a question. He knew Greta's body was in that trunk! And he didn't show any emotion. Do you know what he said?"

"What?"

"He said it was a shame Greta was dead. A shame? It's a shame when your dog chews up your sandals. But it's a tragedy when your former lover is found dead in a trunk."

A loud thump sounded, as if he'd pounded on his desk, followed by a sharp outcry.

"Kyle, if Burke knew about Greta's body, he must have been involved in her murder." An icy chill slithered through her.

"We need to find Burke," Kyle said. "He's probably with his uncle, since that text came from Doyle's phone. Maybe I can trace it. What's the number?"

She recited it from memory.

"Does Burke know your camping trip plans?"

"We discussed the details at the reunion dinner."

"Rox, you need to stay in touch with me every day—"

"We're camping in a remote area. I might not have cell service on the river."

Another thump sounded.

"Kyle, you don't seriously think Burke will come after me in the forest, do you?"

"I don't know. He's a wealthy piece of scum with a cushy lifestyle. But you shouldn't take the risk. You can't go on this trip, Rox."

"What do you mean, I can't?"

"It's a ridiculous idea, anyhow. You've never been camping, and your friends are just as clueless as—"

"Ridiculous? Clueless? Thanks a lot!"

"Rox, it's foolish to risk—"

"So, now I'm foolish?"

"Stop twisting my words!" He paused and lowered his voice. "Look, I don't like the idea of you and your friends alone in that forest—"

"We won't be alone. Trent and his brother will be camping near us—"

"Trent? Why is he going—"

"He's worried about Bri. She has MS and he's an EMT—"

"It doesn't matter! You can't go, Rox!"

"Don't tell me what to do!"

"Okay, I guess there's no reasoning with you! Do what you want!"

"I will! Bye!" She hung up and took several shaky deep breaths as she listened to the rain's monotonous drumbeat. The heat of her anger quickly cooled, and she regretted the way the call ended. She glanced at her phone. Then she sighed and slipped it back into her pocket. They both needed more time to calm down.

Burke came to mind. He murdered Greta! Before last night, she never would have believed it. Now she knew how violent he could be. She turned and looked out the passenger window. Rain slid down the glass in winding streams, giving the dimly-lit parking lot a shifting, surreal look. Nobody knew where Burke was. He could be anywhere. Chill bumps rose on her skin.

She zipped her rain jacket and flipped up the hood. As she climbed out of the truck, sheets of rain sprayed her face, blurring her vision. She clicked the lock button and closed the passenger door. When she turned, she bumped into someone standing directly behind her.

Roxy screamed.

"Hey, it's me!"

Roxy blinked and saw Jo's face against the backdrop of an open umbrella.

"Come on, Rox. Let's get out of this rain." She held the umbrella over their heads as they splashed through the puddles. They entered the café's mudroom, where dripping rain jackets and umbrellas hung from wall hooks. "Sorry... I didn't mean to scare you, Rox. I got worried when you were taking so long, and I knew you didn't have an umbrella."

Roxy nodded, still trembling. Cold droplets slid down the back of her neck as she took off her wet jacket. She hung it up and shivered.

"What did Kyle say about the text?"

"I gave him Doyle's cell number. He's going to check it out. He thinks Burke might be with his uncle."

"Should we tell the others about this?"

Roxy read Jo's worried expression and made a snap decision not to tell her about Burke's connection to Greta's murder — at least, not right now. She shook her head. "Why should we worry them? Burke isn't likely to come after me in the forest. He likes his creature comforts too much. I'll talk to Kyle again tomorrow. Maybe he can trace Doyle's cell phone and find out where Burke is."

Jo eyed her for a moment, as if she suspected she hadn't been told the whole story. Then she turned and opened the café's entry door.

Roxy breathed in the delicious aroma of fried food as she followed Jo inside the cozy dining room. Her soggy hiking sandals squeaked as she walked on the wood plank floor. The décor looked rustic, with honey-colored log walls, huge wooden chandeliers carved in the shape of moose antlers, and mismatched tables and chairs. The group had been seated at a large round table. Jo sat down, and Roxy took the empty seat next to her. The paper placemat served as the café's menu, listing all the specials. She lifted her coffee cup and realized it was empty.

"I didn't want your coffee to get cold, Rox." Jo pointed across the room. "See that man over there in the plaid shirt? That's Harvey. He poured our coffee, and he said he'd keep an eye out for you."

A tall slender woman in her forties walked up, wearing a denim shirt, jeans and sandals. Her dark hair had been swept back into a braided bun, and a moose-shaped name tag with the name Minnie was clipped to her shirt pocket.

"Cute t-shirts," Minnie said, looking around the table. She grinned at Jo. "I wouldn't want to ride in your canoe."

Everyone laughed, except Leeann. Worry lines creased her forehead as she glanced at Jo's shirt.

Tara asked, "Why does the café have a moose theme? There aren't any in Florida."

Minnie smiled. "My maiden name is Moose. I used to get teased about it when I was growing up. Minnie Moose... Minnie Mouse, that sort of thing. But I've always liked my name. That's why I kept it after I married Harvey." She pointed out the specials listed on the placemat and recommended the fried largemouth bass with rice and a side salad, along with homemade key lime pie for dessert. Minnie looked pleased when they all ordered it. "I'll send Harvey over to refill your coffee." She turned and headed toward another table.

Leeann spoke up. "Sal, I've been wondering about the lodge. Why is it called Dusty's Last Resort? That name sounds kind of... desperate."

Sally grinned. "The lodge is located at the end of a long gravel road, and Dusty has a great sense of humor. Matt and I have known him for years. We like staying at his lodge because it has a private river landing. He's giving us all a discount on our rental canoes and equipment. We'll start out tomorrow after breakfast and paddle about eight miles to the campsite."

"Eight miles?" Bri asked.

"It's an easy paddle," Sally said. "A gentle current will carry us downstream. We'll have plenty of time to set up camp and make dinner. It's a primitive spot, but Matt and I have done things to improve it. Last year, we created a nice seating area by smoothing the bark off some huge fallen tree trunks."

"Sounds comfy." Tara grinned.

Sally ignored her. "On Tuesday, we'll break up camp and paddle about a mile downstream to Gore's Landing. It's a public landing with an overnight parking lot. Dusty will meet us there and pick up our canoes and packs. I plan to leave my car at Gore's Landing before we set out on Monday morning. That way, I can drive everyone back to the lodge on Tuesday."

Harvey appeared with a pot of fresh coffee and refilled everyone's cup. His plump face sported a black beard, and thick bushy eyebrows nearly covered his eyes.

Roxy added a generous amount of cream and several sugar packets to her coffee. She took a sip of the sweet creamy brew and began to relax.

Kyle hit a dead end when he checked out Harmon Doyle's phone number. He decided the ex-con must be using a burner phone—a disposable prepaid device that's hard to trace. He turned to his laptop and ran a check on Harmon Doyle. He located several files and downloaded a few to print out. He winced as he pulled the pages from the printer and stapled them together. The pain in his bandaged finger spiked with every movement.

He set down the print-out on Doyle and then stared at it. His gut burned with worry about the camping trip. Fatigue from his sleepless night had made him irritable, and he regretted losing his temper with Rox. Kyle thought about calling her back, and then he shook his head, thinking it probably wouldn't do any good. He knew how stubborn she could be.

Sam strode into his office and plopped down in a guest chair. "I got your message. What did Rox tell you about Burke?"

Kyle briefly summarized their phone conversation.

Sam's eyes widened. "Is Rox sure she didn't say anything about Greta's body?"

"She's positive, and I believe her," Kyle said. "Burke told her he talked to me about it. We know that's a lie. And I just called Earl and Claudia. They confirmed they haven't had any contact with Burke since our meeting on Friday."

Sam shook his head. "So, Burke murdered Greta! He probably killed her out of revenge, for targeting him in the hit and—"

"Sam, I believe Greta's killer was also involved in that hit and run."

"Burke?" Sam shook his head. "He was in that darkened alley with Vance. He's lucky he wasn't killed, too."

"Lucky? Take a look at this." Kyle winced again as he picked up the print-out.

Sam flipped through the pages, summarizing Harmon Doyle's previous convictions and prison record. "Who is this guy?"

"He's Burke Devlin's uncle. He was in town last Friday. He met with Claudia to look at rental condos, but she said he was more interested in asking questions about Burke and Greta—"

"He was asking questions, so what? The news about Greta's car had just been released. Everybody in town was talking about it." Sam paused as he studied one of the pages. "How do you think this Doyle character is connected?"

"I think Burke hired his uncle to be the hit and run driver, and then he put himself in danger to make it look like he was the target."

Sam frowned. "That sounds like a movie script. Why would Burke kill Vance? It doesn't make sense."

"Didn't you say motives don't always make sense?"

"Point made." Sam went quiet as he scanned the entire print-out. "Doyle has a long criminal history, but it's mostly small stuff... car theft, burglaries, assault. The aggravated robbery conviction sent him to prison. But he has no murder charges, attempted or otherwise. And in the past few years, he's been clean."

Kyle leaned forward. "Take a closer look, Sam. Doyle's criminal history reads like a textbook case, showing a gradual escalation in violence. Then a miracle happens. After serving his prison sentence in Georgia, he becomes a model citizen." He paused, keeping his gaze on Sam. "Last Friday, he was driving a Ferrari convertible around town, and he and his female partner were wearing expensive jewelry. Where does an uneducated ex-con with a record like Doyle's get that kind of money?"

Sam's skeptical look disappeared.

"I want you to track down Doyle's parole officer," Kyle said. "You've got top notch interviewing skills and even better instincts.

Find out as much as you can. Burke was living in Atlanta while Doyle was in prison. I want to know if they were in touch with each other."

"I'm on it," Sam said.

Minnie returned with their individual checks after they finished dessert. "You can pay Harvey at the checkout counter, up front." When Sally handed Minnie the large cash tip they had pooled for her, she beamed a smile and thanked them.

They lined up at the checkout counter, near the café's entrance. A woman with short graying hair walked in. She commented on their matching t-shirts and said, "I've seen your website, and I love it!"

Leeann turned to Roxy and whispered, "I thought our website was fake."

"It is," she said, as they exchanged grins.

Roxy stood last in line. After she paid Harvey, she retrieved her soggy rain jacket from the mudroom and stepped outside. The rain had stopped, but humidity lingered in the warm evening breeze.

Leeann was standing on the sidewalk, gazing at the sky. A hopeful expression had replaced the worried look she'd worn during dinner. "Look at that rainbow, Rox." She pointed to the colorful arch, illuminated by shafts of sunlight streaming through breaks in the clouds.

"That's a good sign," Roxy said. They headed toward the rest of the group, gathered near Sally's SUV. The breeze carried the sound of Sally's voice. "...and cell service can be sketchy around the lodge, Jo. If we get separated and your GPS stops working, just stay on the highway. The turnoff to Dusty's Last Resort will be on the left, after you cross the bridge over the Ocklawaha River." She turned toward the others. "Okay, group. Let's go. The lodge is about an hour's drive from here."

As Roxy walked to the truck, she gazed at the scattered clouds, tinted pink by the setting sun. "Hey Jo, it might be dark by the time we reach that turnoff to the lodge."

"I know. I'll be counting on you to help me find it, if my GPS goes out."

As soon as they got into the truck, Jo started the engine. Before leaving, she turned to Roxy. "I called Charlie after dinner, but I didn't mention that scary text. It didn't make sense to worry him, especially if Kyle can find out where Burke is." She paused. "I'm still worried. Aren't you?"

Roxy nodded. "I'd feel better, knowing where Burke is."

They fell into a companionable silence as they left Ocala and drove through Silver Springs. The highway soon narrowed to two lanes, winding past thick stands of sand pine, scrub oaks and sabal palms. Jo pointed to a vehicle up ahead, parked on the shoulder. "I wonder if that driver is in trouble."

Roxy focused on the silver Lexus SUV, but she couldn't read the license plate in the fading daylight. "I saw an identical car drive by your house this morning. It was moving slowly, and I figured the driver was a house hunter, looking at the rental-wreck."

Jo passed the SUV and glanced in the rear-view mirror. "It pulled back onto the highway, and now it's following us. I don't like this."

"I don't, either." Roxy turned around. "I see two men in the front seat, and they're both wearing baseball caps."

"That narrows it down," Jo quipped. She switched on the turn signal. "I'm pulling over. This is giving me the creeps." After the SUV drove past, she checked for traffic and pulled back onto the highway. "Sorry I got so rattled, Rox. There are a lot of SUVs like that around. I guess Burke's text made me jittery."

"I was nervous, too, until it drove right past us."

Minutes later, they crossed the bridge over the river, and Roxy spotted the sign marking the turnoff to Dusty's lodge. Jo slowed the truck and turned left, onto a gravel road. Tall trees lined both sides of the narrow road, blocking what little daylight remained.

The headlight beams lurched up and down as the truck bounced over the road's rutted surface. The wind had strengthened, and the moving beams illuminated the violent swinging of tree limbs as they drove by. It gave the road a spooky look, as if the trees were waving their arms, warning of danger ahead.

The road dead-ended at a circular gravel parking lot. As Jo made the sharp turn into a parking spot, the truck's headlight beams swept across a wide two-story A-frame lodge, flanked by two smaller A-frame log cabins. Sally had parked her SUV nearby, and she was standing by the open cargo door with Tara, Leeann and Bri.

Jo shut off the engine and turned to Roxy. "I'm still worried about Burke. I want to pray for our group's safety, in private." Roxy bowed her head and listened to Jo's soft voice in prayer, against the background of the wind rustling through the trees. After she finished praying, they climbed out of the truck and joined the others.

Sally pulled the small day pack from the jumbled pile of overnight bags in the cargo area. "I've got our papers in here. Let's go check in." She closed the cargo door and led the way up a gravel path to the lodge. A floodlight mounted near the door to the lodge's screen porch clicked on. Leeann let out a shocked cry. They all stopped and stared.

To the right of the door, the screen had been ripped apart. The ragged opening was large enough for two adults to walk through.

"Come on, group. What are we waiting for?" Sally strode up the porch steps. The screen door squeaked on its hinges as she pulled it open. Tara followed her inside, and Jo held the door open for the others.

"What a mess!" Roxy pointed to a shredded fifty-pound bag of dry dog food; the same brand Buddy liked. Kernels crunched under her hiking sandals as she walked across the porch's wood floor.

Sally opened the lodge's double doors and led the way into the spacious lobby. Its décor reminded Roxy of the Minnie Moose Café, with its honey-colored log walls and wooden moose antler chandeliers. Two tall windows flanked the stone fireplace across the room. Oversized couches and chairs filled the lobby's large seating area. A black lab got up from an oval rug near the fireplace and trotted toward them, his tail wagging. Roxy stroked the smooth fur on his large head. He reminded her of Kyle's dog, Clyde.

Sally rang an old-fashioned bell on the check-in counter. The door behind the counter opened, and a man in his mid-forties walked out, dressed in a plaid shirt and jeans. He resembled Harvey from the café, with his black beard, bushy eyebrows and stocky build.

"Sal, good to see you again."

"You too, Dusty."

Loud barking rang out. A Rottweiler dashed around the counter and stopped, facing the women. The dog uttered a low growl as his lips curled back, revealing sharp teeth.

Bri backed up and bumped into Jo, who backed up and stepped on Roxy's foot.

Dusty issued a sharp command, and the dog trotted behind the counter. "Sorry about that. He looks fierce, but he's really gentle as a lamb." He stepped toward the open door and shouted, "Zach, come out here and get the dog!"

A college-age boy with longish black hair appeared at the doorway. "Come on, Killer. You know better than that." The Rottweiler trotted inside, and the door closed.

Roxy whispered to Jo, "If he's gentle as a lamb, why name him Killer?"

Tara was standing behind them, petting the black lab. "What do you call this dog?"

"That one?" Dusty smiled. "He's Lucky."

Jo nudged Roxy and whispered, "Yeah. He's lucky he hasn't been torn apart by Killer."

Tara giggled behind them.

"The bunk room upstairs is all ready for you gals," Dusty said.

"What's the story behind that hole in your porch screen?" Sally asked. "We saw the open bag of dog food when we came in."

"Is that dog food still out there?" Dusty opened the door and shouted, "Zach! Get that screen porch swept up, or we'll have another bear tonight!"

"A bear?" Leeann asked.

"Yeah," Dusty said. "Zach left the dog food on the porch after he came back from the store yesterday. About four in the morning, a bear ripped open the screen and tore into that bag. I chased him away with my shotgun. One shot toward the sky was all it took. You know, a bear can smell food as far away as twenty miles, upwind. That's why you have to take precautions when you're camping. This bear was a big'un. I'd say if he stood up straight, he'd a been close to six feet."

The hair rose on the back of Roxy's neck.

"Sal, we've expanded our restaurant hours. Have you gals eaten yet?"

"We had dinner at the Minnie Moose Café."

"Great place. Minnie's my sister-in-law."

Roxy nodded. That explained the similar décor.

"Are you and Harvey twins?" Jo asked.

Dusty shook his head. "Harvey is a few years older, but I'm better looking." He let out a throaty laugh that sounded like a chugging train engine.

"We have some frozen steaks in a cooler," Sal said. "Can we store them in your freezer tonight?"

He nodded. "You gals sure know how to eat well when you go camping."

Sally led the group back to her SUV. After everyone found their overnight bags, she retrieved a package wrapped in butcher paper from the cooler. When they entered the lodge, she handed the package to Dusty.

Roxy yawned several times as she slowly climbed the stairs. Lifting each foot to a higher step required an enormous effort. The bunk room and the bathroom looked identical in size, but their ceilings slanted in opposite directions. Four bunk beds sat against the high wall in the bunk room, and wooden chairs were lined up against the low wall. A dresser sat at the end of the room, below a large window. The bathroom held three toilet stalls and three sinks with mirrors. A cupboard displayed towels, wash cloths, soap and toilet paper.

The stairs creaked behind her. Sally was in the lead, and Jo was following her.

"Hey Sal, the bathroom doesn't have a shower," Roxy said.

"There's a shower room downstairs, inside the restaurant's bathroom."

"We have to walk into the restaurant to take a shower?"

"It's not so bad," Sally said, yawning.

Jo caught her yawn and said, "I don't care if I have to walk into a dungeon. I'm taking a shower tonight."

One by one, they entered the bunk room. Roxy and Jo sat on chairs next to each other. Sally tossed her overnight bag on a bottom bunk and sat down. Leeann and Bri sat on the bottom bunks on either side of her. Tara walked in and looked around. She appeared to be the one with the most energy.

"Okay, group." Sally looked at each of them. "There are only four lower bunks. Two people need to volunteer for a top bunk." She waited. "I'd take one, but I'm an early riser, and I might wake everyone climbing down from a top bunk."

"I have a problem with balance," Bri said. "I need a bottom bunk."

"I'm afraid of heights, and my legs are too short," Leeann said.

"I don't mind a top bunk," Roxy said, yawning.

"I'll take the other top bunk," Tara said.

They started unpacking their overnight bags. Roxy went into the bathroom and got ready for bed. She returned to the bunk room, wearing workout pants and an old, faded postal uniform shirt, too worn to wear on the job. She sat on the nearest chair and rested her head against the paneled wall as she eyed the bunk beds. The wooden bed frames didn't look all that sturdy.

Sally came out of the bathroom, wearing her swimsuit and holding a bath towel.

"Going to the beach?" Tara grinned.

She grinned back. "I'm going downstairs to use the shower. There are only two stalls, and unless you get up early tomorrow morning, you won't have much time to get ready. Oh, and before I forget, you should charge your cell phones tonight. We probably won't have cell reception, but you'll want to use your camera and the flashlight." She slipped on a pink floral-print bathrobe with puffed sleeves and large buttons shaped like roses.

"Oh my gosh," Tara said. "Grandma's calling, she wants her bathrobe back."

Sally shot her a look. "It's not a bathrobe, it's a duster. It's perfect for traveling... lightweight, comfortable and easy to pack."

"Not to mention stylish," Tara said.

Leeann glanced up as she unpacked. "Who needs style, here in the forest?"

"I think you should always look your best," Bri said. "I have all my makeup with me." She held up a cosmetic bag. "I also brought makeup and lipstick samples from the spa. We can have fun trying out new colors."

Jo looked at her. "Okay, let me get this straight. We're going to a primitive campsite in the middle of the forest so we can try out new lipstick colors."

Bri nodded. "Why not?"

"I like the idea," Leeann said.

"Wait a minute," Tara said. "Didn't you just say we shouldn't worry about style in the forest?"

Leeann shrugged. She draped an oversized yellow t-shirt over her arm.

Sally took a step closer. "Is that one of the sample t-shirts for the Scoop Troops?"

"Yeah," Leeann said. "It's the t-shirt with Greg's first slogan."

Sally groaned. "You mean the worst slogan."

"Let me see it," Jo said.

Roxy sat up; her curiosity awakened. "I want to see it, too."

Leeann held up the shirt. Under the silhouette of a dog's head, were the words, "Scoop Troops. We like taking crap from you."

A round of giggles followed.

"That t-shirt drags the concept of style to a new low," Tara said.

Leeann grinned. "I would always rather be happy, than dignified."

"Okay, which author?" Tara asked.

"Charlotte Bronte, from Jane Eyre," Leeann said.

"Hey Sal, wait for me. I'm showering tonight." Jo hurried into the bathroom and returned, wearing her swimsuit. She searched through her overnight bag. "I forgot my shampoo."

"You can use mine." Leeann handed her a large plastic bottle.

"Look at this." Jo held up the shampoo bottle, as if she was pitching it on a TV commercial. "There's a photo of a golden retriever on the label."

"It's dog shampoo," Leeann said.

"Seriously?" Jo stared at her.

"It's just regular shampoo, Jo. Greg says the manufacturer bottles the same formula for people and animals. He buys it in bulk for the vet practice, and we use it at home. It's economical."

"I told Matt there's no way I'd use dog shampoo just to save a few dollars," Sally said.

"It's not just to save money," Leeann said. "This shampoo makes my hair feel silky."

Jo giggled. "Does it have... Woof! any side effects? Woof! Woof!"

Leeann did an eye roll.

Jo was still barking and giggling as she and Sally walked downstairs.

Roxy finally worked up the energy to climb into the top bunk next to the window. As she hoisted herself up, she heard the alarming sound of wood cracking. The bunk springs squeaked as she snuggled under the covers. She closed her heavy eyelids. As she drifted into sleep, she thought about the hungry bear that had ripped apart the porch screen.

Monday morning

Roxy woke and stared at the slanted wood ceiling inches above her head, illuminated by the warm light of sunrise. She heard the mismatched sounds of breathing, mixed with light snoring. She peered over the side of the bunk. Everyone was sleeping, except Sally. Her bed had been neatly made, as if she hadn't slept in it.

She propped herself up on one elbow and pushed aside the gauzy curtain covering the window next to her bunk. Trees cast long shadows on the path leading to the river. The water's blue rippled surface sparkled in the sunlight. Roxy smiled. She slid off the bunk, trying to minimize the squeaking and cracking. She landed barefoot on the wood floor and glanced at Jo, who was sleeping in the bottom bunk.

After using the bathroom, Roxy dressed in her swimsuit and used her workout pants and postal uniform shirt as a cover-up. She retrieved a bath towel and wash cloth from the cupboard and returned to the bunk room to slip on her sandals.

Jo looked up with sleepy eyes and whispered, "Are you going down for your shower?"

"Yeah."

"Wait, and I'll go down with you."

"Didn't you shower last night?" Roxy asked, keeping her voice hushed.

"I did." She yawned. "But someone needs to guard the door. The lock on the shower room is broken."

"Oh, great."

Jo went into the bathroom and quickly dressed in a pair of tan cargo shorts, the group t-shirt and hiking sandals. She fixed her hair into a ponytail and tied the pink bandana around her neck.

As they walked downstairs, Roxy detected the aroma of fresh coffee. "I'm having trouble waking up. I think I'll take a mug of coffee into the shower room."

Jo yawned as she followed her. "I'll need to drink at least two mugs, if I want to stay awake on guard duty."

Sally stood at the check-in counter with Dusty. She was dressed in camouflage cargo pants, the group t-shirt and hiking boots. Her pink bandana had been tied around her head in 'Rosie the Riveter' style, as if she planned to fix a few things around the lodge before breakfast. Sally glanced up and smiled when she saw them coming down the stairs. "Good morning, you two. Dusty and I just checked the weather. That tropical storm is stalled out in the Gulf, but it's not predicted to head toward Florida."

"You gals should have nice weather today," Dusty said. He eyed Roxy's shirt. "You a mailman?"

She nodded. "I work a mail route in Riverside Bay."

"Harvey used to be a mailman," Dusty said. "He and Minnie opened up the café after he retired. If you want to know the truth, I think he misses working out on his own in that mail truck. But don't tell Minnie I said that." He let out a chugging laugh.

The restrooms and showers were located at the far end of the restaurant, near the kitchen. A self-service coffee bar stood nearby. Roxy and Jo took turns filling a mug from the large coffee urn. They both added a generous amount of cream. Lucky trotted over and sat next to Jo as she took up her guard post.

Roxy entered the restroom, took a few hurried coffee sips and placed the mug on a bench. Leeann's dog shampoo sat in the soap basket inside one of the shower stalls. The golden retriever on the label resembled Buddy, and she realized how much she missed him.

Jo lifted her coffee mug in a mock salute as Roxy walked out of the restroom. "All quiet on the restaurant front."

"Thanks for standing guard, Jo." Roxy stood for a moment and finger combed her damp waves. "I just tried Leeann's dog shampoo, and my hair feels really silky." She grinned. "There's only one problem... I feel a sudden craving for Kibbles and Bits."

Jo giggled. "Woof! Woof!"

The group walked into the restaurant together and headed toward the self-service coffee bar, where Dusty was refilling his mug. "Look at that. You're all wearing those matching shirts again." His gaze rested a moment on Jo's shirt, but he made no comment. "After breakfast, I'll meet you gals in the equipment shed and help you pick out the right size life jackets and paddles."

"I have my own jacket and paddle, but I'll send the others down," Sally said. "I just dropped my car off at Gore's Landing, and Jo drove me back. She left her truck bed cover unlocked, so Zach can start unloading our packs."

"Okay, I'll let him know," Dusty said. "He'll bring all your packs down to the landing."

Roxy entered the breakfast buffet line and briefly chatted with a young couple who were staying in one of the log cabins. She loaded her plate with scrambled eggs, bacon and fruit and then sat at a long table. Bri sat across from her. Roxy glanced at the carton of yogurt and the small serving of fruit on her plate. "Are you feeling okay, Bri? You look tired, and you're not eating much."

"This is all I ever eat for breakfast. Mornings are hard for me, sometimes. I'll be fine in a little while." Bri gave her a cheery smile that looked forced. The others joined them, one by one, and the conversation centered around their excitement about beginning the trip.

Roxy and Jo finished eating before the others and left the restaurant together. As they walked through the lobby, Jo said, "You didn't say much at breakfast, Rox. What's bothering you?"

"I've been thinking about Kyle," Roxy said. "We argued on the phone yesterday, and the call didn't end well."

"How did that happen?"

"I guess we've both been on edge, lately." She glanced at the counter, where Dusty was standing. "I don't have cell service here. Do you think I could use the lodge's landline to call Kyle?"

"Sal used it this morning to call Matt. Go ahead and call him," Jo said. "I'm going to lock up my truck. Zach has probably unloaded our packs by now." She walked past the counter and headed out the lobby's double doors.

Dusty smiled as Roxy approached. "Did I hear you say you need to use the phone? You're not calling Timbuktu, are you?" He let out a chugging laugh.

She grinned. "Just Riverside Bay, to talk to —"

"Anywhere in Florida is fine." He set down his coffee mug and slid an old push button phone toward her. "Looks like you gals are done eating. I'll head out to the equipment shed."

She punched in Kyle's number, hoping it wouldn't go directly into voicemail.

He picked up after the first ring. "Rox, I'm sorry about—"

"Kyle, I'm sorry..."

Their voices had overlapped. An awkward silence followed.

"Rox, I shouldn't have gotten so upset yesterday. I'm just worried about your safety."

"I know..." She paused. "Were you able to trace Doyle's cell number and find Burke?"

"No. Doyle must be using a disposable phone," Kyle said. "Sam and I searched Burke's condo yesterday. Earl let us in. His laptop is gone. But he has so many clothes, it's hard to tell if any are missing. We found no notes, no receipts in his trash, nothing to tell us where he went."

"Did you tell Earl that Burke knew about Greta's body?"

"No. We need to do more investigating, Rox. It's probably best if you don't talk about it, either."

"I haven't said anything. I don't want to worry the others."

"Good. What time are you setting out on the river?"

"In a few minutes. I guess I should get going so I don't hold everyone up."

"Stay safe…"

"I will, don't worry. I'll call you tomorrow night, after we get back to the lodge."

"Okay…" A brief silence. "I love you, Rox."

"Love you, too."

Roxy hung up, and then she stood a moment, thinking about Kyle. She pulled her fishing gloves from a pocket in her cargo shorts and smiled as she slipped them on. When she walked out into the lodge's porch, she glanced at the large hole in the screen. Then she opened the squeaky screen door and headed down the stairs.

Sunlight filtered through the trees surrounding the lodge. A hot, sultry breeze tossed the leafy branches around, creating a shifting pattern of light and shadow on the gravel lot. She put on her sunglasses and fixed her hair into a ponytail as she headed toward the equipment shed. The doors stood open. Neon orange life jackets were hanging on one wall of the shed, grouped by size. Paddles of varying lengths hung on the opposite wall. Dusty was helping Leeann select her paddle. He smiled as Roxy entered. "There she is. You're the last one."

Roxy and Leeann headed down the path to the river landing, carrying their life jackets and paddles. Jo, Tara and Bri were already standing at the shoreline with Zach. Their life jackets and paddles were stacked on the ground next to the group's Duluth packs. Three canoes were tied up near shore, two red and one forest green. They gently rocked on the river's surface.

"Hey, wait up!" Sally hurried down the path and caught up with Roxy and Leeann. She was carrying a package wrapped in butcher paper. "I almost forgot our steaks in Dusty's freezer."

When they joined the others, Sally opened the food pack and stuffed the frozen steaks inside.

Jo frowned. "I can't believe you're adding food to that huge pack. It's already too heavy to carry."

Dusty walked up and eyed the Duluth packs. "What's in that big canvas pack?"

"Our food," Sally said.

He grabbed one of its shoulder straps and lifted it. "Sal, you're going to have to hang this heavy pack from a tree tonight, and I don't think you'll find a limb strong enough to hold it. You know it has to hang at least eight feet off the ground and six feet away from a tree trunk, to keep the bears from tearing into it."

"We'll eat the heavier food today… frozen steaks, cheese-stuffed potatoes, and baked goods. The pack will be a lot lighter after dinner."

Dusty shook his head.

A stubborn look crossed Sally's face. "If it's still too heavy, we can split the food into two packs. The equipment pack will be mostly empty after our tents are set up. We can load half the food into it."

"Then you'll have to hang two packs," Dusty said.

Sally shrugged. "I brought extra rope."

Dusty appeared to give up. He and Zach lifted the food pack and struggled to hold onto it as they waded into the river. When they loaded the pack inside the green canoe, it shuddered and sank several inches lower in the water.

The women worked in teams as they loaded the rest of the packs into the red canoes. Roxy entered the river with Jo, sharing the weight of the equipment pack. She shivered as the cold spring-fed water swirled around her lower legs and seeped inside her hiking boots. After all the packs were loaded, Sally gathered the group together at the shoreline.

Dusty stood nearby and stroked his thick beard as he gazed at his heavily-loaded canoes. He wore an uneasy expression, as if he thought it might be the last time he'd ever see them in such good condition.

"Thanks, Dusty and Zach. We can take it from here," Sally said.

The two men nodded and wished everyone a good trip, before walking back to the lodge.

Sally turned to the group and read from the list in her hand. "Do you have a water bottle, snacks and a rain jacket? Sunscreen and bug spray?"

Tara spoke up. "I put on sunscreen, but not bug spray. I don't want that greasy DEET all over my skin." She pulled several white dryer sheets from a pocket in her cargo pants and tied them to the belt loops. "I read an article that said the lavender scent of fabric softener repels mosquitoes."

Sally shook her head. "Dryer sheets won't repel bugs."

Bri smiled. "Even if they don't work, they'll make you smell great, Tara."

"Yeah. Just like clean laundry," Jo said.

Tara shot Jo a look. She slipped a beige safari hat over her curly hair and snapped the brim up on one side.

"You look like you're planning to paddle all the way to Australia," Roxy said.

Sally grinned. "People living 'down under' don't tie dryer sheets to their belt loops."

Tara lifted her chin. "You'll be begging me for dryer sheets when you see how well they work."

Jo stepped forward. "Before we go, I'll send us off with a prayer." The group gathered in a circle and held hands as she prayed: "Loving Father, we thank you for the friendship we've shared for so many years. Please keep us safe as we journey through this beautiful forest. Go before us as our guide, stay beside us as our friend, and travel behind us as our shield. We ask this in the name of your son, Jesus. Amen."

The women pulled the loaded canoes into deeper water, so they wouldn't bottom out when they climbed inside. Tara and Leeann climbed into a red canoe, and Sally and Bri climbed into the other one. Roxy and Jo had the dubious honor of paddling the green canoe, weighed down with the massive food pack.

"I'll sit in the back," Jo said. "The stern paddler does the steering, and Charlie taught me how to do that last summer, when we rented canoes and paddled down the Indian River with Rachel. You should sit in front Rox, because the bow paddler propels the canoe forward, and you have stronger arms."

Roxy gave her a look. "Are you saying that you're the brains and I'm the brawn?"

Jo grinned. "You climb inside first. I'll hold the canoe steady."

Roxy hoisted herself over the canoe rim and slid onto the bow seat. Her soggy boots dragged muddy water inside the rocking canoe. When Jo climbed into the stern seat, the canoe tipped. The rim momentarily dipped below the surface, and water rushed inside. Roxy fought a surge of panic when the canoe quickly tipped in the opposite direction, and water sloshed over the other rim. The rocking slowly subsided as Jo settled into her seat.

"Don't make any more sudden moves," Sally said. "You're already riding low, and you can't afford to take on more water."

Roxy looked over her shoulder and cast a nervous glance at Jo.

"It's okay. We got this, Rox." Jo pumped her fist in a victory gesture and gripped her paddle.

Kyle set down his pen and rubbed the throbbing index finger on his left hand. It had been awkward, but he'd managed to take notes during his long phone call with an Atlanta homicide detective. Before ending the call, the detective agreed to email a PDF file on Erika Devlin's car accident. Kyle stood and stretched his back muscles before heading to the break room to get a coffee refill. As he walked back down the hallway, he glanced inside Sam's office and saw him sitting at his desk. "Did Quint and Alan show up for their voice stress testing?"

"They both came in, right on time." Sam swiveled his chair toward the doorway. "Kendra conducted the tests, and I just finished reviewing the results with her. You know voice stress analysis isn't foolproof, but the results showed no signs of deception. It's likely both men had nothing to do with the hit and run or Greta's murd—" His ringtone sounded. Sam glanced at his phone screen. "It's Doyle's parole officer, calling back."

Kyle nodded. "Come to my office when you're finished." He sat at his desk and checked his email. Nothing yet from the Atlanta detective. He took a sip of fresh coffee, and then he leaned back in his chair and closed his eyes. He thought about Rox and her camping trip. She and her friends were probably paddling down the Ocklawaha River, right now.

"Earth to Kyle..."

He glanced up.

"You were off somewhere, lost in space." Sam shot him a grin as he sat in a guest chair. He flipped open his notebook and leaned forward. "The parole officer was sure we were calling because we had Doyle in custody. She had a hard time believing he's been clean for so many years. When I asked her about Burke, she confirmed he visited Doyle in prison, and he even helped him find a job and a place to live while he was on parole." He looked up. "What did you find out when you called that Atlanta law firm?"

"I talked to one of Burke's former co-workers. She claimed she didn't know him well, but I heard the lie in her voice. After I pressed her, she admitted she had a relationship with Burke before Erika died. But she insisted she hadn't had any contact with him recently. I asked her to call me if she heard from—" He stopped when his desk phone rang.

"Lieutenant?" Kendra's voice. "There's a woman in the lobby, and she's upset. She wants to report a missing person, and she insists on talking to you. Her name is Isabel McGraw... hang on... what is it, ma'am? Okay. She says her partner's missing. His name is Harmon Doyle."

"Bring her back to my office." Kyle hung up and smiled at Sam. "Speak of the devil. Want to meet Harmon Doyle's female partner?"

Moments later, a jingling sound grew louder in the hallway. Kendra appeared in the open doorway, accompanied by a much shorter blonde woman.

Kyle was struck by the differences in their appearance. Kendra was dressed in a blue police polo shirt, dark slacks and black athletic shoes. She'd applied minimal make-up to her dark brown complexion, and her black hair was gathered into a precise topknot. The blonde woman's black spandex outfit stretched over her ample curves, and her high-heeled sandals sparkled in the office light. Heavy make-up covered her attractive face. Gaudy gold earrings dangled from her ears, and she wore a ridiculous number of gold bracelets.

Kendra introduced Isabel McGraw to the two detectives and started to leave. Then she paused at the open doorway, glanced back at Kyle and shrugged her shoulders.

Sam pulled out a guest chair for Isabel. He scooted his chair close and sat down, facing her.

Kyle hoped Sam wouldn't start drooling. He turned to her and said, "Ms. McGraw, you're here to report a missing—"

"Call me Izzy. Everyone does." She spoke in a high-pitched tone.

Kyle averted his eyes from her large bosom. "Your partner's name is Harmon Doyle?"

"That's right." She lowered her head and smiled at him through amazingly long lashes.

"How long has he been missing?" Kyle asked.

"Two days, almost. He's gone on some kind of business trip, and that's very unusual. Harmie and I are almost never apart, you know. Except when we are."

Kyle nodded, thinking, "That makes no sense."

"Harmie's insanely jealous, you know. He calls me all the time when we're apart. He wants to know about everything I'm doing when he's not around, and who I'm doing it with." She smiled at Sam.

He smiled back. "I can understand that."

Kyle willed himself to be patient. "Can you tell us about this business trip?"

She turned back to him. "He's working for his nephew. He's a lawyer, you know."

"Burke Devlin?" Kyle asked.

She nodded. "Harmie and I have been staying at a beach hotel outside town... I'm still staying there. Burke called us late Saturday night. He asked Harmie to meet him at the Orlando airport."

Sam straightened up. "What time was this?"

"I drove Harmie there around three in the morning."

"Do you know why Burke asked him to go to the airport?" Kyle asked.

"Harmie never tells me his business."

"Okay," Sam said. "You drove Harmie... ah, Harmon to the airport early Sunday morning. Today is Monday." He glanced at his watch. "It's almost noon. He's been gone less than two days. I don't understand why you're so worr—"

"He hasn't called me at all! I called him over and over and he never called back! That's not like Harmie! Something's wrong, I just know it!" A quiver had entered her voice. "I went to the Silver Building today and talked to Earl Silver, Burke's other uncle. I thought he might know where they are. Earl told me to talk to you." She looked at Kyle.

"We'll do our best to locate them." He gave her a reassuring smile and then turned to Sam. "Take her to the officer on duty so she can file a missing person report."

Izzy stood and leaned heavily against Sam as he escorted her out of the office.

Kyle got on the phone and contacted the airlines. He found no reservations for Doyle. On a hunch, he called the rental car agencies near the Orlando airport with round the clock operating hours. The third agent he spoke with confirmed a car rental made by Harmon J. Doyle on Sunday morning, shortly after 4:00 a.m.

Moments later, a ping sounded, indicating a new email. Kyle swiveled toward his laptop and opened the PDF attachment sent by the Atlanta detective. He was reading the last page when Sam walked back into his office and sat in a guest chair.

"Did you find a plane reservation for Doyle?" Sam asked.

"No, but I talked to a car rental agency near the airport. Doyle rented an SUV early Sunday morning."

Sam nodded as he unwrapped a snack-size candy bar and popped it into his mouth.

Kyle glanced at the police report on his laptop screen. "Do you know how Burke's wife died?"

"Yeah, a car accident." Sam's words came out garbled as he chewed. He crumpled the candy wrapper into a ball and eyed the trash can as he raised his arm.

"It was a hit and run," Kyle said. "Erika and Burke were walking toward their fitness club around dawn. Burke said the car came out of nowhere. It hit her but missed him. He was the only witness, the car was never found, and the case went cold. Sound familiar?"

Sam lowered his arm and set the crumpled wrapper on Kyle's desk. "I don't believe in coincidences."

"I don't either," Kyle said. "Burke inherited a fortune from Erika's estate. She was the trophy wife of one of his wealthy law clients. They married shortly after her husband died."

"How did her husband—"

"Heart attack. The man was in his eighties." He paused. "I knew Erika. She and Burke came into town to celebrate holidays and birthdays with the Silva family, and Josh and I were always invited. Erika was a beautiful woman and surprisingly shy."

Sam shook his head. His eyes reflected a sad cynicism, as if he knew people were capable of all sorts of twisted behavior, and he found it depressing. "Burke had it all... a prestigious job with a law firm and a beautiful, wealthy wife. I guess that wasn't enough for him. He probably killed Erika to get full control of her money. And I'm guessing he murdered Greta for revenge. But why would Burke set up a hit and run to kill Vance?"

"His trust accounts," Kyle said. "I've always suspected they fit in, somewhere. Remember what Earl said about that flash drive Greta told Vance about? She copied files from Burke's computer that would prove he'd been embezzling from his clients. Greta arranged to show that flash drive to Vance on Sunday, the day before the hit and run. But she texted him that morning and cancelled, saying she had a migraine—"

"Burke sent that text, using her phone!" Sam sat up straight; his eyes animated. "He found out about that flash drive and killed Greta to shut her up. Then he probably destroyed it."

"But Burke still wasn't in the clear," Kyle said. "Vance called him on Sunday and set up a meeting early the next morning to review his trust accounts. Burke didn't have enough time to clean up the transactions, so he called his uncle in Miami. The hit and run worked with Erika, why not with Vance?" Kyle turned to his laptop and brought up Erika's police report. "Sam, when did Doyle finish serving his parole?"

He flipped through his notebook and read the date Doyle's parole officer had given him.

"That's exactly two weeks before Erika's murder," Kyle said. "Burke waited to set up that hit and run until Doyle was released from all parole restrictions. That way, he could freely leave Georgia after her murder."

"And Doyle moved to Miami, of course," Sam said. "You know what they say... the bad guys move to Florida so they can commit more crimes in better weather."

Kyle frowned. "I'm sure Burke paid Doyle a small fortune to act as the driver in both murders."

"Maybe Doyle wasn't satisfied with a one-time payment," Sam said. "I did some checking on his expensive lifestyle. Besides the Ferrari, Doyle has a yacht and a penthouse condo in Miami. I think Burke had to keep paying him, so he'd keep quiet about Erika's murder... and Greta and Vance, too." He paused. "Doyle was in town last Friday, the day after Greta's car was discovered. He knew we'd find her body in the trunk. I'll bet he came here to squeeze more money out of Burke."

Kyle nodded. "And when Doyle couldn't meet with Burke in person, he started calling him, pressuring him for more money to keep quiet. Rox happened to be with Burke on the night of the reunion when he got one of Doyle's calls."

Sam's face took on a puzzled look. "Then why did Burke contact him on Saturday night and ask him to rent a car at the airport?"

"Burke called Doyle after he assaulted Rox. He probably hid his BMW in one of the airport's parking lots, and asked Doyle to rent a car early Sunday morning, so we couldn't track him." Kyle flinched as he made the connection. "Rox got a threatening text from Doyle's phone number on Sunday afternoon!"

"Hold on, Kyle." Sam held up his hand. "Burke's not crazy enough to go after Rox again. He knows we're on to him. My guess is, he's trying to get away... maybe out of the country. He needed Doyle's help to rent a car and give us the slip." Sam paused. "That threatening text was probably just a cruel bluff, something a scumbag like Burke would do to torment Rox."

Kyle sat back and blew out a sigh. "You're probably right."

"Burke has sailed that fancy yacht of his all around the Caribbean," Sam said. "He knows we're keeping it under surveillance. Maybe he's planning to use Doyle's yacht. I'll call the Miami marina and check it out."

"And I'll put a BOLO on that car Doyle rented," Kyle said. He glanced at his notes, where he'd written the license number of the silver Lexus SUV.

With each paddle stroke, the heavily-loaded canoe rocked from side to side, tipping close to the water's surface. Roxy's anxiety gradually eased as she grew accustomed to the canoe's swaying movement and the gentle pull of the river's current. She soon slipped into a comfortable rhythm—slice into the water with the paddle's narrow edge; flatten the blade as you pull it back; then lift and start again. Slice; flatten; pull back and lift.

Sunshine warmed her face as she propelled the canoe forward. She breathed deeply, savoring the fresh scents in the humid air; the scents of moist earth and vegetation. Trees, palms and shrubs in varying shades of green lined the banks of the winding river, while blooming cardinal flowers provided vivid splashes of red. The trees growing closest to the shoreline—bald cypress, Carolina ash, and swamp tupelos—tended to lean over the river. Their leafy limbs created the illusion of arches overhead. In the shallow areas, the white starburst-shaped blooms of swamp lilies rose above the green vegetation.

Roxy let out a soft sigh as she gazed at the pristine beauty surrounding her—Florida's wild, unspoiled beauty; free of development and tourist attractions. No posted signs or billboards... no housing developments... no paved streets or traffic noise. Just the soothing sounds of nature; birds chirping, the wind rustling through the trees, and the musical sound of water swirling around her paddle blade.

The canoe abruptly shifted direction. Roxy glanced back and saw Jo using her paddle as a rudder.

Jo smiled. "Rox, it's the bow paddler's job to be on the lookout for hazards ahead. The river is spring-fed, so the water is fairly clear, but the rocks and fallen trees underwater can be hard to spot in the shady areas. We don't want to hit anything."

Roxy faced forward and peered below the water's surface. The number of submerged tree trunks surprised her. One thick trunk protruded above the water, and she counted five turtles resting on it. Up ahead, she spotted an alligator, lying motionless on the riverbank with his mouth set in a sinister smile. She pointed the gator out to Jo.

"That's the second one I've seen, Rox."

The gator slid into the river as they paddled forward. Roxy shivered, aware of how low their rocking canoe was riding in the water. The heavy food pack slowed their progress. She and Jo exchanged waves with several people paddling past them in canoes or kayaks. Roxy had lost sight of both red canoes. But every so often, when they rounded a bend in the river, she'd catch a glimpse of them in the distance—red spots riding the river's surface, accompanied by bright flashes as the moving paddles caught the sunlight.

"Hey, Rox. I'm ready for a water break."

"Okay." She pulled her paddle out of the water and lifted her legs over the seat as she swiveled around to face Jo. The toes of her soggy hiking boots pressed against the massive food pack. The boots were supposed to be waterproof, but she guessed that didn't apply to total immersion. And her moisture-wicking socks were useless, sealed inside the waterlogged boots.

Roxy searched for her water bottle. She found it under her seat, rocking back and forth in the muddy water. She unscrewed the cap and used the bandana around her neck to wipe it off before taking a long drink. "Hey, Jo. Our bottled water will be gone by the time we reach the campsite. I know we'll fill our collapsible water jugs when we set up camp. But if the Ocklawaha River is spring-fed, why does Sal want to use purification tablets?"

"There's pollution in the river... bacteria from animals and people, and runoff from fertilizers that encourages algae growth." Jo unscrewed the cap on her water bottle and took a long drink.

The current drew them toward a downed tree trunk. Roxy picked up her paddle and used side strokes to steer the canoe away from it. "Do the tablets give the water a strange taste?"

"Sal says they don't. But I brought lemonade flavor packets, just in case. The only thing Sal has ever complained about is the water temperature. Sitting in a jug at the campsite, the water is always warm. After every camping trip, she and Matt stop at a drive-through on the way home and order extra-large cold drinks, heavy on the ice." Jo picked up her paddle. "Let's try and catch up with the others. It's getting close to lunchtime."

After several minutes of steady paddling, Roxy pointed out the two red canoes, tied up at the shoreline. Jo steered their canoe toward shore and called out, "I'm glad we finally caught up with you. We're both hungry."

Tara giggled and pointed to the extra-large food pack. "You had a year's worth of food in your canoe."

Sally carefully rose out of the stern seat and climbed over the canoe rim. She waded in the shallow water and met their canoe. "Rox, hand me your bow rope."

Roxy pulled it out of the brownish water sloshing in the bottom of the canoe and glanced at her wet boots. She thought about how good it would feel to take them off, along with her wet socks. She longed to dangle her bare feet over the canoe rim, so they could dry out in the warm sunshine.

Sally took the soggy rope from Roxy and tied it to a fallen tree trunk near shore. Before she climbed back into her canoe, she calmly pointed out a snapping turtle the size of a turkey platter swimming in the clear water near her boots.

"Good thing you're not wearing sandals," Jo said. "He looks like he could bite all your toes off."

"Eeeuuw," Bri said. "I'm keeping my boots on if I go swimming."

"I always keep my boots on," Sally said. "There are water moccasins in the river."

Roxy looked down at her waterlogged boots and decided not to take them off.

"Did you see all the gators?" Tara asked. "I counted six of them."

"I counted seven," Jo said.

"That's another reason to keep your boots on," Bri said.

"Hey, everyone. Make sure you wash your hands before lunch." Leeann held up a pocket-size hand sanitizer bottle. She cleaned her hands and then passed it around.

"You usually carry a bigger bottle than that," Tara said, as she slapped a bug on her arm.

Leeann smiled. "I put a huge bottle in our personal pack."

Sally opened the day pack and pulled out two zip-top bags containing pita bread sandwiches; turkey and cheese, and cucumber and cream cheese. She passed the bags around, along with a package of dried fruit. They ate sitting in their canoes, floating near shore.

"I see a bald eagle," Leeann said, looking upward.

Roxy spotted the eagle soaring high overhead. Its outstretched wings stood out against the deep blue of the cloudless sky.

"Look! Something's moving in those branches over there." Bri shaded her eyes as she waved toward a stand of trees. "I see monkeys! Little gray monkeys!"

"Bri, you've been out in the sun too long," Tara said.

"They're rhesus monkeys," Sally said. "Back in the 1930's, a glass bottom boat operator at Silver Springs released some into the wild, as a tourist attraction. Now there are colonies of them. They've become a dangerous nuisance, mostly because people feed them, and that encourages aggressive behavior. They also carry the deadly Herpes B virus. Don't even think about going near one."

"There's no way I'd do that," Leeann said.

"It seems like everything in this forest can kill you," Bri said. "Gators... virus monkeys... bears..."

"Don't forget the water moccasins," Tara said.

"Snakes! Eeeuuw!" Bri and Leeann responded in unison.

While she ate, Roxy gazed at the trees on each side of the river. She spotted several grayish-brown monkeys scurrying along the tree limbs.

Sally stowed the leftover food in the day pack. "Okay, group. The campsite is only about three miles from here. It shouldn't take us long."

Slice; flatten; pull back and lift. Roxy's shoulders ached as she repeated the sequence again and again. The trees arching over the river provided welcome patches of shade, relief from the sun's intense heat. Ever since their lunch break, she'd been glancing up at the leafy branches, searching for monkeys.

"Rox, we lost sight of the others a while ago. Haven't we paddled three miles, by now?"

"Seems more like thirty miles," Roxy said. As they rounded a bend in the river, she spotted the red canoes tied up near shore and pointed them out to Jo. All the packs had been unloaded, and the women stood at the shoreline, drinking from water bottles.

"I'll steer us in," Jo said. "Keep looking for hazards in the shallow water."

Roxy spotted a cluster of cypress knees just below the water's surface. She used her paddle to push away from them. Moments later, the heavily-loaded canoe shuddered as it bottomed out in the mud.

"The eagle has landed," Jo giggled.

"I don't think the lunar module landed this hard." Roxy slowly rose and leaned forward, gripping the bow rim with both hands as she stepped out of the wobbly canoe. She stood in the shallow water and held the canoe steady while Jo climbed out. Then she tied the soggy bow rope to a fallen tree trunk near shore.

"Look over there, at that gigantic tree." Bri pointed her water bottle toward a massive brown tree trunk several feet away.

Jo's eyes widened. "The trunk has to be eight or nine feet in diameter."

"That's about right," Sally said. "Matt estimates it's around seventy feet tall. It's an old growth bald cypress, probably over a thousand years old."

"Seriously?" Roxy asked.

Sally nodded. "This area used to be full of them, until loggers came in over a hundred years ago. Matt thinks this tree was probably spared because it was too hollow. I'll show you the opening on the other side."

Everyone followed Sally as she walked around the huge trunk. The opening, shaped like an inverted V, was large enough for a person to duck through. They took turns investigating the hollow space. Their voices echoed as they stood inside and made comments.

Leeann's brown eyes held a look of wonder as she walked out. "That's amazing. It's large enough for all of us to fit inside, if we bunched together."

Jo nodded. "It's like a tiny house inside a tree trunk."

Roxy entered the space after the others. She stood for a long moment and listened to the gentle sound of the wind rustling its branches, high overhead. Shafts of light streamed inside through cracks in the trunk, illuminating the vast hollow darkness. A feeling of awe overwhelmed her, as if she was standing in a holy place.

Sally called her back to the shoreline. "Let's start carrying packs to the campsite. Rox and Jo, you need to stay here and unload that food pack from your canoe."

"Lucky us," Jo frowned.

"I know it's heavy," Sally said. "Just set it on shore and wait for me. I'll empty the equipment pack at the campsite and bring it back. We can load it with half the food."

Sally strapped on the equipment pack. Tara shouldered a personal pack, and Leeann wore the day pack. Bri slung life jackets over her shoulders. They followed Sal up a narrow trail and disappeared behind a stand of palm trees.

Jo stared at the food pack. "I guess it isn't going to jump out by itself."

They waded into the shallow water on opposite sides of the canoe. Each of them gripped a shoulder strap with both hands and began lifting. Roxy's shoulder muscles quivered from the strain. It took several tries before they finally lifted the pack onto the bow seat. After a short rest, they hurled the heavy pack toward shore. It landed with a thump at the water line. They dragged it toward the large fallen tree trunk near shore.

"That was fun." Jo plopped down on the tree trunk. "I'll need back surgery if I have to lift that pack one more time."

Roxy retrieved both water bottles from the canoe and sat on the trunk next to Jo.

"Thanks, Rox." Jo reached for her bottle. "The water's warm, but I'm too thirsty to care."

After they both took a long drink, they sat quietly and looked out at the river. The breeze stirred its shimmering blue surface, creating shifting patterns of ripples. Roxy watched as a great blue heron made a graceful landing in the shallow water near the opposite shore.

"I'm surprised we haven't seen Trent and Seth, yet," Jo said. "I spotted two men wearing baseball caps paddling by in a canoe, while you were getting our water bottles. At first, I thought it might be them. But the guy wearing the bright red shirt looked too fat."

Footsteps thumped behind them. Roxy turned and saw Sally emerging from the narrow path, carrying the empty equipment pack. "I left the others at the campsite so they can start setting up our tents. My tent has the set-up instructions, but I couldn't find anything in your orange tent bag, Jo."

"We lost the instructions a long time ago, but I know how to set it up."

"Okay, you'll need to come back to the site with me." Sally looked out at the river. "I don't see anyone around right now, but it's not a good idea to leave any packs unguarded."

"Why?" Roxy asked.

"We had our food pack stolen last summer, while we were carrying our other packs to the campsite. It happened late in the day, so we went ahead and camped overnight. Matt, Nolan and I had to split a granola bar for our dinner." Sally shook her head. "I guess people can commit crimes anywhere, even in the forest."

Burke's image flashed into Roxy's mind. She glanced at Jo, who also looked spooked.

Sally handed Roxy the empty equipment pack. "You can stand guard and split up the food while Jo and I take the last two personal packs to the site. You should be done by the time I come back. Then you and I can each carry a food pack."

After they left, Roxy unfastened the rusty buckles on the huge canvas pack and began transferring food into the empty pack. Loud cracking sounds caught her attention, followed by a muffled cry. She stopped working and listened, but all she heard was the wind rustling through the trees, the sound of birds chirping and the squeaking chatter of squirrels.

Roxy continued working until she was satisfied she'd transferred enough food. After closing up the canvas pack, she grabbed the shoulder straps and tested its weight. It was still heavy, but she felt encouraged when she was able to lift it onto the fallen tree trunk. She decided to strap it on and see if she could walk with it. She sat on the trunk with her back toward the pack and slipped her arms through the shoulder straps, being careful not to scrape her bandaged stitches. She fastened the chest strap and then rose to her feet. The pack's heavy weight tipped her backward, and she had to lean forward to keep her balance.

She started up the narrow dirt path Sally and Jo had taken. When she passed the stand of palm trees, she glanced to the side and was surprised to see a steep sandy hill leading down to a small creek.

With each step forward, the pack seemed to grow heavier, until it felt as if she was carrying Aunt Nell's French door refrigerator on her back. Roxy's heart pounded from the exertion. She stopped and blew out a frustrated sigh. This pack was still too heavy to carry.

Twigs snapped. She tensed and stood still, listening. A prickly chill traveled down her spine when she heard loud crunching sounds behind her. Roxy glanced back and caught a glimpse of a large dark form moving between the trees. Fear knotted her stomach. She pictured a bear with long sharp claws lumbering toward her. How far away did Dusty say a bear could smell food? Twenty miles! A hungry bear had ripped apart the lodge's porch screen to eat a bag of dry dog food. And here she was, strapped to a food pack as heavy as a refrigerator, filled with thawing steaks, cheese-stuffed potatoes, and cartons of homemade cookies.

Heavy footsteps thumped behind her. Roxy tried to run, but the pack's immense weight held her back, giving her the feeling of moving in slow motion. Something grabbed the pack and yanked it, throwing her to the ground. She landed hard on her left side. The impact forced all the breath out of her. Dazed and in pain, she struggled to refill her lungs.

She heard gruff, growling sounds. Adrenaline surged, giving her the strength to roll her body into a tight, crouched position, like a turtle with a heavy canvas pack shell. Her beating heart thundered inside her chest as something wrestled the pack back and forth. A hot pain ignited in her upper arm and she let out a scream. Instinctively, she lurched herself sideways, off the narrow path. The heavy pack pulled her down the steep hill. She struck her head and abruptly stopped.

When she opened her eyes, she saw leafy branches, inches away from her face. She was lying under a tree, with the lumpy pack beneath her. She tried lifting her hands to unbuckle the chest strap, but both shoulder straps had slipped down her arms. They dug into the soft skin below each elbow, restricting her arm movement.

She squirmed, but the straps gripped her arms tightly, and the pack's heavy weight kept her pinned to the ground.

Branches cracked. Lumbering footsteps approached, accompanied by growling, guttural sounds. A dark form loomed over her, obscured by the leafy branches. Wild panic gripped her, and she began screaming. Something struck her head, triggering a pulsing pain. A low humming sound began pulsing with the pain. The humming penetrated deep inside her brain, drowning out the sound of her screams. The branches overhead whirled around, spinning faster and faster until their dizzying speed resonated with the loud droning hum. Roxy closed her eyes and sensed a comforting Presence. Peace settled over her like a warm blanket, as the Presence tucked her in. She breathed out a long sigh, and the world went silent.

The bright light hurt her eyes. Roxy squinted and let out a groan. The harsh glare vanished, and her eyes slowly focused on a face... a handsome face. His hair looked white against the light. An angel?

"Rox! You're awake!"

How does he know my name? Oh, of course, he's an angel.

"Hey Rox, how do you feel?"

Jo's voice. Is she in heaven, too?

Something cold touched her forehead, startling her. Her senses sharpened and she felt pain. She lifted her hand.

"Don't touch your forehead, Rox. I need to clean that cut." Jo kneeled down, and the man's face disappeared.

"I want him to take care of me… the angel."

The deep sound of laughter rang out somewhere above her.

Roxy realized she was lying on the ground and her head was resting against something lumpy. She felt a cold pressure on her forehead, and a dizzy feeling overwhelmed her. She closed her eyes and listened to the sound of familiar voices around her, fading in and out.

"Rox? Wake up."

She opened her eyes and focused on Trent's face.

"Do you think you can stand up?"

"I'll try."

"Put your hands behind my neck." He slid his arms around her and supported her as he lifted her to her feet. Roxy gasped at the stab of pain beneath her ribs. She leaned against him as the world spun around. Trent kept his arms around her for a long moment. "Are you still feeling dizzy?"

"Not as much." She wobbled as he let go, and then she regained her balance.

"Rox, look at me." Trent stood in front of her. "Follow my hand movement with your eyes, without moving your head."

She tracked his hand back and forth, feeling as if she was being mesmerized by a snake charmer.

"That's fine," Trent said. "Do you have a headache or any other pain?"

"No headache... but my ribs hurt."

"Can you give the pain a number, from one to ten?"

"Um... five or six..." Roxy glanced at Jo and blinked. She looked around at the concerned faces of her friends and smiled. Everyone seemed to breathe out a sigh.

"What happened, Rox?" Tara asked.

"I strapped on the food pack to see if it was still too heavy, and I heard noises and growling. I got hit from behind and I fell. Then I rolled down a hill. That's all I remember."

"Do you think it was a bear?" Bri's eyes widened.

"It's possible," Trent said. He turned to Jo. "Her ribs don't feel broken; they're probably bruised. Her eye tracking is normal, but she did lose consciousness for a time. Maybe I should take her back to the lodge—"

"No! Please, I'm feeling okay. Jo can keep an eye on me. She'll know if I start acting weirder than normal."

"Rox, how can I possibly know what's weirder than normal for you?" Jo was grinning, but the rims of her eyes looked red and swollen, as if she'd been crying.

Sally was standing behind Jo. "Rox, if you're sure..."

"I am, Sal. I'm fine to stay." She looked at Jo. "Can I take something for the pain?"

"Let's wait and see how you do. I can give you acetaminophen, later."

"Rox, I'm so glad you're all right!" Leeann held up her sunglasses.

"Thanks." Roxy slipped them on and then glanced down the steep hill. "How did I get back up here?"

"I carried you," Trent said. "Seth and I heard your screams as we were paddling to meet up with your group. We found you down by the creek, unconscious."

"The rest of us got here right after they did," Jo said. "When I saw you, and you weren't moving—" She shook her head and went quiet.

Roxy pictured the dark growling form looming over her. Chill bumps rose on her skin. She sent up a silent thankful prayer that she'd escaped without major injuries.

"We were all scared for you," Bri said. Her eyes also looked red, as if she'd been crying. "I'm glad my brothers are here."

Seth looked down at his sister and wrapped his arm around her thin shoulders.

"Oh... Hi, Seth. I didn't see you there." Roxy smiled.

He greeted her with a smile and a nod. Seth wasn't as talkative or outgoing as Trent. He stood slightly taller, and he was the only member of the Thorson family with brown hair, like his dad.

Bri looked at her brothers. "Can you stay and have dinner with us?"

Sally's posture stiffened. "We only have enough steaks for—"

"We can't stay," Trent said. "Seth and I caught a couple of nice bass, and we're going to fry them up for dinner."

"Where are you going to camp?" Bri asked.

"We'll find a good spot across the river," Seth said.

Before they left, Trent leaned over and kissed Roxy's cheek. "Babe... take it easy. Don't overdo it."

"I'll make sure she doesn't," Jo said.

"We'll all look out for her," Tara said. She took off her safari hat and used it to slap a bug on her arm.

"Okay, group. Let's go back to the campsite and get dinner started," Sally said.

"What about the food packs?" Roxy asked.

"Seth and I carried them to the site while Trent and Jo took care of you." Sally looked at her. "It's about a five or six minute walk. Are you up to it?"

"I am. But I probably won't be setting any speed record."

"I'll hang back with you, and walk at your pace," Jo said.

Sally nodded. "Okay group, let's get going."

Roxy's ribs ached as she walked with Jo down the narrow path. When they stopped a moment to rest, she ran her fingers through her tangled hair and frowned when she saw the dirt and bits of leaves in her hand. "Falling against trees is starting to become a habit." She touched the bandage on her forehead, aware of the stinging pain. "How bad is the cut, Jo?"

"It's a few inches long, but it's not deep enough for stitches. It's at the hairline, so the scar won't show." Jo dug out her pocket mirror.

Roxy gasped when she saw her reflection. Besides the large bruise on her cheek, tiny red scratches now covered her face. She tilted the mirror and saw the dark red spots on her t-shirt, above the setting sun graphic. The bloody sight triggered a mild wave of nausea. "My shirt is ruined!"

"I'll bet mom can get those stains out," Jo said.

Roxy shook her head as she handed Jo the mirror. "I'm an absolute mess!"

Jo wore a sympathetic grin. "Rox... I hate to say this. But you actually look like you were caught in a fan."

She laughed out loud, and then she doubled over and gripped her aching ribs.

Jo sat next to Roxy on a fallen tree trunk at the campsite and gently cleaned her scratched face with antiseptic wipes. She helped her remove her bloodstained t-shirt, and then she handed her a faded denim button-down shirt with Christmas trees embroidered on the collar. "I pulled this out of our personal pack."

"Thanks." Roxy slipped her arms through the sleeves and winced at the sharp pain in her ribcage. She buttoned the shirt one-handed, while Jo removed the dirt-covered bandage from her left arm.

"Your stitches look okay, Rox. No sign of infection. I have a bandage in my kit that's large enough to cover them and the new cut in your arm just above them. It's deeper than your forehead wound, but I think stitch strips will close it." After Jo cleaned and bandaged her arm, she tucked the first-aid kit inside the day pack.

Roxy shifted her position on the tree trunk to ease the soreness in her ribs. The trunk's smoothed surface held multiple hatchet marks. Two smoothed fallen trunks had been placed on each side of it, forming a U-shaped seating area around the campfire pit. Rocks had been placed around the circular pit, and ashes from a long-dead fire remained in the shallow depression.

Sally was kneeling a few feet away. She spread a bright green vinyl tablecloth over another fallen tree trunk, creating a lumpy work surface. She set the package of steaks on the tablecloth and began unwrapping the butcher paper. "Hey, Rox. Could you look through that pile of camping gear from the equipment pack and find the cooking grate? It goes inside the fire pit."

Roxy stood carefully, to minimize the pain. She walked to the spot where the equipment pack had been unloaded and retrieved the aluminum grate. She unfolded the legs, snapped them in place and set it inside the pit.

"Sal, I can't find the cheese-stuffed potatoes." Bri was on her knees, rummaging through the canvas food pack. "Oh! Here they are. They're squashed flat. All the food in here is smashed."

"That's the pack Rox was carrying when she fell," Sally said, as she opened a small salt container and seasoned the meat. "These thawed steaks are flattened, too."

"Doesn't pounding tenderize meat?" Roxy asked.

Sally grinned. "Rox, these are the most tenderized steaks I've ever seen."

"Look at this." Bri held up a canvas shoulder strap. "It's sliced, part way through."

"Trent pointed that out to me," Sally said. "He thought a bear claw could have sliced it, since the strap is so frayed."

Roxy shivered.

Tara walked into the campsite, carrying two clear one-gallon water jugs by the handles. The water in the jugs sloshed as she walked. Leeann followed her, carrying their life jackets. Both of them looked weary.

Sally glanced up. "Did you fill the jugs with deeper water, away from the shoreline? And did you turn over all the canoes, so they won't fill up if it rains?"

Tara nodded.

"Thanks. Now we need to purify the water."

"I have the tablets in my pocket," Jo said, as she walked up. "I'll take care of it."

"Good." Tara set both jugs next to a tree trunk in the seating area.

"We need to get the campfire started," Sally said. "Tara, you and Leeann can gather the wood. I brought some organic pine fire sticks to use as kindling."

"I'll need the hatchet," Tara said.

"It's over here." Roxy rummaged through the equipment pile. She found the hatchet and removed the leather sheath from its blade.

Tara took the hatchet from her and grinned like a child with a new toy.

"Remember," Sally said. "You can only chop downed limbs, not limbs from live trees."

Tara made a face. "I'm not trying to be a lumberjack, Sal."

Jo sat on a tree trunk and opened the water jugs. She counted out the purification tablets as she dropped them inside each jug. After replacing the caps, she shook the jugs to dissolve the tablets.

"In a half hour, this water will be ready to drink. I brought flavor packets we can use."

Roxy heard chopping sounds and glanced over her shoulder. Tara was leaning over a downed tree and swinging the hatchet. She whispered a prayer for her safety.

Tara carried several thick chopped limbs to the fire pit. Leeann followed, carrying an armful of smaller branches with shriveled dead leaves. Tara kneeled by the pit, placed the pine fire sticks inside and topped them with small branches and a few chopped limbs. Tara lit the pine sticks, and then she and Leeann fanned the tiny flames until the branches caught fire. Sally brought over the seasoned steaks and forked them onto the cooking grate, while Bri placed the smashed foil-covered potatoes in between the steaks.

After a few minutes, the flames roared up and licked the bottom of the elevated grate. The pungent scent of burning wood mingled with the delicious aroma of grilling steaks. Roxy gazed at the cooking meat and realized how hungry she was.

"Dinner's ready," Leeann said. "There's a bottle of hand sanitizer on the green tablecloth."

After everyone cleaned their hands, they gathered together as Jo said grace. They served themselves, like a buffet line and then sat on the tree trunks, balancing paper plates on their laps. Each plate held a steak, a cheesy smashed potato, snack-size raw carrots and an apple. An aluminum coffee pot sat on the cooking grate. A ribbon of steam poured from its spout as the coffee brewed with a percolating rhythm.

Roxy squeezed another ketchup packet on her meat. "This steak tastes great. I love the smoky flavor."

"Good thing you do," Sally said. "That's how all our cooked food is going to taste... like smoke."

"These potatoes are good, too." Tara dug her fork inside the crumpled foil and took another bite. She slapped a bug on her arm as she chewed.

After dinner, they sat around the campfire, eating Jo's chocolate brownie cookies and drinking decaf coffee in plastic travel mugs with lids, to keep out the bugs.

"The mosquitoes haven't been bad today, but I'm seeing more of them now," Jo said.

"They're always the worst at dusk and dawn," Sally said. "That's when they feed."

Tara let out a shout. She jumped up and tore the dryer sheets off her belt loops. "They've been feeding on me all day long! I need DEET!"

Leeann handed her a bottle of bug spray. "There is nothing I would not do, for those who are really my friends."

Tara stood a few feet away as she applied the spray. "Charlotte Bronte again?"

"No. Jane Austen, from Northanger Abbey," Leeann said.

Tara walked to the campfire and leaned over to toss in the dryer sheets.

"No! Don't throw them in the fire," Sally said. "There may be toxic chemicals in them."

Jo grinned. "Toxic chemicals that obviously don't repel mosquitoes."

"Tara, put all your dryer sheets in the garbage bag," Sally said. "Don't keep them in your tent tonight. The lavender scent might attract bears."

"But I've been wearing them all day. I'm covered with the scent."

Roxy and Jo exchanged glances. Tara would be sleeping in their tent tonight.

When they finished eating, Sally organized them into clean-up teams. While they worked, she kneeled by the two food packs. "This old canvas pack has been damaged, so I'll try to squeeze all the remaining food into the equipment pack." After she transferred the food, she stood and brushed the dirt off her camouflage pants. "Okay, round up anything with a scent that might attract bears, like snacks, gum and even breath mints. After you brush your teeth, bring your toothbrushes and toothpaste, too. They need to go in the pack."

Minutes later, they reported back to Sally. She held open a large zip-top bag as they dropped in their items. She zipped it shut, tucked it inside the food pack and tied up the garbage bag liner before closing the pack.

Tara grabbed a shoulder strap and tested its weight. "It's not crazy heavy, like the monster food pack. But it's still heavy."

Sally sighed. "Let's just hang it up." She retrieved a coiled rope from the equipment pile and tied one end around the pack's shoulder straps with a double square knot. Then she tied a rock to the rope's other end. "Tara, you're the pitcher on our Pet Wellness softball team. Can you toss this rock over that tree limb up there? It looks strong enough to hold the pack."

"No problem." Tara gripped the rock and threw it hard. It sailed over the limb. The group clapped for Tara, and she took a bow.

Sally grabbed the dangling rope and untied the rock. "Okay group, let's lift this." They all took hold of the rope and pulled hard, as if they were in a tug of war with the heavy pack. As it rose off the ground, its weight caused the outer flap to gap open on both sides. "Stop for a minute," Sally said. "We should cover those gaps, or the pack might give off a food odor."

"Let's use the green tablecloth to cover the pack," Leeann said. She let go of the rope while the others held on tight. The pack swung at waist-height as she unfolded the tablecloth. "I'll need help to tape it on."

"I'll help." Roxy let go of the rope and retrieved the silver duct tape. She applied strips of tape to the green tablecloth, while Leeann held it in place. After they finished, they took hold of the rope again. Everyone pulled together in spurts, lifting the pack a little higher each time. The rope finally snagged on a branch and wouldn't budge. Sally tied the rope around a nearby tree trunk. The huge pack swung back and forth just above their heads.

"Didn't Dusty say it was supposed to be twenty feet off the ground?" Leeann asked.

"No," Sally said. "Only eight feet."

"That's about six feet," Roxy said. "Close enough."

"Yeah, close enough for a bear to get at it," Tara said.

Bri gazed at the dangling pack. "You know, it's kind of pretty, wrapped in that bright green tablecloth."

Jo giggled. "It looks like a lumpy piñata at a bear cub's birthday party."

Everyone laughed except Sally, who wore a frustrated look. "It's the best we can do."

"Hey, look at the sunset." Leeann pointed through a large gap in the trees. The sun hovered over the horizon like a glowing orange ball in the sunset sky, and the river's calm surface reflected the vibrant colors. "It reminds me of the graphic on our group t-shirts."

"Without the canoe," Jo said.

Roxy grinned. "Floating or overturned?"

"The sky is clear, perfect for star gazing tonight," Sally said. "The best spot to see them is over there, where the path to the river begins. It has less tree cover."

"The mosquitoes are swarming." Tara used her safari hat to wave them away. "Let's put on our bug suits."

Several minutes later, they were sitting around the campfire, wearing hats with nets covering their faces, and nylon net jackets and pants over their clothes. As darkness settled around them, Tara stoked the fire, and its yellow flames roared upward.

"Look at us, in these bug suits," Roxy said. "We look spooky in the firelight."

"It's these netted beekeeper hats," Tara said.

Sally grinned. "We look like invaders from another planet."

"Yeah," Jo giggled. "Invasion of the alien beekeepers."

Roxy heard high-pitched buzzing sounds around her. Dozens of mosquitoes landed on her netted suit and moved around, as if they were looking for an entry hole. She watched them, feeling a mixture of repulsion and fascination.

They went quiet. The burning limbs snapped and cracked against the background of crickets chirping. Glowing red sparks rose from the gyrating flames and merged with the gray smoke curling upward toward the dark sky. Heat from the crackling campfire warmed Roxy's face, arms and legs. As she sat in the flickering firelight and gazed at the netted faces of her closest friends, a powerful feeling of love and gratitude surged. She remembered something she'd learned in her grief counseling group, about savoring the special moments in life.

This was one of them.

"I like the sound of crickets," Leeann whispered. "What I don't want to hear tonight is a bear growling. That food pack is like a gift-wrapped bag of treats."

"Don't worry," Sally said. "If a bear wanders into our camp, he'll be more interested in our food pack, than us."

"You hope," Bri said.

Roxy shuddered, picturing the growling dark form. She rubbed her aching side and turned to Jo. "Can I take something for the pain now?"

"Do you have a headache, or any dizziness?"

"No, it's for my ribs."

"Okay." She pulled a plastic bottle from her pocket.

Roxy took two tablets with a long drink of decaf coffee.

Sally yawned. "It's been a tiring day, but a good day."

The others responded with yawns.

"Looks like we all need sleep," Sally said. "Tara and Leeann, pour the leftover coffee on the fire to douse it and then bury the coffee grounds. The rest of you can help me cover our packs with a tarp in case it rains tonight."

When the last chores were done, they bid each other goodnight and then broke into two groups. Inside Jo's orange tent, flashlight beams gave the interior a soft glow. Three sleeping bags sat side-by-side, on top of foam mats. Jo's bag sat in the middle. The four-person tent gave them extra room for their water bottles, rain jackets and sandwich bag purses. Shadows moved on the tent walls as the three women got ready for bed. One by one, they snuggled into their sleeping bags.

"Lights out," Jo said. She switched off her flashlight, and the tent went dark.

Roxy fidgeted until she found a position that didn't put pressure on her sore ribs. Then she relaxed and listened to the crickets chirping and the muted voices in the other tent.

"It's stuffy in here." Jo unzipped her bag. "I'm going to open the window flaps so a breeze can flow through the screens." She stood and walked to the window above Tara's sleeping bag.

"Ouch," Tara said. "You stepped on my leg."

"Sorry," Jo said. "I'm so tired, I'm loopy."

"Where's your flashlight?"

"I forgot it." The zipper on the window flap made a metallic buzzing sound.

"Watch out, Rox. She's heading your way to unzip the other one," Tara said.

"I'll sit up, so you won't trample my legs." Roxy rose to a sitting position and let out a soft groan as pain pinched her ribs.

Jo unzipped the window flap above Roxy and then settled back into her sleeping bag.

"It feels cooler in here, already," Tara said.

Roxy heard a high-pitched buzzing sound near her ear. She slapped at a hot sting on her neck. More buzzing sounds followed, and slapping sounds filled the dark tent.

Tara groaned. "There are a lot of mosquitoes in here."

"That's strange," Jo said. "We were careful to zip up the door right away, when we all came inside the tent."

Roxy slapped at another sting. "This is awful! I'm putting on my bug hat." She propped herself on an elbow and winced at the pain in her side as she felt around for her hat in the dark tent. She found her flashlight and switched it on, sweeping its light beam across the tent walls.

"Hey, Rox. I just saw something." Tara unzipped her bag and scrambled to her feet. "Shine the light over here."

She aimed the beam and caught Tara looking out the tent window. "Jo, I don't see a screen on this window. Did you unzip the window flap and the screen?"

"How stupid do you think I am?"

"We won't answer that," Roxy said.

Tara stretched her arm out the window. "Jo! The screen is unzipped!"

"It can't be!" Jo rose to her feet so fast, she stumbled against Roxy. "Ouch!"

"Sorry, Rox." Jo hurried to the window. "Oh my gosh! The screen is unzipped!" She stepped on Tara's foot as she reached for the zipper and then giggled.

"Ouch! Jo, what is wrong with you tonight?" Tara started giggling as she helped her zip the screen closed.

Roxy swung the beam around and aimed it above her head. "News flash! This window screen is unzipped, too!" Pain stabbed her side as she stood and zipped it closed. Then she sank to her knees, feeling utterly worn out and weary. She'd endured a bear attack, her ribs ached, her arm and forehead throbbed, and now mosquitoes were swarming all around her. "This isn't a tent, it's a torture chamber!" Her frustration triggered a burst of hysterical laughter. Then she groaned at the pain in her ribcage.

Tara giggled. "This is a torture chamber! Look at that!" She aimed her flashlight beam at the scattered dark patches of insects crawling on the tent's orange ceiling.

"We're in a mosquito horror movie!" Jo said, in between giggles.

The giggling continued as they swatted mosquitoes and searched for their bug hats. After they put them on, they settled into their sleeping bags and switched off their flashlights. High-pitched buzzing sounds filled the dark tent.

Tara whispered, "Now that the screens are closed, the mosquitoes are trapped in here with us."

"Don't you mean, we're trapped in here with them?" Roxy asked.

The giggling started again.

"What's going on over there?" Sally sounded irritated.

"Houston... we have a problem," Jo said, as another giggle escaped.

Roxy giggled. "Our tent is full of mosquitoes, and we're absolutely miserable."

"If we weren't laughing, we'd be crying," Tara said.

Muffled giggling began in the other tent. Leeann and Bri.

"You're making us miserable," Sally said. "Quiet down so we can sleep!"

The three of them giggled softly and then hushed each other, like guilty children after a scolding.

After a moment, Jo whispered, "I forgot to put on my night braces." She switched on her flashlight and pulled a plastic case and a mirror from her jacket pocket. She took off her bug hat and aimed the beam at her mouth as she put on the braces. Then she switched off the flashlight. "Okay, all done."

"Jo," Roxy whispered. "Something's glowing in your mouth!"

"What?"

"There it is, again," Roxy said.

Tara sat up. "Let me see it. Smile, Jo."

"Like this?" She made a wide smile, and her teeth glowed like yellow dentures, suspended in the pitch darkness.

Tara and Roxy burst out laughing and then shushed each other.

"Rox, what is it?" Jo asked, as her glowing teeth moved.

"You look like a jack-o-lantern!"

Jo giggled. "It must be my invisible night braces."

"Well, they're not invisible," Tara said.

Jo aimed the flashlight beam at her teeth again and switched it off. Her teeth glowed even brighter as she looked into her mirror. "Wow! I got these new braces two weeks ago. Why hasn't Charlie said anything about it?"

"Maybe Charlie isn't interested in looking at your teeth when you're in bed," Roxy said.

They all burst out laughing.

"Will you quiet down?" Sally's voice.

They giggled softly in the darkness, and then they went quiet. Against the backdrop of crickets chirping and mosquitoes buzzing, an owl let out a deep hooting call.

Roxy awoke in total darkness and heard hushed voices outside. Tara and Jo. She felt around for her flashlight and switched it on. Their sleeping bags sat crumpled in a corner, and their mats were gone. She grabbed her mat and slowly unzipped the door. After she crawled out, she zipped it closed. Her ribs ached as she sat on the damp ground and strapped on her hiking sandals. As she stood up, the pain sent tears to her eyes. She followed her flashlight beam as she walked over to Tara and Jo, who were stretched out on their mats, gazing at the night sky.

"Take off your bug hat," Tara whispered. "The mosquito feeding frenzy is over."

Roxy positioned her mat next to Jo. She removed her bug hat, switched off her flashlight and gingerly stretched out on her back.

"Look at all the stars..." Jo's hushed voice carried a tone of reverence.

Starlight filled every inch of the panoramic night sky. Its stunning brilliance held Roxy spellbound. In the densely-packed areas, the stars resembled glittering clouds. In other areas, pinpoints of light pulsed with an intense clarity, giving the illusion the stars were suspended within easy reach. A bright streak of light raced across the sparkling sky.

"I just saw a shooting star," Tara whispered. "This sky is so beautiful... it shows just how awesome the universe is."

"It was designed by an awesome God," Jo whispered. "In my nursing classes, I remember being amazed at the intricate design of the human body… the brain, the heart, the nervous system… the way everything works together."

"Yeah," Roxy said, keeping her voice hushed. "And then there's the complexity of DNA, unique in everyone."

"Ian told me something amazing the other day," Tara said, her voice unusually soft. "He said he can hear colors. Every color has its own tone, and a rainbow is like a harmonic musical chord. I think it makes sense, colors having musical tones. I mean, tones have distinct audible wavelengths and colors have visual wavelengths. Children with Asperger's have a heightened sensitivity. Ian can hear the music in colors, while the rest of us can't."

Roxy gazed at the mesmerizing starry sky, feeling a childlike sense of wonder. Its vast staggering beauty gave rise to thoughts about God… the cycle of birth, death, and rebirth into eternal life. She thought about the people she had loved and lost, especially Vance. A warm tear streamed down the side of her face. The air immediately chilled its wet track. She whispered, "Heaven must look like this."

"I'm sure heaven is more wonderful than we can imagine—" Tara's voice choked.

Roxy sighed, knowing she was thinking of Nikki.

They gazed at the sky in silence for a while, speaking only to point out shooting stars.

"This is beautiful, but I'm having a hard time staying awake." Tara rose to her feet and picked up her mat.

Roxy kept her focus on the brilliant sky as she listened to Tara's footsteps on the hard-packed ground, the buzzing zipper on the tent door and the rustling of her sleeping bag.

"Rox, when you talked about heaven, you were thinking about Vance, weren't you?"

"I was…" She paused and let out a sigh. "You know how hard it was… losing him like that. For a while, life seemed so hopeless. Every day, I forced myself to get up, get dressed and show up. But I was just going through the motions. Some mornings, I didn't think I had the energy to face another day."

"Oh, Rox..."

"Yeah. It scared me, too."

"What do you think helped you the most, the grief counseling or the antidepressant?"

"They both helped, in different ways. But I think my healing really started when I figured out the root cause of my hopelessness." A bright shooting star caught her attention. It streaked across the glittering sky, as if an unseen hand had tossed it.

"What was the cause, Rox?"

"My grief... not just for Vance, but for everyone I've lost. Feelings of sadness and loss overwhelmed me, and my focus got stuck on it. Through counseling, I realized I've always felt alone... like an outsider, without my parents. Aunt Nell and Uncle Cal were wonderful. But you could call them mom and dad, and I couldn't. When Vance and I tried to start a family, I had two miscarriages. Then I lost him, too. And before that, Trent left me, and I gave our daughter up for adoption."

"You've had a lot of loss..."

"We all have loss, Jo. It's part of living in this imperfect world. We can't choose what happens to us, but we can choose how we respond to it. Our attitude... our focus. I realized I felt hopeless because I was focused on me. It was like I was staring into a mirror, and I couldn't see anything but myself... my pain... my grief. I began healing when I chose to shift my focus away from that mirror."

"How did you do that?"

"I started my gratitude journal and began focusing on my blessings, not my losses. It helped me to appreciate the people in my life and the good things God has given me, out of His great love. As soon as I shifted my focus away from myself, I didn't feel as lonely. I saw the people around me again, and I became aware of their needs, their pain, and their grief... not just mine. And I saw ways I could help. When I started reaching out to them and making a positive difference, I regained my hope... a sense of meaning and purpose in my life."

"Rox, that's what Jesus taught."

Both of them sighed softly. The breeze stirred the leafy branches overhead, as if the trees were whispering to each other. Roxy's eyelids closed and fluttered open. She struggled to view the dazzling stars and finally gave up. "I need sleep," she said, yawning.

Jo caught her yawn. "Me, too."

As they picked up their mats and bug hats, Roxy whispered, "I can't believe we haven't been bothered by mosquitoes out here. Maybe it's that breeze off the river."

"Or maybe all the mosquitoes are trapped in our tent," Jo said, giggling.

They giggled and then hushed each other as they walked in the darkness, following the waving beams of their flashlights.

Tuesday morning

Roxy listened to the breeze rustling through the trees and the musical chirping of songbirds. One of them chirped a repetitive three-note song, "get up now, get up now." She glanced at Jo and Tara, who remained snuggled inside their sleeping bags, breathing softly. When she slowly sat up, pain stabbed her ribs. She clenched her teeth together to keep from crying out as she slid out of her sleeping bag. She unzipped the door in short spurts, crawled out and slowly zipped it closed.

Roxy strapped on her hiking sandals and gripped her side as she rose to her feet. Humidity weighed down the warm morning air. She walked to the spot where they had seen the sunset and gazed at the river. Its mirror-like surface reflected the overcast gray sky.

Jo emerged from the tent and slowly zipped the door closed. She joined Roxy and whispered, "How are you feeling? Any headache or nausea?"

"I'm fine, nurse Jo." Roxy gave her a smile. "Can I use your dry shampoo this morning? My hair smells smoky, and I still have dirt in it."

"I put the shampoo inside the food pack because of its vanilla scent," Jo said. "Let's lower the pack and get our toothbrushes and toothpaste, too. We can go down to the river and clean up."

As they untied the rope holding up the pack, it slipped through their hands. The pack hit the ground with a forceful thump. A flurry of leaves landed on top of it. They stood still, listening. When they heard sleep breathing coming from both tents, they giggled and then hushed each other. They gathered items from the food pack and then retrieved clean clothes and chamois towels from their personal pack. After filling travel mugs with water, they headed down the path to the river. Roxy piled her items on an overturned canoe and then sat on the fallen tree trunk near the shoreline. "Jo, I might need help with the shampoo. My side aches, and it's hard to lift my arm."

"You should take off your shirt, first. That shampoo can be messy, and I want to check your bandages." Jo helped her slip her arms out of the sleeves and then stared at her. "Look at that huge bruise on your left side! No wonder you're in pain." She quickly probed the area.

"Ouch! Don't touch it, Jo! Trent said he didn't think I broke anything."

"Sorry." Jo checked the bandages on her forehead and arm. "They look okay. No need to change them, right now." She stood behind Roxy and gently ran a comb through her tangled waves. Then she sprayed on the shampoo foam and worked it through her hair. "Remember, I charge a twenty-percent tip for my beauty services."

Roxy grinned. "Your check is in the mail."

They washed their faces with biodegradable soap and brushed their teeth. Then they stood behind a thick stand of trees as they changed into clean clothes. When Roxy returned to the overturned canoe, she heard the sound of paddles in the water. A canoe was heading toward shore. Trent sat in the bow seat, looking at her.

"I don't see fishing poles," Jo said, as she joined Roxy. "Is this a social call?"

"Sort of," Trent said. "We remembered to pack a coffee pot but forgot the coffee. Can we borrow some?"

"Sure, we have plenty of coffee in our food pack," Roxy said.

"You must have plenty of everything in that heavy pack," Seth said, as he steered the canoe toward shore. "I carried it to your campsite yesterday."

Roxy watched as they landed the canoe and stepped out. Both brothers wore cargo shorts and fishing shirts. She pictured Kyle wearing a similar outfit on Saturday, when he came for breakfast. That was only three days ago, but it seemed like weeks.

Trent tied the bow rope to a tree and then walked over to Roxy. "Babe, are you feeling okay?"

She nodded.

"Aren't you rushing the season a bit?" He pointed to her t-shirt.

Roxy glanced down at the smiling Santa Claus graphic. "Oh, I packed for the trip in a hurry. This is a Salvadore Armani shirt."

Seth looked puzzled. "It's a what?"

"She bought it at a thrift shop," Trent said, grinning.

"Come on, we'll get you some coffee." Jo led the way up the path. "Keep your voices down. The others might still be sleeping." At that moment, loud chopping sounds rang out. "Well, Tara's awake."

When the brothers reached the campsite, they stopped and stared at the huge lump on the ground, partially-wrapped in a bright green tablecloth and silver duct tape. Their expressions wavered between curiosity and amazement.

"What is that?" Seth asked, his voice hushed.

"Our food pack," Roxy said.

Trent let out a soft laugh. "It looks like the gift sack Santa carries in his sleigh." He nodded at her Santa Claus t-shirt. "It fits with the Christmas theme you've got going."

Seth continued gazing at the pack, as if he thought it might contain a Christmas gift he'd been hoping for.

Tara and Leeann called out a greeting as they walked toward the campfire pit, carrying branches and chopped limbs.

"What's going on out there?" Sally's voice held a sleepy, irritated tone.

Jo said, "Trent and Seth came over—"

"What were they doing here?"

"Sal, they're still here."

The zipper on her tent door opened, and Sally peeked out and smiled. "Hi, there. I'll come out in a minute." She snatched both pair of hiking sandals sitting outside the tent and disappeared inside. Moments later, she crawled out, wearing red hiking sandals, camouflage cargo pants and a pink flowered bathrobe with rose-shaped buttons.

Trent let out a laugh and then coughed violently. Seth had a coughing fit of his own.

Bri crawled out after Sally, wearing gray cargo pants, a pink t-shirt and her pink and gray hiking sandals. Her hair had been styled in a French braid, and she was wearing full make-up, including bright pink lipstick. She looked at her brothers. "How long have you been here?"

"Not long. We came to borrow coffee." Seth smiled at her. He looked as if he was tempted to tousle her hair but thought better of it.

"Why don't you stay and have coffee with us?" Bri asked.

"Look at this mess!" Jo was kneeling next to the food pack. She held up a coffee package covered with white dust. "The box of pancake mix got crushed inside the pack, and flour exploded everywhere."

"We have pancake mix in our food pack," Trent said.

"Go get it," Bri said. "We can all have breakfast together."

Trent and Seth looked at Sally.

She smiled. "Sounds like a plan."

After the brothers left, Roxy filled the coffee pot, added the grounds and set it on the metal grate. Flames rose up from the campfire and brushed against the bottom of the pot.

Tara glanced at Bri. "You weren't kidding about wearing makeup out here."

"I like that lipstick color," Leeann said.

Bri smiled. "It's called Tickled Pink. I brought several samples of it." She reached into her pocket and handed Leeann a miniature lipstick tube. She turned to Roxy. "Would you like a makeover?

I brought foundation cream with aloe. It'll help the scratches on your face to heal."

Roxy sat on a tree trunk near the campfire while Bri worked on her face. A few minutes later, she gazed at her reflection in Bri's pocket mirror. "Thanks! What a difference."

"Rox, you look great," Sally said. She had spread the green tablecloth over the fallen tree trunk, and she was kneeling next to it, spreading oil on the surface of a fry pan. Remnants of duct tape remained stuck to the tablecloth's vinyl surface.

Jo was kneeling next to her, peeling and sectioning oranges. She glanced up and gave Roxy an approving smile.

Bri turned to Leeann and Tara. "Which one of you wants to be next?"

Trent and Seth walked into the campsite.

"I was wondering what happened to you two." Sally stood and took the box of pancake mix from Seth. She started reading the directions.

Trent moved toward Roxy and rested his hand on her arm. "We still haven't had a chance to talk, alone. Can we do that now?"

"I guess so..."

He placed his hand at the small of her back as they started down the path to the river.

Roxy stepped to the side and then walked slightly behind him.

Trent sat on the fallen tree trunk near shore and patted the spot next to him.

Roxy chose a spot that put more distance between them.

He swiveled to face her. The breeze tossed around his longish hair, and his facial stubble had grown into a light beard. Trent smiled. "Babe, you look great. Bri said she planned to do makeovers."

Roxy read his intense gaze and looked away, toward the river. The overcast sky appeared darker, and the humid breeze held the scent of impending rain.

"Have you had any headaches?" Trent asked.

"Don't worry. Nurse Jo has been watching over me, like a guardian angel."

He chuckled. "You called me an angel yesterday, after you regained consciousness."

She turned and looked at him. "Seriously?"

He nodded. "Nobody's ever called me that, before."

"I must have been delirious."

Trent laughed out loud, and then he went quiet, as if he wasn't sure what to say next. "Rox, tell me about your life. Do you like working for the post office... when you're not rescuing poodles from sinkholes?"

She smiled. "I've had the same mail route for so long, everyone on it seems like family. My favorite mail stop is the Senior Living Center, where Grandpa Leo lives."

"Does he still call you Roxy-girl?"

She nodded. "What about you? Do you like being an EMT? You always said you wanted to be a doctor."

His expression soured. "I had a wife and son to support. There was no way I could pay for college, let alone medical school. But I like my job. It's never boring. Sometimes people go out of their way to thank us. Women have even given out their phone numbers—" He stopped and glanced away.

"Have you called any of them?" The question came out before she could stop herself. She let it hang in the air. When he glanced back, she read the answer in his eyes. It didn't surprise her.

"Rox, why did you give up your scholarship? You had your heart set on college."

An image of their newborn daughter flashed into her mind, and she tensed. They were alone now. It was time. She took a deep breath and said, "There's something I need to tell—"

"Did I really hurt you that bad?"

She blinked. His question had struck a raw nerve. "What do you think? You ran off with Celia without saying one word to me. Of course, that hurt!"

He leaned down and picked up a small flat rock. He stared at it as he rolled it in his hand. "I just couldn't face you, Rox. The family pressured me to marry—"

"Come on, Trent! You got Celia pregnant while we were engaged."

He frowned and threw the rock into the river. It skipped the surface, creating a pattern of ripples, radiating outward.

She sighed. "It hurt, thinking of you with Celia. But it hurt even more when I called you, and you were so abusive to me."

"You called me, after I was married?"

"I called you about a month after you eloped. You and Celia had just moved to St. Paul. Don't you remember?"

He shook his head. "How was I abusive? What did I say?"

"You told me to stay out of your life. You sounded drunk... you were shouting and cursing."

He sighed and gazed at the river. "I was drinking a lot back then, drowning my sorrows, as they say. I had a lot of anger inside, Rox. I'm not trying to make excuses, it's just the way I was... a binge drinker. I stayed sober when I pulled my shifts, and I drank on my days off. Drinking only made me angrier. I'm still trying to patch things up with my son, TJ." He paused. "I stopped drinking three years ago."

"After you got shot?"

He nodded, and then he opened the top buttons on his shirt and revealed his upper left chest. "Two bullets. One barely missed my pulmonary artery."

Roxy caught her breath when she saw the ugly scars of violence; two dark cratered areas, connected by a jagged discolored line.

"There was a brawl outside a St. Paul bar at closing time, and we were called to assist a shooting victim. Someone shot at us, and I was the unlucky one." He paused. "When I was recovering from surgery, I had a lot of time to think about my life, and how alcohol was controlling it. I gave AA a try, and now I'm an AA sponsor." He buttoned his shirt and looked at her, searching her face.

Roxy sensed he expected to see disappointment or condemnation. She smiled and said, "You chose to reclaim your life... after you almost lost it."

His handsome features relaxed.

"Kyle is an AA sponsor, too."

Trent briefly frowned, and then he reached for her hand, her left hand. As he held it, he brushed her empty ring finger with his thumb. "It was always so good with you. I wish there was some way to turn back time and change what happened between us."

"Don't." She pulled her hand away.

He looked directly into her eyes. "Babe, I've never stopped loving you—"

"Stop calling me that!" She shook her head. "You say you love me... but I've been single for two full years, and you never reached out to me. Not once. Not even to offer your sympathy. I don't get it. You were divorced, there was nothing stopping you."

"I thought about you, a lot. I even started to call you a few times, but I wasn't sure you'd want to hear from me. I mean, the last time we talked, you hung up on me, and—"

"Trent! There's only one time I ever hung up on you." She stared at him and read the guilty look on his face. "You lied about not remembering my phone call!"

He glanced away.

"Lies! You told me so many lies, and I was so in love with you, I believed them all! You haven't changed!"

He turned back to her. "I have changed! I'll never treat you like that again—"

"No! I don't want to hear it!" Roxy heard the vibration in her voice. She rose to her feet. "Trent, there's something you need to know. I called you after you were married to tell—"

"Rox, I was drunk—"

"Let me finish!"

His eyes widened. He stood and faced her, as if he suddenly realized the importance of what she was about to say.

"I called to tell you I was pregnant."

He stared at her. "Rox... we could have had a child together..."

She startled. "You think I had an abortion?"

"Didn't you?"

"We have a daughter, Trent."

He gripped her arms. "Where is she?"

"I gave her up for adoption."

He let go of her and stood, looking dazed. "Bri said she suspected you were pregnant, when you moved to Orlando to live with your grandparents."

Roxy nodded. "She was born in late January, the day your mom..." She paused. "I'm sorry. I didn't hear about her funeral until a few days later."

Trent's face contorted with emotion. He kicked the fallen trunk. "Why didn't you tell me I had a daughter? I had a right to know!"

His anger acted like a match, and flames roared up inside her. "I tried to tell you when I called you, but you never gave me the chance! You were shouting at me! You said, 'Get out of my life and stay out!' Those were your exact words!" She paused, as her pounding heart sent blood rushing past her ears. "Do you think it was easy for me, carrying your baby for months after the way you threw me out of your life? I listed the father as unknown on her birth certificate, so I could sever all ties with you! That's what you wanted, wasn't it?"

Trent wore a shocked look, as if she had slapped him.

His stricken expression unleashed a flood of regret, dousing the fire of her anger. Tears blurred her eyes as she looked at him. "Oh, Trent. Here we are... still hurting each other, after all these years." She turned away and hurried up the narrow dirt path. She nearly bumped into Jo and Bri. They each held a travel mug, presumably bringing fresh coffee to them.

Bri's expression told her she had overheard everything.

Roxy let out a sob. "I'm sorry... I should have told you and your family a long time ago."

"It's okay," Bri's voice came out in a whisper. "I've always wanted us to be sisters, and now we are, in a way." She reached out, and they hugged each other for a long moment.

Roxy blinked away tears. "I shouldn't have gotten so angry when I told Trent about her."

"I'll go talk to him." Bri's eyes glistened with emotion. "Rox, everything in the past... how Trent hurt you... how you hurt him, it's over and done. You two have a daughter. And I have a niece, somewhere. That's an incredible blessing, and I'm going to make sure my brother understands that." She headed down to the river.

Roxy covered her face and let out another sob. "Jo, why didn't I tell Trent about her years ago? And Vance... why didn't I tell him?"

"Bri is right, Rox. You need to let go of the past." Jo handed Roxy the travel mug. "I think your coffee's still warm, and there's a decadent breakfast waiting for you. We added crumbled chocolate chip cookies to the pancake batter."

The pancakes tasted even more decadent, drenched in maple syrup. Roxy sat by the campfire and ate another forkful, savoring the sweet combination of maple and chocolate. She had just finished telling everyone about her daughter with Trent, and she felt a sense of profound relief. She looked around, taking in everyone's expression. Seth's look of surprise had melted into a smile, but the others hadn't appeared surprised at all. They sat quietly, their complexions glowing after Bri's makeovers.

"Rox," Sally said. "I knew it had to be something like a pregnancy, to make you give up your scholarship."

"We suspected it, too," Tara said, glancing at Leeann.

Bri walked into the campsite. She gave Roxy a quick smile, and then she turned to Seth. "Trent's waiting for you by the river. He wants to get back to the campsite and pack up."

Seth stood and thanked everyone for breakfast. He glanced at Roxy and his smile widened as he gave her a nod. Then he and Bri headed down the path to the river.

Roxy fought the urge to follow them and smooth things over with Trent. She regretted her angry words, but she also sensed he needed more time to adjust to the shock of learning about his daughter.

A gust of wind blew a stack of paper plates off the green tablecloth and bounced them along the ground. Tara and Leeann scrambled to retrieve them. Sally pointed to the dark clouds rolling in. "Let's start packing up. Gore's Landing is only a mile downstream. We might have enough time to paddle there before the rain starts."

Tara doused the campfire and cleaned the coffee pot and grill while the others worked together, packing up the food and equipment and taking down the tents.

Minutes later, Bri ran into the campsite. She stopped, breathing heavily. It took a moment before she could speak. "People in kayaks paddled by... they have a satellite phone... that tropical storm in the Gulf... made landfall at Cedar Key... it's heading our way!"

"Okay group. Let's pack up fast. Put on your rain jackets and take off your hiking sandals. Your boots will give you more traction in the mud."

It took three round-trips to carry all the packs to the shore-line. On each trip, the wind tore through the tree branches with increasing violence. When they reached the shoreline on the last trip, the sky grew suddenly darker, as if someone had turned out the lights. The wind increased, whipping the river's surface into a white-capped frenzy. The black clouds unleashed a downpour. Rain pelted Roxy's face with stinging force. Tree debris swirled around her. A leafy limb struck her leg.

Cracking sounds rang out, and the ground shook as a nearby tree toppled over. Bri screamed and gripped Roxy's arm. Sally pointed to the old growth cypress. The roaring wind extinguished the sound of her voice. She herded them around the massive trunk, and they ducked inside the hollow space, one by one. They sat on the hard ground, huddled close together with their knees drawn up and their backs pressed against the rough trunk. Roxy and Sally sat on each side of the opening, with one shoulder exposed to the pelting rain. They raised the hoods on their rain jackets and hunkered down.

The wind's eerie howling and the ground-shaking thumps of falling trees reverberated inside the hollow void. Fear squeezed Roxy's stomach like an icy hand. Her entire body trembled as she whispered the same prayer, over and over. A deafening crack sounded, followed by a thundering crash that sent a vibrating shock wave through the cypress trunk. Screams rang out. Roxy glanced over her shoulder at the profusion of green branches blocking the opening.

Sally shouted, "A tree fell right next to us." Her voice produced a strange echo.

After what seemed like hours, the wind's howling eased. Roxy heard the ragged, uneven breathing of her friends and an occasional whimper. Sally brushed against Roxy's shoulder as she crawled outside, over the tree branches. Moments later, she let out a startled shout.

Roxy turned and followed her. Pain pinched her ribs as she pushed aside the sharp broken branches and climbed over the fallen tree trunk. She rose to her feet and then stood, stunned by the startling devastation. Fallen trees covered the ground, some stacked on top of each other. Cracked limbs dangled from the trees snapped in half. Their jagged trunks pointed toward the overcast sky. Only the most resilient palms had escaped destruction.

The others began crawling out. For a wild moment, Roxy felt as if she had crash landed on another planet, and her fellow explorers were emerging from the wrecked spaceship. They exchanged looks of shock and disbelief as they viewed the strange new landscape.

Sally stood with her hands on her hips. She wore a determined expression, as if she was creating a list in her mind, figuring out how to work around this setback. "Is anyone hurt?"

They all shook their heads.

Roxy stepped toward the old growth cypress and rested her hand on its massive rough trunk. It had remained standing, firmly rooted through this storm... and countless other storms, for a thousand years. Yesterday, its hollow trunk had felt like an ancient holy place. And today, it had served as a sanctuary for all of them. She offered up a silent thankful prayer.

Sally pointed to the overturned canoes, covered with layers of soggy tree debris. "Our canoes aren't damaged by any fallen tree trunks. That's a relief."

"But a huge tree fell on top of our packs," Jo said.

Tara headed toward the spot. Her boots produced sharp cracking sounds as she stepped on the leafy tree debris. She leaned down and tore branches off the tree's upper limbs. "I can see our equipment pack. If we break off a few more branches, we can drag it out and get the hatchet. Then I can free the rest of the packs."

Sally stepped over the tree debris and joined her. "I knew you had a secret desire to be a lumberjack."

Tara looked at her and grinned. Together, they began tearing away branches. Roxy pitched in, feeling grateful for the sturdy gloves Kyle had given her. Jo, Leeann and Bri began removing the layers of branches covering the canoes.

"Ouch!" Sally held up her left hand. Blood trickled from her palm. "These cracked branches are as sharp as knives!"

"You need to get that cut taken care of," Roxy said.

Sally continued tearing off branches with her right hand. "First, we need to find the day pack. The medical kit is inside it."

After they freed the equipment pack, Tara dug around inside until she found the hatchet. Then she began chopping away the larger limbs.

"I see the day pack!" Roxy tugged hard, freeing it from its leafy prison. She handed it to Sally and convinced her to take a break so Jo could bandage her hand.

"There's a water jug!" Tara pulled it out. "It's still half full."

Leeann retrieved the travel mugs from the equipment pack, and they all took a water break. Bri took a drink, and then she tensed, choking on the water. She coughed and pointed toward the river. "I see my brothers!" Tears rolled down her face as she waved her arms.

As their canoe neared shore, Trent shouted, "Is everyone all right?"

"We're okay!" Bri called out.

The brothers landed the canoe. Bri stumbled over a pile of branches as she hurried toward them. As she hugged them, she broke into loud sobs.

Seth pulled a hatchet from his equipment pack and worked with Tara to retrieve the rest of the packs. They freed the food pack last. Sally suggested they have something to eat before starting out.

Leeann passed around hand sanitizer, while Roxy opened the milk carton containing Jo's caramel bars. Everyone ate standing up and talked about the storm.

"The wind was really howling," Sally said. "That tropical storm must have spawned a tornado, to blow down so many trees like this."

Trent nodded and glanced at Seth. "We think so, too. The wind kicked up, and trees started falling as we were getting ready to load our packs into our canoe. We pulled it out of the water and turned it over. Then we stretched out on the ground next to it. One tree fell so close, we had to chop off its limbs to free the canoe."

While Sally described how they sheltered in the old growth cypress, Roxy turned and gazed at the river's gray choppy surface. The rolling waves made slapping sounds as they reached the shoreline. It suddenly struck her how quiet the forest seemed. A damp wind propelled the waves toward shore, but no leafy branches rustled overhead. There were no birds chirping, no chattering squirrels. She thought about all the destroyed habitats, and she wondered how many birds and animals had been killed.

Trent walked over and whispered, "I've been thinking about everything you said. Can we step away a minute?"

Roxy nodded. "I'm sorry for the way I—"

"No. It's okay." Trent walked ahead of her as they made their way down the shoreline, stepping over leafy tree debris. When he reached a downed tree that blocked their way, he turned and faced her. He shoved his hands in his pockets, like an awkward teenager. "It was a shock, learning I have a daughter, after all these years. And even more of a shock, realizing how angry you were." He paused and shook his head. "I never really thought about that before. And I... ah, I want to thank you for having my baby... our baby, after the way things ended with us."

She gazed into his pale blue eyes; the eyes of the man she had once loved with all her heart.

Trent took hold of her hands. "I know you still have feelings for me."

"I'll always have feelings for you, strong feelings, but—"

"I've always loved you, Rox. I didn't marry Celia because I wanted to—"

"Don't!" She pulled her hands away. "It's all in the past—"

"But I want to explain." Trent waited until he saw her nod. "You know Celia's mom and my mom were close friends. Celia wanted us to get married, but I didn't. My mom was the one who put the most pressure on me. I would have put up more of a fight, but mom's cancer had come back, and I didn't want to cause her any more stress. That's why I eloped with Celia. I know it was wrong, leaving you that way. But I just couldn't face you. I messed up the good thing we had, and I was angry at myself. That night, when you called me, I was drunk. I unloaded all my anger on you, and it wasn't right... hurting you like that."

Roxy had never seen this kind of honesty from Trent. A feeling of sadness welled up inside her. He was being truthful at this moment, but she knew his character. She glanced down at their boot prints in the mud, prints that overlapped and then diverged. Her sadness intensified as she recalled the love, the passion, and the dreams they had once shared, and lost.

"Rox, I want a second chance with you, more than ever."

She looked up at him. "It's too late, Trent. We have separate lives, now. You're in Minnesota and I'm—"

"We still have feelings for each other. We can find a way to make it work."

"No. It won't work. There's someone else in my life, now."

"Kyle?"

She nodded.

"Hey, Rox!" Jo shouted. "Last call for food, before we pack everything up."

Trent leaned close and brushed his lips against her cheek. "We'll talk about this later."

As they turned to walk back, something bright red caught Roxy's attention. She peered beneath a leafy tree limb and saw the sleeve of a red shirt. A gray hand protruded from the sleeve. When she recognized the enormous gold dragon ring, her heart stopped.

"Trent! There's someone here—" A surge of bile choked off her words. Roxy swallowed back the sour-tasting liquid as she pointed at the gray hand.

He squatted down and cleared away the branches, revealing the man's bloated head. "His throat has been slit. It's a deep wound."

"I know him!" A sick chill washed over her, and she turned away from the grisly sight. "He's Harmon Doyle, Burke's uncle."

Trent stood and cursed under his breath.

Roxy startled, as the truth came into sudden focus. "Trent! A bear didn't attack me... it was Burke, wielding the same knife he used on his uncle!" Bile surged again. She sank to her knees and clutched her sore ribs as she vomited.

Trent helped her up and supported her trembling body as they walked back. He gathered everyone together and told them about the body they found.

Roxy's trembling intensified as she described Harmon Doyle's relationship to Burke; the threatening text she'd received from Doyle's phone number; and the suspicion that Burke had sent the text using his uncle's phone.

Sally's eyes opened wide. "So, you think Burke attacked his uncle out here... and you?"

Trent wore a grim expression. "We'll have to notify the Marion County Sheriff's Office."

"Okay," Sally said. "Let's load the canoes and get going."

Slice; flatten; pull back and lift. Roxy's ribcage ached with each paddle stroke. Dark clouds hovered overhead as they fought their way through the choppy water, filled with floating tree debris. The uneven pattern of the storm's destruction amazed her. Trees had toppled over on both sides of the river in the area around their campsite, but as they approached Gore's Landing, only a few downed trees were visible.

Dusty waded out to meet their canoes, and Zach followed him. "Good to see you, Sal. We were getting ready to paddle over to that site you and Matt always use, to check on you gals. This storm was a bad'un."

"We think a tornado touched down at our site," Sally said, as her canoe bottomed out near shore. "A lot of trees were blown down."

Dusty's thick eyebrows shot up. "Anyone hurt?"

"No, we found shelter. I'll tell you about it after we get back to the lodge."

While Dusty and Zack loaded the canoes on their trailer, Seth and Trent helped the women load the packs inside the bed of Dusty's pickup truck. They formed a caravan on the way back to the lodge, with Dusty and Zach in the lead, pulling the canoe trailer. Seth followed in his pickup truck, with Bri and Trent as his passengers. The rest of the group rode in Sally's SUV. Tree debris littered the road on the ten-mile drive, and they had to swerve to avoid hitting the larger limbs. As they approached the lodge, the dark clouds opened up again. Wind-driven rain pummeled the vehicles as they entered the gravel parking area. Dusty drove his truck and trailer to the equipment shed, while Seth and Sally parked near the lodge.

Jo led the way up the gravel path. She climbed the stairs and then stood inside the porch, holding the screen door open. As Roxy hurried up the slippery wooden stairs, her muddy boot slid sideways. She fell hard against the edge of the top step, striking her left side below the ribcage. A blinding pain pierced her body, and she cried out.

Jo reached under Roxy's arm, steadying her as she struggled to her feet. "You all right?"

"I hit… my bruised ribs." Roxy took shallow breaths, as the pain throbbed in spasms. She double over and gripped her left side as she walked into the screen porch.

After Jo took off her wet jacket, she helped Roxy remove hers. She hung both of them on the porch's wall hooks. They slipped off their hiking boots and socks, placed them on the plastic boot tray and entered the lodge barefoot. Roxy walked slowly, to minimize the pain in her ribs.

Rain pelted the tall windows flanking the large stone fireplace in the lobby's seating area, while a roaring fire radiated warmth and a soft flickering light. The moose antler chandeliers weren't lit, but the battery lamps placed on the mantle and the end tables gave off a cozy glow.

Roxy let out a soft moan as she pulled her sandwich bag purse out of the side pocket of her wet cargo shorts. She extracted her phone from the waterlogged plastic bag, and her spirits sank when she saw additional cracks in the blue dolphin case. She double tapped the screen, and nothing happened.

Jo looked over her shoulder. "Is your phone broken?"

"Probably," Roxy said, as her rib pain throbbed. "I need to sit down." She headed toward the nearest couch, and Jo sat down next to her.

One by one, the other women walked barefoot into the seating area and gathered near the warm fireplace. Lucky wandered over, wagging his tail. He moved from person to person, acting like the lodge's one-dog welcoming committee.

Leeann stroked his black furry head and looked around. "I wonder where Killer is."

"Don't worry, he's back in our living quarters." Dusty's wife Eleanor walked out of the restaurant. The plump woman wiped her hands on a kitchen towel as she greeted them. Short dark hair framed her face, and she was wearing a Dusty's Last Resort t-shirt and dark blue jeans. "We were worried about all of you. Dusty said a tornado touched down at your site. It's a blessing you're all right." She glanced at the rain-streaked windows. "The power lines are down, but we have generators running our kitchen appliances and our water heaters. I'm sure you'll want to take showers and get settled in before you have something to eat. I just made a big pot of chili, and there's homemade bread in the oven." Eleanor gave them a brief smile before heading back into the restaurant.

Roxy heard Sally's voice and turned toward the check-in counter. She was talking to Matt, using Dusty's phone. She asked him to call the other families to reassure them everyone was all right.

Trent and Seth stood at the counter, waiting. Both men looked weary. When Sally hung up, Trent asked Dusty for the number of the Marion County Sheriff's Office.

Roxy winced as she got up from the couch.

"Where are you going?" Jo asked.

"I should call Kyle. He needs to know about Harmon Doyle."

Jo nodded and visibly shuddered.

Roxy walked up to the counter and listened as Trent described the body they found and then answered questions. After a brief back and forth exchange, he ended the call and blew out a long sigh. "The Sheriff's Office is crazy busy right now, handling storm issues. It's raining hard and it'll be dark soon. They'll send deputies here tomorrow morning to take our statements, before heading out to examine the body."

Dusty leaned on the counter. His shirt collar looked soaked, and his wet hair had been slicked back, away from his plump face. "Are you sure that fella you found was murdered? Things like that don't happen around here. He could'a run into a bear. Their claws are razor sharp."

Trent exchanged glances with Seth and Roxy, but he let it drop. "Dusty, do you have a room available tonight?"

"No, but you fellas can use those couches in the lobby, no charge. Eleanor will get you set up with blankets. There's coffee in the restaurant. You both look like you could use a cup."

"Thanks." The brothers spoke in unison. Seth headed toward the restaurant, but Trent lingered, looking at Roxy.

She turned to Dusty. "Can I use your phone? I need to call a detective in Riverside Bay. The body we found is connected to an investigation he's working on." In her peripheral vision, she saw Trent frown before he walked away.

Dusty slid the phone toward her. "That reminds me. You got a call this morning from your cousin. He wanted to know if you made it back to the lodge."

"My cousin? The only cousin I have is sitting on that couch over there." Roxy glanced at Jo as she lifted the phone's receiver.

"Don't you have a cousin named Vance?"

The receiver slid out of her hands. She caught the cord before it hit the floor.

"Vance came here with a friend yesterday, right after you gals left," Dusty said. "They rented a canoe and fishing gear."

Roxy turned toward the seating area. "Jo, could you bring your phone over here? I need to show Dusty a photo."

"Okay." Jo pulled out her phone as she walked over.

Roxy swiped through the reunion photos until she found one of Burke. "Is this the man who rented the fishing gear?"

Dusty eyed the photo. "Looks like him. But he had the start of a beard, and an ugly scratch ran down the side of his face. It looked to me like it was infected."

Roxy smiled. "What did his friend look like?"

"He was shorter, bald, and he had a pug-nose, like a mobster in the movies."

"That's Harmon Doyle," Roxy said.

"Doyle, that's right. I issued him a fishing license, and that was the name on his ID."

Jo blurted, "Burke and his uncle were here?"

"Burke rented a canoe and fishing gear yesterday," Roxy said.

Dusty's brown eyes narrowed. "His name is Burke? He showed me a driver's license with his photo, and the name on it was Vance, ah..."

"Silva," Roxy said. She shivered, realizing Burke must have taken Vance's driver's license from his wallet after the hit and run. "Dusty, when did he bring back the canoe?"

He scratched his head. "Yesterday afternoon, late."

"Burke was alone, right?"

"Zach checked in his gear. I'll have to ask him—" A startled look crossed his face. "Is Doyle that dead fella you found?"

Roxy nodded.

Dusty's expression hardened. "When Vance, ah... Burke came back, Eleanor sold him a first-aid kit. She said his hand was cut bad, and his shirt was bloody. He told her his knife slipped when he cut a snagged fishing line."

Roxy's stomach went queasy as she punched in Kyle's number.

Kyle's ringtone sounded as he sat at his desk. He picked up his phone, and his pulse quickened when he recognized the number.

"Hi, Kyle. Remember me?"

The sound of her voice sent his mood soaring. "I've been thinking about you. How bad was that tropical storm?"

"The wind was awful... a lot of trees fell... but we're okay..."

Kyle heard her labored breathing. "Rox, what's wrong?"

"I found Harmon Doyle's... dead body near our campsite!"

"What?" Kyle struggled to process what she'd just said. "A dead body? Are you sure it was Doyle? Maybe another camper got caught in the storm—"

"I know it was him! His throat was cut... but I recognized him... he was wearing a gold dragon ring... I saw it the day I met him."

Kyle opened a page in his notebook and began scribbling notes.

"Dusty said Burke and Doyle... rented a canoe and fishing gear... and Burke used Vance's ID... when he bought a fishing license!"

Kyle startled. "He had Vance's driver's license?"

"That's not all... I was attacked yesterday..."

Anger surged as Kyle jotted down details of the attack.

"... Burke's hand and shirt were bloody... when he came back yesterday... Trent called the Marion County... Sheriff's Office. They're going to... take our statements tomorrow."

"Rox, are you okay? You're stopping to breathe every few words."

"I bruised my ribs... and they're a little sore..."

"Okay. Let me talk to Dusty." Kyle briefly interviewed him, and then he gave him his cell number and told him to call if he had any new information. When Roxy got back on the phone, he said, "Call me tomorrow, after you give your statement to the deputies."

"I'll call you on Dusty's phone... or Jo's phone."

"Why not yours? Oh! Did you—"

"Yeah... I broke another one."

Kyle couldn't help smiling. "Rox, I miss you so much."

"I miss you, too."

Wednesday morning

After breakfast, the women carried mugs of coffee into the lobby's seating area. Electrical power hadn't been restored, but sunlight streamed in through the tall windows, giving the lobby a cozy glow. Zach entered the lodge and walked over to Sally. "I just finished loading up all your packs. They dried out pretty well in our equipment garage last night. Dad gave me your list, and I split the packs up the way you wanted, between your SUV and that bright red pickup."

"Thanks, Zach." Sally gave him a smile, and then she turned to Tara and Leeann. "I guess it's time for us to get going."

Roxy, Jo and Bri exchanged quick hugs with them.

"Drive safe," Jo said.

After they left, Roxy and Jo sat on the couch nearest the fireplace. Bri sat on the couch across from them and checked her smartwatch. "Seth and Trent are outside, waiting for the deputies. Our truck is all loaded up. We'll start back to New Smyrna as soon as the deputies are finished. I hope it won't take too long."

"Me, too," Jo said. "Rox and I are eager to get home."

Roxy raised her coffee mug to her lips and then set it down. The creamy aroma prompted a wave of nausea. Even though Jo had insisted on giving her the lower bunk last night, she hadn't slept well. Her rib pain had tormented her. And this morning, even shallow breaths brought on twinges of pain.

Jo looked at her. "You didn't eat anything at breakfast."

Roxy yawned. "I'm not hungry. I didn't sleep well."

"As soon as we get back to Riverside Bay, I'm taking you to the Clinic to have your ribs checked out."

Lucky jumped up on the couch. He rested his large black head on Roxy's lap, as if he sensed her pain and wanted to comfort her. She stroked his soft fur and thought about her sweet Buddy. She longed to hug him. And Kyle.

They all turned toward the lobby as Dusty, Trent and Seth walked in. Three male Marion County deputies wearing dark green uniforms followed them inside, along with a slender woman dressed in a dark green polo shirt and black jeans.

Lucky jumped off the couch and trotted next to Eleanor as she walked over and greeted them. After taking their coffee orders, she ushered them into the lobby's seating area.

The tallest man introduced himself as Lt. Garrett Reddick, the lead investigator. He reminded Roxy of her postal supervisor Mack, with his dark brown skin and close-cropped graying hair. When he shook Roxy's hand, he told her Kyle had called him earlier that morning, to give him the background information on Harmon Doyle and his nephew, Burke.

Lt. Reddick introduced Deputy Dunn, a lean muscular man with a shaved head, and Deputy Cunningham, a shorter and heavier man with brown curly hair. The young woman introduced herself as Hildi Brun, a Marion County forensic technician. Her blonde hair had been swept away from her attractive face and styled into a long braided pony tail.

The deputies split up and took detailed statements from Roxy and Trent, along with Dusty, Zach and Eleanor. After all the statements were taken, Lt. Reddick asked Dusty to outfit two canoes and take them to Gore's Landing, since motorized boats weren't allowed on the Ocklawaha River. He explained that Trent and Seth would paddle one of the canoes to the spot where the body was found, while he and Hildi Brun followed in the other canoe. After Hildi's on-site forensic examination, the body would be bagged and transported back to Gore's Landing, where a morgue van would be waiting. Lt. Reddick instructed the two male deputies to remain at the lodge, in radio contact.

Dusty and Zach left the lodge to begin loading the canoe trailer. Roxy, Jo and Bri walked back to the seating area and took the same spots on the couches. The two deputies sat in the armchairs flanking the fireplace and began talking about the investigation, while Lt. Reddick and the others waited at the check-in counter.

Jo leaned over and whispered, "Look at Trent, over there. He hasn't changed."

Roxy turned and saw Trent and Hildi standing close together, talking. They appeared to be flirting with each other. Their smiles and body language clearly demonstrated a mutual attraction. They both turned when Dusty stepped back inside the lodge and caught Lt. Reddick's attention. As the small group headed outside, Trent guided Hildi out the door by placing his hand at her lower back.

Roxy gave Jo a weary nod. The pain in her ribs had spread to her abdomen. She felt suddenly limp and weak, as if a plug had been pulled and all her strength had drained away.

Jo stared at her. "You look pale, Rox. Your rib pain is worse, isn't it?"

"It hurts a lot... every time I breathe."

"Why didn't you tell me?" Jo sprang to her feet. "Lie down so I can examine you."

Roxy winced as she stretched out.

Jo kneeled beside her. She felt her forehead, and then she took hold of her wrist for a long moment. "Your pulse is rapid, over 120. Do you feel nauseous?"

"A little..."

Jo pressed the bruised area on her left side.

"Ouch! Ow, ow, ow!" The pain sent tears to Roxy's eyes.

"I'm sorry, Rox. But I need to do that one more time." Jo probed a slightly different area and Roxy cried out again. "Your abdomen is swollen and hard. This is serious, Rox. I think you're bleeding internally. We need to get you to the hospital right away."

Eleanor walked over. "I can call an ambulance."

"How long will that take?"

"They'll be coming from Ocala General."

Deputy Dunn rose to his feet. "Trees are still blocking the road to Ocala. It's only one lane in several places. The round-trip for an ambulance could take a while." He looked at Jo. "We came in two cruisers. Lt. Reddick took one of them. I can drive her to the hospital in the other cruiser and use the sirens."

"Thanks," Jo said. "I'm a nurse... I'm coming with you." She reached into her pocket and handed Bri a key fob. "Will you ask Trent to drive my truck to Ocala General?"

"Okay..." Bri's voice trembled. She cast a worried glance at Roxy.

"I'll call the hospital and let them know you're coming," Eleanor said.

Jo nodded. "Tell them to have a surgeon ready."

Jo blinked away tears as she stood in the hallway outside the surgical waiting room. She had just finished a long call with her mom, and she could still hear the tone of anguish in her voice. The phone in her hand buzzed. Kyle's name appeared on the screen, and she quickly read his text message:

"Jo, will you ask Rox to call me? I want to find out how things went with the deputies this morning. I also want to wish her a Happy Birthday. I forgot to do that yesterday."

Fresh tears coursed down Jo's cheeks. Rox's birthday was yesterday, and nobody remembered it! She wiped her face with the back of her hand and took several deep, cleansing breaths before calling him back.

Jo was still holding her phone when she entered the surgical waiting room. Anxiety rolled through her stomach in nauseous waves. She sat in the nearest chair, bowed her head and prayed. When she looked up, she exchanged nods with the others in the small room; a middle-aged couple with a young boy, and a thin man in his thirties. Jo tried reading the text messages that had downloaded once she got back into cell service range, but she couldn't maintain her focus. She fidgeted and checked the time on her phone every few minutes.

A dark-haired woman wearing blue surgical scrubs opened the door and called her name. She leaped to her feet and followed the surgeon into the hallway. Jo had briefly spoken to Dr. Soniat in the ER, describing the circumstances of Rox's rib injuries.

The surgeon looked at Jo and said, "We performed a partial splen—"

"Hey, Jo!" Trent hurried down the hallway toward them. He looked like someone who had been living off the grid, with his shaggy hair, wrinkled clothes and mud-caked boots.

Dr. Soniat frowned as she eyed him.

Trent extended his hand. "I'm Trent Thorson, Rox's fiancé."

Jo's mouth dropped open.

The surgeon's expression relaxed as she shook his hand. "I was telling Jo… Roxy's partial splenectomy went well. Fractures in her lower left ribs caused a splenic rupture. I don't know if her first rib injury caused the rupture. If so, it bled slowly. The second impact either caused the rupture or widened an existing one, accelerating the bleeding." Dr. Soniat turned to Jo. "We gave her three pints of blood. I'm glad you didn't waste any time getting her to the hospital."

"What about her spleen? How much was removed?" Jo asked.

"Only a small portion, because of the rupture's location and size."

Jo sent up a silent prayer of thanks.

"She's in recovery now," Dr. Soniat said. "You'll be able to see her once she's been moved into a room." She gave them a nod before walking away.

Trent blew out a sigh. He reached into his pocket. "Here are your keys. I parked your truck next to ours in the visitor lot. Bri and Seth went to the cafeteria to get coffee."

Jo eyed him. "Did you lie about being Rox's fiancé, so you could talk to her surgeon?"

"Maybe..." Trent shrugged. "It might not be a lie for long. I asked Rox to give me a second chance, and she said she'd think about it."

Jo saw the arrogance in his smile, but she let it go. "Let's go to the cafeteria. I could use a cup of coffee, right now. You can tell Bri and Seth about Rox's surgery, and I'll call my mom." She paused. "I'll need to call Kyle, too."

Trent's expression soured.

Thursday morning

Nell sat in a recliner next to Roxy's hospital bed. She gazed at her niece's sleeping face and watched the slight movement of her chest as she breathed. The vital signs monitor by her bed beeped in a rhythmic pattern as its moving white line registered Roxy's heartbeats. Memories surfaced—sad memories of sitting in her husband's hospital room, ten years earlier. Cal had collapsed with a heart attack while mowing the lawn. Two days after leaving the hospital, he suffered a second heart attack that took his life.

The door opened, and a nurse dressed in navy blue scrubs entered the room. Nell heard a rattling noise in the hallway. Before the door closed, she caught a glimpse of a large rolling cart holding breakfast trays. The nurse slid a glance at Nell and smiled as she replaced a bag on Roxy's IV pole.

As the nurse was leaving, a dark-haired woman entered the room, wearing a white doctor's coat over dark slacks. She switched on the light over Roxy's bed, and Nell squinted at the glare. The woman walked over and extended her hand. "I'm Dr. Soniat."

"Nell Dowling." She stood and shook the doctor's hand.

"You're Roxy's mother?"

"I'm her aunt. But I raised her like my daughter."

Dr. Soniat smiled. She leaned over the bed and said, "Roxy, how are you feeling today?"

Roxy stirred and whispered, "Auntie Nell?"

"I'm Dr. Soniat, Roxy. Can you tell me how you feel? Do you have any pain?"

Her eyes fluttered open and then closed. She let out a soft moan. "It hurts... when I breathe."

"Can you give your pain a number from one to ten?"

Roxy's eyes remained closed. She appeared to be sleeping again.

Dr. Soniat moved to the foot of her bed. She glanced up when the door opened and smiled as Jo entered.

"How is Rox doing?" Jo asked.

"She has strong vitals and her hemoglobin count is steady. She's receiving IV antibiotics, and we're giving her narcotic sedation to alleviate her breathing pain. That's why she's been so sleepy. We'll start lowering the dosage of her pain medication this morning." Dr. Soniat turned to Nell. "I want Roxy to get up and walk today. It'll strengthen her circulation and help prevent blood clots. She's physically fit, and that'll speed up her healing. But she'll be sore for a while, until her fractured ribs heal."

Nell nodded. "How soon can she be released?"

"That depends on how well she does, after she starts walking. I want to keep an eye on her hemoglobin count. If it remains steady, we'll know there's no residual bleeding."

After the doctor left, Jo switched off the harsh overhead light and opened the window blinds, revealing a view of leafy treetops and blue sky. She smiled at her mom as she tucked her t-shirt into her denim shorts. "Thanks for remembering to bring clean clothes." She sat in the recliner next to Roxy's bed.

Nell glanced at a visitor's chair, and then she decided it felt good to stand and stretch her legs after sitting in that recliner all night. She stifled a yawn as she asked, "Where's Charlie?"

"He and Kyle are finishing breakfast. I just had toast and coffee, but they ordered eggs, bacon and pancakes."

"Did Kyle make a room reservation for tonight?"

"He plans to do that after breakfast, before he goes to the Sheriff's Office to meet with Lt. Reddick." Jo paused. "Kyle sure looked rough when he came to our motel room to shower and change this morning."

"He hasn't had any sleep," Nell said. "He drove directly to the hospital, and then he sat in this room with me all night."

"Mom, you look tired, too. Why don't you go down to the cafeteria and grab some breakfast? I can stay with Rox."

Roxy opened her eyes and saw Jo sitting next to her bed.

"Hey, Rox. How are you feeling?"

"Like I've been hit... by a truck..." She tried raising her head, and then winced at the pain in her side.

Jo pressed a button, and the head of the bed slowly rose. She fluffed Roxy's pillows and then wheeled the breakfast tray in front of her and coaxed her to eat.

Roxy ate some applesauce and drank a few sips of juice. Fatigue weighed down her eyelids. She settled back against the pillows, closed her eyes and listened to the monitor's repetitive beeping. She heard Nell's voice and opened her eyes. The sight of her aunt's smiling face comforted her.

"You're awake," Nell said. "You slept after your surgery and all night long. I thought you might sleep the morning away, too."

Jo nodded. "You didn't even wake up when Trent and Bri came to visit you yesterday, before Seth drove them back to New Smyrna. Trent's going to stay in Florida an extra week. He plans to come and visit you after you're released from the hospital."

"You slept the whole time Kyle was here, too," Nell said.

"Kyle was here?"

"Don't worry," Jo said. "He's coming back to see you, after his meeting at the Sheriff's Office."

Roxy smiled.

"I'd like to circle the hallway one more time, Aunt Nell. It feels good, being out of that stuffy hospital room." Roxy gripped her wheeled IV pole and walked slowly to minimize the pinching pain in her side. It was her second hallway walk of the day. Each time she rose out of bed, it felt as if hot nails were being driven into her ribs. She'd had to stand a few moments, until the pain and lightheadedness eased.

As they rounded the corner near the nurse's station, the door leading to the elevators swung open. Jo entered the hallway, carrying a takeout cup from the cafeteria. "How many laps this time?"

Nell smiled. "Twice as many as the first walk."

Jo walked alongside them until they reached the hospital room. When they entered, Charlie looked up from his phone screen.

"I just set a new hallway distance record," Roxy said. She noticed the food tray on her overbed table. "Is it lunchtime already?"

Charlie glanced at his phone. "It's almost one thirty."

"I guess we could go down to the cafeteria," Nell said.

Roxy gazed at her aunt's weary face. "You've been stuck in this hospital all night and half the day. Why don't you go out for lunch?"

"You shouldn't be left alone," Nell said.

Roxy grinned. "I'm in a hospital filled with nurses and doctors. Go ahead, I'll be fine."

Jo looked at Charlie. "Let's take mom to the Minnie Moose Café. She'll love it."

"Sounds like a plan." Charlie ushered Nell out the door before she could protest.

Roxy wheeled her IV pole around her bed and glanced at the blank screen on the vital signs monitor. She wasn't in any hurry to be hooked up to it again. The room seemed peaceful, without those irritating beeps. She stood at the window and gazed at the clouds changing shape against the blue sky.

The door opened, and a male voice laughed softly. Roxy glanced over her shoulder, and her heart leaped against her sore ribs.

"Hi, sunshine." He stood in the doorway, wearing jeans and a blue Riverside Bay Police polo shirt.

"Kyle!" She swiveled around and tripped over a roller on her IV pole. Hot pain sliced through her ribs. She let out a moan and doubled over.

"Rox!" He hurried toward her. "What can I do to help?"

She slowly straightened up as the burning pain eased. "You can start by giving me a hug... a gentle hug."

His expression relaxed. He leaned down and tenderly kissed her bandaged forehead. "You've only been on vacation a few days, and look at all the trouble you've gotten into." He wrapped his arms around her.

She leaned her head against his chest. "I missed you."

"I missed you, too. You gave me quite a scare, Rox."

Roxy felt the vibration of his deep voice through the soft fabric of his shirt. She closed her eyes and rested in his arms for a long moment. Then she stepped back and looked up at him. "Remember when I told you I needed time to sort out my feelings?" She paused as Kyle nodded. "Well... I've sorted out the most important one."

He waited, searching her eyes.

She read his hopeful expression and smiled. "Yeah... I'm in love with you, Kyle."

His face lit up like a sunrise. He leaned down and brushed his lips against her forehead, the tip of her nose and then her mouth, where his kiss lingered. The delicious feel of his lips warmed every part of her.

Roxy sighed, as he drew her into another hug. "Good thing I'm not hooked up to that monitor. My heart is beating so fast, the nursing staff would be rushing in to check on me."

He laughed... and kept on laughing.

"What's so funny?"

"Instead of sunshine, I should call you moonlight."

"Oh!" She reached around to cover her backside and then winced at the pain.

"I'll take care of it." Kyle reached around her and tied the strings on her hospital gown.

"That's why you were laughing when you came in."

"I should have kept my mouth shut. I was enjoying the view." When he stepped back, he stared at the plastic IV line wrapped around his arm.

Roxy giggled. "Looks like I caught a big fish on my line."

He grinned as he untangled himself.

"Kyle, I need to sit down. I've done two hallway walks, and then you came in and sent my heart rate skyrocketing."

He pulled two visitor's chairs together, facing the window. Then he sat next to her and draped his arm around her shoulders.

She looked up at him. "What did you find out today at the Sheriff's Office?"

"The fingerprints taken from the body are a match with Harmon Doyle. Garrett Reddick put a rush on the autopsy, and they did it early this morning. He showed me the preliminary report. The coroner estimated his death probably occurred early this week, which fits with Monday, the day you were attacked near the campsite. The deep slash in Doyle's neck severed his carotid artery. But there were multiple knife wounds... Burke was angry."

Roxy pictured the vicious look in his eyes, when he assaulted her after the reunion. Then another image flashed—Burke, much younger, dressed as a groomsman and smiling as he stood next to her and Vance on their wedding day. "Kyle, how could I have known Burke for so long, and not seen what a cold-blooded killer he could be?"

"None of us saw it, not even Vance," Kyle said.

"Burke was always kind and caring with his mother. And yet, he's a murderer. How does that happen?"

"People are complicated, Rox. Life is all about choices." He paused. "I took a philosophy course in college, and I've never forgotten Saint Augustine's views on evil. He basically said good and evil aren't opposites. You can't turn to evil, because it doesn't exist on its own. Evil comes into being when you choose to turn away from goodness, or when you do something that blocks the goodness. If you think of good and evil in terms of light and darkness, a shadow can only be created by blocking a light source. And the further away someone moves from the light, the larger the shadow becomes."

"Kyle... if it's a matter of choices, then why would someone like Burke choose to do evil?"

"I don't know why people make that choice. I have to deal with them every day, in my job." He let out a sigh and turned toward the window. "I've decided that most crimes are based on selfishness, focusing on yourself, your wants and desires, without regard for others. The evil is not caring for others."

"Not loving your neighbor as yourself," Roxy said.

Kyle looked at her and nodded. "I guess the way to overcome evil is to keep focused on the light... the goodness of God." He reached for her hand.

They sat quietly for a long moment, holding hands. Roxy gazed out the window and watched the treetops swaying in the breeze. "Where do you think Burke is, now?"

"I talked to Sam this morning. Someone made a large withdrawal from Harmon Doyle's checking account last night at an ATM in Miami. Sam hasn't seen the ATM transaction photo yet, but we think it was probably Burke."

"He used his uncle's ATM card?"

"Why not? Burke assumed we'd be searching for him, not Doyle. He hid his uncle's dead body in a remote forested area, and he didn't know it had been found... until about two hours ago, when he called the lodge and asked about you."

"Burke did that?"

Kyle nodded. "Dusty called me right after he hung up with Burke. Unfortunately, he lost his temper and told Burke he didn't appreciate being dragged into Doyle's murder investigation."

She read the worry in Kyle's deep blue eyes. "Do you think Burke's planning to attack me again? You just said he was in Miami."

"We don't know that for sure, Rox. Burke's already attacked you twice. What other reason would he have to call the lodge again and ask about you?"

Roxy took a moment. "Okay... maybe that was the reason Burke called Dusty again. But now that he knows his uncle's body has been found, wouldn't he just want to get away?"

"Maybe. But I don't want you to take any chances. When you get back to Riverside Bay, you're not staying in your house alone."

Footsteps sounded outside the door.

Roxy squeezed his hand. "If that's Aunt Nell, don't say anything to her about this. She's already worried enough about me."

The door opened, and Dr. Soniat entered. She cast a quick glance at Kyle and her smile faded.

He stood and introduced himself as they shook hands.

The surgeon focused on Roxy. After asking her a few routine questions, she smiled and said, "I'm glad you've been walking the hallway. How's the pain, on a one to ten scale?"

"When I walk, about four or five. Sitting here, maybe one or two. How soon can I be released?"

"If your hemoglobin count remains stable overnight, you can probably go home tomorrow." She headed toward the door, and then she turned. "Roxy, where's your fiancé? I haven't seen him around today."

Roxy shrugged.

After the surgeon left, Kyle sat down again. He turned to Roxy and raised an eyebrow. "Is there something you need to tell me?"

She sighed. "Trent lied about being my fiancé, so he could talk to Dr. Soniat after my surgery. Jo said he seemed confident we'd get back together, even though I told him there's someone else in my life, now."

He nodded. "Rox, you've never told me the story about your broken engagement with Trent."

"I guess it's time I did."

Friday morning

Roxy sat in a wheelchair as an aide pushed her toward the hospital's exit doors. Nell walked beside them, wearing a belted denim dress and matching sandals. The glass doors automatically slid open, letting in a blast of hot, humid air. As the aide pushed her wheelchair outside, Roxy saw Kyle standing next to his black truck, parked at the curb. She stood and thanked the aide, who gave her a brief smile before pushing the empty wheelchair back inside.

Kyle leaned down and kissed Roxy. "It's good to see you in regular clothes again, but I'm going to miss that peekaboo hospital gown. It provided an unending source of entertainment."

"Un-end-ing?" Roxy giggled, ignoring the pain in her ribs. She glanced down at her outfit, a Master Gardener t-shirt and khaki shorts. "Good thing Jo and I wear the same size."

Nell smiled. "Charlie and I were in a hurry to drive up here, so we just packed things from Jo's closet."

Kyle opened the truck's passenger door for Nell and helped her climb inside. Then he opened the back door for Roxy and practically lifted her into the roomy back seat.

Nell's phone chimed. After reading the text, she glanced over her shoulder. "Jo and Charlie got home an hour ago, Rox. They haven't heard from Ava yet, so they don't know when the church van will be arriving. Jo said she's on her way to pick up your birthday gift. It's a surprise."

"Haven't I had enough surprises, lately?" Roxy's last word disappeared into a yawn.

Kyle parked his truck in Nell's driveway and heard Roxy moving around in the back seat. He turned and stifled a laugh when he saw her hair flattened on one side.

Roxy yawned as she asked, "Are we there yet?"

Nell looked over her shoulder and smiled. "There's my sleepyhead."

They got out and walked to the rear of his truck. When Kyle opened the tailgate, Roxy started reaching for Nell's suitcase.

"Roxelle Anna! Don't you dare pick up any luggage! You're not supposed to carry anything heavy for the next few weeks."

"Is this too heavy?" Roxy held up her sandwich bag purse.

"Don't give me any attitude, young lady." Nell glanced at Kyle and winked.

Kyle carried Nell's suitcase into her house and set it in the laundry room, as she'd instructed. When he walked outside, he greeted Jo, who was standing on the driveway with Roxy and Nell.

Jo handed Roxy a canvas tote bag. "Your birthday gift isn't wrapped. I wanted to give it to you right away, so you can start using it. I can't believe we all forgot about your birthday while we were on the trip."

"That's okay. I forgot about it, too. Crazy things were going on—"

"Like a tropical storm and a tornado," Nell said.

Roxy reached into the tote bag and held up a large shampoo bottle with the picture of a golden retriever. She laughed out loud and then visibly flinched.

Jo grinned. "Sal and Leeann brought it over this morning. They said they want you to have silky hair when we take you out for your birthday lunch next week." Woof! Woof!

"Rox, isn't that shampoo for Buddy?" Kyle asked.

She grinned. "I'll tell you about it, later."

"There's something else inside." Jo's eyes sparked with anticipation.

Roxy pulled out a brand-new phone with an aqua blue case. She wore a stunned expression as she stared at it.

"I went to the phone store this morning. They examined your broken phone and found your SIM card was still intact, so they transferred everything to this brand-new phone. The whole group chipped in to buy it. But mom and Kyle paid the largest share."

Roxy looked at them and her eyes welled up. "Thanks… I don't know what to say."

"It has lots of cool features, Rox. You should check them out." Jo's ringtone sounded and she pulled out her phone. "It's Charlie." She swiped the screen, and her expression went serious as she listened. "What time are you leaving? Okay, I'll come home right away." She looked up as she pocketed her phone. "Charlie just got a call from Ava. The church van broke down, and the mission team is stuck in Lake City. He's going to drive the church bus there and pick everyone up. I'm riding with him."

"I want to go, too," Nell said. "I haven't seen Rachel for over a week."

Roxy glanced at Kyle as he turned onto Main Street and merged with the slow-moving traffic. "I've really lost track of time. I didn't realize the Early Third celebration is tonight." She gazed at the patriotic red, white and blue banners affixed to the art deco streetlights. "Do you remember the first year Quint and Greta scheduled the Fourth of July fireworks on the night before the holiday? Everyone in town thought they were crazy, but it's become a huge success. Look at all this traffic. The sidewalks are already crowded."

"Sometimes I agree with Leo, about all the tourists in town," Kyle said. "The crowd is predicted to be bigger than ever tonight.

That's why the Chief wants us to do street patrol with the other officers. I'll have to report to the station right after we have dinner at Claudia's. I hope you don't mind stopping at my house first, so I can shower and pick up my uniform."

"That's fine with me. I can't wait to see Buddy." She paused. "It was nice of Sam to volunteer as an in-home dog-sitter."

"He knew I was in a hurry to get to Ocala. His wife is still out of town, so I told him he could stay in my guest room and make himself at home." Kyle glanced at her and grinned. "Sam's probably cleaned out all the food in my fridge."

Roxy gave him a brief smile.

"What's wrong?"

"I'm thinking about Claudia. I wish you hadn't called her. I don't mind staying at her condo tonight, but it's probably not necessary. I feel guilty, making her drive back to town. Paul's leave isn't over yet, and she wanted to spent time with him alone, at Amelia Island."

"Claudia insisted on driving back, Rox. She said Paul made plans to visit his parents in Charleston this weekend, without consulting her. I think she was happy to use you as an excuse to avoid going with him. You know she doesn't get along with Paul's mother."

"That's an understatement," Roxy said.

Kyle parked in his driveway and retrieved his suitcase. As they walked toward his house, frenzied barking started inside. When he inserted his key, the barking grew louder. As soon as he opened his back door, Buddy dashed toward Roxy. She went down on one knee and burst into tears as she embraced her sweet dog. She held his furry trembling body close, ignoring the pinching pain in her ribs as he lavished her with sloppy kisses.

Kyle's low-pitched groaning drifted out the partially-open door.

Roxy carefully rose to her feet and ventured inside to investigate. Buddy trotted close beside her.

Kyle stood in his kitchen, holding a bag of peppermints the size of a watermelon. "Sam ate almost everything, but he left this." He stared at the candy and looked as if he was going to be sick.

"Maybe Milo can give out the peppermints at the diner, as a freebie for customers."

"Great idea. I'll do anything to get them out of my house." He carried the huge bag to his truck. When he returned, he snapped a leash on each dog. "I'll take these two for a quick walk before I get cleaned up. You can stay here and study all the features on your new phone."

"I can walk my own dog, Kyle. I'm not an invalid."

He grinned. "Don't give me any attitude, young lady."

After Kyle returned with the dogs, he headed upstairs. Roxy prepared their dinner and refreshed their water bowls. While the dogs ate, she sat at Kyle's kitchen table and continued reviewing the features on her phone.

Footsteps sounded on the squeaky stairs. Kyle walked into the kitchen, dressed in a white t-shirt, jeans and patrol shoes. His thick hair still looked damp, and he was carrying his dark blue police uniform in a clear dry-cleaning bag. "I'll change into this later, after I get to the station."

Buddy trotted over and nudged Roxy's hand, as if he sensed she was about to leave. She leaned down and stroked his soft furry head. "Hey, sweet guy. I'm going to have to leave you here. I'm staying at Auntie Claudia's tonight, and there will be fireworks at the marina, across the street. You know how that scares you. It won't be as loud here at Uncle Kyle's house."

Buddy wagged his entire body, as if to say, "No problem, mommy. I'm with you now, and I love you, I love you, I love you."

Roxy glanced up and read Kyle's tense expression. "Is something wrong?"

He frowned. "Sam called me a few minutes ago, before I came downstairs. Harmon Doyle's yacht went missing from a Miami marina yesterday. Sam tracked down a witness who saw a man loading supplies on that yacht. The description she gave matches Burke, but she insisted he had light hair."

"If Burke has disguised his appearance, he must be trying to get away... maybe far away," Roxy said. "I really want to see him caught and brought to justice for everything he's done. But I have to admit, it's a relief right now, knowing he's sailed off somewhere."

Kyle looked at her. "Burke could have sailed back here, Rox."

Roxy sat in Kyle's truck and watched him unlock her back door. She folded her arms and tapped her foot on the floor mat, while she waited for him to check her house.

He returned and opened the passenger door. "It's clear, Rox. I'll wait for you in the family room. No hurry."

Pain pinched her ribs as she climbed the stairs. After she packed a few things in a small suitcase, she slipped on a blue and white striped sundress and red sandals, in honor of the Early Third celebration. She washed her face and then studied it in the mirror. The bruise had begun to fade to a lighter shade of purple, and the tiny scratches were almost healed. But the scabbed wound at her hairline would take much longer. She brushed her hair to conceal it. Then she applied a fresh coat of cover-up cream and the rest of her make-up, including bright red lipstick.

Kyle got up from the couch as she reached the bottom of the stairs. He took the small suitcase from her hand.

"It's not that heavy, Kyle. I didn't pack much."

"I know." He tossed the suitcase on the couch and pulled her into an enthusiastic kiss.

A knock sounded at the front door, and they both startled. Kyle walked over and looked through the peephole. "It's Trent." He stepped back as Roxy opened the door.

Trent smiled as he took in the sight of her. "Babe, you're looking really good—" He stopped when he glanced over her shoulder.

Kyle stepped forward and extended his hand. "Good to see you again."

Trent wore a pained expression as they shook hands. He slid a glance at Roxy. "I was going to take you to dinner, but I see you have other plans. Sorry to interrupt." He turned and strode away.

"Trent, wait..."

He kept walking.

Roxy let out a sigh as she closed the door. When she glanced up at Kyle, she saw the bright red lipstick smear on his face.

CHAPTER 46

Burke set down his binoculars after watching Kyle's truck back out of her driveway. He smiled as he looked around the comfortable living quarters on his uncle's yacht, anchored within wi-fi range of Quint's marina. This spot on the river gave him a clear view of her house and the Silva Building downtown. It also allowed him to hide in plain sight, surrounded by dozens of other yachts, sailboats and motorboats waiting to view the town's fireworks display.

He could see his own yacht docked at the marina. It irritated him, knowing it was being watched. This yacht wasn't as large or luxurious, but it was available. He'd kept an extra set of keys when he purchased it for his greedy uncle, and he knew where it was docked, since he'd been paying the monthly fees to that Miami marina.

It was easy, luring his uncle into that forest on the pretense of kidnapping Rox. He was eager to help... too eager. That remote area seemed like the perfect place to hide his body; a place where alligators and decomposition would destroy all traces of it. When he sailed out of Miami yesterday, he had no idea the body had been found. He didn't call that bearded hillbilly at the lodge until he was already heading north on the Intracoastal Waterway.

Burke finished off his whiskey and frowned as he set down the glass. Nature had conspired against him, twice. First, a sinkhole drained that pond, revealing Greta's car and her dead body. Then a freak storm blew down trees, uncovering his uncle's body. Had the police traced him to this yacht? He shrugged. All he had to do was stay hidden for a few more hours.

Last night he did a trial run, rowing to shore in the skiff around midnight. He spotted the police cruiser parked near the Silva Building, so he walked around and unlocked the back door to the parking garage. The security cameras didn't cover that door or the stairwell. He quietly entered his condo and retrieved a few things hidden under the floor in his closet; things he wanted to bring with him to the Caribbean. He'd already made plans to take on a new identity.

Burke raised his binoculars again and searched the downtown area. He tensed when he saw Kyle's truck driving into the Silva Building's parking garage. He'd seen Kyle loading a small suitcase into his truck before leaving with Rox. And earlier today, he spotted Claudia's car entering the parking garage. She'd obviously driven back from Amelia Island a few days early. Rox must have arranged to stay with Claudia tonight.

He hadn't expected that. But it shouldn't be too hard to figure out a new plan.

Burke scanned the shoreline. Around sunset, he could row the skiff to shore and tie it up near Ozzie's Seafood Grill. The place was already packed, and he could hear the live band playing. With all the people in town, he'd simply blend into the crowd.

The Silva Building's elevator doors opened, and Roxy stepped out ahead of Kyle. As she started down the second floor hallway, she realized he was lagging behind. She turned and watched as he picked something off the floor. He briefly examined it before slipping it into his pocket. When he glanced at her, he flashed a smile, but it wasn't quick enough. She caught the worried look on Kyle's face.

"Are you two coming in? I heard the elevator ping." Claudia was standing at her open doorway, wearing a white sundress, a red scarf and navy sandals. "Rox, how are you feeling?"

"A little tired, but I'm okay."

Claudia gave them each a quick hug and then ushered them inside. Her condo's open layout reflected her contemporary taste, with its pale gray walls, wood-look tile floors and sleek white leather furniture. A long panel of sliding glass windows overlooked the marina across the street, and beyond that, the wide expanse of the Indian River.

"It smells great in here," Kyle said.

Roxy breathed in the aromas. "Is it rosemary and thyme chicken?"

"You got it," Claudia said. "I used fresh spices from my rooftop herb garden."

Kyle beamed her a smile and then carried Roxy's suitcase into the guest room.

A muffled ping sounded. Claudia opened the door and stepped into the hallway as she greeted her dad and Leo.

"How's my Roxy-girl?" A smile lit up Leo's wrinkled face as he entered the condo, gripping his walker.

Roxy wrapped her arms around his stooped shoulders and offered up a silent thankful prayer for the blessing of seeing him again.

Earl followed Leo inside. "Rox, I've been so worried about you." His brown eyes glistened with emotion as he pulled her into a hug. She hugged him back, ignoring the pinching pain in her side.

Claudia placed the roasted chicken on a platter, along with rosemary-roasted potatoes and broccoli. She set the platter on her dining table, which she'd decorated with a flag-themed linen tablecloth, red dinnerware, and cobalt blue glassware. They all sat down and then bowed their heads while Earl said grace.

Claudia had taken the seat next to Roxy. She abruptly stood and retrieved a bottle of ketchup from the refrigerator.

Roxy grinned as she took it from her. "I thought you considered ketchup an abomination to healthy eating."

"It is." Claudia shrugged her shoulders as she sat down.

Roxy leaned over and whispered, "Thanks. I love you, too."

"Tell us about your camping trip," Leo said.

Roxy described the beauty of the forest around the Ocklawaha River. She inserted touches of humor as she talked about the gift-wrapped piñata food pack and the mosquito torture tent. When the conversation shifted to the tropical storm and the tornado, she described how they sheltered inside the massive old growth cypress.

"I remember seeing those huge cypress trees, when I worked at the CCC camp," Leo said. "I'm glad you and Jo-Jo didn't get hurt in that storm. A bad one hit our camp one night, and the wind hurled tree branches like spears through the windows of our barracks."

The conversation tapered off. During the brief silence, the atmosphere grew suddenly tense. Burke's invisible presence had been hovering over them, like a toxic black cloud. And everyone seemed anxious to avoid talking about him.

Earl's face contorted with emotion, and he threw down his fork. A sharp metallic clank rang out as it struck his porcelain plate. "If I ever see Burke again, I'll—"

"Dad! Don't get so upset." Claudia rested her hand on his arm. "Burke's gone away somewhere, and we'll probably never see him again."

"Good riddance!" Leo spat out the words.

Earl sighed. "I'm glad Lydia isn't around to see what a cold-blooded monster her son turned out to be. Burke's just like his father, that Red Devil!" He glanced down at his plate and appeared surprised to see the large chip in it.

During dessert—fresh berries with whipped cream, Leo began talking about the fireworks display. "The Senior Center's top floor balcony has the best view in town. Anyone want to join me? We can go back to my apartment and play cards after the fireworks."

"I'm in, Leo." Earl looked at Claudia and Roxy.

Claudia shook her head. "Rox looks tired, dad. If we want to see the fireworks, we can go up on the rooftop terrace."

Everyone stood and thanked Claudia for dinner. Leo patted Roxy's shoulder and said, "You get some rest, Roxy-girl."

Earl kissed Roxy on the cheek before he stepped out into the hallway.

Kyle followed him. "Earl, wait up. I have a quick question."

Roxy started to clear the dishes, but Claudia waved her off. "You relax. Everything can go in the dishwasher. It won't take me long."

Roxy moved to the sliding glass windows and gazed at the large number of watercraft anchored in the river, waiting for the fireworks to begin.

A few minutes later, Kyle walked back inside and shut the door. "I don't think it's a good idea for you to watch the fireworks on the rooftop terrace."

Claudia stepped out of the kitchen. "Why not? The rooftop door is always locked. Only family members have keys—" A startled look crossed her face. "You think Burke might be in town?"

Roxy stared at Kyle. "He'd be crazy to come after me again."

"Burke is crazy, Rox!" Kyle pulled a strip of paper from his pocket. "After Sam and I searched his condo on Sunday, I slipped a small piece of paper between his front door and the door frame, low enough where it wouldn't be seen. When we got off the elevator tonight, I found it lying in the hallway outside his door. It's definitely the paper I left; the top portion of my Brew Be receipt."

Roxy read Claudia's blank expression. "Kyle and I like to watch old black and white detective movies with Grandpa Leo. That's a trick a private detective used in one of them. When he came back and saw the slip of paper on the hallway floor, he knew someone had entered his apartment while he was gone."

"It was probably the cleaning crew," Claudia said.

"I just talked to Earl," Kyle said. "He told the crew not to clean Burke's condo this week."

"It wouldn't be the first time they ignored dad's instructions."

Kyle shook his head. "Earl just let me into Burke's condo. Several items have been moved and there are unwashed dishes on the counter. They weren't there last Sunday." He paused. "Burke could have anchored his uncle's yacht with all the other boats in the river. We know he's changed his appearance. If he came into town, he could easily slip by our officers in that crowd, especially after dark." He turned to Roxy. "Remember that SOS feature I showed you on your new phone?"

She nodded as she rubbed the chill bumps on her arms.

His eyes softened, and he wrapped her in a hug. Before leaving, he said, "I'll make sure our officers keep an eye on the building. Stay inside and keep the door locked. Don't open it for anyone, except me or Sam."

Now Claudia was rubbing her arms.

Roxy sat on the couch facing Claudia, who was leaning against an oversized pillow in her favorite white leather chair. During the past hour, Claudia had been acting like a tabloid reporter, asking a series of questions about her relationship with Trent and their broken engagement.

"I saw Troy in the class reunion photos, and he's still a hunk," Claudia said. "What about Seth... has he aged well?"

"He's still a hunk, too." Roxy smiled, amused by her curiosity about Seth and the fact that she couldn't seem to get Trent's name right.

"Rox, I can understand why Troy still loves you. But how can you still have feelings for him? He treated you like dirt, eloping with someone else."

"I haven't forgotten what he did. I've just decided to move past it. Trent and I have known each other since childhood. He was my first love, and I'll probably always have feelings for him. But I understand him much better, now. Even if we'd gotten married years ago, I don't think it would have worked out." Roxy paused. She looked at her sister-in-law and decided it was time. "Trent and I have another connection, Claudia. We have a daugh—"

They flinched, as explosive pops rang out.

Claudia glanced at the sliding glass windows. "The fireworks have started."

Roxy blew out a relieved sigh. She got up and moved to the windows. Claudia joined her, and they stood together, watching the bright patterns of light exploding in the dark sky.

The doorbell rang. Claudia crossed the room and looked through the peephole. "It's Melody. What's she doing here? I can't believe she has a problem with a real estate transaction tonight." She unlocked the deadbolt.

"No, Claudia! Don't open the door!"

CHAPTER 48

The loud bursts sounded like gunshots. Kyle stood on the sidewalk outside the Brew Be coffee shop and glanced at his watch. It was three minutes past the scheduled start of the fireworks. The tall buildings on that side of the street blocked his view, but he heard the oohs and aahs of the crowd at the marina, in between the popping sounds. Quint always cleared a large area of the parking lot, so people could set up chairs and view the display.

An uneasy feeling burned in Kyle's gut. Burke was in town. He could almost feel his presence. Kyle had given photos of Harmon Doyle's yacht to the officers in the Riverside Bay Police patrol boats. But he knew they'd be busy tonight, keeping all the watercraft a safe distance away from the fireworks barge, anchored offshore.

A scream rang out, and Kyle recognized the tone of panic. It wasn't someone enjoying the fireworks. He heard scuffling, and saw people fighting in the narrow alley between the Brew Be and Shyanne's Boutique. He dashed toward them.

Burke shoved Melody inside, holding her in a one-armed choke-hold. He locked the door with his free hand—the one holding the knife. As he turned to face them, he brought the knife up to Melody's throat and held it there. She whimpered and visibly trembled, as tears and black mascara streamed down her cheeks.

Roxy hardly recognized Burke with his light hair and gold-rimmed glasses. A purple scratch ran down the side of his face, disappearing into his bleached beard stubble. He was dressed in a gray sleeveless hoodie and cargo shorts.

He shot an angry glance at Claudia, who was staring at him with her arms folded tightly against her stomach. Then he turned toward Roxy.

She stood, shaking violently as she met his gaze. His dark eyes looked like black voids behind the clear lenses. An image of Burke's vicious attack after the reunion flashed into her mind. It triggered a surge of anger. Roxy lowered her shaking right hand and felt the shape of her phone inside the pocket of her sundress. Her index finger located its power button. She hesitated, knowing he'd take her phone away, if he saw what she was doing. She started turning away.

"Stay where you are!" Beads of sweat slid down Burke's face as he dragged Melody toward the dining room table. His knife blade waved up and down, close to her throat.

"Don't hurt me!" Melody's pleading voice came out as a shriek.

"Shut up!" Burke threw her into a dining chair and stood over her, breathing heavily. He pulled a roll of duct tape from the pocket of his cargo shorts and began taping her mouth.

While Burke was focused on Melody, Roxy swiveled away and pressed her phone's power button three times, fast. Her phone's SOS feature was programmed to send a five-second audio recording and her GPS location to her designated recipient. She swiveled back to Burke, realizing she needed to keep him distracted until Kyle arrived. "What are you doing here? What do you want, Burke?" She raised the volume of her voice, so it would be recorded over the loud fireworks explosions.

He looked at her. "I came for you."

A sick chill washed over her. Stay calm... stay calm. "Okay... let Melody and Claudia go, and I'll come with you."

"I'm giving the orders!" He tossed the duct tape at Claudia. "Finish taping her hands and feet to the chair. Now!"

Claudia stooped down and picked up the tape. As she straightened up, she glared at him and lifted her arm, as if she was going to throw it.

"Don't get any ideas." He waved the knife at her.

Claudia kept a wary gaze on his knife as she moved toward Melody. She kneeled next to the chair and used her manicured nails to peel the tape. The sound of ripping duct tape mingled with the popping sound of fireworks and Melody's high-pitched whimpering, muffled by the tape covering her mouth.

Burke let out a harsh laugh as he looked down at Claudia. "Hey, cuz. It's good to see you on your knees. You and Vance always thought you were better than me, didn't you?" He turned to Roxy. "Vance was always the favored one. I was smarter... I was better looking... I had a better education, but I could never measure up to him."

"What do you mean? You built a successful law practice—"

"Vance was going to destroy everything! He and Greta, they pushed me too far. She accused me of embezzling! Vance claimed he didn't believe her, but then he insisted on reviewing my accounts!"

Burke was shouting now. "He said he was only going to do a quick review! Who was he kidding? I knew what he was planning to do! I had to stop him!"

Claudia leaped to her feet and threw the roll of tape at him. "You killed my brother!"

Burke ducked as the tape sailed past his head. Then he lunged forward and thrust his knife into her side. Claudia let out a cry and gripped her mid-section as she sank to the floor.

Roxy recoiled in shock. When her breath returned, she slid her hand to her pocket and pressed her phone's power button again, three times.

Burke stood over Claudia and made angry, guttural sounds.

Roxy cringed. She'd heard those sounds when she was attacked near the campsite.

He gripped the knife in his hand and raised his arm as he leaned toward Claudia.

"No! Don't hurt her!" Roxy screamed. "I'll do whatever you want!"

Burke straightened up and waved his bloody knife at her. "Too bad you didn't have that attitude the night of the reunion. I should have taken this with me, to persuade you."

Roxy's blood went ice cold. She thought, "Kyle, where are you?"

After handcuffing the skinny bearded man, Kyle turned his attention to the middle-aged couple who had been attacked. When they assured him they weren't injured, he instructed them to follow him to the police station. He escorted the cuffed man through the crowd and across the street. At the station, he briefly described the mugging. Then he handed the man over to the officer on duty, to be booked into a temporary cell. Another officer took the couple aside and began taking their statements.

Kyle's phone buzzed a second time in his pocket, and he pulled it out. When he saw the two SOS texts, his gut hardened into a rock.

Roxy stared at Claudia, lying motionless at Burke's feet. The red stain on her white dress had grown larger, and blood had begun pooling on the floor. She suppressed a surge of nausea. "Please, Burke! Claudia needs medical help!"

"Shut up! You said you'd do anything I want!" Burke pointed the knife at her. "We're leaving, right now!"

Her heart leaped against her sore ribs. She needed to stay here and keep Burke talking. "Where are we going?"

"To a yacht, offshore. I bought it for my uncle, but he won't be using it anymore."

"You killed him! Why?"

Burke's eyes narrowed. "He got too greedy."

"You could have sailed away in his yacht. Why did you come back for me?"

"Can't you guess? You're the perfect trophy. Vance's devoted wife."

Melody whimpered, and he pointed the knife at her. "Shut up!"

He turned back to Roxy. "I saw how attracted you were to me, and I was willing to play your little waiting game for a while. But after Greta's car was found, I knew the game was over. I flew to Tallahassee, but I skipped the conference. I used that time to get my finances in order and make plans to get away. If my plan had worked out on the night of the reunion, you and I would already be together, somewhere in the islands." He focused his cold black eyes on her, and his lips curved upward.

An icy chill slid down her back. The handsome smile that used to remind her of Vance, now looked hideous and disgusting.

"Don't look so worried. I won't keep you around forever." Burke grabbed her arm and pulled her to the front door. He opened it and shoved her into the hallway. He stood behind her, holding the tip of his knife against the base of her spine. "Feel that? If you make any sudden moves, you'll feel even more of it. We're going to walk down the stairs and leave through the garage's back door. Then we'll move through the crowd, like a normal couple. My skiff is tied up at Ozzie's."

The stairwell door flew open. Kyle emerged in uniform; his gun drawn. Sam and another officer stood slightly behind him.

"Claudia's been stabbed!" Roxy shouted. "She needs help!"

Burke wrapped his left arm around her neck in a chokehold. He held the knife in his right hand against her throat. "Get back in that stairwell or I'll kill her! You know I'll do it! I have nothing to lose!"

Kyle's gaze locked on them. "Let her go! You can't get away!"

"That's what you think! She's my getaway ticket. You'll negotiate with me. You don't want anything to happen to her, do you?" Burke tightened his hold on her neck, choking her. "I mean it! Go downstairs, all of you, and wait for my call! Now!"

Kyle nodded at Sam. They backed into the stairwell and the door closed.

Burke pulled Roxy back into Claudia's condo and locked the door. He paced the floor and took short rapid breaths, mumbling over and over, "They're out there, waiting for me." His pacing abruptly stopped, and he turned to Roxy. "We'll go to the rooftop terrace, where there's only one entrance and exit!" He shoved her out the door and held her arm in a vice-like grip as he dragged her down the hallway toward the stairwell.

Roxy held her breath as he opened the door. The stairwell stood empty.

Burke pushed her up the stairs ahead of him. He held her against the rooftop door and pressed his body against hers as he unlocked it. She gagged as she breathed in the sour odor of his sweat.

When the door opened, he pushed her onto the open terrace, and she stumbled. The motion-activated lamps clicked on. Each lamp was mounted on a tall post set in the center of a waist-high decorative planter. Claudia had ordered these expensive lamppost planters, so she could grow her cooking herbs on the sunny rooftop. At night, the lamps cast a cozy glow on the terrace for dinner parties.

The warm humid breeze feathered through Roxy's hair. Dim stars sparkled in the clear night sky. The fireworks had ended, and she could hear the traffic noise on Main Street. Occasional shouts and peals of laughter rose above the hum of the crowd. Three stories below, people were celebrating.

Burke shoved Roxy into a patio chair. He kept his knife pointed at her as he pulled out his phone and thumbed the screen, one-handed. His phone shook as he held it to his ear. "We're on the rooftop, now... just Rox and me. Yeah, she's all right." He paused and then shouted, "Don't tell me what to do! You listen to me! I want to talk, face to face. Come up here alone and unarmed. If you try anything, you know what I'll do!" As soon as he ended the call, he yanked Roxy to her feet and pinned her tightly in front of him, like a shield.

Burke's chest moved rapidly with each ragged breath, and she could feel his fast, erratic heartbeats. She sent up a silent prayer, "Burke's coming unglued! Please God, don't let him kill us."

Knocking sounded on the rooftop door, followed by Kyle's muffled voice. "Let me in, Burke. You know the door automatically locks."

"Are you alone?"

"I'm alone. Open up!"

"Don't try anything! I have a knife to her throat!" Burke moved forward, pushing Roxy.

She felt a hot sting in her neck as his knife blade sliced into her skin.

Burke opened the door and then backed up, pulling her with him.

Kyle walked onto the terrace, and the door slammed shut behind him. He stopped, and his expression hardened as he focused on them. His blue eyes briefly met hers, and she read the anguish in them. He pointed to his empty holster and held up both hands. "I'm unarmed. Now let Rox go so we can talk."

"I'm not letting her go... not until we make a deal." Burke pulled her back a few more steps.

Roxy's right hand brushed against the rim of a planter. Instinctively, she dug her fingers into the loose dirt. She jerked her foot back, kicking Burke's shin with the heel of her shoe. As he loosened his grip on her, she swiveled around and hurled the dirt into his face. Someone pushed her out of the way. Kyle!

She gripped the edge of the planter as she watched them struggle. The blade of the knife caught the light as it dug it into Kyle's shirtsleeve. She screamed.

Kyle got a two-handed grip on Burke's wrist. "Drop it!" The knife fell, and he kicked it away. Then he punched Burke, hard. Blood spurted as he fell onto the terrace's tiled surface.

Burke blinked as he looked up at Kyle. Then he propped himself on an elbow and said, "You wore an ankle holster. That's not playing fair."

Roxy realized Kyle was holding a small gun in his left hand.

"You've never played fair, Burke!"

The ruthless tone in Kyle's voice sent a shiver through her.

"Was it fair, the way you killed Erika... Greta... Doyle? And was it fair, what you did to Earl? He welcomed you into his home! He paid for your first-class education! And what did you do? You killed his only son... my best friend! You stabbed Claudia tonight, and you would have killed Rox, too! You don't deserve to live!"

Kyle shouted the last words, and then he raised the gun, aiming it at Burke.

"No! Vance wouldn't want this, Kyle!"

He held the gun steady.

Burke's lips curled into a macabre smile; his teeth smeared red with blood. "Go ahead. Do it!"

"Please, Kyle! The killing has to stop!" Roxy held her breath.

Kyle stared at Burke for a long moment, and then he lowered the gun.

Roxy slowly exhaled. She became aware of pounding on the door and Sam's muffled voice. Still shaking, she moved to the door and opened it.

Sam ran onto the terrace. He quickly assessed the situation and issued an order as he holstered his gun. Officers rushed from behind him and took Burke into custody.

Roxy gripped Sam's arm. "Claudia's hurt, in her condo—"

"I know." Sam kept his gaze focused on the officers handcuffing Burke. "We sent in the EMTs as soon as we knew you were on the roof."

Kyle turned toward them, and his eyes widened. "Rox, you're hurt!"

At that moment, she became aware of the stinging pain in her neck. She touched the area, and then she stared at the warm red liquid dripping from her fingertips. The terrace briefly spun around and everything went dark.

Friday, one week later

Roxy climbed into Kyle's truck. "Have you been waiting long?"

"Not long." He leaned over and kissed her. "How was your first day back?"

"I was busy all day, working behind the counter." She let out a sigh. "I miss my mail route. I can start driving next week, but I'll be stuck working as a clerk for another month, until I'm released from the ban on lifting heavy packages."

"The time will go fast, Rox." He started the engine. "Did any reporters bother you?"

"No. Mack dealt with them. He knows you advised me not to speak to the press, since I'll be testifying at Burke's trial." Roxy strapped on her seat belt.

"Melody has been ignoring my advice," Kyle said. "She's enjoying all the media attention."

Roxy nodded. "She's been exaggerating the way I handled Burke, like I'm some kind of hero. People stepped into my line today, even when the other clerks were available. Grumpy Hiram from the Senior Center came in and bought stamps from me. I gave him my usual cheery smile, and guess what? He smiled back! At least, I think it was a smile. Hard to tell, with Hiram."

Kyle let out a soft laugh. He checked for traffic and then pulled out of the parking lot.

"How was your day?"

"Good. We finally arrested the gang involved in those burglaries at Riverside Bay Estates. Remember that bearded guy, the one I caught mugging that couple during the fireworks display?"

She nodded.

"His thumbprint matched the print we found on a jewelry case at one of the houses. After his lawyer negotiated a deal, that guy gave us the names of the others in the gang, and he told us which one of them shot and wounded the homeowners."

"That's great. I'm glad you finally caught them." She looked at him. "Did you have court today? You're wearing a shirt and tie."

"No. I got off work early, so I picked up Buddy and brought him to my house. After I walked and fed the dogs, I showered and dressed up. I want to take you out to dinner, to celebrate your first day back at work."

Roxy smiled. "Can we go to Gemelli's Italian Café? I love their lasagna."

"Anywhere you want."

"I promised Claudia we'd come and visit her after you picked me up today. She's only been home from the hospital two days, and she's already going stir crazy. Paul had to report back to duty at King's Bay yesterday. He'll have a few months of shore duty before he goes out to sea again."

"I'll call Claudia and tell her we'll come over for a short visit before dinner," Kyle said, as he pulled into Roxy's driveway. "Would you mind wearing that dress you wore at Josh's graduation dinner? I like that one."

"The black belted dress? Okay..." Roxy eyed him for a long moment. He usually didn't care what she wore. She got out of the truck and pulled a stack of letters from her mailbox at the end of the driveway. After thumbing through them, she said, "Nothing important." When she walked into her kitchen, she tossed her mail on the island. She hurried upstairs, changed into the dress and slipped on black high-heeled sandals. After refreshing her makeup, she ran a comb through her waves and put on her favorite lipstick.

Kyle was standing in the family room, gazing out the windows facing the Indian River. He turned as she reached the bottom of the stairs and his expression softened. "You look beautiful, sunshine." He gave her a tender kiss. "Go into the kitchen and check your mail again. I think you missed something important."

Roxy's heartbeat quickened when she saw the white satin box sitting on top of her mail. She opened the box and stared at the brilliant round diamond, surrounded by tiny diamond chips.

"You brought the sunshine back into my life, so I chose a sunburst pattern. Do you like it?"

She nodded, feeling too overwhelmed to speak.

Kyle picked up the ring and went down on one knee. Emotion glazed his sky-blue eyes as he took hold of her hand. "Roxelle Anna, I love you so much. Will you marry me?"

Tears welled in her eyes. "Kyle Ransom, I'd be a fool not to marry you."

His hand shook as he slipped the ring on her finger. Then he stood and gave her a soft, lingering kiss. The touch of his lips sent hot shivers through her. He wrapped her in his arms, and she leaned against him, her heart pounding. "I assume you've talked to Josh."

"We had a long talk last weekend. He said it was about time I asked you to marry me."

"Sounds like he's been talking to Claudia."

Kyle stepped back and grinned at her. "Actually, he has."

"I wonder what kind of wedding she's planned for us," Roxy said. "Let's tell her we want a simple ceremony, very soon."

"The sooner the better."

She looked up at him and smiled. "Roxy Ransom. I like it. The name Ransom brings up images of swashbuckling pirates… sailing ships… and maps of buried treasure."

He laughed out loud. "Pirates? That's a new one."

"Doesn't the name Captain Ransom sound pirate-like?"

He pulled her into another hug. "Rox, you have a quirky way of looking at things. That's one of the reasons I love you."

They entered Claudia's condo and took turns giving her a gentle hug. She was dressed in an oversized white shirt and black yoga pants. Her makeup couldn't disguise the dark hollows beneath her eyes. She stood a moment, looking at them. "You two are all dressed up. What's the occasion?"

Roxy held out her left hand. The ring's faceted round diamond sparkled as it caught the light.

Her eyes opened wide. "Congratulations! I can't wait to tell dad! When are you—"

"Soon," Kyle said.

Claudia smiled. It was a satisfied smile; the smile of a match-maker whose plan had finally come together.

"How are you feeling?" Roxy asked.

"It hurts if I take a deep breath, but otherwise, I'm healing fine. My doctor says I can go back to work on Monday, mostly because our realty office is only an elevator ride to the first floor." As Claudia headed into her living room, she avoided walking near the spot where she had fallen. The grout around the wood-look tile still bore dark stains. "That knife narrowly missed an artery when it punctured my lung." She sank into her favorite white leather chair.

They sat on the couch across from her. Roxy pointed to the vase of colorful fresh flowers sitting on the coffee table. "Did Paul give you these before he left for King's Bay?"

"No. Jo brought them over today, along with some homemade oatmeal raisin cookies, your Grandma Anna's recipe." Claudia paused. "Duke and Melody also came over and brought me a huge sack of my favorite chocolate glazed donuts. Those two seem really happy together."

Roxy read the look in her eyes and wondered if she'd already started making plans for their wedding."

"Melody asked about you, Rox. She's grateful for the way you handled Burke, and she's convinced you saved our lives—" Claudia's voice choked, and she cleared her throat. "... and I agree."

Kyle put his arm around Roxy and kissed her cheek.

Claudia turned to him. "How's the investigation going?"

He leaned forward. "We found several incriminating items Burke had hidden on Doyle's yacht—Vance's driver's license, Doyle's wallet, Greta's passport, tablet and phone, and that infamous flash drive she made. Our forensic team found traces of dried blood beneath the handle of Burke's knife. We sent it off to the lab. If the blood matches Doyle, that strengthens our case. The judge denied Burke's bail, so he's going to have to remain behind bars during his trial, or trials, rather. He's generated a long string of murders and assaults. Sam suggested we look into Betty Norman's death and her sister Jane's, too."

Roxy and Claudia exchanged surprised glances.

"We've been searching through Burke's computer and piecing together the spider web of his financial accounts. Burke had an online gambling addiction, and his losses were massive. He gambled away everything he inherited from Erika, and the income from his law practice wasn't enough to feed his addiction and sustain his expensive lifestyle, while financing his uncle's hush money payments. Burke needed a new money source, and Betty and Jane had wealthy trust accounts. He embezzled from them by setting up phony charitable trusts. And after they died, he skimmed off even more money as the executor of their estates."

Roxy's phone chimed. She pulled out her phone and read the text. "It's Jo. She's with Aunt Nell and Rachel. They want to do a video call with me. Do you mind, Claudia?"

"No, that's fine." She smiled, and it looked genuine.

Roxy kneeled next to Claudia's chair and propped her phone against a stack of coasters on the end table. Images filled the screen. Jo's face came into focus, seated between Rachel and Nell. The three women bore a striking generational resemblance.

"Hi, Claudia." Jo's smile appeared sincere.

Rachel gave a shy wave. "Hi, Aunt Rox and Claudia."

Nell spoke up. "Rox, how was your first day back at work?"

"It went fine. I miss my mail route, but I guess I can put up with clerking for another month." Roxy paused, realizing she had an opportunity to surprise them, for once. "Kyle gave me something today." She held her left hand close to her phone's camera, and she smiled when she saw their reactions.

When Kyle opened the back door of his truck, Buddy and Clyde leaped onto Roxy's driveway, as if they were shot from a cannon. They raced down to the river and splashed into the shallow water near the fishing boat.

Roxy balanced the box of leftover lasagna in her hand as she unlocked her back door. "Kyle, I think this is a little crazy, going for a sunset boat ride with the dogs. We're all dressed up." She turned to him and smiled. "I'll come down to the boat as soon as I put this in the fridge and change my shoes."

Kyle headed down to the river and strode out onto the dock. The sun hovered low in the pale orange sky. He gazed at the river's rippled orange surface and let out a sad sigh as his thoughts turned to April and Vance.

They had driven to the church cemetery after dinner at Gemelli's. They visited April's grave and the small grave next to her, bearing the inscription: Suzanne Kay Ransom, beloved daughter. Then they visited Vance's grave and the two tiny graves nearby. At each gravesite, he held hands with Rox as she spoke—in between tears— telling April and Vance how much they are still loved and that their memories will be cherished, always. Her soft voice mingled with the gentle sound of the breeze rustling through the moss-draped limbs of the towering live oaks.

Kyle rubbed the stitched wound where Burke's knife had pierced his arm, and he recalled those critical seconds on the rooftop when he stood, aiming his gun at Burke. He had turned away from the light and allowed his rage to take over. But the sound of her voice broke through the darkness, restraining him from pulling the trigger. Kyle shook his head and thought, "Burke's a cold-blooded murderer, but seeking my own vengeance wasn't the answer. By taking his life, I would have ruined my life, and the lives of everyone I love... especially Josh and Rox."

"Hey, Kyle! I made coffee for us." Roxy hurried toward the dock, carrying two travel mugs. She flashed him that wide dimpled smile that always quickened his heartbeat.

He whistled for the dogs, and they clambered up on the dock, dripping wet. They shook their bodies, spraying water everywhere. Roxy shrieked and then giggled. The dogs leaped inside the boat, and then they stood, panting, as water dripped from their matted fur.

Roxy stepped into the boat and set the travel mugs inside the cup holders in the cockpit. Kyle untied the mooring ropes and followed her. She wore a playful grin as she pointed at the dripping dogs. "Captain Ransom, I see you have a motley crew. Are you taking me for a ride on your pirate ship?"

He gave her his best imitation of a pirate growl as he drew her into his arms.

Roxy giggled as she reached up and wiped the lipstick smudges off his face. She moved to the cockpit and sat in the passenger seat. The dogs curled up on the deck behind the seats as Kyle steered the boat away from the dock.

She gazed at the orange sky and recalled the beautiful sunset she'd seen with her friends in the Ocala Forest. Then her mind brought up another image — trees blown down around her, with only a few jagged trunks left standing. She thought, "Beauty and destruction, in the same forest. Just like good and evil, on this earth. Why do people like Burke choose to do evil? And what can we do to overcome it?"

An image flashed — the Bible verse Aunt Nell wrote on her chalkboard the first Sunday of every year:

"Oh people, the Lord has told you what is good, and this is what he requires of you: to do what is right, to love mercy, and to walk humbly with your God." Micah 6:8

Roxy closed her eyes and offered up a prayer of thanks for her life, and the lives of Claudia, Kyle and Melody. When she opened her eyes, she realized Kyle was looking at her.

He gave her a smile as he steered the boat into the main channel. Then he poured on the speed, and the boat bounced on the river's surface, sending up sprays of water. Feelings of joy and exhilaration bubbled up inside her as they sped west, toward the setting sun.

CHAPTER 53

Roxy's ringtone sounded as Kyle finished tying up the boat. Jo had told her she'd call later this evening, so they could start planning the wedding. She sat on the bench at the end of the dock and answered the phone without looking at the screen.

"Hello... ah, my name is Dani… Danielle Pierce. Is this Roxelle Anna Rode… ah, I mean, Roxy Silva?"

Roxy's intuition sparked when she heard the trembling teenage voice... and her full maiden name.

"This is Roxy Silva. Can you tell me what this is about?" She glanced at Kyle, who appeared to read the look in her eyes. He sat on the bench next to her.

"I found you on a class reunion website. I'm calling about an adoption, fourteen years ago."

Roxy's body tensed. "Is this about my daughter?"

"I—" A choked sob escaped, followed by hiccups. "... I'm your daughter."

"Oh, my sweet child..." Tears stung Roxy's her eyes as she pictured her tiny newborn baby.

Kyle wrapped his arm around her shoulders. Roxy leaned close to him and blinked away tears as she listened to the lovely sound of her daughter's voice.

-End-

* 9 7 8 1 9 5 2 3 6 9 8 1 0 *